LION

BLOOD RIVER DOWN

DANIEL R. HORNE
86

LS 53785-8 • $2.95
CAN 53786-6 • $3.95

ISBN 0-812-53785-8

>>$2.95

I NEED SOMEONE

Glorian stirred and held up a finger to prevent his interruption. "Now you're asking yourself, Why you? Why of all the people in the world, your world, should I pick you—"

"Stop," Gideon said, pushing himself into a sitting position. "I don't know if I want to know the answer to that burning question."

Glorian smiled. "That's good, because I don't have one."

Gideon couldn't help himself. "Then why?"

"Chance," she said, with a shrug. Glorian moved again, out of his grip and into the meadow. She was *in* the pantry, and was impatiently waiting for him. He thought to himself, How bad is it here that I have to lose my mind to keep my sanity?

"Hey," he said as he took a deep breath and stepped through the wall, "what am I looking for anyway?"

Glorian paused. "Oh that. What you're looking for is a duck."

"A duck? Forget it," Gideon bellowed, turned around and started back for home. And stopped.

Home was gone.

BLOOD RIVER DOWN

LIONEL FENN

A TOM DOHERTY ASSOCIATES BOOK

BLOOD RIVER DOWN

Copyright © 1986 by Lionel Fenn

First printing: November 1986

A TOR Book

Published by Tom Doherty Associates, Inc.
49 West 24 Street
New York, N.Y. 10010

Cover art by Daniel Horne

ISBN: 0-812-53785-8
CAN. ED.: 0-812-53786-6

Printed in the United States

0 9 8 7 6 5 4 3 2 1

Dedication

To the memory of my late darling, Felicia Andrews, who started me on this fantastical road;

And to Kate Little Bird, a loon in her own write.

ONE

On a Wednesday evening in the middle of May, Gideon Sunday opened his pantry door, took one step over the threshold, and shrieked.

All things considered, the reaction was a natural one even for a not-quite-middle-aged man who used to play football for a living, and he wasn't the slightest bit ashamed when he jumped back into the kitchen and slammed the door, put his back to it, and closed his eyes as tightly as he could. After all, he had only gone in there to fetch a jar of his late sister's plum preserves, a perverse treat to cap the end of a dismal and rainy evening. Seeing the rear wall of his small New Jersey home unceremoniously replaced by something so monotonously pastoral that it would test the soul and sanity of any human being was, to say the least, rather unexpected.

The shriek, then, was justified.

And that, he thought as he opened his eyes slowly and was reassured by the familiar sight of the stainless-steel sink with its dripping cold-water faucet, is what I get for tampering with tradition.

Normally, instead of being in the kitchen at this hour in the first place, he would have been in the living room, where he would have opened a bottle of mediocre but serviceable liquor, sat in front of the portable black-and-white television, and watched an old movie while he read the sports sections of the local and national newspapers

1

and tried to figure out the daily crossword puzzle. Having not seen his name yet again in any of the sports sections' syndicated columns, and having given up on the crossword but not the liquor, he would have made himself satisfactorily sleepy by ten, would have gone to bed by ten-thirty, and would have been asleep by eleven, forgetting, for the nonce, the unpleasantly undeniable fact that he was slumping dangerously into his ninth consecutive month of unemployment.

Tonight, however, as he was changing into his pajamas after mowing the lawn by moonlight to get a jump on his neighbors, who consistently woke him at dawn with their own trimming and gardening, he had come across an old wallet-sized photograph of his sister, lying at the bottom of his jewelry case. It had been taken at the Jersey shore when she was twenty-four, ten years before her death. She was beautiful, her cockeyed smile defying the camera's attempts to freeze it into a wooden snapshot pose. He had held it for quite some time, remembering, before deciding that in her honor he would break down and break open some of her godawful preserves, make some toast, and toast her memory.

She would have appreciated that—he had never touched the stuff while she was alive.

But now even that bit of solace had been taken from him.

After testing the pantry doorknob several times to be sure nothing untoward would happen when he moved, he passed a harsh knuckle across his eyes, sat at the kitchen table, and stared at the door.

It didn't seem to have changed since the last time he'd seen it. He wasn't in the wrong house because he recognized it the moment he came into the room. And behind its peeling but still presentable white surface were hundreds of memories of his mother and father, his sister, his childhood . . . and a meadow that didn't belong there.

The memories he could deal with; they were so ordinary he often used them to put himself to sleep when he struggled with bouts of insomnia.

It was the meadow that threw him.

It's got to be the preserves, he told himself. Just the thought of ingesting them had probably triggered a subtle chemical reaction which had, not surprisingly, induced hallucinations in an already weary brain.

He sat for ten minutes.

The door didn't change.

He wondered if the hallucination might have been brought on by the fact that he was worrying himself grey over finding a new job before the generous but not bottomless inheritance from his sister ran out. What he had seen might be the perfectly logical result of wish fulfillment on the part of a desperate man, a piercing and not inexplicable desire to escape to an untroubled world where he was not bothered by the realities of feeding, housing, and clothing himself.

There were not, as he had unhappily discovered, many lucrative or even marginally pleasant positions available in the real world for a professional football player whose team franchise had been disbanded. All but eight of the team members and coaching staff had been gleefully and cheaply swallowed up by other organizations within a month of the announced dissolution; four of the remaining players went into insurance, one found hope in men's shoes, one married a senator, and the seventh opened a sports bar in Kansas City.

He, however, the seldom used backup to the backup quarterback, discovered that his average physical skills and tendency to bruise before the ball was hiked prevented him from being asked to tryouts even for the semipros, while his liberal arts degree in ancient history, *cum laude* graduation notwithstanding, wasn't worth the fake lambskin it was printed on in today's high-tech, low-literacy market.

He sat for ten minutes more.

The door still didn't change.

He considered the remote possibility that he had mistakenly thought the postage-stamp backyard he had known for over three decades was a meadow. It was an idea that might have been convincing, had he not then looked over his shoulder at the clock over the sink and seen that it was only twenty-four minutes shy of ten.

Either the moon was damned bright for this time of night, or he was still in his easy chair, sleeping and dreaming.

"Hey!" he said, smiling at himself.

Speculation was worthless if one only speculated and never acted.

With a determined squaring of his shoulders, he walked around the table and put his hand on the knob. He tilted his head and listened. He kicked the door lightly, once.

Then he flung it open and stood boldly on the threshold.

The shriek this time was more like a squeak.

On the left and right pantry walls were the white-painted shelves that held his fading larder; the narrow floor was still a pale green-and-red-checked linoleum; and the back wall where the window used to be, looking out on the backyard, was gone.

So was the backyard.

"All right," he said, stepped back, and closed the door a second time.

He rubbed his eyes methodically with the heels of his hands, went to the sink, splashed water on his face, and dried it with a succession of harsh paper towels. He drank out of his palm. Then he walked into the living room, opened the cabinet under the stereo turntable, and pulled out the bottle of scotch he had given himself on his birthday, three months ago. This, he knew, would solve nothing and most likely only add to his confusion; on the other hand, it might provide him with the stimulus necessary to face whatever it was that had invaded his pantry.

He eyed the level of the bottle, nodded, and returned to the kitchen. A deft twist of his fingers had the top off; a deft turn of the wrist filled his mouth; a swallow made him bold once again.

His next move was not unlike the only thing he did

better in the league than anyone else—the "last second, the team's behind and we need a score" Hail Mary play. He had been known, on more than one spectacular occasion, to throw a ball over a hundred yards when he was feeling particularly pressed by approaching tacklers; he was also known for not always being able to put it where he aimed it.

A bold desperation play that once in a while even worked.

Gideon flung open the door.

"Incredible," he said when he saw the meadow waiting.

He took another drink, rather larger than the first, and decided to investigate; what the hell, you only live once, and who knows what the morrow may bring. He propped the pantry door open with his chair, the table, and the portable dishwasher. A run to the hall closet got him a baseball bat since he didn't own a gun.

A sudden and embarrassing thought occurred to him, and he opened the back door to look out at the yard. It was there, it was dark, and it wasn't anything like a meadow.

"Nuts," he said.

Then he turned off all the lights, set the bat on his shoulder, and walked into the pantry.

"Calm," he ordered himself when his knees threatened to turn the rest of him around. "Think of it as an adventure."

He took a deep breath, sneezed, and put out a hand—no glass, only warm, summerlike air that caressed his palms and made his fingers curl in anticipation of a nymph's kiss.

"So far so good."

He withdrew the hand, examined it for signs of rotting or alteration, then inserted a foot through to the grass and tested the ground—firm, slightly damp, the grass coming softly to his ankles and twinkling with a dew that should have evaporated shortly after dawn.

He retreated, thinking he was pressing his luck and shouldn't stick out his neck. Further examination was necessary before he went any farther.

He held out the bat and waited for laser beams to char it.

He called out a "Hello!" to see if the natives were responding.

He searched for large, ominous shadows on the grass that would indicate someone lurking suspiciously just to the side of his peripheral vision.

He pressed himself against the righthand shelves and squinted into the bright sunlight beyond, half hoping he could spot the tops of the screens on which the scene was painted, or the lights that passed for the sun, or the wind machine hidden just around the side of the opening.

The meadow was, he judged, several hundred yards wide, equally as long if not longer, and marked by gentle undulations of the ground which gave it a vaguely sealike appearance. It was surrounded by a dense forest of towering pine, which he could smell disturbingly clearly. Directly ahead, beyond the forest, was a range of high mountains, peaks hazed by distance. There were flowers in colorful abundance, a few darting insects that made no attempt to fly into the pantry, and a flock of dark birds wheeling about in the sky.

He shook his head with a disgusted groan.

"This," he said, "is crazy."

He turned around immediately, went back into the kitchen, moved the chair and the table and the dishwasher back into their places, put the bat on the table, closed the door, and went to bed.

In the morning he would get the preserves. When he was sober.

But sleep refused to come when he wanted it. He spent several minutes punching at the pillow, rearranging the covers, stretching stiffly in order to relax more fully, punching the pillow again, and counting black-faced sheep. None of it worked. He went into the bathroom and took a drink of water, examined his eyes for signs of age lines, his neck for signs of sagging, his chest and arms for signs of deterioration—not, he told himself glumly, that he was all that marvelous a physical specimen. He was, in proportion, like his abilities as a player—adequate. He was a nice guy who tried to talk tacklers out of hitting him and never once argued with a ref about a lousy call.

He grinned at himself, shook his head, and returned to bed.

In more than one way he was relieved that he had never become a star, or even a journeyman player. At least now he didn't have scrambled brains, a destroyed knee, and a few fused discs in his back.

All he had were zero prospects for the future, and a meadow in his pantry.

Things, he thought, could hardly get worse.

Unless, he thought further when he heard the crash of crockery downstairs, someone has broken into the house and is going to clean me out of my furniture, too.

He scrambled out of bed and moved silently into the hallway, his head cocked as he listened, almost convinced he had been dreaming when he heard it again—a plate dropping onto the kitchen floor and shattering. Muffled footsteps. A soft muttering.

Halfway down the stairs he paused and swore when he remembered that he had left the bat on the kitchen table. Quickly, he turned into the dining room at the bottom of the staircase and picked up a vase from a corner table. Then he returned to the foyer, listened again, and made his way down the short hall.

The light was on.

He distinctly remembered turning it off.

He pressed against the wall and took a deep breath, prayed the burglar wasn't armed, and rushed into the room.

No one was there.

But the pantry door was open.

TWO

"That," Gideon whispered, "is impossible. No way. I shut it. I know I shut it."

He closed his eyes tightly to produce painful sparks behind his lids, rubbed his free hand hard and fast over his face to be sure he was awake and not still in bed having another one of his unemployment nightmares, and opened them again, one at a time and slowly.

The door was still ajar.

Definitely out of the question, he told himself as he took a tentative step forward, changed his mind, and stepped quickly back again; I simply don't do things like that. Everybody knows that. I just don't.

Even his dead sister, who had been lovingly tolerant about many things in his life—and had even politely called them foibles instead of idiocies—had laughingly chided him more than once about his meticulous attention to such details as closing a door and turning out all the lights as soon as he left a room, even if he were going to return in five minutes. And more than once, she also tended to remind him not so laughingly, he forgot there were other people still in there.

She, however, had been just as notorious at home before she'd run away to California, and during her career, for leaving her purses in restaurants, keys in the ignition, money and credit cards in department stores, and five or six pieces of luggage on airport carousels, then practicing her hysterics until all items were recovered.

Gideon never listened to her.

Shortly after his mother died and left him this house, he had been more than close to fanatical about making sure all the doors and windows of his various apartments, homes, and motel rooms were securely locked against all intrusion save the eventuality of a determined tank in the outer hallway. It drove his room- and teammates crazy.

But it was, his mother had told him sternly on too many occasions to mention, the only way to insure one's tenuous safety against the encroaching viciousness of the crime-ridden jungle engulfing the universe and driving all decent people to Arizona. Do this, she offered, and you will never regret it, though the hardships be great.

As a child he had performed the task out of habit, his mother's teaching, and fear of his father's large-buckled belt ominously hanging on a meat hook beside the back door; as an adolescent he had done it because the nightly chore was necessary for the Friday collection of his meager allowance so he could go to the movies just to get out of the house; and as an adult he had done it because he couldn't sleep until the ritual had been completed.

So he was positive that, aside from the improbability though not impossibility of divine intervention in terms of his kitchen environs, he had closed the pantry door when he had decided to go to bed.

Positive, however, did not account for what he was seeing.

His first thought was to back stealthily into the living room, find the telephone in the dark, and call the police; his second was to cancel the first because he didn't think he would be able to explain the meadow in his pantry or the empty liquor bottle on the counter or the consequences of the empty liquor bottle on his breath. Nor could he simply retreat to the upstairs and pretend it hadn't happened since it obviously had or he wouldn't be here now. Nor could he rush to any of his neighbors for assistance since they never had appreciated his mowing by moonlight, and besides he was obviously big enough to take care of himself, being a football player and all; not, he recalled somewhat bitterly, that they had ever asked for his autograph.

Despite the glare of the fluorescent light in the ceiling, the doorway was filled with a soft golden glow.

His nose wrinkled and he shuddered when he caught the distinct odor of pine.

Maybe, he thought, it's a poor lost deer or some other meadow creature looking for food; and maybe the manager of the Green Bay Packers will call first thing in the morning and make you his starting quarterback next season, complete with a record bonus, a new car, and options.

"Hell," he said.

Stuck then with the flimsy vase in his right hand and no alternative but to proceed, he bolstered himself with vengeful thoughts of the potential violation to his dead sister's preserves and eased into the kitchen, following as best and as silently as he could the contours of the refrigerator and the dishwasher until he reached the pantry door.

He listened.

There wasn't a sound.

He tried to ignore the prickling that had started to erupt along his spine and paid no attention to the fact that the house wasn't talking anymore.

He listened again, leaning hard against the wall as though he might be able to hear right through it, and swore silently when he knew there was only one thing left to do.

Snatching up the bat in his left hand and holding the vase over his head, he leaned swiftly around the frame to expose the intruder in the act of doing whatever the act was, holding his breath, his shoulders and stomach tightening as though expecting a blow.

"Damn," he said, and lowered his arms.

The pantry was empty save for the can of pork and beans on the floor; and the meadow was still there, cheery as ever.

There was no sign of anyone, any thing, or any distressing combination thereof; nor were there signs that anyone had been in here since he had left over two hours ago.

Yet he knew he had shut the door, and he knew he had heard the sounds of dishes breaking.

A slow turn of his head and a look to the floor stopped him from giving in to the temptation of relief. Lying in front of the sink was what remained of a plate that had been in the drying rack since he'd washed up after dinner; a foot or so away were two others in similar states of breakage, along with a handleless cup and a chipped and cracked saucer.

The bat swung tightly at his side like a spooked cat's tail.

He knelt to look under the table and saw only more pieces of more dishes he could ill afford to replace even if they had been less than a dollar apiece. It was, he thought as he straightened, a crime for which someone is going to pay.

The refrigerator coughed on, and he spun around, barely able to check his swing before the bat dented the top.

"Take it easy," he told himself, patting the appliance to make amends for his mistake. "Take it easy."

The vase he placed on the table as he walked over to the back door and checked the lock, rattled the knob, peered around the white curtains that covered the panes. The backyard was still dark, the houses behind unseen.

He examined the high window beside it and discovered the lock still in place; he checked for telltale signs of little people or expert illegal contortionists in the cupboards over and under the counters; and, as long as he was at it, he checked the oven and the refrigerator and thanked the ceiling for the fact that the house had no cellar.

He closed the pantry door because the golden glow was making him nervous. It had occurred to him fleetingly that he might go in there and check the meadow as well, for a clue to whatever was happening here tonight. That was discarded. Coward or not, he would just as soon not know.

And when he was positive he was alone, he tapped the

bat thoughtfully against his left palm. This, he reminded himself, was not the only room in the house. And in the time it had taken him to get down here, whoever it was might have even fled out the front door, giggling to his friends about the fool he had made of the sucker who lived alone in the house and never came out except at night, to mow the lawn.

And maybe not.

The meadow aside, the idea of calling the police and letting them do all the work was becoming increasingly seductive, even if they would eventually question his sobriety and his pantry decor. Unfortunately, there was no phone extension in the kitchen, and once again he couldn't count on his neighbors for help.

"Gideon," he muttered, "you'll never get some sleep if you don't get your ass in gear."

Thus inspired, he moved cautiously down the hall toward the living room, aware that he had not put on slippers and that the floor where it wasn't covered by throw rugs was skin-tighteningly cold, the constant jumping of his nerves promising to make his calves cramp.

He slowed even further, his breathing more a faint hissing, and dropped into a slight crouch and raised the bat for a quick and devastating strike to his opponent's kneecaps when he reached the foyer and looked to his right.

The lights were out, but the waning moon was still bright enough to cover the few pieces of furniture in shimmering silvered grey, to put unpleasantly shifting shadows in the mouth of the fireplace, and to show him that unless the intruder was substantially smaller than the average midget, there was no one here, either.

He double-checked the dining room, just to be sure they weren't hiding under the table or in the china closet, and tried the front door, which was still locked from the inside.

He frowned and scratched the side of his neck.

A board creaked overhead.

It was entirely possible, he thought as he stared glumly at the ceiling, that his night visitor—who seemed now to be less dangerous than intriguing—had hidden in the living room until he had gone into the kitchen, then left the living room to run furtively upstairs into either of the bedrooms or into the bathroom as soon as his back was turned. Unless he or she or they found the stairs to the attic and went up there instead, though it was little more than a crawlspace and held nothing of interest to even the most myopic of thieves.

In that case, his search was not yet finished.

In that case, he ought to stop trying to be a hero and call the goddamned police and be done with it.

Another board creaked.

Remember, Gideon, he told himself, the meadow and the bottle; that kind of publicity you do not need when you're trying to make a comeback.

Of course, it could be just the house.

For as long as he had known it, it had talked to itself at night, groaning and settling and releasing its warmth, shifting and shrinking and snapping as it contracted with the night's chill; the floorboards made noises all the time, even under the carpets, not to mention the walls and a couple of the ceilings, especially when a good wind was blowing and the eaves found their voice.

The fireplace and its flue were a veritable orchestra of whistles and moans, and when the furnace turned on, the ducts added a basso blowing that even reached into the closets.

A board cracked.

On the other hand, he thought, I could just be stalling because I'm in a bathrobe and bare feet and carrying a baseball bat for protection against god knows what that's creeping around my house.

There was nothing else to do, again, and he headed for the staircase, moved up as quietly as he could, and when he reached the second floor decided that boldness was the best way to keep the intruder off guard.

He stepped into the spare bedroom and switched on the light, looked under the bed, the dresser, and in the tiny closet—they were empty; he stepped into the bathroom and switched on the light, threw back the shower curtain, checked under the sink, and shook his head when he found himself staring at the toilet's water-tank lid; he hesitated before stepping into his own bedroom and switching on the light—it was getting personal now, and he was beginning to feel like ten kinds of a fool.

But when he did, it was empty.

The door to the attic was closed, and locked.

"Gideon," he said, "you have earned a rest. Put the stupid bat away and forget this ever happened."

Something moved downstairs.

With a revelatory snap of his fingers, he realized he must be drunk. Not nearly four sheets to the wind, not by a long shot, but at the very least struggling with a good-sized pillowcase. Four good, healthy swallows in his tired and forlorn condition could very well have caused an interruption of rational thought, a short-circuiting of reality perception, and a muzziness that began to make him feel as if he were wading through wet cotton. That would do it, no question about it, and the only logical solution would be to get back into bed, sleep, and sort it all out in the morning, when he wasn't jumping at every shadow that moved in every corner.

It wouldn't be the first time he had done something stupid after drinking; it would be the first time he was glad of it, though.

Someone, or something, knocked the vase off the kitchen table.

"Well, Jesus," he said angrily, and took the steps down two at a time, ran down the hall, and barely stopped himself in time from slicing his bare feet open on the pieces of vase that lay jagged on the floor.

"You know," a voice said behind him, "this isn't getting us anywhere."

Gideon shrieked.

THREE

Nimbly treading a fine line between bolting for the back door and skipping over the shards of crockery and pottery on the floor, Gideon stumbled backward until a chair caught him behind his calves. He sat heavily. The baseball bat dropped unnoticed from his hand, and most notions of imprecations were driven away by the sight of the woman standing in the hall shadows.

When his lungs started working again and his heart slowed down, he swallowed and said, "I haven't got anything. You're wasting your time."

She said nothing.

He peered at her and didn't see a gun. "You can look around," he told her, "but like I said, you're wasting your time. The most valuable thing I have is this bat, believe me."

"I don't want anything, nothing that belongs to you, that is," she said.

"Thank god."

"If you choose, go ahead."

Her voice was pleasant and soft, but oddly strained. Though she remained in the hall, he could see she was wearing some sort of plain long white dress with something gold tied around her waist. He could not see her feet, nor could he see more than a suggestion of her face. It was disconcertingly like talking to a decapitated mannequin.

He waited.

She remained silent.

15

"Well?" he said.

The ghostlike figure stepped forward into the light, and he couldn't for the life of him understand why she would want to hide a face like that. Her eyes were wide and violet, her eyebrows dark to match the dark of her hair; her cheeks were full and flushed, her mouth naturally red, the whole destined to plunge every cosmetics firm in the country into a depression.

And she was bleeding.

At first he had thought it was some sort of decoration, there under her arm, just to the side of her left breast. Then he realized the decoration was moist, red, and spreading. He looked up and saw a faint glaze spreading over her eyes.

"Damn," he said, and jumped to his feet.

She took a hasty step backward.

"But you're hurt!"

She looked at her wound as if seeing it for the first time and nodded. "Yes, I suppose I am."

"But how?"

Her answer was a slight swaying that alarmed him, though she showed no evidence of the pain she must have been feeling.

Again avoiding the cutting edges on the floor, he took her hand and, slapping on lights along the way, guided her to the upstairs bathroom. She did not protest, and by the time he had lifted her easily to the counter beside the basin, she was leaning heavily against him. The pain was there now, and it made her look far too old for her years.

"Look," he said, fumbling open the medicine chest and staring inside, "I'm no doctor, but I know a little about cuts and things because I was always getting cut and things." He grabbed out tape, ointment, gauze, bandages, scissors, tweezers, and his straight razor. He looked at the blood on her dress and held his breath for a moment. "I think you'd better get to a hospital. I don't have a car, but I can call a cab. Really, I—"

"Do what you can," she said flatly. "Please."

"All right. But I'm afraid I'm not . . ."

The cloth, of some shimmering material far softer and less slippery than the silk it resembled, would not part when he tried to cut it away from the wound. He cursed, blushed, then saw the line of lacing down her spine.

"We're going to have to . . ."

"Whatever you must," she said.

Gently he pushed her hair over one shoulder and undid the lace's knot at the top of the dress. When the material parted sufficiently, he eased it down over her shoulder until her arm was free. She held the dress to her chest with her right hand and lifted the arm.

"God almighty," he whispered.

It was more than a scratch. It was a four-inch slash that ran across the ridge of one rib. He looked at her in near panic, and she smiled back encouragement.

"It's crazy."

"It hurts."

He filled the basin with cold water, soaked a towel, and used it to staunch the bleeding. When the wound was as clear as he could get it, he realized it wasn't as deep as he had thought; it was, however, unpleasant enough to make his stomach queasy.

"I think you'll need stitches."

"Just do what you can."

"Sure."

After a deep breath he blew out in a rush, he drenched several lengths of gauze with antiseptic and placed them over the cut. She didn't wince, hiss, or try to slap his hand away. Quickly and awkwardly, then, he taped the gauze in place, washed as much of the blood away as he could from around the wound, and stood back, his hands trembling as he tried to dry them on his jeans. His breathing was shallow, and there was cold perspiration on his face he patted off with a towel, and perspiration on hers he washed with a face cloth.

"You're still going to need a doctor."

She examined the repairs by lifting her arm high over

her head, her other hand prodding at the tape and thick gauze mound. Accordingly, her dress dropped away from her chest.

"Oh my," he said, and being no fool took a careful look before turning away modestly.

"It will do," she decided, and slipped her arm back into its sleeve, slid off the counter, and turned for him to relace the back.

He did, albeit reluctantly, aware that she was watching him closely in the mirror.

"Gideon," he said, fumbling with the laces. "Gideon Sunday."

"Glorian," she told him with an amused smile.

"Pretty name."

"Yes."

His hand brushed over the drying blood, and he grimaced and pulled away as soon as he was finished. She thanked him with a nod and walked out of the room, forcing him to follow as she returned to the kitchen and headed for the pantry.

"Hey, wait a minute! What about the doctor? I can have a cab here before—"

She turned. "What are you talking about? Aren't you coming with me?"

He blinked. He looked at the bat on the floor, the glow in the doorway, and decided that this woman, whoever she was, could not possibly be part of whatever his sour-minded destiny had in store for him. She was, alas, nothing more than a puzzling but nevertheless evident part of the nightmare he was having, or the DTs he was suffering, or the letdown he was feeling from finding no one in the house.

He leaned against the jamb and folded his arms over his chest. "I don't think so."

She seemed suddenly bewildered. "What?"

"I said, I don't think so."

"But don't you want to help me?"

"With what?"

She gestured vaguely toward the pantry. "With that. You know, the meadow."

He frowned and looked at her slightly sideways for a new and perhaps more illuminating perspective. Then he smiled. He grinned. And he laughed once and loudly.

"I get it!" he exclaimed happily. "By god, I get it!"

Clearly impatient, and more bewildered than ever, Glorian looked anxiously into the pantry, then back at him. "What do you get?"

"This," he said, relief and a twinge of fear battling to keep his voice unnaturally high. He coughed and cleared his throat. "This is one of those Connecticut Yankee things, you know what I mean? You get hit on the head, you wake up in a different time and have all sorts of fantastic adventures, bring modern technology to a medieval country, and then, just as you fall in love with the heroine and you're going to live happily ever after, you're sent back to where you came from. Or you wake up. Or you come out of the anesthetic because you've been having a terribly serious operation that means life or death to you, and you work out all your fantasies and wishes while you're under, thus saving yourself in more ways than one.

"Boy, am I stupid. I should have known."

Glorian stared at him. "You mean . . . are you trying to tell me you don't think I'm real?"

"Of course you're real," he said earnestly, failing miserably to keep a quivering smile from his lips. "But you're not real here"—he rapped a knuckle against the wall lightly—"you're real in here"—and he tapped a finger to his temple. "It's a hell of a difference."

"You shit," she said.

The smile wavered.

She strode across the room and stood in front of him, glaring until he wondered if perhaps he had made a slight error in perception.

Then she punched him.

His head rebounded off the wall and she punched him again, catching his chin just right. His hand came up to stop her, but he missed her wrist and took the blow instead. His knees buckled and he had to press his palms against the wall to keep from sliding to the floor. Getting tackled was one thing; getting slugged by a woman in a bloodstained dress was something else again—a clear symptom that he had misjudged not only the strength in her slender arms, but also the depths to which his self-pity would sink in order to teach him some small measure of humility and gracious behavior.

When his eyes cleared she was at the pantry door again, hands on her hips. "I am Glorian," she said angrily, "and I don't like being pushed around and laughed at."

Gingerly examining the condition of his face with one finger, he managed an apologetic wince; in all his years as a football player he had never once met a cheerleader who could slug like that.

"Now if you're coming, come! If you're not, go back to bed."

His tongue found a loose tooth; when he swallowed he could taste a hint of blood. Wonderful, he thought sourly; and tomorrow someone will call to give me an interview and he'll ask me where I got the bruises on my jaw and I'll have to tell him I got them from a woman who lives in my pantry. Wonderful.

Glorian gave him a look of supreme disgust, whirled around, and stalked into the pantry. He would have followed, but there was still a stubborn part of his mind that refused to believe he wouldn't wake up in the morning with a clear face and a hangover. After all, that's what happened, in a way, to Alice when she fell down the rabbit hole and ended up not playing with a full deck of cards. The whole thing was standard Freudian problem-solving and escapism, and while it might have been nice to escape, he still had enough pride left, not to mention his sister's legacy, to carry on a while longer before he gave in to—

Glorian screamed.

"Christ," he said wonderingly, "she's still here."

He moved into the kitchen with every intention of finding out what was wrong this time when Glorian, still screaming, raced out of the pantry, shoved him aside, and charged down the hall toward the staircase.

"Hey!" he shouted.

"Run!" she ordered.

"What?" he said.

And froze when he heard something he knew had to be large and ugly topple the pantry shelves. Jars shattered, cans cracked and thudded, and that same large ugly thing let loose with a bellow that made him think of an oversized lion that had just discovered its prey.

Glorian, from the relative safety of the second floor, screamed at him again, but Gideon didn't move.

He had been afraid before on many occasions, and he was afraid now as he saw the gold glow in the doorway blotted out; but he was also getting a little annoyed at the way his house was being used as a traffic lane for fantasies. In fact, as he reached out and picked up the bat, he was beginning to lose his temper, which, as his sister had often despairingly told him, was the one thing about him that made him somewhat undesirable company for those who triggered it.

The wall shook and the refrigerator gurgled off.

Using one foot as a brush, he pushed aside the pieces of broken crockery he could see and eased his way toward the door, keeping the table between him and whatever was trying to bull its way through.

When he saw it, he decided that perhaps Glorian was the wiser of the two.

It was much larger than the tiny room it was trying to squeeze through—its head was long and narrow on a thick stumpy neck, its eyes were set high and were of a green so dark they were almost black, and its mouth when it opened it to roar its anger again was filled with two rows of teeth a tyrannosaurus would die for. It had horns that curved back from its crown. It had two front legs that ended in claws that gouged through the wood and linoleum as if they were paper. The rest of it he couldn't see; it was wedged in the opening.

And it was black.

The black of winter midnights that intensified cold and drew the warmth from a hearth and turned the edges of dark dreams into the edges of dark razors.

It saw him, and it bellowed.

It tried frenziedly to push itself forward and shook its head wildly from side to side, slamming it mindlessly into the frame, cracking the wood, spilling chunks and flakes of plaster onto the floor.

Gideon's mouth dried, his heart stopped, and he knew that if he stood there one more minute, his bowels were going to loosen and his stomach was going to empty.

It bellowed again, and a lone jar fell from what remained of the bottom shelf. It rolled into the kitchen and the creature opened its mouth, flicked out a tongue as thick as a man's thigh, and scooped it up, crushed it in a curl, and let the preserves drip between its teeth like slow-moving blood.

Gideon lost his temper.

His pantry, his kitchen, and now his dead sister.

He didn't give a damn now if he were dreaming or not, if he had been thunked on the head or not; he had had enough of it, enough of every damn thing, and he shoved the table aside, raised the bat over his head, and brought it down squarely between the black beast's eyes.

It bellowed in pain and tried to draw back, changed its mind, and tried to get him with its tongue.

He struck it again, cracking several of its teeth, struck a third time, and a fourth, and heard bone splinter, heard leathered skin split, heard screams he wasn't sure were his or its. But now that he had started all he could do was swing and dodge the teeth and the tongue, and swing again without thinking about what he was doing.

It bellowed.

He bellowed back.

It became the failure of providence to give him more

than ordinary skills as a player; it became the failure of the
world to give him his due; it became the crush of futility,
the anger at a sister who had left him too soon; and it
became the image of himself, waiting for fortune to knock
on the door, hold out the silver tray, and present him with
his millions.

The bat splintered.

The jagged edges dug into the creature's now bloodied
and ragged head, making it more difficult after each swing
for Gideon to retrieve it.

The head sagged, and he moved closer, stabbing now in
a frenzy that made him dizzy, made his eyes close, made
him finally stagger backward and fall on the floor, legs
splayed and trembling, arms limp in his lap.

A crashing, then, nails screeching out of wood and metal,
and when he looked up he saw the pantry empty, and the
meadow clear beyond.

He heard a sound to his left and barely had the strength
to move his head around.

"Damn," Glorian said. "Boy, you don't fool around."

FOUR

"I want you to know before you even try to explain that I'm still not convinced," he said.

"What do you have to do?" she asked. "Die?"

They were in the living room, moving there at his request since he didn't want to have to look at the carnage in the kitchen anymore. He didn't turn on the lights, only opened the curtains more to catch the last of the moon and a glimmer of streetlight. She sat in his favorite armchair, her long legs curled comfortably beneath her, the hem of the white dress pulled demurely around her ankles. He lay exhausted on the couch, head on a lumpy throw pillow, one arm limp over his eyes. His shirt was gone, his boots and socks off, taken by a shaken Glorian, who had insisted on bathing the odious blood from his face and chest, his arms and hands. Miraculously, none of it was his, but he was too weary to offer a thankful prayer for the favor.

"You really are stubborn, aren't you?"

He shrugged.

"If you want, I'll go out again and bring back another."

"No!" he said quickly. "No. Just give me a chance to get my breath back so I can think."

He inhaled deeply, feeling the pull of aching muscles across his ribs, through his arms, along the backs of his legs. There was the sting of several clumsily extracted splinters that had lodged here and there when the bat had broken. There were the bruises on his jaw where Glorian had hit him. And there lingered in his nostrils the stench of

24

the black beast, the smell of its blood, its breath, the fear it induced.

His arm lowered stiffly, his legs hated him for even thinking about moving, and he shifted to his side so he could look at her without causing a cramp in his neck. And it saddened him to think that at the moment he could not appreciate how lovely she was.

"I hurt," he said with a wry smile.

"I know."

"It isn't going away."

"It will."

"Hurt in dreams doesn't last."

"I've noticed."

"What I mean is, if this whole thing isn't a ridiculous dream and I'm not drunk and I haven't been clobbered over the head and I'm not dead already and just waiting for someone to take me where I'm supposed to go and it isn't some lousy practical joke, then what the hell is it?"

She considered him for several long seconds, enough to make him feel uncomfortable about watching her so intently, before she slipped down off the chair and sat catlike on the floor beside him. She said nothing; she only hummed tunelessly for a while before falling silent.

He shifted again. The moon was finally gone, but the leaf-shrouded streetlamp outside gave him just enough light to see the color of her eyes, and the lines of her hair, and the set of her mouth while she thought and touched his hand.

"Are you a princess or something?" he asked finally.

She gave him a look: *knock it off, this is serious*.

"I mean, are you here to . . . that is, are we talking about going on some grand quest to find a magical talisman that will save your . . . country from destruction or something?"

She gave him the look again.

"Oh."

It was evident she had no idea how to say what she had

to say, and just as evident that when she said it she knew he wouldn't believe her. And he probably wouldn't because, in spite of her touch, he didn't believe it himself.

The problem was, he couldn't rid himself of the image of the creature in the next room, the battering it took, and the very real blood that was still on the floor.

"Try me," he said.

"I can take care of myself," she said by way of prologue.

"I wouldn't doubt it."

"But I can't do this alone."

"I gathered that."

"I need someone who can . . . well, fight a little, talk a little, think a lot." She stirred and held up a finger to prevent his interruption. "Now you're asking yourself, Why you? Why, of all the people in the world, your world, should I pick you for this job? What demonstrative qualities do you, Gideon Sunday, have that are so unique that I am willing to risk my life to contact you and bring you back with me? What is there about you and your existence—"

"Stop," he said, pushing himself into a sitting position. "I don't know if I want to know the answer to all those burning questions."

She smiled. "That's good, because I don't have any."

He was suddenly disappointed. "You don't?"

"No."

He couldn't help himself. "Then why?"

"Chance," she said with a shrug.

"What? You're kidding."

"No," she said. "I'm not kidding."

"Damn. That's not very flattering, you know."

"It wasn't meant to be."

His smile twisted, but he kept silent.

"There is little personal control over the Bridges, you see," she explained. "In fact, there's barely any at all that I'm aware of. When it seems as if you need one badly enough, they happen. Most of the time, that is. And then you either choose to go across, or to ignore it. If you ignore it, it lifts, as it were, and can't be summoned again for whyever you got it in the first place. If you cross, you have to hope that there's a reason why it is where it is, and you also have to hope you can figure it out fast enough to do you some good if it isn't immediately evident. And if what you need is in fact on the other side, then all you have to do is bring it back and hope that it will take care of things for you. It doesn't always, though. Sometimes it's a mistake. Sometimes it's deadly. And sometimes everything works out just fine. There's no telling. No telling at all.''

"Chance?" he said when he thought he had untangled everything she'd said. "You mean, I'm a random choice?"

"Not a choice," she told him. "An event."

"Oh. I'm an event."

"Yes."

"And now you have to decide if I'm right for whatever it is you wanted the Bridge for, whatever that is."

"I already told you what it is."

"But you didn't tell me how it happens."

"Yes, I did."

"But . . . ." He put his elbows on his thighs, cupped his face in his hands, and rubbed at his temples, hoping that if he rubbed hard enough, the pain would help him think, or make her go away so he could go back to sleep and wake up screaming. "But what you're saying, then, is that it's something like . . . like magic."

"Sure. Something like."

"I don't believe in magic."

"You have a meadow in your pantry."

He had an idea. With a gesture that asked her to stay where she was, he went to the front door, unlocked it, and went outside. The night was cool, dark now that the moon had finally set, and he shivered as he went down the steps and across the small front lawn. The blades were cold, the dew colder still, and he was hugging himself by the time he reached the side of the house.

He stopped, looked at the high untrimmed hedge that separated his house from the next, then stepped quickly forward and turned right.

The house was normal.

Ignoring the wet grass, he hurried to the pantry window and looked up. There was no break that he could see, no bulges, no screens, no lights, no sophisticated projection equipment, no signs of anyone's elaborate tampering. He touched the clapboard below the sill, pushed at it, thumped it lightly with a loose fist, and stood back, frowning. He cocked his head, he squinted, he cocked his head the other way and squinted again. He considered checking it upside down and told himself he was being stupid. Then he returned to the foyer, looked at Glorian still on the floor beside the couch, and went to the kitchen doorway.

There was blood spattered on the floor, the remains of the bat lay in front of the stove, and a golden glow pulsed dimly from the pantry.

"You're a hard man to please," she said when he sat on the couch and shrugged. "Are you satisfied?"

"I'm satisfied that I don't think I'm any crazier than I used to be."

"It's a start."

"Now what?"

"I guess we go." She stood, hesitated, then leaned over and kissed the top of his head. "Thanks."

"Don't mention it," he muttered, put his hands on her waist, and eased her to one side. He rose, looked down at himself, and shook his head. "I'm really going to do this, I think."

"Great," she said with a remarkable lack of enthusiasm.

"Yeah, well, if I am, I'm not going like this."

"I don't have much time."

"I'm not going to pack a trunk," he told her, and ran up to his room, pulled his aluminum-frame backpack from the closet, and dropped it on the bed. He moved quickly to prevent himself from thinking, every so often looking at the picture of his sister and asking her what in hell he was getting himself into this time?

She didn't answer.

He didn't think she would.

He dressed in boots, jeans, and a dark shirt; he packed another pair of boots, two more pairs of jeans, underwear, and two shirts. He figured anything else he needed he'd pick up along the way. A shrug, and the pack was on, and after he locked all the windows and pulled all the plugs, he closed the door and hurried into the hall. As he passed the bathroom he paused and looked in, wondering if he should take his razor, his deodorant, his brush, his shampoo. Then he reminded himself that he was not on his way to play in Los Angeles or Detroit. He was going somewhere else; the fact that he didn't know where, or what name it had, didn't make him feel any easier.

Glorian was standing in the kitchen doorway. When she saw the pack, she shook her head. "That isn't necessary."

"Is it a nudist colony out there?"

"No."

"Then it's necessary." Before she could turn he took hold of her arm. "Glorian, you said you never knew if what you found on the other side of the Bridge was what you wanted until you got there. I still don't know what you're after, but, just for the sake of my ego, am I what you want?"

"As opposed to what?"

"Never mind."

With exaggerated care they crossed the littered floor and moved into the pantry. The meadow was still filled with a gold light, somewhat dimmer now that the sun was nearing the distant mountains. A breeze rustled across the top of the grass, and the birds he had seen earlier were gone.

"Wait a minute," he said as she moved to step through.

"Now what?"

"How do I get back?"

"The same way you get in."

"Through the pantry."

"On this side, yes."

"Is there a limit?"

"What?"

"Is there a time limit? That is, do I have to do what I have to do in less than twenty-four hours or the Bridge goes up and I'm trapped on the other side? Or do I have a month, maybe a year? For that matter, now that I think about it, is time the same out there as it is in here?"

She frowned. "You sure have a lot of questions."

"I've never done this before."

Her lower lip pulled slowly between her teeth, and she bit down lightly. Her frown was disturbing. "Well, to tell the truth, neither have I."

"Oh."

"What I mean is, I don't know about the time question. I assume it's the same on both sides. I do know that there isn't a limit on what you have to do."

"Which is?"

"Stay alive long enough to help me."

Why, he wondered, am I not surprised.

"And what do I have to do to help you?"

"Find something for me."

"Ah," he said, smiling at last. Now, at least, she was treading familiar ground. "It is a quest."

"No, not really."

"Do me a favor," he said. "Let me think it's a quest, all right? It'll help me cope."

"All right, if you insist."

She moved again, out of his grip and into the meadow. There was no shimmering of light, no thunder, no music. She was in the pantry, and she was standing in the ankle-high grass, waiting impatiently for him.

How bad is it here, he thought, that I have to lose my mind to keep my sanity?

He looked over his shoulder and raised an eyebrow.

Pretty shitty, he thought.

"Hey," he said as he took a deep breath and stepped through the wall, "what am I looking for, anyway?"

"Oh, that," Glorian said.

"Yeah, that."

"What you're looking for is a duck."

FIVE

"A what?" he yelped, stumbling over the threshold and nearly falling to the ground.

"A duck," she said as if he should have known, and headed straight for the mountains.

"Forget it," he told her, turned around, and started back for home.

And stopped.

Home was gone.

Instead of the gap in the pantry wall, there was a tree. A rather large tree with a rich thick crown fully sixty feet above the meadow. Its wide bole was a dark green so smooth and glossy he was able to see a vague unflattering reflection of himself when he stood up to it and slammed it with a fist. It didn't give. He slammed it again, then walked around it, hoping to find some sort of break that indicated a doorway, or a clue, or a sign, or a knothole through which he would be able to squeeze. But there was nothing but the bark, and when he put a palm to it his hand slipped away, negating the possibility of climbing up to the nearest branch some twelve feet over his head.

It smelled strongly of pine, but he wasn't comforted.

He stood back and scowled, and checked the other trees around it in case he had made a mistake.

None of them, however, looked like his pantry.

"I thought," he said to Glorian when she returned to fetch him, "that I'd be able to go back."

"And I told you I've never done this before."

"Then how did you know that?"

"Hearsay."

"Wonderful."

"Come on," she said, tugging at his arm. "We've got to get across before the sun sets."

"Why?" he said sourly. "More monsters?"

"Right."

"Damn."

He followed her, but not gladly, as she strode across the rolling land. More than once he was tempted to tell her to go on ahead, that he wasn't having any part of this fantastic nonsense, that he was going to by god wait by the tree until he figured out how to locate the Bridge that would take him home; and more than once he changed his mind because he didn't like the looks of the birds that lifted from the trees to the south. They were the same ones he had seen before, but now that he was here and not there, it was easy to see they were considerably larger than he had thought. So much so that he wished he had brought his bat with him, a notion that reminded him cruelly that he hadn't bothered to think about bringing a weapon—all he had were his feet for running and his fists for punching and his head for butting up against the nearest wall for talking him into doing this.

A glance back when they were halfway across, and he saw another mountain range, this one much higher than the one ahead, much more rugged, and darker despite the fact that its uneven slopes received the full brunt of the setting sun. He walked on, but he couldn't help looking again, and again. Were he superstitious, he knew he would have thought that a goose had danced a drunken jig on his grave.

There was something up there.

He didn't know what, but there was something up there, miles away yet still able to watch him and definitely unhappy about his being where he was.

Glorian moved more rapidly.

The sun lowered to touch the highest peak.

The birds had wheeled over the meadow and were flocking, more than a score of them, and they were silent.

A duck, he thought angrily. A goddamned duck.

But there had to be more to it than that. Nobody went through all the trouble Glorian had to find someone to help her unless this duck wasn't, maybe, a real duck after all. Perhaps it was a symbol of her people—about whom she had said nothing at all, he reminded himself—and had been taken by their enemies; or perhaps "duck" in her language means something else, except that her language seemed to be his in every respect, including the nuances of truth and honesty that make life so exciting when the nuances are lies; or perhaps it was some sort of treasure, a statue or statuette that has her people's wealth literally attached to it in the form of jewels and precious metals.

The air began to cool, and the shadows of the forest ahead began sliding toward him, darkening the grass, turning the sky indigo. The sun was red. Behind him, the dark slopes had become unpleasantly touched with what looked like running blood.

Something was up there, watching.

He shifted the straps on his shoulders and hastened his pace until he was walking beside her. She did not look at him; her gaze was directed at the trees ahead, once in a while darting upward to check on the birds, who were flying in a tight circle now, and decidedly lower. The fact that she was obviously disinclined to talk increased his ill humor, but he turned his concentration to his feet instead, noting that the meadow was considerably wider than he had previously estimated and that it was taking them much longer to reach the forest than he hoped. But then, he had always been a poor judge of critical distances, which is why he had found himself flat on his back so many times in the few games he had played—the other guys seemed farther away than they really were, and it became a fascinating point of locker room and newspaper discussions as to why Gideon Sunday always looked so surprised when he was tackled; surely the jerk knew he was about to be hit; did he think he had some sort of invisible shield around him?

The birds dropped lower, and he could hear them now, muttering cries that were rasping and clipped. As though they were talking to themselves, debating the meals they saw hurrying below them.

And Gideon, without a doubt in his mind, knew they weren't the sort of avians who dined on insects and flowers.

"Glorian," he said, panting a little as the pack gained weight and his legs grew tight.

"What?"

"Those birds."

"Not good."

"Right."

The trees were a hundred yards distant now, and the sun was below the peak. The meadow was dark, the air under the trees darker still, and only the sky still held a touch of light.

"I think," she said, and began to run.

He was a step slower in starting but soon found himself racing beside her, one part of him admiring the way she took the ground in strides that made it seem as though she were floating, the other trying not to feel the talons and beaks of the predator birds tearing into the back of his neck, the top of his skull, his face, and his eyes.

The ground leveled and they moved even faster, and faster still when a grating shriek ripped through the twilight and he knew the creatures were diving.

He looked up and back, and saw them stringing out in single file, the lead bird already plummeting toward them, the others following a roller-coaster curve.

Glorian looked at him, and he took her hand and lengthened his stride, pulling her now and tensing not only for the assault but for her stumbling. He could hear her gasping, could hear his own breath hissing, and had to shake his head to clear his vision of a blur that had settled over it like a veil.

A bird screamed.

He whirled suddenly and pulled Glorian to him, whirled again and threw her in a spin past the first row of trees, spun himself and followed, and dove for the ground behind the nearest bole. The lead bird couldn't dodge in time, and it screamed as it struck the trunk head on, shaking leaves and twigs loose and causing a split to form jaggedly around the bark.

The others pulled away, silently, not even the sound of their wings beating the air.

The ground was virtually clear of underbrush. Glorian was lying on her back at the base of a sapling, rubbing her hips and glaring at the leaves, muttering unpleasantries Gideon tried not to hear. He waited until he was sure the birds wouldn't enter the forest, then crawled over and sat beside her, keeping an eye on one large brown wing he could see on the other side of the trunk where he'd hid.

"Are you all right?"

She sat up, brushed dirt from her dress, and checked her arms and legs. "I think so, yes."

"Good. What were they?"

"Ekklers," she said, panting only slightly from her exertion. "They're kind of like vultures, only they don't wait for someone else to do their killing for them."

He pulled the straps off and let the pack fall behind him so he could use it as a pillow. "I take it they don't come in here."

"Not often, no. Only when they're really hungry."

He scanned the high foliage and nodded; there was room for them if they were desperate enough. The trees were not all that close together, and now that he was inside the forest he could see that the higher branches were not as densely packed as they appeared from a distance. Fragments of sky were still visible, and he imagined that daylight would not be much diffused. The ekklers could, in fact, follow them rather easily if their eyesight was keen and their determination high.

"How hungry are they?" he asked, nodding toward the meadow.

"Not hungry enough."

He rested a moment longer, then grunted to his feet and moved cautiously toward the meadow's edge. A check of the sky proved it clear, and he peered around his protector tree to examine the bird that had nearly taken off his head.

"Jesus," he whispered.

A dark smear ran the length of the trunk from the point of impact to the ground, and a few feathers fluttered in the breeze. Other than that, there was only the wing. He looked up quickly, thinking the creature had somehow survived and was waiting to ambush him; he knelt and without leaving the forest's rim stared at the grass, searching for a place where the ekkler might have crawled off to recuperate; he looked down at the wing again and stepped away when he saw it quiver and begin to sink into the black earth.

A closer look in spite of himself, and he realized it wasn't sinking at all, it was falling apart, into a deep grey dust that danced across the ground and was scattered in an eyeblink.

"They do that," Glorian told him when he hurried back to her and explained what he'd seen—or not seen; he wasn't sure.

"Do what?"

"They don't hang around after they're dead. They decompose right away so they can return."

He obeyed a gesture and retrieved his pack. "Return?"

"Well, not really return. You'll only find them in places like this. They're born of it, Gideon, and they come back when they can."

"From the ground."

She nodded.

"The meadow is a breeding place? Like some sort of . . . egg?"

"Sort of."

She would have gone on, but his expression told her he

wanted time to think, and she gave it to him, taking his arm and leading him deeper into the forest as she did, following a convoluted trail he could not see himself and did not ask about. Instead, he awkwardly pulled a jacket from the pack when he felt dusk's chill and wondered how Glorian, in her dress, was able to keep warm. A look told him she wasn't, and he scowled away her protests when he draped the jacket over her shoulders.

"Where are we going?"

She pointed. "There's a place not far ahead. We should reach it before midday tomorrow."

"And when we get there?"

"We find a couple of lorras, you get the duck, and you can go home."

"You weren't kidding about the duck, were you?"

She grinned. "No."

"You pulled me into this . . . place just to find a duck?"

"Well," she said, "it's not just a duck."

"A big duck? A jeweled duck? What?"

"No, a white duck."

It was indicative, he thought glumly, of the way things were going. No princesses, no treasures, no talisman that would destroy a world unless found and returned to the rightful owner. A duck. A white duck.

He sighed.

She patted his arm and smiled.

"What's a lorra?"

She shrugged. "You'll see."

"Is it going to kill me?"

"Not unless you tell it to."

He sighed again and kept silent.

The air darkened as the last of the light receded, as the wind died, as shadows sifted down from the leaves and laid a deeper chill over his shoulders. He was about to suggest finding a place to sleep when Glorian, barely visible now, stopped at a tree and stroked the smooth bole. He stared, thinking of the ekklers and wondering if these trees were about to become some sort of exotic pet. Then he saw a light, faint and tinged with blue; it was coming from the bark she had been caressing, and the more she did it the more it flowed, up and down until it formed a pulsing globe the size of his hand. She cupped it without touching it, blew on it lightly, and it broke free to float at eye level in front of her face. A nod, and she blew again, pushing it ahead until it was some twenty feet in front, where it stayed.

"Incredible," he said quietly, as if afraid his voice would startle the thing into feeling.

"We need another one." She moved to the next bole, and the globe moved away, maintaining the same distance, the same height. "Your turn."

"Can't you do it for me?"

"The lamps belong to the maker, Gideon. If we get separated, you'll need one for yourself."

"Well . . ." He touched the bark, and it was cold; he ran his hand along its surface, and it was colder still; a second time, and the dark green began to fade, to shift, and the more he rubbed the more the blue was drawn to the surface, colder, just shy of burning his hand. A touch from Glorian, and he let his hand drop away, shaking it to bring back its warmth while he watched the globe form. Then, following her example, he cupped it and blew on it, and the cold vanished as if snapped back into the trunk. He blinked at its brightness, blew again, and it settled some ten feet away and slightly higher than hers.

"Fascinating," he said, walking again, the illumination a narrow path from him to the lamp. "How long do they last?"

"Till sunrise."

"Ah." The weariness that had made his limbs heavy and his vision unsteady receded as he stared, trying to figure out how the things worked and deciding that if he did, he probably wouldn't understand it anyway. "And what if we want some privacy, or we don't want to be seen, or we want to sleep, or—"

She snapped her fingers, and her lamp extinguished.
"Wow."
She snapped them again and the bluelight returned, exactly where it had been, no dimmer, no brighter.
He had no idea how long he was mesmerized by the phenomenon, an hour or two, no longer, but he was soon beginning to stumble over his own feet, over shadows on the ground and he pleaded with her to stop.
"Why?"
"Sleep would be a good thing," he suggested.
"I want to get home."
"For crying out loud, don't you ever sleep?"
"Every so often."
"Well, I sleep every night, thank you," and his legs gave out. He toppled slowly, twisting so he could land on the pack, his arms and legs sprawled, a foolish smile on his face. "I feel like I'm drunk."
She stood over him, shaking her head. "You'll get over it."
"Only if I can get some sleep. A couple of hours, that's all. Then I'll be good as new."
"Oh, god," she said, sinking down beside him, "I hope not."
He would have asked her what the hell she meant by a crack like that, but as soon as he closed his eyes he could feel sleep beginning to draw up the blanket. He didn't even bother to open them again when he snapped his fingers; he just did, and it was darker. Then Glorian did the same, and there was no light at all; and when he saw the two pinpoints of red up in the branches he had no time to check for stars before he was unconscious.

SIX

"So it's like this," he said with maddening patience to his agent on the phone, trying to remember the guy's name and at the same time temper his growing exasperation. "I just can't come to Dallas any time soon for the tryout because I'm hunting for this duck. No, not duck hunting, hunting for a duck. There's a difference—subtle, but a difference. Yes. A duck. It's a special duck. No, not for the zoo. No, I don't know where it is. For that matter, I don't even know where I am. What do you mean? I'm not drunk. I may have been before, but I sure as hell aren't now.

"Look, it's really very simple when you take the time to think about it. I met this woman, who has a bitch of a temper, by the way, and a hell of a right cross, who was in my pantry, and I followed her after beating some really bad-news creature half to death and now I'm—"

The agent yelled.

"Now we're not going to get anywhere if you act like that," he said, shaking his head at the man's lack of trust and faith. "Just tell the manager I'll be there as soon as I can, and tell him for me that I appreciate more than he'll ever know this chance to make a living again. Hell, I'd even tote the water, but don't tell him that, for god's sake, he'll think I'm desperate.

"When? I don't know. How can I give you a date, I told you I don't know. The best I can do is tell you I'll be

41

back soon. No, I do not know when, damnit! As soon as I find this stupid duck and find out how to get back. No, I don't have a map. No, I can't ask a cop. I don't know if there are any around here. No, I can't take a plane. As far as I know there are no planes here. No, no cars either. Look, I haven't even seen a road, for god's sake, so give me a break, okay?"

The agent yelled again.

"You really aren't cooperating, you know," he said, beginning to lose his own temper. "You may think you have a problem, but what about me, huh? I'm in the middle of literal nowhere. You think that's fun? You think I'm doing this because I want to play hard to get? How can a guy who hardly ever plays play hard to get? That doesn't make sense."

The agent screamed his name as an obscenity, and Gideon slammed the handset back into its cradle, rolled over, and punched at his pillow in hopes that the agent would get a telepathic black eye. The pillow wouldn't give. In fact, it felt as if he had punched a block of concrete.

He groaned and sat up, and rubbed his face with his hands, ran his tongue over his teeth to rid them of their cotton coating, and stretched.

And froze.

He was in the middle of a forest, a forest whose trees had dark green trunks, whose branches began far over his head, and whose foliage was sparse enough to permit him a good look at a sky so blue his eyes began to water.

"Oh hell," he muttered, and lowered his head.

Not a dream. It wasn't a dream.

No agent, no offer lucrative or otherwise, no chance for him to make another stab at a comeback. He grunted then and scratched his scalp and chest vigorously. He was, of course, kidding himself anyway. Had he been a star, he would have been able to find at least a decent backup position on a contending team; but he was, like most of his colleagues, only average, and only average players who are dragged bellowing over the age of thirty do not get asked to come back to the game and help save a team's ass in the home stretch.

In that sense, he knew the dream was very much a nightmare.

It told him things he did not want to know.

His back ached, his legs ached, his head ached, and he took his time getting to his feet, swayed a little for balance before he dropped into a fast series of deep-knee bends and toe-touchers in order to fool his muscles into thinking he wasn't quite dead. And when he thought he would move around without falling over, he put his hands on his hips and looked for Glorian, the first thing on his mind a bit of persuasive technique to force her, if necessary, to give him more information about this place and about what the hell he was doing here.

She was gone.

He grunted softly, rubbed a finger over his nose, and looked again.

She was still gone.

She had been standing over him when he'd dropped off, he remembered, but as he walked slowly around the area he realized he couldn't find a single sign that she had slept there. Maybe, he thought, she was modest and slept over there. Or over there. Or back here.

She hadn't.

Then he remembered the screaming, and a vague thought that the agent—which he didn't have in the first place— had a curiously high voice.

"Glorian?"

Using his backpack as a hub, he walked a hundred paces in several directions. He looked up, he checked the hard ground for footprints or marks of scuffling; he widened the radius of his search and with a hard swallow looked for blood or torn cloth; he widened it yet again and found, nearly an hour later, a small scattering of leaves and broken twigs. He tilted his head, squinting through the soft daylight at the nearest leaves, and saw a branch that had been almost stripped. And the one above it the same. Measuring the distance between it and the ground told him that unless Glorian had leaping skills she hadn't told him about, she hadn't climbed up there. On the other hand, something could have been waiting there and carried her off.

The ekklers weren't large enough.

The black beast, however, was.

"Glorian!"

But all he could hear was the sound of his voice fading and the soft call of singing birds too high for him to see.

He ran to his pack, cursing the lamented lost bat, and swung it onto his shoulders. He had no intention of staying around for whatever it was that had taken Glorian, or had chased her off, to come back and get him; and he didn't feel as if he were deserting her, either. She was gone, and he was without a weapon. The best thing for him to do was go somewhere else—keep on in the direction she had been guiding him. Maybe, when he reached the town or city or whatever, someone would be able to help him, to come back with him to find her.

Though he doubted seriously such a search would succeed.

An hour later he suspected he had made a mistake.

Though he followed as best he could the invisible trail she had been using, keeping the sun at his back and trying to walk a reasonably straight line, he realized that there were a number of rather vital things she hadn't told him about her world, among a great number of other things. Like how to distinguish between the edible and the poisonous plants and berries he saw occasionally, like how to find water because his throat was filling rapidly with sand every time he took a breath, and like what to do once he got where he was going.

He rested more frequently than he knew was necessary.

He spent as much time looking up and behind him as he did ahead.

And nothing he did, from counting the trees to counting

his footsteps, could keep him from remembering the screams he had heard in his dream. Each time they returned they were more horrifying; each time they returned he was less able to tell if they were screams of anger or fear; they were screams, and they forced his expression into a perpetual wince of guilt—if he had awakened, if he had been more alert, if he had driven himself on as she had wanted . . .

Too many ifs.

Too many things he did not understand.

And too often, in spite of the oddness of his surroundings, he found himself thinking he was only hiking through some little used national park in some remote western state. Any minute now he was going to come across a ranger who would caution him about forest fires and not feeding the bears; or he would stumble upon a twenty-foot camper filled with midwestern tourists roughing it in the wilderness as they watched their portable televisions, listened to their portable radios and tape decks, and cooked their canned food on portable gas ranges. They would offer him a beer, he'd accept with a smile, and they would trade harrowing stories of their adventures, how the traffic was getting worse every year, how the park fees were unpatriotically going up until they could scarcely afford them, and how it was getting increasingly difficult to find a place truly cut off from civilization so that they could get back to nature and feel the atavistic pull of the land their ancestors had settled the century before.

Then he'd remember the screams.

And he'd take a close look at the trees and remember the lamps, the ekklers, and the face of the black beast.

He played word and history games in an effort to test the reach of his sanity and decided that he was too crazy to know if he was crazy or not.

When the sun was almost directly overhead, he stopped at each bush to test their leaves, pinching them in hopes of getting a dab of moisture onto his tongue. He figured that if he had a meadow filled with them, he just might be able to get a mouthful, if he were lucky.

Then, suddenly, he stopped.

He looked at the brush to his right, to his left, and realized that the trees were now much farther apart and the underbrush was growing thicker, forming itself into red- and cobalt-blossomed hedgerows that almost too patly defined paths for him to follow. Though the forest continued, he could see by looking only slightly up that the mountains were much nearer and much higher than he'd estimated. The slopes, what glimpses of them he could get, were not as precipitous and were streaked with green and what may have been running water—streams or small rivers spilling out of creeks midway toward the peaks.

By midday, he remembered Glorian saying by midday they were supposed to be where they were going. Wherever that was.

He sat crossed-legged where he stood and stared at the winding path ahead. Being a somewhat reluctant tourist in this place, he decided he would have to have some sort of plan, some way of greeting these others—if others there were—so that they didn't think he was the one who had . . . The word wouldn't come. He substituted "lost" instead and hoped they would understand that he was new at this game, that he was less a babe in the woods than a babe in someone's arms, and sooner or later, and preferably the former, he was going to need a patient tutor who bordered on the genius for dealing with strangers.

A plan, then.

But he couldn't think of one.

It did cross his mind to return to the meadow, wait until dawn, and then cross in a hurry. When he reached the other side, he might be able to figure out how to locate the Bridge and get back to his own house. Explaining the damage to the kitchen and pantry would be a minor consideration when he had someone in to fix them—the fact that he would be there and not here would be sufficient incentive to lie through his teeth.

On the other hand, there was Glorian.

Or rather, there wasn't Glorian. And he finally decided that if the people she knew were as open-minded as she had been about his presence, he would have a much better chance not turning back. A decision that did not ease his mind a whit but at least severed another option.

He sat until the sun nearly shone directly in his face, and he couldn't think of a damned thing to do finally but get up, stretch, shift the pack to a more comfortable position, and move on. Sitting wasn't getting him anything but a damp rump, and when he heard the first faint cries of ekklers swooping above the trees, he decided that the best plan was to get where he was going before they got him, too.

Maybe, he thought, he would be able to get some food. His stomach was embarrassingly loud, and the hunger had become close to a physical ache. He didn't fear starving to death, but when he stumbled over nothing and the weight of the pack almost dumped him on his face, he worried. As the hedgerows grew taller, then, he was more inclined to examine them more closely and saw, nestled in the center of the cobalt-and-red blossoms, clutches of berries the size of his thumbnail; they were round, though not perfectly so, and of a deep purple he imagined would leave a stain like blueberry juice. They also looked inviting.

His step slowed.

He glanced behind him, glanced ahead, and licked his lips. The leaves surrounding the flowers were deeply serrated and prickly, but a quick snatch had a bloom in his hand without more than a small scratch on a knuckle. He held it close to his face, sniffed, admired the somewhat pungent perfume for almost a full second before plucking the berry from its stem and popping it into his mouth.

It was sweet, its juice thick, its meat pulpy. He held it on his tongue, waiting for the stabs of poisonous agony to course through his system and leave him dead where he stood; when it didn't happen, he swallowed it with a loud gulp and froze. Waiting again. Looking heavenward in preparation for a swift final confession just in case. When still nothing happened, he narrowed one eye and took another. The worst he could feel was his stomach demanding that he stop sending such paltry amounts down when, as if he didn't know, it was starving.

"Well," he said, pleased with himself, and silently blessing the land for bringing some luck at last; and he renewed his walking, reaching out to pluck a berry, to stuff a berry, to admire the way the hedgerow thickened until, after several miles, it was nearly impenetrable.

Then the path, the brush, and the forest ended.

He halted and slowly brought the pack off his shoulders to dangle from one hand.

Ahead, perhaps two or three days' walk at the rate he was going, was the slope of the nearest mountain, gentle, covered with grass and what appeared to be grazing animals moving across it. A scattering of trees unlike those he had just passed under. A line of low, intensely green brush that marked the course of a stream. A narrow band of deep red, which, when he stared at it long enough, he decided might well be a road that left the valley floor and climbed in a gentle switchback toward a notch in the mountain's side, just to the east.

And directly in front of him, a village.

He corrected himself. It was much too small to be a village, more like a compound without walls. The path resumed after a hundred yards of low grass that encircled the colony like a wind-rippled moat, passing between a row of greystone, two-story houses whose slate or stone roofs were only slightly peaked. There were, as best he could count, four on either side, the windows he could see paned in glass and circular, the walls untouched by paint and weathered smooth. A low stone wall surrounded each one, and though he could see nothing in any of the yards, he could hear the sounds of bleating and barking.

People, he thought with a grin; my god, there are people.

Without regard for the niceties of approach, he broke

into a run across the grass, dragging the pack at his side and readying himself for a friendly wave as soon as the first man or woman showed a face to him.

He managed only twenty yards before the ground opened up and he plunged flailing into a pit.

SEVEN

His first reaction as he fell windmilling and kicking was one of extreme disappointment; his second was one of only slightly less pain when he slammed shoulder first into the pit's far wall and rebounded to its bottom, striking the other shoulder just as hard. His elbow felt split in half as it filled his arm with a tracing of fire. The pack landed on his right leg. A clot of dirt broke across the small of his back. A shower of dirt and dust greyed his hair and got into his mouth. He spat and rolled to his knees, shook his head to clear it, and looked up.

"I'll be damned," he said.

The hole was easily six feet deep and twice that on a side; a trap, he imagined as he himself shakily to his feet, for something as large as . . . not the black beast by any means, but perhaps a smaller cousin, or a band of stupid marauders. A cursory look around, however, showed him no scattering of bones, no fragments of rotted clothing, no feathers or fur that would vindicate his theory. Maybe, he thought, the people who dug it clean it out every night.

Noting that the top of his head was not two inches from ground level, he raised himself up on his toes, his hands gripping the edge.

There was no one in sight, no alarm given, no guard to see that unknowing strangers didn't fall into the trap. The distant bleating and barking continued. The sun was already teasing the top of the mountain. He glanced around the pit, grunted, and fetched his pack, threw it out, and hauled himself out behind it. After dusting off his shirt and jeans, and stretching his legs to be sure they still worked, he tried to imagine, if there was no one immediately on hand to render the trapped unconscious or dead, what possible use it might have. A dog could jump out of it. So could a determined rabbit.

He took another dozen steps and fell into another one.

"There's got to be a trick to this," he muttered as he pulled himself and his pack out a second time, but nothing on the grass betrayed what he knew had to be the next line of defense. Yet he couldn't keep walking and falling like this, or one of these times he was going to break a leg; then he wouldn't be able to get out, and he would have to spend the night in one.

Oh, he thought.

Immediately, he lowered himself by stages to his hands and knees, hooked the pack around one ankle, and began a cautious, probing advance, slanting to his right and glaring at the ground to find seams, the telltale rims, the slightly discolored blades that would keep him from falling again.

When he found the next one, only his arm dropped, the ground coming up to give him a fair clip to the chin that stunned him for several seconds and made him check his tongue to be sure he still had it. A test for the pit's perimeter, and he moved on, more confident but no more rapidly—he didn't want to take the chance. A fourth pit was discovered, and a fifth he nearly tumbled into on his own when he heard a faint skreeing over the forest that spun him around in a panic. The hunting ekklers were out again, and though he was sorely tempted to leap to his feet and run like hell, he only looked up, saw them flocking above the trees, apparently not able or willing to leave their meadow sanctuary. Being thankful for small favors, then, he continued crawling until he had reached the path's smooth cobbles again.

He stood.

He waited.

He didn't expect a band, but he couldn't credit no one
having heard him at all. A call brought no response from
any of the eight doors or any of the sixteen windows; it
did, however, shut the bleating and barking up.

He sniffed, rubbed at his neck thoughtfully, and checked
the houses again before moving. Nothing had changed.
They were well kept, clean, upper and lower stories without shop signs or family designations of any kind, and the
stone walls with only a single break for entry were neither
crumbling nor broken. In all, the hamlet could have been
just completed for all the indications of habitation it gave.

A self-consciously casual stroll to the last pair in line
brought him no attention; a faster stroll back showed him
his shadow arrowing toward the forest, and he realized
with a start that the sun had already drifted behind the
range and, when he checked, the flock or herd was gone
from the pastureland. If it was a flock or a herd. And if all
that grass was only pasture and not another obstacle course.

A yell this time produced no more reaction than his first
call, and he decided it was time he stopped thinking about
the right thing to do and act on instinct instead—unfortunately, a race for home was out of the question, so he
walked through the gap-gate of the first house on his right
and knocked on the thick, banded door. When there was
no answer he reached for the knob and his fingers closed
around air, reached for a latch and found nothing.
Trusting sorts, he thought, and backed away to peer up at
the windows, the roof, around him again before he returned to the door. Another knock for form, and he pushed.
The door swung open noiselessly, and only after he had
scanned the street and the other buildings did he step
inside.

There was no one home.
There may never have been anyone at home.
The room he walked into was large, its walls done in
soft white, its ceiling the same, the floors wood and
polished, and not a stick of furniture or a single framed
painting caught his eye anywhere.

There were two narrow doors side by side in the back wall. He chose one and found a switchback staircase that led him to the second floor, three more large rooms, and not a thing else. The second door below led him down a short hall off of which he found four other rooms, all the same though smaller than the first. A back entrance showed him an ill-tended band of grass, the wall again, and to the north low hills he had not seen before. This place, then— the meadow, the forest, the deserted hamlet—was in a bowl valley, and for some reason the thought was not comforting at all.

It didn't occur to him until he returned disquieted to the front that he had seen neither kitchen nor bath anywhere, nor anything that might lead him down to a cellar or up into an attic. He didn't much care for the way his bootheels sounded on the floor, or the way his breathing seemed magnified, ragged, and echoed; the curtainless round windows were covered with a light dust, but the panes weren't broken, nor was the glass rippled with age, and when he caught his reflection in one, and realized who it was, he also didn't like the way he seemed more like a ghost than a human being looking for help.

The house across the way was the same, though the floorplan was slightly different.

He searched every building, and every building gave him the same empty answer.

By the time he had reached the last one and was sitting on the wall outside the front door, he guessed that he wasn't going to have any better luck here. No plumbing, no refrigeration, no facilities for internal or external relief. Dollhouses, he thought with a shudder and a quick look to the sky for the giant child who might soon come tramping over the mountain to take her toys home; they're like dollhouses no one wants to play with.

Dollhouses, or a ghost town.

Twilight hazed the air; the eastern range turned to blood.

He could see more clearly here that the meadow, the forest, and the colony were in a bowllike valley, and the northern and southern arms of the two ranges were considerably lower than those to his right and left. Empty; large, verdant, and empty. A pricking at the base of his spine. He glanced eastward and knew, as he had before, that something was there on those blood-red slopes. Something was there, knew he was here, and was watching.

Glorian, he thought, this isn't fair at all.

He found himself searching the sky for contrails and, as the stars began to appear when twilight turned to dusk, familiar constellations. He didn't know many back home, only a handful at best, but what he saw up there made no sense. The moon, when it finally appeared in an unpleasantly pale form, seemed like the one he was used to, but he couldn't be sure.

So what else is new? he thought, and spun himself off the wall into the yard, where he picked up his pack and went inside the last house.

It was the same, no surprises, but it was out of the night's chill and it didn't take him long to find a way to use the clothing he had brought to make an unreasonable facsimile of a bed and lie down, facing a front window, hands cupped behind his head.

He decided as he watched the track of the moon that the first thing in the morning he would see if he could uncover whatever it was that Glorian had intended to do after she brought him here; then, if that failed, he would head on toward the slope to see if he had really seen grazing animals there, or if those tiny moving spots were only perverse tricks of the mind. If they did exist, and if they weren't undomesticated, there would probably be someone around to watch them, and that someone might be inclined to give him a direction or two. Assuming he didn't run into anything else first.

Maybe, he thought, sitting up suddenly with eyes wide, he ought to first do something about a weapon. He hadn't the slightest idea how to use a sword or a gun except in the most theoretical manner, and he supposed there wasn't going to be much use for a good blind-side tackle now and then. What he would have to do, then, is find himself something equivalent to a baseball bat; it had worked before, and it might just work again. It was, on any slate you cared to write, better than his bare hands, and a damned sight more comforting.

He lay back again.

He listened as a wind slid down the mountainside and began muttering to itself in the gaps between the houses, over the peaks of the roofs, through the grass that sounded like a colony of serpents moving out for an evening's hunt; he watched as the roof of the house across the way began to fade into black; and he wondered just what it was he would have to do in order to make things normal again.

"Shit," he said softly. Not because he was feeling pangs of homesickness or regret that he had been so ridiculously foolish as to begin this idiotic nonsense, but because, startlingly, he wasn't much homesick at all. He hadn't time to be, and now that he was letting his mind do a bit of free-lance roaming, when he had the time, he wasn't. Not a lot, anyway. He was, if he were going to be truthful with himself, a little excited. It beat all to hell the frustrations of failure, and his inability to make a choice about his future, and his refusal to look inside instead of outside for the reasons why he couldn't function the way he wanted; and it was certainly different, on a scale he never imagined existed.

That he was also considerably frightened and uncertain only made the episode all the more real.

A pact with himself, then: he would work on two fronts as close to simultaneously as he could—he would continue his attempt to locate someone who could tell him what Glorian was after, and he would also try to find his way home.

At sunrise, then . . . And he blinked in astonishment.

The sun was already up, shadows retreating in the opposite direction, the night's chill full in the house and making him shiver. He had slept, and he had not dreamed, and it

Lionel Fenn

was time to stop lying about making plans when there was work to be done and a world to be explored.

"God," he said for the sound of his voice, "you sound like a goddamned coach, for god's sake."

He repacked in a hurry, used the back of the house in lieu of more sanitary facilities, and sat on the front wall again. The day promised to be warm, and from what he saw of the land that rose gently toward the mountain, he wasn't going to get much in the way of shade if he started out that way. On the other hand, there wasn't much he could do here, either. From a pocket in the pack, then, he pulled out a handful of the berries he'd had the foresight to gather on his way here and popped them into his mouth one by one, taking as long as he could over them, knowing he was stalling and for the moment not caring.

After he was finished he slid off, shouldered the pack, and stared back the way he had come. When no one appeared in the short street to stop him, he grunted, turned, and began walking toward the slope.

And had taken less than five steps off the cobbles onto the grass moat when he fell into another pit.

"God damn!" he said, pushing at the dirt wall and rolling his eyes. "You're gonna be dead in an hour at this rate, dummy."

He climbed out, rolled over to stand, and dropped again.

Maybe, he thought, I'll just stay here. I'll eat bugs and roots and drink rain water and weave my clothes from bits of grass the winds brings down and maybe dig another room with my bare hands, a den for a quiet night when I don't want company.

"Damn!"

He crawled, tested, fell in one more time before the moat ended. There was no path now, only a broad stretch of field whose grass was higher, coarser, and relieved now and again by high, isolated bushes like those that had made up the hedgerows on the other side of the hamlet. The going was more difficult as the ground climbed and grew more uneven, but he was able to avoid sprained

ankles and unseemly tumbles by keeping his eyes down
most of the time. It made for more plodding than strolling,
and to prevent himself from slowing time down by counting the seconds, he passed the time by counting his steps
instead, ignoring the beat of the sun on his back and the
aches in his limbs, which seemed to fade once he had put
an hour and two miles behind him. The thought that he
might actually be getting used to this was pleasant to
contemplate; the thought that he might have to do this for
the rest of his life was considerably less alluring.

But since he had no choice, he moved on, pacing himself as the land rose more steeply, pulling at his legs and
adding weight to the pack.

And when he was high enough so that he could look
back, and down, he shook his head slowly.

The view across the valley was as beautiful as he'd ever
seen, as perfect as a place could get if one didn't mind not
having any conveniences at all. And he supposed that, if it
came to it and he were forced into it, he could probably
live down there until he died of natural causes, or until he
was utterly and unendurably bored to death.

Then he turned around to look at the mountain, to see if
he could find any sign at all of the road he thought he'd
spotted the day before.

He didn't see the road.

What he saw was the giant goat.

EIGHT

Gideon took a startled step back, and his right foot sank into a shallow depression that buckled his knee. He fell, and the weight of his pack toppled him over. He was too astonished to yell, and too busy trying to find his footing again to notice that the animal had moved closer to him. When he finally stood again, he wondered what sort of food the thing ate—with luck, it would be grass.

It didn't move again.

Gideon backed off another pace but didn't attempt to run. There was no threat in the creature's stance, and he had a feeling there was only curiosity.

It also wasn't precisely a goat.

It stood a good three times taller than a goat—about the size of a healthy horse on legs somewhat longer and thicker than normal—and though it had the long filmy hair and bearded muzzle of a caprine, its horns were those of a mountain ram's—thickly spiraled, curled back aside each large ear, and as solid-looking as the rock from which the houses below were made; the elongated tips also seemed to have a disconcerting habit of pointing directly at his chest. Its head was the same shape as a billy, but its eyes were much larger and nearly entirely white, and when it shifted sideways as though to find a better perspective on what it was staring at, he saw a tail half as long as the thing itself.

The hair was a soft and downy white at the body and shaded to black at the tips; the tail was all black, and there the hair was short, barely stirring as it switched back and forth. The hooves were hidden in the grass, but he suspected they were cloven and, aside from the horns, a potent weapon against whatever preyed upon it in the mountains.

Assuming, he thought, there was anything large and dumb enough to try it.

All in all, then, a harmless-seeming creature, though he did not like the pointed, horselike teeth that were bared when it lowered its thick neck to pull at a clump of grass.

Gideon cleared his throat.

The animal raised its head expectantly.

Gideon smiled, reached out carefully, and pulled a handful of grass out by its roots; a gentle clearing of his throat, and he held the offering out, hoping the beast wouldn't notice how much his arm trembled. A test for negotiation; his feet were killing him, his legs were preparing a wildcat strike, and the idea of going over the mountain by shank's mare was almost as unappealing as listening to the war cry of the ekklers. And if he was careful, the most he would lose would be a fingertip or two.

"Hey, fella," he said.

The goat-thing snorted, raised its head higher, and sniffed the air.

"It's okay," Gideon told it, taking a step forward. "Hey, I'm not going to hurt you, believe me."

The head lowered and it snorted again, and when Gideon moved still nearer it closed the gap in a single stride and wrapped its thick upper lip around the grass. Gideon held it for a moment, then released it.

"Not bad, huh?"

The creature backed off, shifted its head from side to side, and lowered it until its lips were touching the ground. Then it straightened and watched.

"Well, look," Gideon said, grabbing another clump and holding it out, "you and I could stand here all day eating like fools and gaining a lot of weight and stuff like that, but I think we ought to make a deal, don't you?

Maybe, but only if you want to, you could give me a lift over there. You know, through that notch up there? I'd be grateful. God, would I be grateful.''

The goat-thing bobbed its head as if it were nodding and took the second offering. This time Gideon reached out his free hand and touched the animal's neck. It shivered but didn't move, and he was astonished at the silken texture of its hair. He patted it, and it purred. Gideon blinked and patted again, and it purred again. He rubbed its nose, scratched between its horns, between its eyes, and moved to its side and stroked the length of its back.

And it purred.

Brother, he thought, and suddenly realized that this must be one of the lorras Glorian had told him they were going to get at the village before they moved on. Interesting, he thought; a beast of burden or just a riding animal, and he guessed without proof that it wasn't used for food. After all, how could you eat something that purred so wonderfully and could, at the same time, puncture both your lungs with one swipe of its horns?

He was trying to figure out a way to get onto its back without having it think he was attacking when something nudged him hard on the hip. He whirled. Another lorra, this one somewhat smaller and shaded dark pink to russet and apparently just as lazy in foraging for its own meals.

He shrugged. One to ride and one to change off on, and he picked up the grass.

A third one shoved him from the back—white to black like the first and considerably larger—and a fourth all white.

They were hungry, and they didn't want to wait their turn.

''Now wait a minute,'' he said, surrounded. ''Hold on, boys, this isn't going to work.''

The first one snorted as the purring became a soft rumbling, and Gideon noticed a slight discoloration in its eyes—they were, the more agitated it seemed to become, slowly turning a hard and flat black. Russet was tossing its head lower and lower, the better to aim the extended points of its horns; White was pawing at the ground.

"Now damnit, knock it off," he said angrily, looking down at the grassless plot of ground he was standing on. "There isn't anything left, can't you see that?"

Russet couldn't; it butted him lightly in the stomach, the points of the horns passing just barely to either side.

Gideon considered yelling for help, then considered vaulting the animals and running like hell, then lost his already shortened temper when one of them nipped his right buttock and slapped Russet sharply on the muzzle with an open palm. It growled and backed off, shaking its head.

"Well, well," he said, and slapped Grey and White the same, with the same results.

When he turned defiantly to the larger one, however, his hand paused in midair. While he could look the others in the eye, this one was taller than he at the shoulder, and he had the feeling that a slap was going to turn him into a marshmallow on the end of a fork over a fire. Instead he only glowered, keeping the threatening hand high.

Dumb as cows, he thought when it backed off a step; a real goat wouldn't put up with this crap for a minute.

Then he unshouldered his pack and let it hang from his left hand. He was beginning to suspect that getting a ride on one of them was a hopeless task. The others might be bullied into it for a few minutes or so, but that monster, who was probably the bull of the herd, would have him full of holes before he could get a leg up.

A nice idea, but fruitless.

"Sorry, fellas," he said. "I guess I'll go it alone."

They made way for him reluctantly, but a stroke here and a scratch there had two of them purring. The big one only watched him with head lowered and black eyes up; and Russet refused to give up—it lumbered easily at his side, every so often swinging its head around to nudge him and remind him it was still there. A dozen yards later there was only the two of them; a dozen more, and he looked back to see the other three grazing as though he hadn't existed.

Without thinking, and still walking, Gideon pulled up another handful of grass and held it out. The lorra took it and snorted its pleasure.

"Y'know, Red," he said, "this could be great if you'd only do me the favor of lending me your back."

The lorra cocked its head at the sound of his voice.

Gideon stopped, frowning in thought. No, he decided, it couldn't be. It was unnatural. It was fantastic. One just doesn't do things like this, not even in dreams.

"I don't suppose," he said, "you'd mind kneeling down or something so I could climb on."

Red did, lowering itself front legs first, then hind, and looking over its shoulder.

"I'll be damned."

Quickly, before the lorra changed its mind, or snapped out of it, or fell asleep, he put on the pack and swung one leg over the animal's back. The hair at the base of its neck was thick, and he buried his hands in it, almost closing his eyes at the softness, tugging at it lightly to be sure he wasn't going to fall off the moment the thing moved; then he took a deep breath.

"I guess we can go now."

Red swung its head back front and lifted, front, then back, so slowly Gideon was easily able to maintain his balance. Then it stood there, chomping the grass.

Gideon waited.

Nothing happened.

Gideon rocked back and forth, side to side, and tugged at the hair wound between his fingers.

Nothing happened.

"Okay, giddyup."

Red didn't move.

Gideon tried some very gentle persuasion with his boots. "Let's go, Red. I don't think I have all day."

Red spat at the ground and reached for more grass.

"The notch up there, see?" He leaned over the lorra's neck and pointed. "I want to get up there. I want to see what's on the other side." He considered, then rapped Red on one horn with a knuckle and winced. It felt like stone and was as abrasive as sand.

He tried wriggling again, various simple and complex permutations and combinations of body English, every word he ever heard a movie cowboy use, and still the lorra wouldn't move.

He looked behind him at the valley, at the rest of the grazing herd, and pictured himself on this beautiful slope, sitting on top of a giant goat and talking to it as if it understood every word he said. He wouldn't have been a bit surprised if a couple of pigeons came along and decided to make him their summer home.

"Red, please."

And Red moved.

It took him a while to get used to the lorra's odd side-to-side gait, but whenever he felt himself growing slightly seasick, or thought his legs were going to fall off from clamping its sides too hard, or wondered if he would spend the rest of his life bowlegged, he considered the alternative and concentrated on not falling. And the moment he stopped concentrating, he managed it with ease.

He was so pleased, it was almost a full five minutes before he noticed that they were moving parallel to what was indeed a road leading to the notch. It was cobbled in dark red stone and worn down its sides by the rush of water, down its center by what had to be the passage of more than a few giant goats' feet.

He sighed and told Red to get on the road and maybe they could move a little faster.

Red stayed on the grass.

He suggested that Red could easily detour to the verge now and then to pick up a snack if his stomach demanded it so much, but the lorra stayed where it was.

"For god's sake, Red, gimme a break."

It stopped at a bush and deftly plucked off the berries with its upper lip without disturbing the blossoms. Gideon remembered those he had in his pack and, with a bit of awkward maneuvering, managed to get some for himself, ate them, and looked at the road now curving away from their line of march.

"Jesus, Red, you're heading down again!"

Red was, and appeared to have no intention of going anywhere else.

"Red, for god's sake, will you please get on the god-damned road?"

Red did.

He looked at the back of the animal's rhythmically bobbing head and shook his own. This, he thought, was not to be believed. And remembered all too clearly his mother telling him, whenever he wanted this and demanded that, to give her the magic word and all would be handed to him—if not on a silver platter, then at least on a plastic tray that didn't contain his still beating heart because he was being rude. Please. Sis, he thought to a chuckling image of his dead sibling, you should be here. He was riding up the side of a mountain looking for a white duck, sitting on the back of a giant goat that did what it was told when you said please.

It was enough to make him laugh, which he did, loudly and long and lifting a hand when Red looked back to signal that he was fine, and if he wasn't, whatever he was didn't feel all that bad.

He laughed so hard his eyes filled with tears.

And when he stopped laughing it was a while before the tears left him alone.

The notch was closer, but he knew by then he wouldn't reach it before sunset. Around him the grass had become more sparse and was pocked now with boulders large and small; above, he could see great patches of bare rock, sheer and gleaming and sparkling with mica that caught the sunlight and gave it back to him in blinding lances. There were no trees that he could see, and when Red ambled over to the side to take more food, he saw, too, that the berry shrubs were gone. The hamlet was so far below that he had to squint to make out the individual buildings. The rest of Red's herd was gone.

"I think," he said when Red started moving again, "that we ought to look for some place to spend the night, okay? It doesn't have to be spectacular. I can hear water up ahead, maybe a place by the stream; what do you say?"

His answer was a grating, prolonged shriek from behind and above him. He twisted and saw a bird coasting out from the side of the cliffs—a large bird, glossy black, and wheeling about in what he knew was going to be a dive.

"Red," he said nervously.

The lorra increased its speed; and the bird shrieked again.

"Jesus, Red!"

The lorra, however, did not break into a gallop and sweep them away to safety; it stopped and turned, so quickly that he was spilled from his seat. The pack fell from his shoulders and rolled down the slope; a snap gave way, and his clothes spilled onto the grass, were caught by a wind that gusted up from the valley, and were pinwheeled away. Gideon gave them only a brief despairing glance before he spun around on his knees in time to see the bird nearing the end of its dive.

Its wingspread was fully ten feet across, its head slanting back to a double-pronged point, its beak hooked out and down over a mouth that opened wide enough to swallow a sheep. Its talons were extended, its eyes platter wide, and Gideon decided the ekklers would be mosquitoes compared to the thing that was about to take off his head.

Then Red reared, and Gideon gaped.

The lorra when extended was a good twelve feet tall, and its hooves when the hair fell away were like claws themselves. It challenged in a tigerlike roar that made Gideon scuttle back quickly and apparently made the diving bird think twice about attacking.

But it was too late.

It was too large and moving too fast, and in a blur

Gideon found almost impossible to follow, Red's right front hoof broke one of the bird's wings at the base, and its horns and head slammed into the thing's exposed breast. There was a scream. There was a roar that reverberated off the slope. Red was driven backward by the force of the collision but stayed on his hind legs, vigorously working his horns deeper into the bird's mangled chest, dancing to the side and using his hooves to drive off, then snap off the bird's talons.

A pause as Red sank back slightly, hesitated, and leapt forward, pulling down his head and landing on his front legs, driving the dying predator onto its back. Then he disengaged his horns and began a methodical, unrelenting trampling from head to tail that included the all-too-clear sounds of bones snapping and splintering, of flesh tearing, of blood running, until Gideon turned away and folded his hands over his stomach, retching, his eyes watering.

When his distress and the bird's screams ended, he stayed where he was, gasping, until he heard hoofbeats on the cobbles. Only then did he turn, and saw Red waiting for him, kneeling, looking, spatters of blood on his hair.

"Aw, Jesus, Red," he said, and staggered to his feet, hurried over, and combed quickly through the coat with his fingers, looking for injuries. He found none worse than a scratch, and his relief had him bury his face in the lorra's neck.

Red purred.

Gideon swung onto his back, said the magic word, and they continued up the road for the next hour, watching both the sun in its descent and the sky in its blankness. At a fortlike configuration of four boulders, he suggested, politely, that they stop for the night. He had seen the mark of the stream beyond, and Red, spying the berry bushes, moved straight toward them.

Gideon knelt on the bank and splashed water over his head, blowing and laughing when Red did the same.

They drank. They ate berries. And they walked to the space in the middle of the boulders, where Red curled his legs under him and Gideon lay with his head on the lorra's side.

Nightfall came swiftly.

And Gideon slept soundly until, somewhere past the middle of a nightmare, he woke in a daze, heard nothing, and saw nothing but a pair of red eyes.

NINE

Gideon yelled hoarsely and threw up an arm to protect himself, then scrambled hastily away from Red, who was lurching clumsily to his feet, a deep catlike growl thundering in his throat. There was a moment of confusion and disorientation before Gideon was able to clear the sleep from his eyes, and when he did the red eyes were gone.

A dream, he thought, and knew it was wrong because he had seen them once before, the night Glorian had been taken, and he had thought that was a dream, too.

"I think," he said to no one in particular, "I don't want to stay around here anymore."

With further sleep out of the question, he noticed that the sky was beginning to lighten and knew that dawn was only a few minutes away. He groaned, rubbed the night's cold from his arms and legs, and staggered with the lorra to the stream, where he ducked his head under the water, drank, and shared the last of the berries with his companion. Then he climbed on Red's back, and they returned to the road, heading for the notch.

The day brightened, but the sky was filled with a low grey overcast that cast rippling shadows on the ground ahead of them. He preferred not to look at them or speculate on what it might have been that had been watching him while he slept. Try as he might, he could not determine if those eyes were animal or human; they were a definite red, dark and slanted upward, but he sensed an intelligence as well, and though he shuddered at the memory, neither could he determine if he'd been in danger or not.

It was a puzzle.

But then, this whole damned place was a puzzle, and he might as well be blind for all he knew about it, and his place here.

They reached the notch shortly before midday, and Gideon dismounted stiffly to let the lorra graze while he stood in the center of the road, rubbing his shoulders thoughtfully while he considered his next move.

The gap he faced was high-walled on both sides, each wall a precarious jumble of massive boulders and fallen rock, and once between them he noted apprehensively they would be easy targets for anyone, or anything, hiding above. As far as he could judge, and reminding himself that he was no judge of distance at all, the narrow passage followed the side of the mountain for at least four or five hundred yards, then swung to the right, probably to drop down the other side.

And that was the rub.

He had come all this way because it seemed the simplest way to go, yet he had no idea what lay beyond or even if he should be going there. He chastised himself again bitterly for not being alert when Glorian had needed his help, wished there was someone he could talk to, to ask advice of. Red was a good sort for a giant goatlike creature, but talking to him was like talking to a wall.

Still, he couldn't think of anything else to do; so, calling Red to him and explaining what was up, he mounted, took hold of the beast's hair, and they entered the notch.

The wind increased before they were a dozen yards in.

It boiled down the irregular rocky slope and snapped at his face, tangled his hair in front of his eyes, and penetrated his clothing as if he were naked. He shivered and leaned forward, hoping to gain some warmth from the lorra's luxurious coat, then decided to ask if the animal might, if he were of a mind, move a little faster. Red evidently didn't mind at all; he broke into a trot that nearly tossed Gideon aside, then into a loping run that made him suggest further, and loudly since he had to be heard over the wind, that getting one of them killed before they reached their destination was not precisely what he had in mind.

The lorra, however, was not to be stopped now. He had gotten into the spirit of the thing and was determined to see them on the other side of the mountain in less time than it took Gideon to complain that he was never going to see it at all at this rate.

Halfway through, the wind nearly blew him from his seat.

Three-quarters of the way to the far side, Red had to gather himself into a masterful leap over a fall of rock and stone, and Gideon, clutching the animal's neck hysterically and getting as low as he could without actually burrowing under the lorra's skin, was amazed at the grace it showed for such a large creature. Formidable, he thought, and concluded it would be a hell of a cavalry ride during a battle. He doubted there was much that would be able to stand in its way.

The road began to curve north and down, and the notch's south wall began to shrink until there was nothing left but a few rocks lying along the narrow verge. At that point Gideon wished aloud and angrily that Red would knock it off and stop, which the lorra did, in such a short space that actual sparks flew up from his hind hooves. Then Gideon dismounted, patted the animal's neck in gratitude, and walked to the edge of the precipice he faced.

The road, as he had guessed, continued on to the right for another hundred yards before slanting back to plunge down the far side of the mountain. Where he stood, however, there was a drop he estimated at easily a thousand feet, if not more, and he wasn't exactly sure what to make of the view.

Almost directly below was a wide white-water river that appeared out of a dim, misty haze to the north and van-

ished into the same many miles to the south; it was marked
by a broad band of intensely green woodland on either
bank, with breaks here and there that indicated regularly
used crossings, though he could see no evidence of ferries
or bridges. Beyond the river was a vast sullen plain that
stretched flatly to the far horizon, itself masked by still
another haze, smoky and tinged with dull yellow and deep
blue.

"I think," he said thoughtfully, "I may have picked the
wrong direction."

There were no cities that he could see, no isolated villages or clutches of homes such as the one he had left
behind. Were it not for the low brown grass, the plain
could easily have been a desert.

"This," he said to Red when the lorra moved more
closely to him, "is not promising at all."

Idly he reached into his jeans pocket and pulled out two
slightly flattened berries. He popped one into his mouth
and gave the other to the lorra. Then he looked down at his
feet and shrugged.

"On the other hand, this road is man-made, so to speak,
and has to go somewhere."

It did.

It swept them down to the base of the mountain and ran
along the outskirts of the river woodland until, at the first
of the breaks he had seen from above, it swung right again
and took them to the water. There was no bridge, nor were
there any signs there ever had been one here, but a quick
wading test proved that the swift-rushing water was less
than a foot deep, at least in this place, and they forded it
without difficulty, picked up the road again, and found
themselves outside the woods on the edge of the plain. The
grass was indeed brown, and low, and sharp-edged enough
to slice his skin neatly when he reached down to pluck up
a blade. He yelped, scowled, and decided that nothing
short of an elephant would be able to cross it with some
semblance of impunity.

Another mile, and he discovered he was wrong.

His first clue came when Red began to act peculiar, snorting and tossing his head side to side, spending more time watching the motionless plain than the road. When Gideon leaned over to stroke his wide neck in hopes of calming him, he saw that the creature's eyes were slowly turning black.

Not, he thought, a good sign.

He wondered if it was the mere fact of the plain. It was certainly eerie enough—the sharp-bladed grass rocklike in its stillness despite the occasional breeze and gust of wind, the length of it, the breadth of it, monotonously the same color and giving off not a single scent that he could pick up, nor a single sound that he could hear. Nothing lived out there, and nothing resembling a knoll or a hillock broke its surface all the way to the horizon.

Yet the lorra edged itself closer and closer to the left-hand verge—so close, in fact, that the reach of the trees soon had them in shade. Gideon didn't dispute the animal's instincts, but he would be damned if he could see anything amiss. Nothing changed, all was the same until, the road following the angles of the woodland and river, they rounded a sharp bend.

Then something moved on the plain.

Red stopped and backed toward the woods, his head down and horns at the ready. Gideon, not wanting to be aboard when whatever was going to happen finally happened, slipped off and stood near a bole that was, he noted, considerably wider than he.

The ground trembled slightly then, and he saw a large mound of grass begin to rise, black earth spilling away, then splitting, then falling away completely as the creature beneath it hove out of its burrow into the air. Red grumbled deep in his throat. Gideon eased farther around the tree and watched openmouthed as the creature shook the remaining bits of dirt from its body and paused to look around.

Well, he thought, I was right about the elephant. Sort of.

It had the bulk and height of a pachyderm, but its dark grey hide ranged back from a broad triangular head in folds much like scales that merged into a taillike appendage it kept arched over its flat back; the head itself was on a short, muscled neck and was broad at the base, where a slash of a mouth slavered and gnashed, and at the apex narrowed to a horn that curved frontward between the wide saucers of its eyes.

Red was set to charge when Gideon whipped out a hand and stayed it with a touch.

He waved at the thing, and it didn't move.

He stepped into the open and waved again; it didn't move.

The creature was blind, or at least blinded by the light. Its head swung in a slow searching arc while its broad nostrils flared and snorted, hunting for the scent that had brought it out of its lair. The arched tail trembled. When it took a short step forward, the leaves overhead quivered and husked.

Gideon kept his gaze on the thing as he backed slowly away, tugging at Red's hair to pull the lorra with him. It was no digging beast, he thought as he put another tree between himself and the plain; there must be burrows underground, a network of them, created by something else that permitted the thing to travel from one place to another. Its teeth marked it as carnivorous, its agitation at being unable to locate them marked it as hungry and getting frustrated, and the tail fully as long as the main body slowly lowered until it thumped repeatedly and lightly on the ground.

The thing moved again, this time sideways, the tail beating the grass harder, sending a hollow booming across the plain that sounded like thunder making its way over a mountain.

Red pawed the ground, and Gideon reached for a horn and with an effort tugged its head around, pulling now and trying to get it to follow. It resisted, then complied, and they hurried toward the river and followed the high bank south, the booming now behind them but still clear until, as they detoured around a thorned thicket, it stopped abruptly.

And was replaced by the sound of the thing crashing through the woods.

Gideon listened only a second before leaping onto Red's back and digging in his heels. The lorra at first thought they were going to meet the enemy head on and began a weaving charge that took them back the way they'd come. He yelled, he pulled, and finally he managed to plead his case politely and urgently enough that Red veered sharply and thundered south again, dodging the trees and underbrush until he reached the road. There he lengthened his stride in a single bound that almost threw Gideon off before he was able to stretch out along Red's neck and hold on, glancing over his shoulder to see the thing return to the plain ahead of a pair of trees it had snapped off at their base.

Gideon wondered if it could run.

It could, but only for a few steps before it lowered its head in exhaustion and lumbered back on the grass, where it pounded a hole in the roof of its burrow and climbed down, the last thing visible the blurred sweep of its tail.

The lorra ran on, and the trees became a green wall, the plain a smear of dirty brown.

Gideon closed his eyes against the wind caused by their passing and tried to clear his mind, to let time pass without a single image interfering, without a single speculation or examination diluting the only thought he wanted to hang on to—that of not falling off and being left behind.

It didn't work.

He suddenly wondered if on its home ground, under the surface, the thing could move faster than when it was out on the road. It had to be possible, otherwise it would never be able to catch its prey, unless its prey was so stupid as to let itself be trapped and caught. Or maybe it didn't need to eat all that often. Maybe its system was efficient enough to hoard and allocate the food it took in for the optimum effect; maybe all it had to be was patient, and let its appearance paralyze its prey long enough to make a move.

The ground to his immediate right exploded upward.

Red growled again and galloped even faster.

The thing trumpeted at them as it surged furiously from its burrow, ran a few steps, and hurried back to the grass.

The road ducked back into the woods, and just as they reached the curve the thing bellowed again, spinning on its hind legs to swing its tail, which hummed over Gideon's head and cracked a tree in half.

Persistent sonofabitch, he thought without an ounce of admiration, and hugged Red's neck more closely, glad they were under the woodland canopy for a time while the road found its way to the river and followed the bank. Red slowed and began panting, a fleck of foam appearing, then flying away from the corner of his mouth. Gideon saw it and urged the lorra to slow up, that as long as the trees were around they didn't have to rush, only hurry without dawdling. Red seemed to understand and paused once at a collapsed portion of the bank to drink his fill before moving on at a fast walk, giving Gideon an opportunity to straighten and take a deep breath that somehow failed to bring him anything remotely like a sense of relief.

The booming started again.

He wondered if there might be more than one of those things in pursuit, the winner getting the ears and tail and the rest the flank steaks.

The idea was discomforting enough for him to tell Red to leave the road when it plunged back into the trees again and stick to the riverbank. The going was slower but safer, and he knew he wasn't going to be happy until that confounded drumming stopped sending its message.

"Well, damn," he said, and looked behind him. "Damn, I think I've got it!"

Red bobbed his head.

Gideon permitted himself a deserved moment of preening.

Then a tree they passed shattered, and a branch knocked him senseless and into the river.

TEN

Given a choice, Gideon decided he would rather die in bed of old age; the river, however, had placed limitations on such dreams, and he flailed in the frigid water, amazed that it had gotten so deep when the fording area had been comfortingly shallow. He was not a good swimmer, but he knew enough to kick upward toward the surface and not attempt to fight the current. As it was, he was being swept along at a considerable rate, and when he was finally able to break into the air, gasping and sputtering and gulping for a breath, he saw nothing but the trees on either bank; Red was gone, the burrow-thing was gone, and if he didn't make his way to shore soon, he would be gone as well.

The trouble was the current.

It sailed him along like a newly hatched leaf, and dog paddling, which was the extent of his swimming stroke knowledge, was not going to break its hold and permit him to land, not without a vast amount of difficulty. The alternative, however, spurred him sufficiently, and he managed to angle himself to the right while swallowing only the occasional mouthful of water until, as luck would have it, he came up against a half-submerged rock and was able to cling to it on the downstream side. He was still an imposing twenty feet from the bank; his arms were filled with lead, and his side was threatening to split open without warning; and every time he tried to focus on something that might help him, he saw double.

The river sped and boiled around him, but after a moment's fumbling he found purchase on the underside of the boulder, a tiny ledge that permitted him to raise himself up until he was waist clear and slumped over the rock's top. A roll to one side, and his mouth begged for more air, spat water he could not hold down, and gasped again. His arms were stiff, both from exertion and the water's temperature, and he felt his teeth chattering, his lips hardening and most likely turning blue, and aches in both ears like the continuous sting of a sadistic wasp. He rolled to the other side; one foot slipped off. A frantic scrambling saved him, some kicking found the ledge, and with a grunt he clambered up until he was sitting high if not dry above the surface.

"Great," he said in short-lived self-congratulation. "Now what?"

The sun warmed him, dried his clothes, made his skin feel as if it were layered in thin mud.

He looked upriver and was astonished at how far he had been carried, and how miraculous it was that he had not drowned in the process. The mountains that ringed his meadow were now behind, and the course of the water had taken so many bends and turns that he had no idea where he had left Red, or even if the lorra had escaped the plain-beast.

The possibility that he hadn't depressed him.

Twice now he had managed to make friends of a sort, and twice they had been wrenched violently from him. It was enough, he thought gloomily, to make a man look deeper into the definition of a walking jinx.

Another ten minutes passed before he decided that he'd have to find the nerve somewhere to get off the rock. The river on its western flow was unbroken though uncommonly swift, and he didn't think he'd have to worry about having his knees bashed in if he tried to swim for it; the question was how long it would take before he could grab for one of the large tubular roots poking out and down from the earth exposed above the water—too long, and he'd drown, if he wasn't first slammed into a boulder not as friendly as this one.

On the other hand, if he stayed here and waited for help from people he had never seen, much less met, he would probably weaken from exposure, slip off the rock, and drown, if he wasn't battered to death by another boulder farther downstream.

Decisions, he thought bitterly, and before he could taunt himself with any more combinations, he drew his legs under him and dove into the water, broke the surface farther from the bank than he'd prayed for, and pumped arms and legs to force himself over.

There were no shallows.

The river at its banks was just as deep as in the middle, and each time he thrust up a hand to grab for a root, he sank, took in water, and surfaced a bit lower than the last time. Once, he actually had one, but the current was unrelenting and he was dragged away, cursing; a second time, a barb where his palm folded made him yank his hand back; and a third time, he simply slid off as if the root had been greased.

A submerged rock cracked against his leg then, and he yowled in pain, sank, surfaced, and flailed desperately at the earth speeding past him. It was hard, however, and the few depressions he felt his fingers meet were too shallow for a grip.

He was going to die.

What the hell, he thought when he found his arms too weak to do anything but drift, and he went limp, let himself sink, waited for the end, and found himself a few seconds later floating on his back, feet aimed downriver. It was comforting, but he didn't like the way the water rose in glassine humps just ahead, or the way it suddenly gouted into white boiling foam when it fell on the other side. The number of rocks was increasing. If he kept on this way, he was going to ram one sole first and end up with his knees behind his ears.

"Hey, are you crazy?"

Of course I am, he answered silently; it was the euphoria one feels when one knows he's going to die, a calm resignation that attends the end of a man's life.

"For god's sake, give me your hand!"

It wasn't God, then, but an angel, and when he shifted his gaze slowly to his right, he saw her. Him. A young angel racing along the riverbank ahead of him, stopping, reaching over with extended hand, then glaring and racing on again. He was dressed in furless hides and in high boots wrapped around with red thongs. A curious angel.

Not, he thought, an angel.

And he sank.

Jesus Christ, not now! he ordered when his legs refused to drive him back up; and he kicked, expelled the last of the air in his lungs, and shot out of the water, his arms high and his voice keening. A hand snared a wrist, the other wrist, and though he felt as if his shoulders were going to part company with the rest of him, he managed to cling to his rescuer until he was dragged onto the bank and flopped on his back.

He closed his eyes.

He doubled over suddenly and retched until his stomach had rid itself of all the water he had swallowed and a few inches of its lining.

Then he lay back again, not caring about the aches, or the cramps, or the shadow that had covered the sun.

When his eyes opened, a young man was staring intently at him, a young man who reminded him unpleasantly of Glorian.

"Are you all right?"

Gideon shook his head.

"Were you trying to swim?"

Again.

"Fell in?"

"Knocked," he said weakly. "I was riding Red, and—"

"Who's Red? Are you cold?"

He couldn't answer. A series of violently painful tremors doubled him again, and he could not stop them, and could not stop weeping until he felt a blanket of fur wrap around him, felt the young man hold him until the reaction passed.

When control returned, he managed to sit up.

And laughed when he saw the lorra coming toward him through the trees.

"That," he said, pointing, "is Red."

The young man looked, went pale, and hurriedly positioned himself behind Gideon. "You rode that lorra?"

"Sure."

"But—"

Red bounded out of the trees and only barely stopped in time to nudge Gideon's legs playfully, snorting softly and purring. Then he looked up and saw the young man, and the purring became a growl.

"Knock it off, Red," Gideon ordered. "The kid here saved me from the river."

Red eyed him doubtfully, then lowered himself to the ground and began munching the grass between his ankles.

"That's amazing," his rescuer said. "The only one I ever knew who could do that was . . . Hey, who are you?"

"Gideon Sunday," he said. "Who are you?"

"Tag."

"Tag? Do you have a last name?"

Tag frowned. "What's a last name? I have Tag, and I have a place, Kori." He pointed at the mountain. "Over there."

It was Gideon's turn to frown. "Over there? Eight houses by a forest? Grey houses?"

Tag sat facing him, his legs crossed. "You were there?"

He nodded.

"And you didn't die?"

"Not to my knowledge."

"Who are you?"

"I already told you."

Tag shook his head; that wasn't the question. And he

shook his head even more when Gideon, glad for a chance to talk to something that could talk back, explained how he had come to be in the river, how he had crossed the mountain, how he had nearly killed himself getting to what the young man called Kori. He said nothing about Glorian; he didn't want the kid dying just when they were getting to know each other.

"And you ate the . . . berries."

"Sure. I didn't want to starve. It wasn't much, but they've kept me going this long."

"And you got away from the pacch."

He shrugged. "If you mean that thing that lives underground over there, yes." He paused. "Well, Red helped."

The lorra lifted its head just long enough to give him a stare, then returned to its lounging graze.

Tag pushed away from him on his buttocks, propped an elbow on one knee and put his palm to his cheek. He clearly doubted the story, but the evidence of his eyes was difficult to discount.

"Where," he asked at last, "are you from?"

Gideon fell into a spate of coughing he claimed was a result of his dunking in the river, but he could not stop Tag from repeating the question or demanding an answer when he tried to stall by asking if the country they were in had a name. He considered a simple refusal and reminded himself that he owed his life to the young man, and probably owed him a more complete explanation.

"Bridge," he said at last. "I came across, or through, or under, or whatever, a Bridge."

Tag's doubt turned to outright scorn. "And what do you know about Bridges, huh?"

"I don't know anything about them except they exist."

"And how did you know that?"

"Are you a lawyer?"

"What's a lawyer?"

"Like a pacch, only they walk on two legs and have more teeth."

"You haven't answered my question."

He almost said he had no intention of answering it unless he was treated with a little more respect, but Tag's left hand moved against his hip then, and a section of his hide vest fell away to reveal a rather large-looking dagger with a hilt made of spiraled horn. Red stirred uncomfortably, and his eyes turned a momentary shade of grey.

"The Bridge."

"Right," said Tag.

"Well, like I said, I didn't even know they existed. Then I found one in my house and came across it."

"You don't just find one," he was told.

"Well, you're right, I didn't exactly just find it. In fact, Glorian showed it to me."

Tag's large brown eyes widened, and he leapt to his feet. "Glorian? Glorian brought you over?" He ran to the edge of the bank and searched the opposite shore. "Where is she?" He whirled, and the dagger was in his hand. "Where is she?"

"I don't know," he said truthfully, and managed not to cringe when he saw the look in Tag's eyes. "I swear I don't know." He explained quickly what had happened the night she had disappeared, how he had searched for her as best he could and had found evidence that something had taken her up into the trees and away. His regret was genuine when he finished by saying he hadn't seen her or a clue of her since.

Tag glared, but he was prevented from precipitous murder by the steady look Red gave him; instead, he stalked angrily along the riverbank, angrily back, and began pitching rocks furiously into the water. With each rock he threw, he uttered what Gideon imagined was an oath, and he kept it up until he could no longer lift his arm. By that time, Red had grown bored, had lurched to his feet, and was browsing for snacks under the trees.

"You knew her," Gideon said when Tag finally dropped and began murdering the ground instead.

"She was Kori."

"Your sister?"

"We shared the mother, if that's what you mean."

Damn, he thought.

Then, suddenly brightening: "Tag, do you have any idea why she brought me here across the Bridge?"

"Don't you know?"

"All I know is, she said something about me finding a white duck before she brought me back."

Tag leaned away from him, his eyes wide again and his lips beginning to quiver. "The duck," he said softly, in a tone near to reverence.

"Right. The duck."

Then Tag smiled. "You're going to get it!"

"That was the plan, I think."

Suddenly, the young man was on his feet and pulling at Gideon's arm. He jabbered about not wasting any time, and Gideon reminded him curtly that drowning was not, in his opinion, a waste of anyone's time, including the person under the water. But Tag was not to be sidetracked. He said they had to be on the road before nightfall, to put as many miles between them and the Scarred Mountains as they could before they would be able to rest again. It was, Tag said impatiently when Gideon balked, a long walk.

"Walk? What for, when we have Red?"

"Red?" Tag looked fearfully at the lorra, who had turned his great head at the sound of his name.

"I am not walking, young man, when I can ride."

He called Red over, asked him if he wouldn't mind, please, taking on two passengers for the rest of their journey, and the lorra promptly lowered himself to the ground. Gideon climbed aboard and scowled when Tag held back.

"C'mon, boy, he's not going to bite."

"He does."

"Maybe he does, but he isn't."

"He won't?"

"No."

"Are you sure?"

"Jesus Christ," Gideon yelled, "will you get the hell on the goddamned animal before we die of old age?"

ELEVEN

At Tag's quavering suggestion, they stayed on the bank of the river for nearly four miles before they swerved back through the trees and onto the road again. The brown-grass plain was still there but intermixed now with struggling green and swatches of wildflowers. When he was assured they were no longer in danger of ambushes by the myopic pacch, Gideon relaxed enough to ask that Tag give him a guided tour of the country they were traveling. It wasn't because he didn't know what he was looking at, but he hoped it would keep the young man's mind off riding the lorra, an event he had decided must be of some import in people's lives around here.

Tag was more than happy to comply.

The Scarred Mountains, he was told in tones generally reserved for angelic women and cathedrals of note, was the only circular range anyone was aware of, and only the Kori had bothered to settle there. The river he had nearly drowned in was called the Rush, the plain the Blades. There was no general land designation comparable to a country; people lived primarily with their families and took place names in order to distinguish one family from another. Some families were very large, some consisted only of parents and immediate children, and movement between the various enclaves was unhindered and encouraged. Tag had no idea why two or three families didn't join together in one large group; it wasn't done, that's all, though he admitted that in some places the communities were almost close enough together to make boundaries virtually meaningless. That didn't happen often. Families like the Kori were jealous of their land, and of their privacies, and though they were cordial enough to visitors and the odd traveler or two, they examined any potential joiner exceedingly carefully before granting them the highest honor of permitting them to build a house and take a spouse and merge their lives with those who had accepted them.

But when he proclaimed rather proudly that war did not exist and was never contemplated by even the meanest-spirited of people, Gideon touched his dagger and suggested that the existence of weapons such as that did not easily lead one to believe they were used solely as defense against something as large and unpleasant as a pacch, or a flock of ekklers, or even a single one of the mountain's winged predators he learned were called deshes.

Tag allowed as how that was a point to be considered.

Gideon dropped the subject and asked him instead where they were heading.

The road had swung off to the southwest while the river had contorted itself southeastward, and they were moving now across another plain, one emerald green and so abundantly filled with flowers of considerable size and coloration that looking at them too long made his vision blur. This, he was informed proudly, was the Sallamin, a land area of considerable size and natural wealth that was controlled, not by any one family, but by a group of them, each using the various resources as their personal economic base. It stretched, he said, from the Rush to the east all the way to the Chey in the south and west.

"The Chey?"

"Of course."

"And what is the Chey?"

"The end of the world; didn't Glorian tell you that?"

He reminded the lad that they'd scarcely had time to learn to get on each other's nerves, much less become part of a roving geography lesson, then wondered aloud if the

Chey was what caused the haze on the horizon. Tag said it was, and they would begin to notice the difference in the air the closer they got.

"Closer? Why? Surely we're not going there."

Tag, who was riding behind and had spoken mostly into his right ear, nodded quickly enough to put a painful dent in his shoulder.

"I don't understand."

"That's where Glorian was probably taking you."

"Probably? You don't know?"

"Who knows anything about what Glorian does anymore?" he said with a faint whine of disgust and, Gideon thought, what might have been envy. "She was always doing what she wanted, she never told anyone where she was or where she was going, and when she was finished she just showed up and expected everyone to treat her like she was somebody important."

"Did they?"

"Of course they did. She was."

Red snorted, tossed his head, and slowed down as he moved away from the road's center toward the less worn cobbles along the verge. Gideon suspected the lorra was hungry and realized with a start that he was, too, but all that had happened since their descent down the mountain had more than driven the thought of eating from his mind. When he mentioned it to Tag, the young man groaned at his forgetfulness and guided them to a cleared area a half mile ahead. It was a crescent of red-clay earth that reached thirty feet into the Sallamin and had scattered about it flat-topped rocks, where he bid Gideon sit. Then he proceeded to wade into the grass, snatching at a blossom here, a stem there, until he returned with a vegetarian bouquet in his arms. Gideon eyed the offering dubiously, but his stomach was the master, and after Tag showed him which parts would fill him and which would put him off his feed, he was forced to admit that while none of it tasted like chicken, neither did it remind him of eating hay.

A light breeze came up as they finished their hasty

meal, and when he looked he could see the slopes of the Scarred Mountains turning red in the setting sun; he could also see why they had been called that—great gouges of bare rock marked the western face, as though quarrying had been begun there and abandoned without thought of the consequences. In contrast to what lay in the bowl, the slopes were depressingly ugly, and the shadows that darkened them further gave them a curious air of angered sorrow.

He shuddered.

Tag asked if he were cold and assured him they would have shelter by nightfall. Well, perhaps not tonight's nightfall, but most certainly tomorrow's. Gideon smiled, and smiled more broadly when he saw the alacrity with which the young man climbed onto Red's back for the trip's continuation. Whatever fear he had of the lorra was gone, and any remnants had been scattered when the animal nudged him playfully for a portion of his meal, which he gave at first fearfully, then gladly, laughing silently and scratching the beast hard behind the ears.

Nice, Gideon thought, not at all sure that the lorra's gesture hadn't been deliberate.

Once more on the road, Tag exclaimed admiration over the cut of Gideon's clothes, and though he professed never to have seen their like before, he was at the same time oddly knowledgeable about denim, cotton, and the hard leather boots. Another question, but one Gideon decided to postpone in favor of finding out more about what Glorian had been up to when she'd caused the Bridge to appear.

"She's always going off," Tag said evasively. "You never know what's on her mind one day to the next."

"I think you already told me that."

"Well, I've told you all I know, then."

Gideon doubted it, but as long as the Kori wasn't about to put a knife in his back or feed him to the pacch, he supposed he could wait another day. But in the morning, he resolved, he was going to dig in his heels. Tag had accepted him without reservation once Glorian's connection was known, and he was puzzled about such an extension of instant trust. It didn't make sense. Unless, he amended, there was something about the Kori and other families that had no analogy to the world he was used to.

Which immediately brought to mind still another query.

"Where are we?"

"The Sallamin."

"No, I mean where are we? Where is here? All this," and he gestured to include everything he could see. "You know, and I know, this isn't my world. And I doubt we're talking about instantaneous corporeal transmissions to another planet. Which means I'm not in outer space, and I'm not in my house, so where the hell am I?"

Tag shrugged. "Here."

He decided to try another tack. "The Bridges. Glorian said they come when they're needed, and sometimes, when you cross them, you come back with something you need for what you needed in the first place."

He could sense Tag frowning through the syntax, then nodding as he finally understood. "The Bridges."

"Right."

"You want to know about them."

"Right."

"I don't know. Sometimes you get them, and sometimes you don't. I don't know how they started or who discovered them or why they're there. They just are."

This, he thought, is getting me nowhere.

"Okay," he said, "then tell me about Kori. You said that's where your family makes its home, but there wasn't anyone there when I arrived. The houses were empty, I didn't see anything growing that looked like crops, and except for those dumb pits in the grass, it could have been a false village for all I know."

"The pits?"

"Right. I kept falling into them."

Tag stretched his face over Gideon's shoulder and gaped at him. "And you got out?"

"Well, sure. Jesus, they're only about six feet deep, give or take an inch. Not much deeper than a grave." Tag withdrew and muttered to himself, and Gideon twisted around. "You know, you seem awfully sure of yourself about a lot of things that concern me, and awfully surprised about a lot of other things. Like those pits, like those berries, like my getting out of that valley in one piece." He lifted an eyebrow, a polite but firm invitation for an explanation.

Tag ducked his head away from a sudden gust of wind and muttered something Gideon couldn't quite hear.

"What?"

"I said, they're all dead but you."

"Who are?"

"The Kori."

"But you're a Kori. And Glorian is."

"Right. But the rest of them . . . we, Glorian and me, we're the only ones left."

"Because of the pits?"

"No."

Gideon took a deep breath and let Red take him a hundred yards before he decided to take it one step at a time. "Listen, Tag, I gather that eating those berries, or fruits, or whatever, is something your people don't do. Probably because they are lethal to you in some way."

"All ways," Tag insisted with a shudder. "It's horrible. I wonder why they didn't kill you? And the thorns—didn't you cut yourself trying to feed?"

Gideon held up a hand; the back was clear. "A couple of times, I guess, but nothing serious. Why? Don't tell me the thorns carry poison, too."

Tag nodded.

"There ought to be signs."

Tag agreed, though he was apparently still perplexed by Gideon's survival.

"The pits," he said, ignoring the speculation by moving on to the next step. "Why should I have died there when the other stuff didn't kill me?"

"The pacch." Tag glanced over his shoulder. "Those pits are part of their burrows."

"But there weren't any of them there!"

"There was, once."

Gideon opened his mouth to ask the obvious question, then closed it when the obvious answer came to him, and, at the same time, he saw the expression that clouded the boy's face.

"I didn't think they could move that fast," he said quietly.

"They can. At night."

"But there was no damage to the houses."

"We weren't in the houses. We were outside."

"Why?"

But Tag was done talking. He stared at the passing landscape with a finality in his posture that made Gideon turn around again. He could see no profit in even pursuing the subject himself since he had only fragments of information, and most of that was incomplete; yet he could not help thinking that the impression Tag had left him with was that someone, or something, had lured the Kori from their houses in order to slaughter them. For what reason he couldn't begin to guess; that would have to wait until the morning, or considerably later from the weight of the silence he felt behind him.

By dusk they had reached another one of the claylike crescents, and with Red grazing contentedly nearby and Tag assuring him they were in no danger from nighttime attacks this far from the mountains, he stretched out on a strand of thick grass and watched as the Kori perched on a rock and stared at the stars. Gideon had no idea how old he was, but sitting there with his face upturned and his hands clutched around his shins, he seemed quite a young lad indeed, perhaps still a boy, or a young man who was still close enough to boyhood to make almost no difference.

It was clear he missed Glorian.

Gideon wondered, suddenly and with an unwanted, abrupt burning at the corners of his eyes, if there was anyone back home who missed him. There were no parents, no wife or currently active girlfriend, and his sister didn't count because she was already dead. She would have missed him were she alive, though she probably would have had a few choice words for him on his return. He only wished there had been a grave to go to, someplace other than the memorial marker that rested coldly in the cemetery in the town where they'd been born.

He sighed and brushed an angry hand over his face. Dead she was, but he'd thought he had long ago expunged the grief that had caused him to weep. It must, he decided, be the situation and the place—the one person he had ever cared about was the one person who wasn't able to know he was gone.

It was a long time before he was able to sleep.

Long after Red nestled down beside him and gave him his flank for a pillow.

Long after Tag had curled up on the rock, his head tucked in his arms, his knees drawn to his chest.

Long after the moon had dropped below the horizon.

And definitely long after he could have sworn he had seen those red eyes again.

TWELVE

They retook the road shortly after dawn, and Gideon was not in the best of moods. Unused to knowing what the sun looked like until it was already a goodly and decent way up into the sky, he and his system were embroiled in minor skirmishes over habit and his internal clock; he was never at his best anyway upon awakening, and doing so before the day even had a chance to take a deep breath bordered on the ludicrous. In addition, while the foodstuffs Tag provided from the Sallamin's abundant fields were nutritious enough and did the job of settling his stomach's rebellion, by the time the road began to rise and fall over a gentle series of low knolls, he would have killed for the taste of a good greasy hamburger or a steak-and-onions dinner or even a bag of overpriced buttered and salted popcorn. Scavenging in the wild was not his idea of a civilized life.

He was also having a difficult time ridding himself of the melancholy that had come upon him the night before. No one likes to think he can abruptly leave the world he knows and not leave some sort of vacuum; but he added to his ration of self-pity the belief that the only notice he would probably get would be a squib in some sports column in some small-town paper that needed a filler under the joke of the day.

It bothered him.

It bothered him so much that he became annoyed with

himself for acting like a child and took it out on Tag, snapping at his good humor, refusing to see the beauty of the day, and snarling at Red whenever the lorra wanted to waste a few minutes tasting the local fodder cuisine.

By midday, Red was sulking and Tag had fallen into a pout he found worse than the constant bright prattling that had preceded it.

You're an idiot, he told himself; the kid only wants to help, and wants your help, and all you can do is bite off his arm. Why don't you stick your head in a bucket and take a deep breath?

On the other hand, he argued back, he had taken a large part of all this on blind faith, assuming that everything would be explained sooner or later. But the more he asked for explanations, the more questions he had, and they were giving him a headache. It was getting to the point where he knew he would either have to scream or just float along as he had on the river, pulling together as much as he could until he could build himself a raft large enough to give him support. Once that was done, he could make up his mind what to do next.

The trouble was, by that time he might not be in a position to make any decisions at all.

Tag poked him in the small of his back.

"What?" he said, making an effort to sound friendly.

A hand snaked over his shoulder and pointed.

The Sallamin, he had noticed over the last few miles, was not as unbroken as it had been near the Blades. There were stands of trees now, and whenever they reached the high point of a rise, he could see that the wildflowers were decreasing in number, that the grass was lower, and that the road itself was considerably more worn. There were also side paths worn across the plain, though he could see no immediate destination should he take one.

Now, ahead as they came over the crest of a knoll, on the far side of a stream that cut across the cobbles, he could see a collection of houses. They were smaller than those of the Kori and appeared to be made of wood rather than stone. They stood facing the road, and there were others behind them—rows and files and low fences between them.

"What is it?" he asked, feeling a swift chill of excitement.

"Pholler," he was told. "They're one of the largest families on the Sallamin."

"Friendly folk, I hope."

"We all are."

"Of course," he said.

At the stream they stopped and dismounted, drank, cleansed their faces, and waited until Red had polished off a clump of grass whose blades had faintly scarlet edges. Meanwhile, Gideon walked to the bank and shook his head. The water was twenty feet across, chillingly clear, and probably knee deep.

"Tag," he said, "don't you people believe in bridges?"

"What are you talking about? Didn't you get here across a Bridge?"

"No," he said. "Not a Bridge, a bridge. Like you put across water so you don't get your feet wet."

"Across water?" Tag looked at him, bewildered. "Why? Can't you swim?"

"Not well," he admitted after a glare that turned the boy's head, "but that's beside the point. Wouldn't it make traveling easier, not to say quicker, if you didn't have to ford every river and puddle you came across?"

"On a bridge?"

"What else?"

"Bridges are for holes, not water. You can't swim across a hole."

"A hole?"

"Sure. Don't you have holes? Big holes?" And he swung his arm at the stream as if the water would vanish and the bottom would suddenly be thirty feet down. "Holes."

"Oh." He reminded himself to be patient; after all, he was the stranger, not this infuriating kid. "Like chasms, canyons, gullies, things like that."

"Yeah. Holes."

"Damned big holes, if you ask me."

"Sure they are. That's why we have bridges."

I will not strangle him, he thought, because then I will probably regret it. Not for long, but I will regret it.

They remounted Red and forded the stream, the lorra's rich hair floating on the surface, their feet submerged to the ankles before the bottom rose and they were on the other side. Then Tag jumped to the ground and walked beside him, one hand lightly touching his right leg.

"What's up?"

"I should walk," Tag said. "I don't want to scare them."

"And I won't?"

"Of course you will. That's important."

"I don't get it."

"You will."

Again, the explanation he needed was forestalled, this time by large and small groups of people hurriedly filtering out of the houses and gathering at the roadside. They were dressed well, in cloth—loose-fitting blouses, long baggy trousers, high boots of varicolored hide thick as leather. The women were dressed the same, except that their blouses had more splashes of embroidered color and many of them wore their hair tied back with bright ribbons.

They were silent.

They stared as he rode past, and he smiled at them, nodded, winked at a child, who instantly ducked behind his father's legs. Tag was right; they were afraid of them, and he had no doubt part of it was because he rode the lorra.

Red seemed to sense it, too. He kept his head high to show off his massive horns, picked up his hooves to sound them loudly on the cobbles. Tag grinned and patted the animal's neck, and someone in the crowd was unable to stifle a gasp.

Gideon, feeling like a last-ditch politician riding into the enemy party's territory, kept the smile at his lips while he looked more closely at the buildings and saw they weren't made entirely of wood—the frames around the squared windows and heavy doors were blocks of stone that strongly resembled marble, and the roofs were sharply pitched and broken at least twice by chimney pots. Some of the houses had flower gardens in the front yard, some of the yards were cluttered with what could only be children's toys, and all had a small pennant flying over the lintel, each one, as far as he could tell, different in design and combinations of color.

Seven houses down, the road branched into a square, in the center of which was a long, low building festooned with the same pennants he had seen over the doors. There were faces in the several windows that flanked blond-wood double doors, and standing in front of the doors were three men and a woman.

Tag tugged on his leg. Gideon leaned forward and whispered, and Red came to a halt, snorting and blowing until he leaned forward again and told him to stop showing off. Then he waited while Tag ran up to the quartet and began speaking with them earnestly. The larger of the three men—as tall as the doors and nearly as wide—appeared unimpressed by whatever the lad was saying, though the others, the woman included, kept stealing glances in his direction, measuring him, he supposed, for whatever guise Tag was putting on him.

Since it seemed he wasn't going to be invited to join the discussions, he took the opportunity to look around, seeing to his left, at the north end of the square, a pair of small buildings fronted by wooden overhangs, under which women and men were passing and returning with baskets and cartons of what he guessed was food; on the south was a similar arrangement, though there was no customer traffic. There was, however, a large sign over one of the shops whose name was in a language he didn't know, but the stylized picture of crossed sword-and-cudgel gave him a fair idea of its wares.

Red shifted and growled impatiently. The three men backed away with scowls, and Tag hurried over.

"What's the matter?"

"The critter is bored," Gideon said. "So am I. What's going on?"

"I'll tell you later."

"I've heard that before."

Tag shook his head. "Look, there's nothing you can do, not now, anyway. Why don't you look around?"

"Will they let me?"

"They'll tell you if they won't."

Before he could respond, the young man had run off again, and with a shrug he slipped off the lorra's back. He stretched and noted that the people who had watched him arrive had returned to their homes. I guess I'm just a fad, he thought with a lopsided smile, and, taking an easy handful of Red's neck hair, he headed off toward the armory. Red followed docilely and bobbed his head when Gideon asked him to please wait outside while he took a look around.

Batwing doors eased aside when he entered, feeling foolishly like a gunslinger stalking the local saloon. But when his eyes adjusted to the dim light inside, he stopped, blinked several times, and checked over his shoulder to be sure the lorra was still there, just so he would know where he was.

There was enough weaponry on the walls, on the square posts supporting the ceiling, in glass-fronted display cases, and on fierce-visaged mannequins, to supply a fair-sized army out for one hell of a good time. He remembered Tag's denial of war situations and made a note to ask the lad what they thought war was around here. He also puzzled over the selection of arms—the lefthand side of the large room was devoted to a selection of very modern-looking rifles, while the right gave itself to swords, great-swords, broadswords, claymores, and virtually everything else that had a blade except a straight razor.

"This is crazy," he said; and as if the words were a signal, a door opened in the rear wall and a man stepped out.

"Good day!" he said cheerfully, hitching at a pair of dark trousers several sizes too large for his lanky frame. His hair was a thicket of unruly brown atop an equine face that beamed as Gideon crossed over to him and took his offered hand.

"You are the hero?"

Gideon didn't know what to say.

"Ah. Modesty."

Gideon still didn't know what to say.

"They call me Whale," he said, using one finger to scratch the side of his wattled neck. He laughed then and thumped a fist against his belly. "I used to be much heavier."

"Okay," Gideon said, grinning.

"And I suppose you want something to fight with," Whale said, immediately heading for his display of swords and dirks. "A good thing, too, since I doubt you'll be able to handle things very well with just your hands." He laughed. "I think that's a joke. Is it a joke? Handle, hands? I don't know. They tell me I don't have a sense of humor, so I have to keep asking if I've found one. I do know how to fight, though, you can ask anybody. Why, just last week—" He stopped, blushed, and picked up a dagger with a curved-horn hilt. "What do you think?"

Gideon, who hadn't the slightest idea what to think about any of it, pointed to the rifles. "What about those?"

"Those?" Whale's face wrinkled in disgust and mild shock as he shook his head. "You don't want those, sir. They're only good for hunting, not killing."

"Oh, I don't know," he said. "I should think you could stop a man pretty well with one, don't you?"

"Never!" Whale backed away as if Gideon had insulted every female member of his family, then had refused to marry any of them. "You don't treat a man the same as you do a pacch, do you? Of course you don't. A man has dignity, isn't that right? A man deserves a chance to defend himself. How can he defend himself if you're going around potting at him from a mile away, huh? What kind of dignity is that?''

Gideon hastily agreed there was no dignity to that whatsoever, though he did not add that neither did he think opening a man's insides with a sharpened piece of steel was all it was cut out to be, either.

"Well, then," Whale said, the matter of propriety settled, "what shall you have?"

He moved more swiftly than Gideon could answer and soon had an impressive, gleaming, deadly array of swords and short blades on the counter between them. He extolled the many virtues of each (made by his own hand) and the few drawbacks of each, especially if one had a short arm, which Gideon apparently didn't, though you can't always tell about these things, fashions today being what they were, and finally ended his spiel by stepping back and spreading his arms with a flourish.

"Splendid, aren't they? Absolutely . . ." His face flushed again. "I'm sorry. I get that way. One grows attached to one's wares after a time, don't you think?''

"I suppose," Gideon said. Then, after passing a hand over several of the weapons, he dropped it to his side and shook his head. "I'm sorry. I can't.''

"Oh. Oh, dear. Oh, my heavens." Whale quickly gathered the blades up and reset them in their places. Then he reached for another group.

"No," Gideon said. "That's not what I meant."

Whale frowned.

"I mean, I don't know how to use any of them."

"You don't?"

"I don't."

"You can't . . ." And he dropped into en garde and swished a bit at the air with his arm. "You can't?"

"Nope."

"Oh. A problem."

"Perhaps something else," Gideon suggested, feeling

foolish for feeling guilty at the man's distress. He had a memory, and an idea. "I have been successful with a bat."

"A bat?" Whale flapped his arms. "A . . . bat? My goodness, how does one train one? It must be awfully difficult. Patience, I suppose, though I can't imagine anyone having the—"

Gideon gripped an invisible baseball bat and put it to his shoulder, then swung in slow motion. "No, a bat."

Whale frowned. "I thought a bat was a bat."

"In this case, no. A bat's a bat." A giggle rose in his throat and he swallowed it hard, then saw a half dozen different-sized clubs on the wall next to the rear entrance. He pointed. "Something like those, only a bit thinner."

"Thinner will break."

Gideon hesitated, then asked for a piece of paper. Whale, still puzzled but more intrigued, provided it, plus a straight pen and a small pot of ink. Gideon, not an artist at the best of times, valiantly attempted a sketch of the bat he had broken over the head of the black beast, and when he was finished, five sheets and two pens later, Whale held it close to his eyes, held it at arm's length, walked to the door, and turned so the light fell full upon it.

"Ah."

Gideon joined him. "One piece of wood, you see. Tapered, but a knob so the hands don't slip off. Fat up here."

"You need . . ." Whale closed one eye. "This isn't enough, you know. Not for really proper bashing without losing it in an awkward spot. You need . . ." He pressed the paper to his chest and walked away in what Gideon could only suppose was a creative daze. He paused, then passed through the back door and closed it behind him.

Gideon shrugged to himself and, since there was nothing he could do but wait, headed for the display of rifles. When he was close enough he felt a chill that was hard to shake off—except for minor variations in the design of the stock, and an addition here and there at the trigger guard and along the barrel for whatever purpose, they looked exactly like those he had seen back home. In the display counter there were boxes of cartridges. And it took him a while to realize there were rifles only; nowhere in the store could he find a single example of a handgun.

Then the rear door banged open just as the front doors swung in.

Whale held up a bat and said, "A beauty, don't you think?"

And the woman he had seen with Tag and the three men looked him up and down, smiled slyly, and drew a dagger from her belt.

THIRTEEN

Gideon stepped nervously back toward the lefthand wall as Whale approached him from one side and the woman came at him from the other, knife and bat all too clearly displayed. He supposed he had transgressed some local custom, but he didn't think that whatever he had done deserved the ultimate solution to public or private ill behavior.

Whale, shifting his gaze from his creation to the expression on Gideon's face, laughed abruptly and shook his head. "No, no, sir, it's not what you think! Please, don't you— My goodness"—he turned to the woman—"it's not at all what he thinks, is it? Of course it isn't, and for heaven's sake, Ivy, what are you doing with that thing?"

Ivy Pholler flipped the dagger over in her hand and gave it to the armorer horned hilt first. "It needs a good sharpening, Whale. The damned thing won't cut a baby's—" She stopped herself. "It won't cut."

"I can take care of it for you in an instant," the man promised, and rushed back out of the room.

"Ivy?" Gideon said breathlessly as he leaned back against a display case in order not to fall weak-kneed to the floor. He was definitely going to have to learn not to judge people and events so precipitously, not if he wanted his nerves to calm down now and again.

"That's right. And you're Gideon, so says Tag."

"That's right." He gestured vaguely toward the back. "Mr. Pholler was making me—"

"I know. I saw it. It looks . . . interesting. What do you do with it?"

After a moment's hesitation, he shrugged. He was going to tell her about his confrontation with the black beast but changed his mind. She didn't seem to be truly interested in his answer, only marking time until Whale returned. Not that he was complaining about her disinterest. Ivy was an attractive woman, and he supposed he could be content with simply looking at her. She was about Tag's height, buxom with long blonde hair sensibly wound into a braid whose feathery tip brushed against the small of her back. Her clothes were similar to Tag's—hide leggings tucked into high thong-wrapped boots and a dull white blouse heavily embroidered in gold. She was green-eyed, strong-looking, and, he guessed, a formidable opponent either with words or deeds. It was clear from the hard lines faint at the corners of her eyes and mouth that she was not one to be shunted into corners.

"Are you finished?" she said with a trace of amusement.

Gideon, not realizing he had been staring, gave her a quick smile and looked to the back for rescue. There was none, and he heard a noise that made him turn his head. Ivy was laughing behind a hand.

"You blush easy, do you?"

"Not that I've noticed, no," he said stiffly, and strode over to the counter where Whale had left the bat.

"Prickly, too."

He ignored her for the bat and ignored as well the surge of temper he felt.

On first and second examination, the thing on the counter resembled an ordinary big-league baseball bat, save that it was flawlessly fashioned from deep green wood and, when he picked it up one-handed, nearly broke his wrist with its weight. It was also a few inches longer, and its rounded tip nearly squared the toe of his boot before he could pull it back. A beautiful piece of work, he thought as he hefted it back to the counter, but I wouldn't be able to swing it even if I wanted to bash my own brains out with it.

"A problem?" Ivy said, coming up beside him.

He pointed at it and shrugged. She made to lift it, scowled at the weight, and shook her head.

"He's done something," she told him.

"I know. He's made a bat I can't lift."

"A bat?"

"That."

She frowned at it, at him, and at the rear door. "Well, he's still done something. You'll have to wait—"

But he didn't. Whale came out at that moment, Ivy's dagger wrapped in soft blue cloth. He handed it to her ceremoniously, and she dipped a finger into a velvet purse slung from her belt. Two silver coins changed hands, and Whale dismissed her with a polite smile and a turn to Gideon. Ivy didn't take the hint.

"It's lovely," Gideon said, nodding at the bat, "but I can't lift it."

"Of course not, it's yours."

"I appreciate that very much," he said, "but what good is it going to do if I can't use it?"

The thin man looked puzzled, then triumphant. "Ah! But you're the hero, you don't know!"

Ivy giggled.

"Know what?" he said, ignoring the woman.

"Stroke it."

Gideon narrowed one eye. "What?"

"Stroke it, sir. It's yours, as you can see since I've just brought it out from my humble workshop, and I've wasted my time if you don't do it, because then no one else will be able to and I'll just have to burn it or give it to the pacch for lunch." He reached out and grabbed Gideon's hand with an apologetic smile, placed it on the bat's grip, and moved it up and down until he got the idea. "Not to worry, sir, it won't bite."

Like the forest lamps, he thought, and looked to Whale, who nodded.

An imprinting of some kind, he concluded, though he felt rather foolish standing in a weapons shop surrounded by a delirious array of swords and knives and rifles and cudgels while he stroked a baseball bat. But he did it because Ivy wouldn't stop her giggling, her face flushed now and tears beginning to glint in her eyes, and because Whale kept nodding silent encouragement, directing his hands first to the top, then to the grip, then to the knob, and back again.

"That's it, sir. Gentle if you will, so it doesn't think you a man of ill intention."

The wood was cool and smooth, feeling like wet glass or, he thought with a deliberate turn of his head away from Ivy, like a woman's soft skin. It was also growing warm, so warm as a pulse of crimson appeared down the bat's central axis that he started to pull his hand away, but Whale's warning hiss kept him at it, hissing himself as he watched the flickering crimson spread, grow brighter, and, as he was ready to pull back because he knew his palms were blistering, suddenly vanishing.

He stumbled backward while Whale applauded, and Ivy gazed at him in a combination of suspicion and wonder.

"Now," the thin man said with a final clap of his hands, "you can use it. Just as if it was your third arm, which, of course, I can see you don't have because you're not from— Never mind. It's all yours. Just pick it up, put it on your shoulder—" He frowned, tapped a long finger on his chin, and tsked loudly. "Oh, no. We can't have that, can we? We can't have you marching around like that. It would be unseemly." He disappeared behind the counter. "Never. I would never live it down. People would talk. Whale Pholler, they would say, can't even provide his customers with a simple but effective means of— Aha!" He leapt up, brandishing what looked to Gideon like a rifle sheath with a narrow leather belt. "Just the thing to add a bit of dash and practicality."

"It's . . . interesting."

Whale, however, hastened around the counter and fastened the contraption to Gideon's waist. Then he nodded to the bat.

Gideon eyed it doubtfully, and somewhat fearfully, but picked it up in both hands, steadying himself for the weight, and nearly tumbled onto his back. It was light. It was virtually without weight. He didn't get it, and put it to his shoulder, stared at the pitcher waiting on the mound by the front door, and swung . . . and gasped at the high-pitched hum the weapon made as it sliced through the air, struck one of the posts, and split it in two; the lower half toppled to the floor, the upper dangled and rocked from the ceiling.

"Oh my," Whale said as he stared mournfully at the shower of dust piling on their feet.

Ivy ran out of the shop laughing.

"Hey, I'm sorry," Gideon said, staring at the bat, then at the shattered post. "Jesus, I didn't think—"

"It's all right, all right, don't worry about it," Whale said hastily as he nudged him toward the exit. "I'll have this mess fixed in a jiff, don't you bother yourself about that. Just test it elsewhere, if you don't mind, and I'll get about . . . Oh my."

Gideon soon found himself under the log overhang, alone, the batwings swinging up behind to shove him gently farther toward the street. He looked back with an apologetic sigh, then looked to the gadget Whale had given him. It was little more than a belt and a holster, but when he placed the bat inside he saw the dark leather close around it snugly. When he reached a tentative hand to the knob, the leather sagged and opened, and the bat fell into his grip.

"I'll be damned."

But he couldn't help feeling again like a gunslinger as he walked over to Red and ran a hand down the side of its neck, patting, watching as Tag backed away from the trio he had been talking to and stomped toward him, his face flushed and his fists swinging hard at his sides. Whatever he'd been trying to do had not been successful, and Gideon kept his mouth shut when the young man gestured brusquely at him and started around the square, heading out of town.

"Red, let's go."

The lorra hesitated before following slightly behind, hooves loud and echoing off the walls of the buildings. There were no watchers now; the houses were silent, the windows empty, and the pennants snapped angrily in a wind that had come up from the south. He felt his nerves tighten, and there was no shame when his right hand touched the bat and the bat became a part of him at his side.

When the last house dropped behind, he called Tag's name, but the lad continued to march on, muttering, gesticulating, punching at the air over his head and spitting at the side of the road. A second call was no more effective than the first, and with a look to the lorra he trotted up and took Tag's shoulder.

"What's up?" he said, refusing to let go though the young man tried to shake the grip off. "C'mon, Tag, what's going on?"

Tag's face was ominously red. "They won't help," he said in almost a wail. "Those bastards aren't going to help us at all! Can you imagine it? They said they took us in because of what happened to Kori, but they won't do anything more. You know, I ought to—"

He shook Gideon's hand away and reached for Pholler, his dagger suddenly in his hand. Gideon hurried after him, but he needn't have bothered—Red put himself squarely in the middle of the road, lowered his head, and growled. Tag yelped and jumped back, demanding at the top of his voice to be saved from the beast. Gideon reached him, snatched the dagger away, and spun him around.

"Now look, boy, this is getting ridiculous. What did you ask them, and why won't they do it?"

"It was nothing," Tag said sullenly. "All I wanted them to do was help us get to Chey. What's the matter with that?"

Gideon looked over his shoulder at the horizon, at the

thickening haze there that dulled the sky above it. "I thought you said that meant something like the end of the world."

"Not something like—it is."

"And you want to go there?"

"We don't have a choice!"

"Why not?"

"Because if we don't . . ." He shook his head in abject sorrow and dropped himself onto the grass at the roadside. "It isn't fair. They're supposed to help us."

Gideon crouched down beside him. "Tag, does this have anything to do with that . . ." He could barely bring himself to say it. "With that duck?"

"It has everything to do with it! God, didn't Glorian tell you anything?"

"Nope."

Tag's eyes widened. "She didn't?"

"No."

"That's like her, you know. That's just like her. She has all these stupid secrets and she never tells anyone and then, when she gets in trouble, she expects us to run after her like she was a queen or something. She's always doing that, always. Sometimes I think I should just forget her and let her get herself out of trouble for a change."

Gideon touched the lad's shoulder. "Tag, you forget— Glorian is dead."

"What? Who said that?"

"You did. When I told about what happened that first night here."

"I never said she was dead."

Gideon looked at him hard. "Then she isn't?"

"Of course not." He paused. "I hope not."

"Then if she isn't, she's . . ." And he pointed toward the horizon.

"She better be. I'm not going there if she's not. That would be too much. I mean, that's asking too much, going to Chey if she isn't there." He stared at the horizon, then at Gideon. "But she has to be there, because if she isn't, I don't know where she is. So she's there. Yes. She's there.''

"And the duck."

"Yes."

Gideon let himself drop to his buttocks, then pulled up his legs and draped his hands over his knees. It was clear enough that the people of Pholler weren't about to give Tag any assistance, which implied that going to Chey was not altogether a healthy journey, unless the journey was all right and Chey itself was dangerous. Or it could be both. Or Pholler, for all its size, was a basically conservative community, which, having discharged its obligation by taking in the refugees from Kori, didn't want to be involved any further in what was probably a family matter. But if it was just a family matter, why had Glorian resorted to a Bridge in order to get help?

"God," he muttered.

And he didn't look up immediately when Tag suddenly scrambled to his feet with a string of his favorite oaths, retrieved his dagger, and raced to the middle of the road. When he did, however, he saw a group of men leaving Pholler toward them; they were armed, making no bones about it, and making it clear they weren't going to parley first before they set about eliminating the last of the Koris, not to mention the Sundays.

FOURTEEN

This just isn't going to work, he told himself; if I wanted a riot, I could have stayed at home and watched the damned team lose again, for crying out loud.

Tag looked over at him then, widened his eyes when he saw Gideon still sitting, and gestured at him angrily before turning around to face the mob.

Suppose I don't want to? he called silently; suppose I'm a peaceful man who never harmed a fly? Then he took a closer look at the mob and realized none of its members gave a damn what kind of man he was like, as long as he was dead when it was over.

He pushed himself wearily to his feet and had the bat in his hand before he knew he had touched it. He looked at it in surprise, then moved to stand beside Tag. And when he saw the delegation, he knew without having to question why that he didn't have the stomach for this sort of work. It was one thing laying your padded shoulder into a center or a guard because you knew he was going to get up, one way or another, for the next play because that was what you were being paid for, and it only happened once a week anyway; or, considering that the reverse was usually true in his case, that he was going to get up for the next play, wobbly but alive.

This, on the other hand, had a definite air of finality about it, and after what he had seen the bat do to Whale's shop, he knew that any man who was struck, no matter

110

where, wasn't going to be going home for dinner that night.

"Maybe," he said, "we ought to talk to them."

"I think we ought to cut their throats," Tag countered. "And even that's too good for them."

There were a dozen or more of them, bunched in the center of the road and holding unnervingly sharp-looking blades of varying lengths in their fighting hands. They did not bear friendly expressions, and the garbled noise that rose from their throats indicated they were working themselves up to the fight they were facing without much conscience for the inevitable results.

"You don't think talking would do any good?"

"Only," Tag sneered, "with the point of your sword at their miserable little throats."

"I don't have a sword, I have a bat."

"Bats are good, too."

He shrugged; it figured.

The advance faltered only once, when Red, growling and snorting as if stoking a fire in his belly, poked his way between Gideon and Tag and pawed furiously at the ground, shaking his head, his eyes already a dead flat black; but when a tall husky man in front spoke a commanding word to those on either side, the hesitation was over.

"That's Shelt," Tag said in disgust. "He's the head of that miserable place, and he's the one who said they wouldn't do anything."

"Then why are they doing this? Why don't they just let us go and good riddance?"

"They're afraid." And he said it so loudly that Shelt, carrying a saber whose blade flared in the sunlight, stopped in his tracks some fifty feet away.

"Afraid!" Tag yelled, slicing the air with his dagger. "But not so afraid that they can't attack two harmless men!"

Gideon looked at the dagger, at his bat, at the horns on Red's head, and decided not to quibble.

"You have a big voice for a Kori rump," Shelt yelled back, and was poked by his friends in approval.

"And you have a lot of friends for just two men," Tag told him with a sneer.

"The man has a Whale club," Shelt said.

"Hell, he probably doesn't even know how to use it without breaking his own arm," Tag said with a mocking laugh. "He's from across a Bridge, you know that."

"Hey, Tag," Gideon said, smiling at the mob.

"He'll probably kill himself before he kills one of you."

"Tag, what the hell are you doing?" he muttered from the side of his mouth.

"Better two men such as you lot than what you'll bring down on us all if you go there," Shelt replied, pointing his sword toward the horizon.

"Oh, yeah?"

"Tag, for god's sake," Gideon whispered harshly.

"Yeah!" Shelt snapped.

"Well, my sister is a better man than the whole bunch of you put together," the lad spat, "and you didn't see her hiding behind a bunch of cowards and snivelers."

"Tag, what the hell are you trying to do, you idiot!" Gideon said, feeling his smile crack holes in his cheeks.

"Get them mad."

"I think they already are."

"But not mad enough. If they get really mad, they'll do something stupid, like attack us."

"That doesn't sound stupid to me."

"But then they'll be so mad they won't fight right and we'll get the whole damned lot of them." He took a strutting step forward and turned sideways to them arrogantly. The mob grumbled. Tag wriggled his buttocks. The mob grumbled more darkly. Tag kissed one finger and touched the tip of his nose. The mob surged forward without moving a step. "C'mon, Shelt, for crying out loud. Gideon and I have work to do. We don't have time to waste on Pholler scum."

Shelt's broad face reddened, the men behind him began

pushing and shoving to get into position, and Tag laughed in delight as he jumped back to put Red at his side. "That got them," he whispered as he swished his dagger back and forth. "Now we'll see what they're made of."

"I know what they're made of," Gideon said miserably.

"That's the spirit," Tag declared with a good-fellow slap to his shoulder.

Tension from the Pholler was almost as visible as the dust they raised beneath their feet.

"Tag, I don't think this is a good idea."

The boy bounced lightly on his toes. "Why not? We'll take care of them and then go on to Chey."

"But you were right."

Tag looked at him. "About what?"

Gideon lifted the bat. "This."

"You . . . you can't use it?"

"Not against that lot, I don't think."

"You mean, you don't . . . you're not . . . that isn't . . ."

"I've never hit anyone in my life, if that's what you're asking."

"Oh, shit," Tag said.

Then Shelt yelled something Gideon didn't understand, and the mob swept forward again, its sudden silence more threatening than the voice of its rage. Red bared his teeth with a toss of his head, dug at the cobbles until sparks flew, and Gideon decided resignedly he could have a worse ally. At least the lorra could charge into them, scatter them, and give him and Tag better odds in the short run.

"All right, Red," he said tensely, "let's get to it."

The lorra reared impressively, opened its mouth, and let go a roar that would have defoliated a jungle. In its wake the mob fell back several paces; then Red roared again and charged them with head down and horns well aimed, stopped halfway to the mark, and turned to run back.

Gideon gaped at him. "That's it?"

Red bobbed his head and wandered off to the grass, where he began to graze.

"Hey, that's it?"

A yell made him turn and hold the bat up, his mouth dry and his stomach looking for someplace else to reside. Another yell, one of astonished pain, and he saw someone on the outside of the advancing men leap into the air and come down with one hand rubbing a buttock and the other brandishing a sword. Behind him was Ivy, who showed the man her dagger, made a tight circle with it as she spoke to him, and the man's free hand wavered unconsciously toward his groin. She wrinkled her nose at him and moved, oblivious to Shelt's shrill demands that she get back to the village where she belonged.

"You need help?" she asked when she reached Gideon.

"I won't turn it down," he told her gratefully.

She looked at him in mild surprise. "But I'm a woman."

"I noticed. I also noticed that you can use that thing."

She looked to Tag, who was concentrating on the mob, and smiled broadly. "I'll be."

"If we live long enough."

Shelt looked at the trio facing him and his men, shook his head, and started toward them again. "You'll die, Ivy," he warned in a booming voice.

Ivy merely flipped the dagger in the air, caught it by the hilt, and smiled.

Suddenly there was an anguished shout from someone at the back, and Shelt, groaning at yet another interruption of his expedition, held up a hand, halted the advance, and waited, though he did not take his gaze from Tag, who was bouncing from side to side, taunting him, gesturing at him, showing him all angles of the weapon he carried.

It was Whale.

He pushed and bulled his way through the mob until he reached Shelt. The village leader glowered at him and stabbed a finger toward Gideon and Ivy before turning the finger toward Whale's chest. The armorer ignored it, turning the arm easily aside, and whispered something in his ear. Shelt leaned away from him and stared, his mouth slightly agape. Whale nodded. Shelt glared. Whale said something else, and Shelt punched his shoulder, hard. The thin man fell back a pace but did not lose his balance; instead, in the abrupt hush that silenced the men, he took a deep breath, exhaled it loudly, and turned his back on the village.

Shelt yelled a command at him, but Whale ignored it, his face granite as he strode away from the silent mob, his arms swinging purposefully at his sides. When he reached the others, he smiled humorlessly at Tag, nodded to Ivy, and pulled to his front a deep pouch on his belt.

"They're fools," he said with a rueful sigh. "They do, on occasion, forget who I am. Long memories were never strong with the Pholler. Never. Sad, don't you think? Doomed to forgetting is what keeps them stupid."

"Look, Whale," Gideon started, and was stopped with a look from Ivy.

With a sharp glance over his shoulder, Whale reached into the pouch and showed Gideon what appeared to be a small black ball four inches in diameter.

He took it and closed his fingers around it. It felt warm and smooth, almost like the wood his bat was made from, though its weight belied its size.

"What is it?"

"Can you throw?" Whale asked.

Shelt ordered his men forward, and they moved with a single yell, no longer willing to be put off by distractions.

"Sure. But don't ask me to hit anything."

Whale seemed puzzled, but he suggested strongly, now that Shelt and his men were running, that Gideon take the black ball and throw it toward Pholler as far as he could.

"That far?"

"This is not a time for boasting," Whale scolded.

Gideon, puzzled but pleased he wasn't expected to put the ball between someone's eyes like an overgrown David with a multiheaded Goliath, handed him the bat, drew back his arm, paused to check for windage, and hoped he was as good with this thing as he had been with the Hail Marys.

He was.

The ball sailed in a perfect arc over the mob's collective head, and that collective head turned to watch it, ignoring Shelt's demand that they stop making fools of themselves and get on with the slaughter.

They watched.

Ivy and Tag watched while Whale looked astounded at the distance the missile covered.

Gideon watched with a gratified smile at his lips and said, "Jesus H.," when the ball landed a hundred yards beyond the mob and exploded into a fan-shaped gout of flame, earth, and burning shards of grass.

The mob threw up its arms and jumped into the air, looked over its shoulder at Gideon and the others, and scattered, leaving Shelt red-faced and alone in the middle of the road, bellowing for their return or else, until Whale handed over another ball; then the big man made one last, indescribably rude gesture and took off across the field.

Ivy applauded and hugged Tag, less in jubilation than to prevent him from tearing off after the nearest attackers.

Whale took back the second ball and placed it delicately into his pouch.

Gideon brushed dirt and grass from his hair, dusted off his shirt and jeans, and put the bat back into its holster. Then he started up the road, whistling for Red, who fell in beside him.

"Wait!" Tag called, and raced after him.

Ivy looked regretfully to the village, to the men running in terrified circles in the fields, and took Whale's arm. Whale sighed and walked.

"Hey," Tag said, "what's going on?"

Gideon looked at him. "Two things," he said when he thought he could speak without bellowing. "One—in a little while those idiots out there are going to stop panicking, figure out what happened, and come after us again, this time with more men and, if possible, more weapons. It would not be advisable to wait to see what they have in mind after that."

"And the other thing?" Tag asked when Gideon paused.

"I could have killed someone back there," he said bitterly. "I could have knocked someone's brains all over Sallamin, or I could have blown someone to bits."

The lad was perplexed. "But that's what you do when you fight!"

"I know that. I'm a fast learner, no matter what you think. But," he added when the boy started to protest, "Tag, I have never killed anyone in my life. Never. Not accidentally, and certainly not deliberately. Those men back there, they're real."

"Sure they are."

"Believe me, Tag, that's easier for you to say than me."

"I don't understand."

"That makes two of us."

And he put his arm around the lad's shoulder and hurried him on, saying nothing, seeing nothing, feeling only Tag under his arm and the reassuring silken hair of Red's neck on his left as he stroked it, seeking to calm himself, hoping he wouldn't have to stop in the middle of the road and start screaming.

FIFTEEN

Shelt and his men did not regroup but spent their energies racing through the high grass until, at some unheard command, they wandered back to the village.

Gideon paused long enough to watch them go, fearing his explanation to Tag was more correct than he wished. He decided, however, that his mother had not brought him up to be a diplomat and so discarded before it was completely formed the notion that he return to Pholler and attempt a healing of the wounds his actions had caused.

Instead, he walked at a steady, swift pace until his legs adamantly refused to take another step and the adrenaline stopped feeding fuel to his muscles. With a weary groan and a look back that showed him nothing but the plain, he dropped on the roadside and waited for Whale and Ivy to catch up. When they did, their silence respectful of the expression he held, Ivy produced from a pouch at her side foot-long lengths of what tasted like dried beef with a tang, and Whale found a stream from which he brought them water in makeshift cups he had woven from wide leaves.

Tag sat apart, clearly working for a reason why the man his sister had found was acting so peculiarly.

Twenty minutes later, Gideon, apologizing for seeming ungrateful because he certainly wasn't, asked why Whale had taken their side against the people he lived with, especially now that it appeared as if he'd not be able to return.

"Dignity," the thin man answered, sprawled on his back with his hands behind his head. A wink and a nod. "Oh yes, don't look so surprised. Dignity. That's terribly important, you know, much more than a few coins lost toward one's guaranteed poverty-laden retirement. Not that I'm trying to make you feel guilty, you understand. Not at all. Just a little, to ease your conscience.

"But it is not dignified to abrogate an obligation just because you are afraid of the consequences. Once you accept one—an obligation, that is—you just see it through to the end because that's what an obligation is, isn't it. And Pholler did not behave in a dignified manner when it sent out those men to stop you. They should have questioned you further, they should have accepted your reasons for going to Chey, and they should have done all they could to assist you in your quest."

Then he winked once, and closed his eyes.

"Besides," he whispered so the others couldn't hear, "my shop collapsed after you knocked down the post. Shoddy builders, the Pholler. No sense of permanence. Lost everything. Why stay?"

Gideon smiled, though he knew the man couldn't see him, and chewed thoughtfully on the last bit of meat. When Whale's breathing deepened into what was unmistakably a rhythmic snoring, he stood and walked into the field, looking up at a sky still alien to him, wondering if he really felt better for what Whale had said or if he was only trying to keep himself from slitting his own throat. A few minutes later he sensed but didn't hear Ivy join him until she slipped a hand around his waist, pinched him lightly, and withdrew.

"Thanks," he said softly.

"Don't mention it. Besides, I did it for Tag and Glorian," she said as if she threatened immediate, and most likely expert, castration every day of her life. "I was one of the first to see them when they came from Kori after it . . . after. I like her more often than not. She's a little bitch sometimes, but I like her. Those idiots, though . . . well, it wasn't right, what they did." She stopped, forcing him to halt as well and face her. "But they didn't mean any harm."

"They wanted to kill me!"

"Sure, but it wasn't personal."

"It would have been to me."

"They're afraid," she said, looking at him steadily. "You have to understand that they are afraid. Going to Chey isn't like going to the mountains or to the Blades. When you go to Chey, especially now, things happen, and they don't want their homes . . . like Kori."

He covered his face with his hands and massaged his forehead, his temples, and lowered his arms slowly. There were fourteen or fifteen questions; he chose one at random. "What do you mean, especially now?"

"Now," she said, "is when the Blood rises."

"The Blood?"

She nodded solemnly.

"I see. And what in god's name does that mean? And don't," he admonished with a raised finger, "tell me that I'll learn about it soon enough. That's what Tag is always saying, and soon enough never happens."

"That's because he doesn't really know."

"Who does?"

"Nobody."

"Then—" He waved off the beginning of an explanation and started slowly back toward the others. Ivy remained beside him, close enough to touch, though they didn't touch at all.

"Okay. As I see it," he said in his best noncommittal manner, "there's a lot of serious trouble you people are expecting from this place Chey, trouble that's going to be stirred up even more because Tag wants me to go there, and it looks like I'm going whether I want to or not. And this trouble started with or was caused by or is a result of Glorian and her lost duck, whatever the hell that is."

"It's a duck," Ivy said, astonished he didn't know what a duck was.

"A quack-quack?"

She giggled and nodded.

"You mean a real, honest-to-god, white-feathered, flat-footed, mean-tempered duck? A quacker?"

She nodded.

He stopped again and held her arms, only vaguely aware that it was not an altogether unpleasant sensation. The woman was softer than she appeared, and, he reminded himself, this was no time to be thinking anything like that.

"Look, Ivy, since Tag won't tell me, and Glorian didn't have a chance to, would you mind letting me know what's so important about a duck that would cause a whole damned town to want to bring dismemberment upon my body?"

"You talk funny," she said.

"That's because I'm crazy."

"Oh."

"The duck."

"I'm surprised Tag didn't say anything."

"Ivy, please . . ."

She glanced nervously toward the road. Whale was still on his back, and Tag was brushing down Red with handfuls of grass. The light was almost gone, and the moon was climbing slowly toward the stars.

"Maybe," she said, toying with one of the buttons on her blouse, "you'll feel better if I take off my clothes."

"What? What?"

She slapped his hands from her arms. "What's the matter, aren't I pretty enough for you?" One eye closed dangerously. "You didn't . . . you and Glorian didn't . . . No. No, she's not the type. Or you're not the type. She's pristine, you know that? At least, she claims she is. I have my doubts, but when it's Glorian, what can you say?" The eye opened. "Or are you prejudiced because I'm not from across the Bridge?"

"What the hell," Gideon demanded, "does that have to do with a duck?"

"It's not a duck, damnit!" she shouted, then covered her mouth and winced as if afraid she'd been overheard.

"It's what?"

"It's not a duck."

"I thought it was a duck."

"Well, it is. And it isn't."

He narrowed his eyes and held his breath. "Are you going to tell me like, if I kiss this duck, it'll turn into a princess or something?"

"I hadn't thought of that."

"Ivy," and he took her arms sternly again, looked straight into those remarkably green eyes, and wondered if the explanation would make any more sense if she were in fact naked. It might clear his mind of extraneous inconsequence; it might also help his apprehension by discovering if these people were as physically human as they seemed. It was an admittedly interesting problem, and he would have explored it further had not Tag suddenly yelled a warning, and he suddenly turned, and they all saw the clutch of torchlights coming at them from the road.

"Too late," Ivy said sadly as she rebuttoned the blouse he hadn't noticed until now she had already unbuttoned almost to her waist.

"For what?" he grumbled as the light parade drew closer.

They ran.

Whale was awake, up and sprinting without needing to be told; Tag was on Red's back and charging headlong toward the haze visible even in twilight; and Gideon and Ivy raced over the grass, angling toward them and joining them in full flight.

The lights as they closed separated to show them a sizable army on the way; there was no noise from the Pholler save for an occasional clatter of metal.

Red kept his pace down so the humans wouldn't be left behind, but it didn't matter—less than a mile later, Gideon found himself running through what felt like an arctic fog, a chilled dampness covering him instantly and sending tremors through his legs that almost pitched him to the ground. He could no longer see the others, though he could hear their footsteps, could hear them calling to each other, could hear Red's nervous growling.

Streaks of blue and gold flared overhead, and he thought he heard the distant sound of thunder.

"Ivy!"

"Keep going," she called, though he couldn't see her. "Stay on the road, it's safer."

"Safer? Than what?" Almost immediately he remembered the pacch lunging hungrily from its burrow, and he stayed on the road, using the rain ditch on the side to warn him when he strayed too far left or right.

The chill increased, and he suspected that if it were daylight, he'd be able to see his breath plume between his lips; the dampness increased as well, cloying and sticky and forcing his lungs to work all the harder for a decent fill of air.

Blue and gold darted on either side, the colors clear, though they gave him no light.

"Ivy! Whale!"

He thought he heard them calling, but he couldn't find a direction to run to, nor, when he glanced back, did he see the lights that had driven them into the black fog. Slow down, he ordered them, before you kill yourself. He sensed that their pursuit was left behind and for one reason or another would not follow them into this place. Whether that was a comfort or not he could not decide, but without the others the devil-you-know did not apply.

He was almost at a walk, his knees weak and his right side burning, when he stumbled and fell off the cobbles into the grass. A yelp, and he scrambled to his feet, dove back to the road, and heard where he had been the sound of something large and sharp digging into the earth.

He didn't look; he started running again.

"Red!"

There was no indication at all that the lorra was still on its feet, much less carrying Tag full speed ahead.

"Red!"

Only his own voice, echoless and flat.

The fog made the road slick, and twice he had to slow down to prevent another fall, twice more spin around when one foot decided to try a different direction than the other.

Then he heard a scream and a feline roaring that faded quickly away—Tag and Red.

Whale shouted next, more in surprise than anguish.

And Ivy was the last, sounding furious and betrayed.

And it was silent.

Not a sound but his own feet running on, the hushed swing of the bat, his breath hoarse and burning between his lips. He slowed because he couldn't see the ground, slowed even further when he couldn't see more than a few feet in front of his face.

He called out.

There were echoes now, but they didn't sound like him.

He turned and looked back, and saw nothing at all but the dark.

He trotted, the bat snug against his chest, knowing he was in Chey and terrified that no one had told him it would be like this—formless, soundless, not even a trace of a scent of anything he knew.

He stopped at last, panting, leaning over to catch his breath, calling out again and hearing nothing but echoes.

Then he looked up, and saw the red eyes.

He yelled, spun around, and ran . . . and was astonished when after less than ten steps his feet were running on nothing but air.

He was falling, and he knew then that Chey was no figurative or mythic place.

It was literal, and he had found it.

He had found the end of the world.

SIXTEEN

I don't think I like this, Gideon thought as he pitched into the dark.

Like the blurred spokes of a runaway wheel, he felt in swift succession terror, rage, terror, puzzlement, terror, and, finally and most chillingly, an odd sense of calm resignation. He was, if the length of his fall and the condition of his luck thus far were any indication, going to die without benefit of an open casket; and this recognition and acceptance, he realized, were not unlike similar sensations experienced when he was in the river, floating on his back toward the rapids and watery demolishment.

Only this time there would be no Tag to save him.

Yet the only indication that he was, in fact, falling was the tug of his hair away from his scalp in the wind of his own making, the annoying thump of the bat in its holster against his thigh, and the watering of his eyes as he faced, he thought, downward. It was difficult to tell. The mist was still thick and, now that the lightning darts of color had vanished, dark as the night he had left above him. The air was cold and clammy, like a November drizzle that promises ice the moment the sun goes down.

By keeping his eyes tightly closed and thus giving them no points of reference, he was able to stave off vertigo with only a mild lurch or two of his stomach trying to wrap itself around his spine; with no sound but the wind, he was at least spared the ignominious and thoroughly understandable screams he thought he was making; and with nothing solid to touch, he could not fool himself into believing there was something to grab on to, something that would break his fall, something out there in the dark that would prevent him from dying upon impact.

Time also lost meaning, but he was sure enough that two or three minutes had passed to begin to wonder if this miserable world had something else in store for him beyond the scattering of his bodily parts across the landscape. It seemed, he thought with a light surge of hope, that he wasn't falling now so much as he was floating, or coasting. And he was undeniably still alive.

He recalled reading somewhere that most people who fall from a great height succumb to heart failure before they hit bottom; it was all theory, of course, since the flyers weren't interviewed or monitored on the way down, but it was a vaguely comforting notion since the only problem his own heart had at the moment was keeping up with his adrenaline.

He also recalled reading that a falling object reached maximum velocity after only a thousand feet or so. Maybe more. Sixteen feet per second, per second. He didn't know what that meant, but it sounded impressive and implied that he was now going as fast as he ever would. Meaningless now, but significant should he encounter a freestanding brick wall.

But again he had the feeling that the falling was now a floating, with a very slight side-to-side swaying as though he were lying facedown on a hammock.

And that, he understood abruptly, was lulling him into the possibility of dangerous complacency. His life might even begin to flash through his mind, and he would perforce fall asleep and miss the grand climax or an opportunity for salvation. There was no question but that he was going to have to stop hiding and take a look. After all, what did he have to lose?

His eyes wouldn't open.

He nodded without moving his head; that was perfectly

reasonable. Why would anyone want to see the future, when the future was about to smash him into his several component parts?

He tried again. One eye opened warily, didn't like what it saw, and closed again with a snap he almost heard in the wind. He clenched his teeth, tightened his lips, and suggested to himself that he was being rather immature, that a real man would stand up, as it were, to whatever cards were being dealt and spit in the dealer's eye.

Besides, there might even be a slim chance that he was going to get out of this alive, which would permit him to find Tag and beat the hell out of him for not telling him about the cliff.

A brave smile, and he opened his eyes, finding himself in what he imagined was a skydiver's classic position— arms outstretched, legs slightly parted and bent at the knees. A sustained effort accompanied by a fair amount of grunting and grimacing drove as much tension from his limbs as was humanly possible under the circumstances, and he drew his left arm slowly toward his chest, noting as he did that he began to roll to the left; when the arm was thrust out again, he stabilized. A similar experiment with his right arm brought similar results. When he tried pulling his right knee toward his stomach, he was canted upright; his left knee made him fall upside down.

It was fascinating.

And not nearly as terrifying as he had feared.

The dark mist had become less so; so much so that he was able to see the face of Chey's cliff rushing past him several hundred yards away. It was irregular and pocked with caves, and he wasn't moving so fast that he missed spotting the ladders and switchback steps that seemed to lead all the way to the top and all the way down. A hell of a climb, he thought sourly, but rather preferable to the method forced upon him.

A wiggle of his hands turned him slowly on his horizontal axis, away from the cliff face.

The mist thinned even more, and the air began to warm.

He blinked away wind-tears, listened to the howling wind, and recognized suddenly the state he was in—almost as though he were experiencing the scene from a seat in a theater, watching it all happen to an actor who had the good sense to look exactly like him. It was, he decided, like the onset of an automobile accident, when time abruptly slows and vision takes on a clarity that enables the doomed driver to see every unalterable move, every spot and dance of dust, every step of the destruction that is aimed straight at him. Or when the center snaps the ball and six or seven tons of padding, snug uniforms, and fresh red meat instantly thunder across the turf toward him while the crowd rises ever so slowly to its feet and the roar it gives is like the drawn-out growling of a hundred prowling beasts. It was a subtle kind of terror, the calm before the end, holding a breath though the lungs were still working.

And he felt someone watching.

He wasn't surprised. Plunging toward the inevitable was bound to have some effect, and with a quick tuck and stretch of his right arm he reversed his position, lying now on his back, staring up into the mist.

Into the huge red eyes that had been dogging him from the beginning.

They were slanted slightly upward, rimmed in black, and each was centered by a flaring speck of gold.

Though no other feature was visible, nor could he spot even a faint suggestion of a body, he knew that whoever or whatever belonged to the eyes was smiling, the quiet pride of an executioner who had no feelings one way or the other toward the condemned at his feet.

"Who are you?" he demanded.

The eyes merely stared.

"What the hell do you want?"

The eyes only watched.

"Don't suppose you'd want to give me a hand."

The gold in their center darkened a little.

Gideon reached for the bat, rolled over until he was nauseated, then scowled and stuck out his tongue.

One eye winked, and both eyes vanished, and he quickly flipped himself back onto his stomach, swallowing at the blade-edged lump trying to climb out of his throat.

A look over his shoulder, and the cliff face had fallen away, replaced by an aerial-view city like no other he had ever seen—a low wall surrounded it, the stone buildings were small and square, the cobblestone streets meandering, and there appeared to be a steady flow of pedestrian and carriage traffic through the open front gates made of rusted spiked iron. And at those gates, and ranged at irregular distances along the fieldstone wall, were creatures of such surpassing ugliness and indescribable meanness that none of the people looked at or spoke to them, none even came within touching distance of them. They remained still as gargoyles contemplating dinner, but the angle at which Gideon watched them was such that he was unable to see their features fully; he only knew that he didn't want to meet any of them, any time, any place— not, he reminded himself, that he was in any position to do so anyway.

He cocked his head, then, and the city vanished, the cliff face returned, and he sighed for the hallucinations his overloaded mind was dumping on him.

Like Ivy over there, standing sideways toward him in midair, one hand buried in the unbound mass of her blonde hair, the other toying coyly with the buttons of her blouse. She pursed her lips and winked at him, turned her back and maddeningly slowly slipped the blouse off, tossed it away, and kissed each of her shoulders. She kicked off her boots. She ran her palms down her buttocks. Then her head turned and her eyes narrowed, a slow bump, a slow grind, and she began to pirouette, dropping into a huddled crouch as she did, so that, when she faced him again, her naked torso was hidden by the protection of her knees. She smiled. She pouted. She reached out her arms toward him and vanished just as she leapt upward.

So this, he thought, is what dying is like.

Then he looked down, and saw the ground.

*   *   *

At first, Gideon was too astonished by the sight to think of anything but how beautiful it was.

Above and beyond him was a massive white cloud through which he had just passed, immense as he fell away from it, but not so large as to cover more than a slight fraction of a painfully blue sky.

The cliffs of Chey had retreated to become the stark, bleak side of a continent-huge mountain whose peaks were lost to the casual observer in broad swirling bands of dark grey and poisonous amber.

Below was a magnificent spread of verdant rolling forestland through which, from the east, west, and south, ran three meandering rivers whose surfaces reflected the bright sunlight in flares and lances that made his eyes tear when he stared at them too long. He could see, to the west, a horizon befogged and hazed much like that he'd seen on the higher ground, but elsewhere there were no signs of high ground other than the one he'd just left— there was only the woodland, the rivers, and an occasional expanse of impossibly green plain.

There was also a huge lake, egg-shaped and, as far as he could tell, perfectly calm.

And in staring at the water, the rivers, the trees, it all snapped abruptly into focus and into a perspective that had him gasping.

Floating through the cloud—once he had determined that death was not terribly imminent—had not been so bad, all things considered. Despite the visions and the frustrating sight of the ladders on the cliff face, he could have been dangling only three or four inches above the floor of his living room. Helpless, cold, unsettling, but not so bad once he'd gotten used to it. In a curiously unfathomable way, it felt almost unreal, almost safe.

This, however, was all too real.

The ground was several thousand feet below, and though he was still floating in the general direction of his demise, able in small ways to control his direction, he was still going down. And those trees there were a lot higher than they looked, and the lake grew into an inland sea, the surface no longer smooth but rippled now with whitecaps whose size he was unable to determine. The rivers, too, were wider, and now that he was closer and the sun was no longer flaring off them, he could see that they were tinted by the landscape; and one of them, which appeared to rise from the base of the mountain, was a disturbing red whose source he could not locate.

Suddenly, he discovered he was afraid to move his head. A single wrong motion now might disrupt whatever forces were working to prevent precipitous plummeting, and he wished he could see signs of life. But there were no roads visible through the woods, no villages or isolated buildings or even signals that would tell him his friends had landed safely.

Worse: no matter how hard he wriggled his fingers, shifted his limbs, or prayed, he was unable to stop himself from drifting directly toward the sea.

When you're in serious trouble, his sister had once told him, whistling doesn't do a damn thing but waste good air, especially if the other guy has a tin ear. What you have to do if you're going to get out of it is think fast, think smart, and then run like hell. It was easy for her to say. Trouble avoided her all her life, until the night he received the call from the state police; they had found her rented automobile on its back in a California river. Apparently, she had driven through the guardrail on an old wooden bridge during a sudden autumn storm. The car was towed out just before dawn, but his sister's body was gone, swept away, the police informed him, to an unknown grave in the Pacific.

Now it seemed as if he had an ocean of his own to contend with, and from the looks of the waves that rolled onto the eastern shoreline, it wasn't going to part for him so he could walk back to the beach.

The trees speared at him, their leaves broad, here and there some with daggerlike needles.

He could see no fording areas as he had along the Rushes, reluctantly concluding that shallows were not part of their makeup.

He shook his hands. He bunched his legs and curled his arms over his chest. He tried positioning himself in a swan dive. But nothing worked—he could neither turn nor slow down, spin away or alter direction. As if strung to a guy wire, he was heading directly for the water.

Which, he thought, was not so bad in itself since he ought to be able to swim to safety; what he didn't like were the shapes he spotted on the surface. Dark shapes, somewhat long and perhaps scaled, and from a hundred feet up he knew damn well they weren't boulders.

Ninety feet.

Fish food, he thought grimly; the quarterback ends up as fish food.

Sixty feet.

The shapes broke the surface in the manner of whales sounding, but their details were obscured by the sun's glare in his eyes. He thought he heard watery snorting, faint splashing, and he strained when he was sure he had heard something snarling.

Forty feet, and he realized with a groan he was moving faster.

Thirty feet.

The trees towered above him, the far shore of the sea was lost in a mist that seemed too much like fog, and he estimated he would land some ten yards from the beach.

And at twenty feet he was released by whatever had held him.

He yelled, and he fell, but he still dropped into the water.

SEVENTEEN

Trying to keep a cool head to prevent undue catastrophe, Gideon let his body sink into the water. The inland sea was cold but not shockingly so, and his system adjusted rapidly, with little more than a single spasm that almost tore his head from his neck—a small price to pay for not drowning, he decided.

Though his eyes were open, there wasn't much to see but a distressing number of bubbles escaping between his lips and the roll of the gentle surf above; the bottom, whatever it consisted of and whatever dwelt down there, lay beyond the reach of the light. He waited several seconds, until his descent slowed, before flexing and thrusting upward, breaking through the surface with a gasp for air and a toss of his head to clear hair and water from his eyes.

He sank again before he could move his arms.

Another thrust, and he broke up again, treading water as best he could while he turned in a slow circle, hunting for the shore and looking up every so often at the sky, the drifting clouds, and the imagined glide path of his landing.

He almost sank when he realized the distance he had fallen, but at last, the push and nudge of the low breakers turned him toward the beach, and he struck out wearily, wishing he were able to swim faster, but for the time content to let the tide do most of the work. He had never realized how tiring falling off cliffs could be, and for a

133

brief moment he feared not being able to make it. The trees and the sand seemed awfully far off, and the way they kept bobbing up and down made him feel a bit seasick. Only a dismal belief that he was fated to die in some more exotic way than drowning in a freshwater lake kept his arms moving, kept his legs moving, kept his mouth closed so as not to admit more ballast.

Then his feet kicked the bottom, and he stood, the water in the troughs barely up to his waist. Bracing himself against the waves, he gulped at the air, touching his side to be sure his bat was still there. Then he walked, half hopped, until he staggered onto the sand.

Soft sand that was a gentle, foglike white with a few flecks of sparkling pink and blue. Warm from the sun. And ahead not thirty yards distant was the edge of the forest—titanic trees that made the woods of the Scarred Mountains seem like mere shrubs, their grey-and-black boles gnarled and twining, their heavy lower branches thicker around than a dozen saplings. There was a mixture of broad leaf and needle, with a few hesitant colorful blossoms that winked in and out of sight as a breeze darted among them. There was no underbrush to speak of, and as he dropped to his knees, he listened and did not hear a single sound other than the waves hissing behind him.

Friday, he thought, I am here, so where's the booze?

No one came to greet him, which did not reassure him; yet nothing came to eat him, which took a considerable load off his mind. Safe again, through no fault of his own.

Slowly, he lowered himself until he was prone, resting his chin on crossed arms while he stared at the woods. He knew that he ought not to stay very long. He was more lost on this beach than he had been above, and with a few hours of daylight still left, it would be prudent of him to begin searching for signs of his friends or for a place to stay for the night.

But the sun was comfortable on his back, and he was having a difficult time keeping his eyes open. His muscles whined for respite, his brain for a few hours' deep and dreamless sleep, and it did not take long for temptation to whisper that a good night's rest wouldn't do him any harm. After all, he wouldn't be any good to anyone if he wasn't fully recovered. It would be, he told himself, the only reasonable thing to do.

A good point, until the sand just a foot from the tip of his nose began to bulge as something beneath pushed its way up.

He raised an eyebrow and decided it was an omen.

When the sand fell away and he saw a crab's pincer thrust redly into the air, he knew he was right—the pincer was a good six inches across, and if the crab itself matched the size of its appendage, this beach wasn't going to be big enough for the both of them.

It was. Twice as large, and growing larger.

Gideon pushed himself hastily to his feet, moving slowly to his left, not taking his gaze from the crab until it shook itself again, dug a claw into the sand, and threw it at him. He blinked in surprise. The crab's eyes waved on their stalks, and it scooped up another clawful and tossed that as well. When he backed up another four feet, the crab clicked at him rapidly; another step back, and the crab, having successfully defended itself, waddled into the water.

Amazing, he thought.

Shortly afterward, a second crab emerged, a shade larger and less inclined to be belligerent when it saw Gideon staring; a third was larger still, at least the size of a healthy dog, and Gideon decided his curiosity had been sated. He turned and broke into a leisurely trot, veering toward the trees as he headed north, looking back only once, to see the last crab standing in the surf and watching him with one eye while the other watched its fellows bobbing on the surface. Then it was gone, the only sign of its passing a pit in the beach rapidly filling with water.

It occurred to him to call out a name now and then, but he decided against it. Until he knew what else lived along this stretch of land, it would be the wise thing to pretend he was invisible. Besides, the silence was beginning to make his nerves stretch for stimulation. For all those trees, all that water, the only sound he heard was the breakers, which were less than thunderous, and the slap of his soles on the sand.

Illogically, he came to believe that the minute he opened his mouth, all hell would break loose.

One of the rivers, he decided finally, would be the best thing to aim for, so he could follow the banks inland. It was reasonable to assume that whoever lived in this part of the world would probably build a community along such a natural road; it was also reasonable to assume that his friends would head for the same place. It would be a simple matter, then, to catch up with them, exchange tales of their adventures, and discover at last his final destination.

On the other hand, simple had never been a hallmark of his life thus far. There also were too many unknowns to consider—like procuring food and drink that wouldn't poison him outright or otherwise, unraveling the false trails he would inevitably find himself following, marshaling the ability to ration his own strength and stamina so that he didn't collapse just when he was on the verge of victory, not to mention puzzling at the way the water out there was beginning to boil.

He slowed but didn't stop.

Beyond the third row of breakers the sea was roiling—fan-shaped spouts of water lifting high into the air, the surface churning into dazzling white foam. Perhaps it was some sort of geyser released from the bottom. Perhaps it was a suddenly risen sandbar upon which the waves were breaking. Or perhaps the crabs he had seen were engaged in one of their mating rituals or had found something that appealed to their crustacean tastes, and that something wasn't in the mood to be eaten just yet.

He bet on the crabs.

Then something large and dark burst out of the middle of the cauldron and landed several feet in front of him, spraying sand in all directions and forcing him to swing even closer to the trees.

The sea still boiled.

He looked down and saw what was left of the largest crab, both pincers torn off and a gaping hole in its back.

He stopped, stared, and poked at the crumpled carapace with the tip of the bat.

"Son of a bitch," he said softly, and wrinkled his nose at a stench that burst from the dead creature when he tried to flip it over.

He stared out at the water.

Through the whirling white foam he could see a long dark shape rising, then abruptly falling down and away as still another portion of crab was flung cavalierly into the air. This piece, apparently unsuited for the unknown predator's taste, sailed over his head into the trees, and its crash through the canopy produced an hysterical avian shrieking. He looked up but saw nothing, peered into the shadows, and thought he saw streaks of red fleeing deeper into the forest.

The boiling subsided.

The foam broke apart and was carried shoreward by the waves.

Gideon stepped gingerly around the crab's body and started running again, fearing to take cover under the trees in case he should get lost. The inland sea was the only thing he had to mark his place in a place he had no knowledge of, and he didn't want to leave it until he absolutely had to.

His progress, however, was not as rapid as he would have liked since he dared not take his gaze from the water. At any moment he expected to see the boiling begin again, and to see whatever it was that had taken on the giant crabs and had beaten them so handily. It affected him so badly that he was soon slowed to a fast walk, the bat swinging like a cat's tail at his side, his eyes narrowed against the sun setting redly in the west; it affected him so strongly he almost wished it would show itself and dispel the suspense. After all, he thought, how bad could it be? He had seen and battled the black beast in his pantry, and there wasn't much his imagination could conjure to rival that hellish creature.

Then he tripped over a fallen tree and fell into a pit.

"Well, hell," he muttered as he landed on hands and knees and spit out the sand that had collected in his mouth. The hole wasn't deep, only waist high when he stood, but he didn't move immediately. Instead, he gripped the bat more tightly.

Ahead, for nearly fifty yards along the beach, trees had been uprooted, smashed, split in half, defoliated, stripped of branch and twig, skinned of bark, and splintered; the beach was pocked with pits like this one, not the result of digging but of a struggle in which the opponents had evidently slammed each other to the ground, spun around on massive legs, and rolled about in a futile attempt to continue living.

As he hauled himself out of the depression, Gideon wondered if whatever he had glimpsed in the sea had been a part of this; then he looked into the forest and wondered if there were more of them living back in there.

Then he looked behind him, at a miles-long stretch of beach on which not a single one of his footprints remained.

Dusting the sand from his jeans, he sniffed and squinted out at the water, turning his head slightly when he saw movement on the surface—a V-shaped rushing, the bow wake of something submerged and moving toward him.

He took a step back.

The bow wave grew, and a black shadow appeared behind it.

The bat lifted to his right shoulder, and he flexed his wrists nervously, not remembering until the sea creature emerged that his weapon was untried, that the only thing it had thus far successfully done combat with was a ceiling post in Whale's armory shop.

And when he saw what he was facing, he decided that this was not the time for a baptism of fire.

EIGHTEEN

The sea-beast stood poised in the shallows, water dripping from its sides, waves hissing and swirling about its feet. With the sun behind it, it was little more than a huge, ominous shadow, but there was still enough light for Gideon to see that it had the sleek, somewhat pudgy lines of a dolphin, its body ending in a forked broad tail more probably fitted to an undersized whale; its head, on the other hand, resembled a German shepherd that ate fire hydrants for breakfast—its ears were high, long, and pointed, its eyes wide and glowering, its needled snout lined with dozens of small, sharp teeth that snapped and glinted as it swiveled about, seemingly testing the air. And it stood nine feet above the water on a pair of thick, dark-furred legs, which Gideon did not doubt ended in claws unpleasantly honed.

From one corner of its mouth a crab leg dangled unnoticed.

Gideon took a step toward the trees.

The sea-beast spotted him.

Gideon brandished the bat.

The sea-beast lowered its head and charged, raising its tail for balance, opening its mouth to save time when it was close enough to swallow.

Gideon bolted, plunging into the forest, zigzagging around boles and propelling himself with branches that might otherwise have whipped his head off. He paid as little attention as possible to his pursuit in case his legs decided the rest of him didn't have a prayer; instead, he leapt over deadfalls, veered around boulders, flew over the sudden appearance of a shallow, narrow ravine at the bottom of which he thought he saw water trickling.

The sea-beast whistled at him, and a branch snapped at its base, barely missing his head.

A shift to the right, a sudden one to the left, and he raced across a wide clearing knee deep in grass.

The sea-beast whistled, and the grass turned brown.

In the forest again he continued angling to his left, ducking as if being shot at whenever he heard the piercing whistle, his shoulders hunching as he expected one of the trees to break in half and pin him underneath.

When the sea-beast whistled a third time, nothing happened, and the sound was definitely farther away.

Gideon didn't slow down. He paid no heed to the screaming his lungs were doing, or to the stitch that was working its way around his waist to his spine. As long as he kept moving, he knew he had a chance, and as long as he didn't brain himself on a branch, he knew he'd soon find the boundary of the beast's range from the sea.

Ten minutes later he was stumbling, and the crashing had been reduced to the occasional snap of a twig.

Another ten minutes, and he was staggering, wiping sweat from his eyes with a leaden arm while his feet tripped over nothings.

Behind him there was silence.

At last there was nothing more he could do. His knees buckled and he fell, hands barely able to reach out and stop himself from striking a fallen log. He rolled over and lay against it, gasping. This, then, would be his last stand. This would be the place where they would erect the monument to the stranger who had failed to rescue the white duck. This would be the forest they would name in his honor, just after they had sent an armada to sea in order to exterminate the beast that had caused his demise.

This, he thought as he fumbled for the bat, is where I make up for all the failures I've been.

He fell asleep.

Several hours later he awoke when something soft brushed against his cheek, causing him to flail about with the bat and smash the log to pieces. And when he realized where he was, and when he felt a leaf clinging gently to his cheek, he slumped forward and rested his forehead on the grass, laughing weakly, sobbing his relief, not noticing the darkness until he tried to stand and tripped over his own feet.

He sat, pulled his knees to his chest, and looked up.

Though the foliage was high and thick, he could still catch a glimpse of the nightsky, the moon, and a handful of stars. As his eyes adjusted to the dim silver light, he saw the trunks and branches oddly flattened, the leaves without edges, his own hands unable to cast a shadow on the ground. Above, he could hear rustling in the canopy, and out there in the dark night-things moved about. But there was no sense of danger, no feeling of being watched. The sea-beast had evidently given up and gone home, and nothing else here was hungry enough to attack him.

Directly ahead, something growled.

"Go away," Gideon told it angrily. "Gimme a break, do you mind?"

It growled again, and the dark was punctured by two pinpoints of green.

Using the bat as a brace, he pushed himself to his feet, looked around, and saw that the tree he had been sitting against had a bole that spiraled around itself and was thick enough that if he had to, he could climb by running around in circles.

The growling deepened, and the green eyes advanced.

Gideon held the bat to his chest, trying to decide if he should stand and fight or try for the tree. His hand stroked the wood absently. Fighting in the near dark was not exactly ideal; on the other hand—of which there seemed to be an awful lot lately—it was entirely possible that whatever the creature was out there, it could climb as well. It might even be some sort of large cat, in which case he'd have just as much chance on the ground as above it.

He frowned; it was growing warm.

Running, of course, was out of the question. Two steps, and he'd break his leg; of that he was sure.

"Damn!" he said then, and snatched his hand away from the bat, looked at it, and grinned. There was a deep blue glow inside the grain, and he quickly brought it to the surface, cupped it, blew on it, and sent the bluelight gratefully ahead.

The green-eyed creature was caught unawares. It looked up at the globe and snarled at it, swiped a paw at it, and whirled when it glided over its head and stopped.

Gideon laughed.

The animal was less than shin high, half that long, and covered with long black fur that dragged on the ground. It was tailless, fat, and though its round head looked to be larger than it should be for the animal's size, there was nothing menacing about it except for its growl.

"Thank you," Gideon said, not to the globe, but to the animal, for being one of the few creatures on this world that didn't seem bent on shortening his life. He was so relieved that he climbed the tree anyway, heading for a flat-topped branch some ten feet above the ground. The lightlamp rose accordingly and enabled him to see that if he braced his back against the trunk and stretched his legs along the branch, only a strong wind or a nightmare's tossing would take him to the ground before he was ready.

It was a chance, but his body needed the rest, and he hoped his reflexes would serve as his alarm.

It sounded convincing, and once he'd clapped the light off, it even felt convincing as he rocked back and forth, flung his arms out, his legs, testing for the limits of balance before the drop.

But it was still a long hour before his nerves relaxed and he permitted the night sounds to lull him to sleep . . . and heard a distant whistling that had him instantly awake and the bat in his hand.

It was daylight, the sun high and bright enough to show him his perch, the forest around him, and the sea-beast looking at him from the base of the tree.

He had no idea how it had followed him so far from the ocean, but it was down there now, snapping those teeth at him as its ears lay back alongside its canine-dolphin head.

Slowly, his hand raised his weapon, his gaze on the sea-beast while it thumped its tail on the forest floor and shifted agitatedly from one clawed foot to the other. Spittle slipped out of its mouth, nictitating membranes winked over its bulging eyes, and finally it lunged forward, butting the trunk and nearly spilling him from his branch.

Instantly, he was on his feet, not bothering to wonder for more than a brief moment why, with its height, it hadn't just reached up and gulped him down. With the bat waving bravely in front of him, he edged out along the branch; the sea-beast followed, a soft mocking whistle slipping between its teeth. It eyed him as if measuring distance, the top of its head level with the branch's underside but too far away for Gideon to swing at without putting himself within range of its mouth.

Sideways it moved, its tail still thumping, the ground still shaking.

Sideways Gideon moved, until he felt the branch beginning to sag and saw culinary excitement begin to shine in the creature's eyes. Puzzled, he stopped. The beast stopped. He looked down the creature's length and lifted an eyebrow. How, he wondered, could such an ugly thing be so damned stupid? The legs, he saw then, were so rigid they were trembling, the claws dug deep into the earth, and its neck was virtually nothing more than a thick stump.

"You poor sap," he said. "You can't jump, can you?"

The beast whistled, a bit louder, and he felt the branch quaver, felt the wood beginning to split.

Gideon cocked his head and took a long stride back

toward it, saw the jaws open and shut in frustration and anticipation, saw a tidal flow of muscles ripple from the back of its skull down its spine to the tail. He was right. It could not leap because its legs were too busy trying to hold up its out-of-water weight, nor could it raise its jaws any higher because it didn't have the means to.

Gideon smiled.

The sea-beast whistled again, and the branch sagged even more.

Gideon raised the bat over his head just as the beast saw the move and started to back away. Before he could bring the weapon down on the skull, however, the branch split with an agonizing scream and he was propelled into the air, twisting as he sought to avoid the snapping jaws, landing with a grunt square on the thing's back. It spun around immediately, trying to dislodge him; he clamped his thighs against its short fur, trying not to be dislodged. It whistled and dropped a tree; he hissed when the tree almost brained him. It began to run, and Gideon began to panic, realizing that once it was back in its element he would have no more chance of survival than one of those giant crabs.

It whistled, and trees parted in its path like the volley of cannons that had wiped out the Light Brigade.

Gideon no longer attempted to dodge the lower branches but rather tightened his legs even more and lifted himself up, took the bat and closed his eyes, swung it, and heard it crunch against the beast's neck.

The beast whistled and stumbled.

He swung again, one eye open now to see the fur part, the flesh part, and the dark red of its viscous blood splatter into the air. With a moue of distaste he struck again, aiming for the head and falling just short, feeling himself slip backward, where the tail was trying to arch overhead and swat him to the ground.

The bat whistled through the air; the beast whistled toward the beach; the trees snapped, crackled, popped out of their way, until Gideon gathered himself and lunged

forward, the bat finally coming down in the middle of the
beast's skull.

It stopped dead.

Gideon kept moving, sliding up the back, the neck, the
skull, and into the air to the ground. He twisted around
and leapt to his feet, the bat at the ready, his breath
coming in short gasps.

The beast eyed him mournfully.

Gideon shrugged and stepped to one side to leave it
plenty of room to fall.

It seemed to appreciate the gesture because it whistled
once again, this time soft and low, and dropped. It wasn't
elegant, but it served the purpose, and Gideon hopped out
of the tail's way when it made one last move to smash him
into a tree.

Shaking his head at that deception in death, Gideon
stepped around the body and headed back into the trees.
He wasn't about to walk the shoreline when there might be
others waiting, and if he were lucky, he wouldn't get too
lost before he died of old age. Besides, he wanted time to
think, and he quickly placed the bat in its holster so he
wouldn't have to feel its power and be reminded of what it
had done, and what it could have done had he been in a
more tenable position.

The idea frightened him, and he moved deeper into the
trees, until the sun was directly overhead and he had
reached the stream he had vaulted the day before. There he
dropped to his knees and splashed water onto his face, his
head, washed his hands, and drank from his palms. It was
no substitute for solid food, but he'd not seen any of the
red berries or anything else he felt tempted to eat, and he
needed something in his stomach to stop it from complaining.

An hour later, when his legs stopped aching and his
arms had lost their cramps, he moved on, aware after only
a few paces that he was listening to a faint, steady roaring
in the distance. Not an animal, but one much like what
he'd heard as he'd floated down the Rushes.

Without running he quickened his step, ignoring animal

noises seeming to keep pace with him in the branches, ignoring his legs. telling him they were tired of all this nonsense and wanted a vacation, with or without pay they didn't give a damn, and ignored the fact that he had once again taken up the bat. Just in case there were surprises.

Then the trees ended, and a river began.

And there, on the opposite bank, was Ivy Pholler.

"Hey!" he called, waving his free hand.

Ivy turned, and he gaped, abruptly realizing she was standing in the shallows, perfectly naked.

NINETEEN

"Where the hell have you been?" she called, hands hard on her hips.

Gideon could only stare dumbly as his right hand gestured vaguely behind him, thinking that perhaps one of his better hallucinations had come cruelly back to haunt him. When she saw the stunned expression on his face and looked down at herself, however, she scowled a clear message and he sighed—she was real, and there she was, scrambling up the bank to yank on her clothes and ruin his fantasies. A resigned lift of his shoulders, and he watched as she returned fully clothed to direct him upriver, where he saw a bridge spanning the deep water. A log bridge. The narrow trunk of a single storm-felled tree that barely made it to the other side.

"Are you kidding?" he said, nudging the trunk with his foot and watching it wobble. "I'll fall in."

"No, you won't," she assured him. "I didn't."

He closed one eye. "Which side did you land on?"

"What a stupid question."

With a glance back to be sure there was no miracle in the offing, no chance that this place would somehow give him a temporary pair of wings, he took out the bat, held it out in both hands for a balance pole, and stepped timidly onto the log. It rocked ominously, and he jumped back with flailing arms, did a deep-knee bend, and stretched his arms over his head. Then he leaned down and plucked

147

some purple moss off the log where his first step out would be.

"Are you finished?" Ivy called.

"I just want to be sure."

She shook her head in disgust and sat down to wait.

A woman doesn't understand these things, he thought as he kicked at the fallen tree again; there's a certain aura a man has to sustain if he wants to keep his self-respect.

"For god's sake, Sunday!"

On the other hand, some women understand men all too well.

With the bat once more in position, he gauged the distance to be traveled and stepped firmly up onto the log. It trembled. He held his breath. It steadied. Ivy hoped he would cross before the seasons changed. Ignoring the jibe, he took a sliding pace forward and set his hips square with the opposite bank. When he didn't fall on the third step, he allowed himself to breathe and to keep moving. The tree took his weight without too much sagging in the center, but he refused to look up, staring unwinking at the slippery bark, one foot carefully sliding in front of the other, swaying every few steps and closing his eyes until the log steadied. Left foot, right foot, until a hand closed around the bat and yanked him to shore.

"I—"

Ivy told him to shut up and embraced him without warning, snuggling her cheek against his chest and squeezing. "I thought you were dead," she whispered. "I really thought I was never going to see you again."

"Nope."

"I thought . . ." She lifted her gaze to his and shook her head. "I was going to have to do this on my own. I couldn't find Tag or Whale, and who the hell knows where that damned lorra is. God, you can't know the feelings I had. You just can't know, Gideon."

"I suppose not."

She frowned and leaned away from him without releasing her embrace. "You're certainly talkative, aren't you?

Aren't you glad to see me, or is that just the bat in your hand?''

He backed away quickly, nearly fell into the river, and sat hard on the bank instead, on a flat-topped rock. Ivy clucked and dropped beside him, and together they watched the river sweep past, glass smooth and silent until it reached submerged boulders under the bridge, then turning into white water all the way to the next bend.

"Rough time, huh?" she asked.

He nodded. It occurred to him that she, too, had probably been through the wringer, but right now he was only concerned with his own self-pity.

"Want to tell me about it?"

"Not really."

"It would help, you know. You shouldn't keep things like that to yourself."

"It's unpleasant."

"Life, too, is unpleasant if you can't see the sun."

He stared at her incredulously, and she giggled.

"Stupid, right?" she said.

"Profoundly so."

"So tell me, and don't leave out the gore."

He did, beginning with the terror and fascination of his fall and ending with his near fatal confrontation with the two-legged dolphin that looked like a German shepherd. When he was finished she was gaping at him, admiration in her green eyes and a rapid pulsing at the hollow of her throat.

"Incredible!"

"It couldn't jump."

"No kidding."

"I'm still alive, aren't I?"

"Well, it just goes to show you, doesn't it?" she said, and scrambled to her feet.

"Now what?"

"Well, we can't stay here, right? We have to move on."

"Where?"

She pointed upriver.

"What's up there?"

"Good lord, didn't Glorian tell you that, either?"

Glorian, it seemed, had a remarkable gap in her already questionable memory when it came to the finer details, and he complained bitterly about it for the next hour as they worked their way along the bank.

"And you still haven't told me where we're going."

"Rayn," she said, swiping at a dull scarlet vine that was curling toward her neck.

He looked quickly up at the sky slowly turning dark, saw no shadows, and wondered if her prediction was part of some sort of weather folklore. Ivy, when she saw him, groaned.

"No, not rain. Rayn!"

"Spell it."

She did.

"What is it?"

"A place."

He gathered that no one in this world had ever heard of the spontaneous narrative.

"A city," she elaborated when he prodded her with a harsh word and the bat. "If Glorian's anywhere, she's probably there."

"Why there?"

"The duck, remember?"

"Ah. The duck's in Rayn."

"I doubt it. But that's where we can find out where it's been taken."

"Ah."

"Unless they kill us first, of course. It's a possibility you have to consider on something like this."

"Ivy, take me home."

She sympathized with a smile, patting his arm in condolence while she casually sliced away branches in their path with the edge of her dagger. Raw cries from deep in the forest made him wary about their digressions when boulders or trees blocked their way, but she assured him they weren't facing anything dangerous. At most they might come across a wandering footh, a tiny catlike creature with black fur and green eyes.

"Oh. I saw one of them," he said, ducking under a branch that aimed for his nose.

"You did?"

"Sure. Just before I fell asleep."

"And you lived?"

Amazing, he thought, how these people expected him to die at any moment and at the same time expected him to rescue their duck.

"Yes," he said when she expressed her amazement again. "And now you'll tell me why I shouldn't have."

"It has a bite."

"I might have lost a finger, not much more than that."

"You would have lost a lot more, Gideon. The poison in its fangs can kill an army."

He stopped.

She looked over her shoulder and raised an eyebrow.

"What's it called again?" he asked.

"Footh."

"Stupid name."

"If it bites you, what do you care?"

A potent if somewhat after-the-fact argument, and another reason to keep an eye on the shadows, on the trees, on the branches overhead, on the leaves that seemed to quiver though he could feel no wind, on the deadfalls in the river, on the path behind him, on the sky in case it had wings, on Ivy's back in case he got lost.

To her unusually restrained and therefore all the more maddening amusement, he kept his weapon constantly to hand from that moment on, testing it once in a while on an unsuspecting bush or a falling leaf determined to do his skull damage, until finally, when he could barely distinguish his shadow from the ground, she brought them back to the river, to a wide shelf of dark rock six feet above the water.

"We'll stop here until morning," she said, looking

around and nodding her approval of the site. "If we go any farther now, we'll only kill ourselves."

He didn't dispute her. His legs were so tired he couldn't have walked another step anyway, and his stomach was growling so loudly they would only have been able to sneak up on a deaf man who had been dead twenty days.

While she foraged for food, he was left with instructions to pull broad leaves from the trees to fashion bedding for the night. It took only a few minutes, once he got the idea to use the bat to loosen the branches. Afterward, he realized that his clothes were sorely lacking in the social graces, and for the first time in days he regretted losing his pack on the slope outside Kori. He sniffed, rolled his eyes, and with a glance toward the woods he stripped and found a series of natural if slippery steps down to the water. There he rinsed out shirt and jeans as best he could, slapped them against the rock until he thought his arms would fall off, then tossed them back up and decided the rest of him might as well get a good washing, too.

With a scan of the surface to be sure there were no shark fins or bathing foothi, he stepped boldly into the shallows.

The water was cold but not icy, and he lowered himself gingerly until he was sitting on the bottom. A little splashing for fun, a kick of his feet, and he understood the first level of an explorer's heaven. The flow eased his muscles, the river's whisper through the reeds made him delightfully drowsy, and it wasn't until he looked lazily toward the opposite bank that he knew he wasn't alone.

It was green, and it was long, and it had a bubblelike head atop a serpentine body.

It also moved rather fast.

He yelped and scrambled to his feet, fell, and thrashed until he was on his feet again.

It was still coming.

A shout now, and he backed up, lashing out with his feet. The watersnake dove, appeared five feet closer, and he could see two pair of lifeless black eyes measuring the distance between itself and its dinner.

He kicked again, reached down, and grabbed a rock from the riverbed; the first throw landed in the trees, but the second caught the thing in the middle of its back. It dove again, and this time when it surfaced it was already twenty yards downstream and still moving.

Damn, he thought; just when you thought it was safe to go—

"Very nice," Ivy said from the rock above him.

Gideon looked down at himself, blinked, and cupped his hands over his groin while he grinned sheepishly and tried to climb the wet steps back to the top.

"Don't flatter yourself," she said, not unkindly, and pointed to the water. "That. It only eats insects, but you did a nice job just the same."

He said nothing. He only glowered and shouldered her to one side before dressing, thinking that someone really ought to sit down and give him a comprehensive zoological lecture before his mind snapped and he found himself battling battalions of crazed and ravenous roses.

Then, as daylight slipped rapidly from the air and filled the forest with a disturbing, premature midnight, Ivy built a fire in a depression of the rock, made a crude spit over it, and fastened to it the corpse of a small headless creature he recognized right away.

"I thought they were poison," he said, pointing to the footh.

"Only when they bite you. This one never had a chance."

He looked to her sheathed dagger, to her gentle hands, to the half smile at her lips. "You're pretty good, aren't you?"

"I have my moments," she said.

"Then have a moment now. There's someone behind you."

TWENTY

Ivy whirled into a defensive crouch with dagger in hand while Gideon jumped to his feet and held out the bat in what he hoped was an attitude of prohibitive menace. The fire was between them and a shadow that moved out of the trees, the details of its features just beyond the light. But it was huge, and it was silent, and Gideon heard the faint ticking of what sounded like claws on the rock.

"You take the left, I'll take the right," Ivy whispered as she sidled into position. "Don't let it kill you."

Good advice, he thought somewhat sourly, and waited for her to be more specific.

Then he heard purring.

"I'll be damned," he said, lowering his weapon as he stepped around the firepit just as Red moved into the light. The lorra blinked once, then pressed its muzzle happily into his chest while his hand went instantly up to its head.

"What about me?" Tag said wearily from the animal's back.

"You want your head scratched?"

"No, but I'm hungry."

The reunion was made quiet by the silence of the forest, but it was enthusiastic and long, and by the time they remembered they were hungry, the footh had long since been charred hard as stone. Not to worry, Ivy assured them, and vanished to hunt again while Tag warmed his hands over the low flames and told Gideon how he had ridden the lorra all the way down to a meadow two days' ride from here. They had come across many promising signs of civilization, but when Tag tried to follow them, assuming the others would as well, Red had refused, plunging instead straight into the forest. Nothing the young man could do had altered the lorra's direction.

Gideon reached behind him, to where Red was lying down, and stroked the lorra's neck. Red purred and yawned.

"Loyalty," he said when Tag looked puzzled. "A unique bonding between man and animal. Red knew instinctively where I was, and he came to find me."

Red snorted.

Ivy returned with a pair of foothi, which she cooked over the fire. Red disdained the offered meat when it was done and roused himself long enough to defoliate a nearby tree. Tag fell asleep before he was finished, leaving Gideon and a nodding Ivy to listen to the river and watch the fire burn down to a handful of glowing embers.

"We're only missing Whale," she said as she lay on the bedding Gideon had provided.

"I would guess he's on his way to Rayn. I doubt if he could find us in this place."

"You found me."

"Luck."

"Nice of you to admit it," she said, closed her eyes and began snoring.

Gideon watched her for a long time before deciding he'd be no good to himself if he didn't sleep too, but when he looked around he realized that Tag had preempted the other bed, and it was too late now to make himself another. The noise he made was a cross between a sigh and a groan, and he crawled over to Red and rested his head on the lorra's flank. The giant goat stirred, sniffed his chest and hair, but didn't wake up.

Suddenly, Gideon sat up and stared at the animal's closed eyes. "He *rode* you down?" he said. "I fell like a goddamn rock, ended up in the goddamned ocean, and had to fight all kinds of beasts in this misbegotten jungle, and he *rode* you down?''

Red snorted in his sleep.

''It ain't never easy,'' he muttered, relaxing again. ''But it would be nice, just once, to see what it's like.''

Ivy hushed him sleepily, Tag moaned in a dream, and he crossed his arms over his chest, closed his eyes, and winced at a sudden bright light that made him roll over and bury his face deeper into the lorra's fur.

''You going to sleep all day?'' Ivy demanded, and he felt the toe of her boot prod his ribs.

He blinked and sat up, not feeling the least bit rested, his stomach lurching when he smelled a footh roasting over the morning fire. Tag was in the river, swimming.

''I think,'' Gideon said as he stretched the knots from his muscles, ''I'll pass on breakfast.''

''You'll pass out if you don't eat,'' she scolded.

He thought to argue when she sliced off a piece of meat and plopped it onto a palmlike leaf. He sought for an excuse to leave the room, the forest, and the world when Ivy grinned at him with a sliver of food dangling from her lips. And he knelt down and ate when his stomach told him not to be an idiot.

It wasn't bad.

It didn't taste like chicken, but it wasn't half-bad.

And by the time they were finished, right down to the bones and a goodly portion of the innards, and the fire was scattered to hide their presence from people and things he refused to ask about, daylight was already two hours strong.

Ivy, after checking the position of the sun and its shadows, led the way along the riverbank. Tag, stiff from sleep, swimming, and riding, followed while Gideon, who told himself he was the eldest and therefore needed the most rest, asked Red if it would be all right to ride for an hour or so. The lorra swung his great head around to give him a baleful look, then lowered himself to the ground so that he could climb on.

Once aboard, he wondered aloud if everyone who dropped

off the edge of the world tended to become as leaves in the wind.

Tag dropped back and shook his head. "You die, usually. You get so splattered you couldn't be picked up with a pacch's tooth in a full moon."

"I didn't. You didn't."

"I know," the lad said.

"Why not?"

"Whale."

He closed one eye in a frown. "Whale?"

"Sure. He's . . ." Tag paused when Ivy looked back at him with a cautionary frown. "But he's going to know sooner or later."

"Sure he is. But does he have to know now?"

"I think he'd better. For Glorian's sake."

"Well . . . I guess."

"Well, I know."

"Excuse me," Gideon said, "but have I left the room without knowing it?"

"It's Whale," Tag told him, brusquely telling Ivy with a gesture to keep her mind on hacking a path through the forest. "He doesn't like everyone to know who he is."

Gideon's right hand brushed over the bat's hilt. "Who is he?"

"I don't know."

"Come again?"

"What I mean is, I don't know his real name. Nobody does. He just showed up one day and asked the Pholler if he could set up shop at the square. But you could tell he wasn't normal. Really strange, if you know what I mean."

"He did magic."

Tag's eyes widened. "Magic? What's magic?"

Gideon looked to Ivy, who kept her back turned. "Magic," he said, "is something . . . well, it's spells and things."

"Ivy has spells."

"What?"

"Sure. Look at her funny and she'll cut your tongue out."

Ivy's back stiffened and she felled a sapling with her dagger.

"That's not a spell."

"Oh. Well, I don't know about magic," Tag admitted. "But Whale does strange things sometimes. Like not falling off the world."

"Whale did that?"

Tag looked at him in disgust. "Well, if he didn't, we would have been dead, wouldn't we?"

Gideon considered it, accepted it, and didn't ask for an explanation. "It might have been the guy with the eyes, though," he said after a few minutes' silence.

"What eyes?" Ivy and Tag asked in unison.

He was startled by the astonishment in their voices, and the startled-deer look that widened their eyes. He had a feeling he should have mentioned the eyes a long time ago. And when he explained what he had seen in the forest beyond Kori, on the mountain, and during the fall, Tag began searching the treetops nervously, and Ivy quickened her pace until she was trotting.

"Is it something I said?"

"Later," Ivy said without looking around. "We'll have to hurry now. We have to get to Rayn before the Blood rises."

Gideon nodded, and concentrated on not falling from Red's back when the lorra began to pick up the pace. He dodged several branches, winced when one slapped back at him, and had to rap Red on the head when Tag fell and the lorra, blithely walking in his sleep, almost trampled him. That night they camped in a small clearing, feasting on a bird Gideon refused to look at before it was plucked and cooked. He slept, but again not well, and the next day was the same until just before sunset.

Gideon was walking beside Red, explaining to the lorra the difference between a hit-and-run driver and a blind-side tackle, when Tag finally ran up to Ivy and tapped her shoulder. She stopped and cocked her head to listen, then grabbed the lad by his hide vest, lifted him off the ground, and tossed him into the nearest bush. By that time, Gideon had caught up with them, and he stared at Tag's struggles, not knowing whether to be amused or not. From the expression on Ivy's face, he read enough to decide to be neutral.

"Well, I can't read your mind," Tag complained, stamping his feet to shake off a coating of pale yellow burrs. "You should have asked me."

"Asked?" Ivy said, almost shouting. "Asked? You should have told me!"

"Asked what?" Gideon said. "Told you what?"

Ivy, her face lightly scratched from her battle with the flora, her chest rising and falling in barely contained agitation, turned on him and jabbed a finger hard into his sternum. "He says there's a road!"

"I know that."

"What?"

"He said that the first day. He found a road, but Red wouldn't let him take it." He grabbed her wrist then, before she managed to drill through to his heart. "If you recall, he said it took him two days to get to us."

"Red got lost."

"So if it took him two days, and he didn't know . . . what?"

"Red," Ivy said, softly and hard, "got lost."

Gideon looked back at the lorra, who began scraping his horns against a trunk to get the mildew off.

"The road," Ivy said, pointing so quickly with her dagger that he had to jump aside, "is over there."

"How far?"

"About two hundred yards."

Gideon turned on Tag, who shrugged. "Red got lost. How was I to know?"

"How did you know the road was over there?"

Tag's eyes rolled up, then he took Gideon's arm and faced him to the left. "You can see it if you look."

Gideon looked.

He could see it—through the woodland's gloom he could just make out a brighter lane of sunlight, which, if you weren't looking for it and didn't know what it was, appeared to be a break in the foliage, nothing more.

"That's a road," he said.

"Right."

"Then why the hell are we playing Frank Buck?"

"Who's Frank Buck?" Ivy asked.

Gideon shook his head, walked over to Red, and grabbed a handful of beard. Slowly, he forced the animal to look into his eyes. "You got lost."

Red purred.

"You didn't come just for me, after all."

Red's purr took on an edge.

"I apologize for the slur," he said hastily when the eyes shaded slightly darker. "But you still got lost."

Ivy, meanwhile, snared Tag's shoulder and shoved him ahead of her, through the underbrush toward the road. Gideon followed with a sheepish Red purring and nudging him from behind until they broke out of the trees and found themselves on a hard-packed dirt road. Tag grinned, Ivy cuffed his chest, boxed one ear, and made an impression on her sole with his left buttock before striding off without looking at anyone.

Tag picked himself up and followed meekly.

Gideon patted Red's neck and brought up the rear, whistling tunelessly to himself until, shortly after the sun passed its zenith, Red stopped and shook his head.

"What," Gideon said, then immediately called the others when he saw the lorra's eyes turning black. Ivy raced back, Tag not so quickly, and they watched the animal raise its head and sniff the air, clawed hooves digging into the ground until it lowered its head and aimed its horns at the trees on their right.

Tag and Ivy immediately had their weapons in hand.

Gideon was a bit slower, but soon enough to bring it to his shoulder when a shattering, warbling war cry burst from the forest and Red replied with a bellow of his own.

TWENTY-
ONE

The lorra's pantherlike bellow of defiance echoed through the dense foliage, and before it had faded, an explosion of leaves and twigs half turned Gideon away; when he looked back there were a half dozen creatures poised on the verge. He stared at them until a half dozen more appeared in the road a dozen yards beyond Tag and a third half dozen on the road to his right. His throat filled with sand, his arms began to tremble, and only an acute sense of self-preservation had him reach around Red's lowered head to thump Tag on the chest, to prevent him from going into his taunting dance again.

"My god," Ivy said with horror-laced fascination, "it's the Moglar!"

And indeed they were—stocky, swarthy creatures dressed in thick leathered vests and pleated kilts run through with glints of polished iron, in each hand spiked clubs that hissed through the air as they glared and grunted. They wore no helmets over their dark hair, and the boots they wore seemed little more than strips of hide wound around them, leaving their prehensile toes ready for emergency gripping.

There was something terribly familiar about them, Gideon thought as he watched those on his right begin a halting, almost simian advance, and when one of them drew himself up and brandished his weapon over his head, Gideon knew what it was—their proportions, the shape of

161

their limbs and torso, the slightly distorted and pudgy features . . . They were dwarves, but of a sort he had never bothered to dream about back home.

Fierce, giant dwarves that towered almost to his shoulder.

Suddenly, as Tag was about to lunge forward with his woefully inadequate dagger, the largest of the brutes crossed his clubs over his chest.

"I am Kron," he announced with a self-satisfied sneer, in a voice that sounded like overfed swine starved for oxygen. "You are my prisoners. You will give over your lives to me without delay."

"Why?" Ivy said dubiously, her own dagger glinting in the last of the light.

"So that you will enter the home of the Wamchu in glory."

Tag paled.

Ivy gasped.

Gideon reached out a hand to pat Red reassuringly, the bat growing warm in his grip, a headache beginning to climb through his scalp from his nape. He didn't much care for the idea of having to fight these creatures, but Kron's attitude and the slavering of the other Moglar suggested rather strongly that he wasn't going to get to Rayn without breaking a few eggs. Assuming he would be able to get there at all.

"You will submit now," Kron demanded.

"You will perform unnatural physical acts upon yourself," Ivy retorted.

The Moglar's already dark face darkened, and he shook his head so that the black stringy hair that Prince Valianted his forehead swung back and forth like serpents seeking prey.

"Ivy," Gideon said cautiously.

"I'll take the left,"`she said, "you take the right, Tag and Red the middle."

"That's not what I meant."

Then Kron, with a bark of unintelligible orders to his band, leapt from his place with clubs high and narrow eyes flashing. The others charged as well, and Gideon could only turn his back to Red and face the onslaught, the bat suddenly and disturbingly snug against his shoulder.

Red wasted no time. He met the charge with horns and claws, and before Gideon had a chance to take his first swing, the lorra had skewered one Moglar and flung three more back into the trees, sending Kron and his lieutenant scurrying for cover. Then he whirled to his left and knocked Ivy aside, gored a Moglar square in the neck, trampled two more, and terrified the remaining pair into a dust-raising retreat.

Gideon closed his ears to the screams of the defeated and the triumphant bellow of the lorra now standing panting at his side. He tried instead to judge the distance between himself and the first of the giant warriors, steadied himself, and tapped the tip of the bat on the ground.

There was no need.

So swift had Red's vicious attack been that by the time he had returned, the remaining Moglar, with Kron posturing in their midst, were having second, more healthy thoughts about the purpose of their ambush. Their eyes flitted back and forth over the quartet they faced; their clubs were not quite as menacing; and despite their imposing size, they backed off a step when Red took a step forward and snorted.

Kron finally held his ground and glared.

Red growled.

Kron growled back.

Red lowered his horns and charged.

Kron leapt nimbly aside, permitting his lieutenant to have all the glory, at the same time swatting the lorra smartly on the hip.

Red shrieked in pain and his hindquarters buckled as he hamburgered the Moglar, and Gideon suddenly found himself charging as well, lowering his head and butting the nearest raider in the chin, spinning over the toppling body to tackle another and drive a fist into his throat. A Moglar landed on his back, and he fell sideways instantly, rolled over and picked up the giant dwarf by the front of his vest, lifted him over his head, and threw him into the trees. Red regained his feet and headed for Kron, who was coolly observing the exchange from a position well behind the others. When he saw the lorra approach, however, he uttered a strange whistle that rallied his remaining men to his side and they then vanished silently and abruptly into the forest.

"Jesus," Gideon said, blowing on his hand, sure he had shattered at least four of his knuckles.

Ivy shook his arm and tugged. "C'mon, we can't stay here now. They'll be back."

Gideon didn't protest. He retrieved his bat and holstered it, then with a soft word and a smile poked through the lorra's long hair to see if any damage had been done. Red whimpered, then purred, then butted him away and hurried up the road after Tag and Ivy. Gideon lagged behind, checking to see that no one followed, listening to the forest for signs of further ambush.

It wasn't until an hour had passed that he was satisfied they were safe for the time being; but it wasn't until full dark had fallen and he was virtually feeling his way along the road with his feet that he tried to analyze why he had abandoned the weapon Whale had created for him and instead treated the deadly attack as if it were a scrimmage.

He had no answers.

All he could do was hope that sometime before this damned world succeeded in murdering him, he would be able to defend himself and his friends properly. Though he had admittedly made a good account of himself, he couldn't help feeling as if he had let them all down.

He didn't stop thinking, however, until he ran into Red's tail and realized that the dark which had fallen over the land had finally forced them to halt.

Ivy made a low fire on the verge as the night's chill worked its way into their aching bones; Red stood guard in the road's center, and Tag began composing an epic, nonscanning poem to his own prowess and the ignominious defeat of the Moglar contingent. Gideon sat by the flames and stared at them, his palms cupping his cheeks, his sighs so loud and explosive they threatened to blow the fire out.

Ivy shook her head. "You certainly have a way of fighting," she said in reluctant admiration.

He nodded glumly.

"What do you call what you did back there?"

"Stupid," he said. "They could have broken my back with those clubs, torn out my throat with their bare hands, picked me up by the ankles, and thrown me to the top of the nearest tree."

"But they didn't."

"I was lucky."

"You were good."

He looked up sharply, a curse on his lips, and swallowed it when he saw no derision in her eyes, heard no sarcasm in her voice. When she smiled, he realized that she was probably right, that he hadn't actually been half-bad at all.

"Not great, though," she said then. "If Red hadn't scared them so much, they probably would have torn you to pieces."

His mouth opened, closed, opened again, and he laughed, loudly and fully, until, with an effort, he was able to regain control. Then he stretched out on his side and let the fire warm him.

"When do we get to Rayn?"

"In the morning, I think. Late."

"Then what?"

"Then we tear down the walls," Tag said as he squatted next to Ivy and poked eagerly at the embers with his dagger. "We'll start on the north side—that's the weakest, I think—and pull the walls down until they give us what we want. We'll have to kill a few guards, I guess, but that shouldn't be any trouble. After that we'll attack the city itself, probably go for the market so they'll starve. Or—"

"Tag," he said.

"—we might go for the armory. Kill the guards there and head straight for the best weapons. Once we have them we'll go right to the Hold and take the Wamchu. Once we do that it'll be no—"

"Tag," he said, more loudly.

"What?"

"What the hell are you talking about? There's only three of us and Red."

Tag looked to Ivy, who shrugged. "So?"

Gideon dropped a twig onto the fire and watched a leaf brown and curl and fall into sparks. "What is the Wamchu?"

"He's not a what, he's a who," Ivy said.

"All right, who is the Wamchu?"

"Which one?"

"The one Tag is talking about. The one that Kron person talked about."

When the others exchanged somewhat wary glances, Gideon did his best to appear impatient and menacing. Then Tag hugged himself as though he'd gone deathly could.

"The Wamchu," Ivy said, "is the one you've been seeing. The one with the red eyes."

"Ah."

"He comes from Choy."

Gideon frowned. "Where's that?"

"The end of the world."

"What? I thought we already went through that. Or over that, as it were."

"Chey is the end of our world," she explained, pointing over his head and upward. "Choy is the end of Chey's world."

He foolishly considered asking if Choy had an end of the world as well and decided against it; esoteric geography was not one of his strong suits. Instead, he went for the obvious: "But what is this . . . this Wamchu doing here if he's from there?"

"He's only from there sometimes. The rest of the time

he's from here, and because we're here, he won't go back there.''

"Just because of us?"

"Close enough.''

"I see.'' He watched a tiny whorl of ash stir into a mound. "It's the duck, right?''

"Right.''

The ash stirred again and scattered.

"This Wamchu. Is he a magician?''

"Huh?'' Tag said.

"I mean, can he do things like Whale can?''

"I don't know. He doesn't need to, I don't think.''

"And who are his friends?''

Ivy looked puzzled.

"You implied,'' Gideon said patiently, "that there is more than one of this Wamchu person, which I assume is a title like a king or something.''

"Oh no,'' Tag said eagerly. "Wamchu is his name. The other ones, they're his wives.''

"He has more than one wife?''

Ivy looked disgusted and lay down, her face a mosaic of light and dark between the flames. Gideon was distracted for a moment by the sight of her, by the snaring of the firelight in her hair, and had to blink once and hard when something Tag was saying slipped past him.

"Again?'' he asked.

"Chou-Li,'' Tag said.

"What's that, the end of Choy's world?''

"No, Gideon. That's his first wife. Then there's Thong, who's supposed to be the nicest one, and then . . .'' The lad glanced around him at the dark, at the snap and sway of the leaves, at the reach of their shadows onto the road. "Then,'' he said in a voice so low Gideon barely heard him, "there's Agnes.''

"Agnes?''

"Shhh!'' Tag said with a finger to his lips. "God, I don't want them to hear us. Even Red couldn't save us then.''

"Agnes?"

"Agnes Wamchu," Ivy said, sounding like a little girl being dragged into a nightmare. "She's the worst."

"Why?"

"She just is," Tag said. "She's the one who's going to kill us, you know."

TWENTY-TWO

Sleep came with great difficulty, and Gideon was not greatly annoyed when Ivy woke him shortly before dawn. They ate a hasty footh breakfast and set off hurriedly, taking turns riding Red, who after his nightlong vigil slept as he walked, his purring snores the only sound in the forest.

By the time the sun was up, the trees had begun to alter shape and composition, growing wider apart, shorter, until they were little more than shrubs on the edge of a fan-shaped plain. As they rushed along the road, Gideon looked behind him and saw what appeared to be a ridgeline of mountains impossibly high, peaks and high slopes permanently encased in billowing cloud; and he was momentarily chilled when he realized that it was the cliff he had fallen off of only a few days earlier.

By midday he began to notice a change in the land ahead of him. Though he could see no mountains on the horizon, there was a definite break in its configuration, a speck that grew to a blot that puffed to a dot that soon broke apart into what he identified as the roofs of houses.

The city of Rayn, temporary home of the Wamchus and, with any sort of luck at all, the end of his search for the mysterious and by now intriguing white duck.

By midafternoon, however, it was clear they were not going to be able to reach the city until long after nightfall, and he suggested they stop now and camp, giving themselves a chance to rest and be fresh for the next day's journey. Tag disagreed, saying that a night assault was the best chance they had of overcoming the Wamchu's armies and rescuing Glorian and the duck. Ivy, on the other hand, was evidently running low on her reserves and took the opportunity to rest with a vengeance—she slumped onto the grassy field beside the road and collapsed into a deep and soundless sleep.

"Women," Tag said in disgust as he watched her. "They just don't understand how it is with a man."

Gideon almost laughed, turned away quickly, and followed Red to a hidden stream, where he drank, splashed water over his face and hair, and stared for a moment at his reflection. I'll be damned, he thought. He was growing a beard. A hand passed wonderingly over his jaw as he turned his face side to side, angle to angle. He had never had a beard in his life, and as he turned his face side to side he decided that he probably wouldn't have one again. He looked less like a roguish buccaneer or a dashing rake than a parrotless pirate who had suffered and not recovered from a childhood disease that had killed off half his facial follicles.

Another burden to be borne, he thought with a resigned lift of his shoulder, and he straightened, rubbed at the small of his back, and turned around to call Tag.

The name remained glued to his tongue.

Tag was standing with dagger in hand over Ivy, who was sitting up and glowering at a portly, green-dressed man with a tricorn green hat; a bow was slung over his shoulder, a quiver filled with green-feathered arrows dangling down his back. His hands were on his hips and he was laughing mightily as Tag darted back and forth like a cub whose genes told it it would soon grow into a full-blown wolf.

Slowly, hoping the man hadn't seen him, Gideon unholstered his bat and crept through the grass, crossed the road, and came up behind them. He didn't bother to look

for Red; the lorra obviously wasn't inclined to fight anything it judged was human.

"My dear boy," the man said to Tag, "would you
please stop that infernal dancing about? You're making me
dizzy, and I'm simply not in the mood for it today."

"Just defend yourself," Tag demanded. "I don't want
to kill you in cold blood."

"Girl, please," the man appealed to Ivy. But Ivy was
trying to get out from under Tag's legs and reach her own
weapon, a move that eventually entangled their legs and
had them both in a squirming, helpless heap.

The man reached for the foil at his hip.

Gideon gently placed the bat on the man's shoulder and
pressed down slightly. "Don't," he said.

"I won't."

Gideon took the foil's gilt-etched hilt and pulled the
sword free, stepped back, and ordered the man to turn
around. Tag immediately made feinting moves with his
dagger, and Ivy scrambled to her feet and ran to Gideon's
side.

"I am, as you see, right and truly outnumbered," the
green man said, spreading his hands wide, his round,
flushed face beaming with a smile. "May I assume that
your current plan is to have me done away with?"

"Yes," Tag said delightedly.

"No," Gideon said.

"Well," the green man said, "you had best make up
your minds before my men make up theirs."

"What men?" Gideon said disdainfully.

"Those men," Ivy whispered, pointing behind them to
a band of similarly dressed though not so rotund woodsmen
whose arrows were nocked and whose apparent skills were
displayed as elaborate notches on their supple bows.

"What if I kill you first?" Gideon said.

"Then my dear and most trusted Croker will take over
and kill you second." The man grinned at the symmetry of
it all. "The remarkable thing about our company, don't
you see, is that none of us is indispensable. I get to carry

the sword because I thrashed poor Croker the last time he tried to take it. Isn't that right then, Boole?''

Croker Boole, a scrawny but well-fed youth whose bow was almost as large as he was, nodded agreeably.

"I see,'' Gideon said reasonably, and after a second's debate with his will to live, lowered the bat and tossed the foil onto the ground at the green man's feet. "Now what?''

"Well, first we shall rob you of all your valuables and life's possessions, since that is, after all, our trade. Then we shall tie you up and leave you for someone to come along and rescue. In a way, you can see that it's a service, can't you—we get what we want, and someone else is rewarded either here or in the grand and glorious hereafter for being kind and charitable to those who are down and out. Since you get to live, you make out as well.''

"We don't have anything to steal,'' Ivy said sullenly.

"You have the lorra,'' the man pointed out.

"Over my dead body,'' Tag declared.

"Damnit, don't give him any options,'' Gideon snapped. Then he nodded, called Red over, and watched calmly as the green man approached the giant caprine, whistling softly and snapping his fingers. Red cocked his head and listened, curled his upper lip, lowered his horns, and turned his eyes black. The green man paused. Red emitted a low but easily translatable growl. The green man swept off his tricorn, wiped his brow with a sleeve, replaced the hat at a jaunty angle, and walked back.

"It appears to be more loyal than others of its breed,'' he said with some amazement. "I can't imagine how you managed it.'' He nodded to his band, who put down their weapons and gathered around. "But manage it you did, my friend, and I am well impressed by your skills.''

Gideon narrowed one eye. "Your name isn't Robin, by any chance, is it?''

"Robin?'' the man said, straightening his back as if expecting an insult. "Robin, you say?''

"Yes. As in Robin Hood.''

The man's eyes widened. "You know Robin?''

"Do you?" Gideon said, equally as astonished.

"No, but I've heard of him."

"No, but I've heard of him, too."

"My god, sir, then we have common ground!" He thrust out his hand. "Vorden Lain, at your service. And I do apologize for the hastiness of my men in thinking to do you harm."

"You were going to rob us," Gideon pointed out.

"But that, sir, is my lot. That lot over there has no lot save to cast their lot with mine."

Gideon rubbed the tip of his nose, decided not to ask, and introduced Tag and Ivy. The next hour, then, was spent in recounting their adventures since their fall from and to Chey; the hour or two after that was spent listening to Lain describe the history of his band of footpads and aspiring brigands and decrying the fact that Lu Wamchu had made things terribly difficult for him these days because of a disturbance among those who would send the man back to Choy with his figurative tail between his allegorical cur's legs.

Ivy, who was attempting not to strangle the man for his not-too-subtle glances in the direction of her chest, let him know that they were probably much of the cause of the unrest since they were attempting to locate a certain woman and a certain fowl.

Boole gasped and glanced uncertainly at the rest of the men.

Lain narrowed his eyes suspiciously. "You do not mean to reference the white duck, do you?"

"Of course," Ivy said. "You think I'm after a chicken?"

Lain rose suddenly and gestured to his men, brought them into a huddle, over which an occasional face rose to check on the strangers. They conferred for nearly half an hour while the sun lowered toward the distant city, but the only voices Gideon could hear were Boole's, raised in obvious dissent, and Lain's, by turns excited and calming. And when they were finished, only Lain returned to the others still seated on the grass.

"You need to get into Rayn," he said.

Ivy nodded.

"We will help you."

She was instantly wary. "Why would you want to do that? You were just trying to rob us a few hours ago."

"A few hours, my dear and most beautitious woman, is a lifetime for the butterfly, is it not?"

"I think," Tag said, "he's calling you a name."

"And a few hours ago," Lain continued, "I did not know you were embarked upon a quest of such import that our livelihood may well depend upon its outcome."

Gideon knew he'd hate himself in the morning: "Why's that?"

"If you lose," the man said solemnly, "we shall all surely die most hideously. Wamchu is most assuredly not a man to be trifled with, and worse—he takes you seriously."

"He does? He doesn't even know—" He stopped, remembering the mocking eyes, and the evil that lurked behind them.

Lain nodded knowingly. "And don't forget those he brought with him."

"Others?"

"He led three wives. Out of Choy, as you have no doubt surmised. You may take my word as fact, m'boy, that it wasn't for love."

They fell silent, then, while Boole led the men on a hunt for their supper. When they returned, strands of footh and other hapless creatures over their shoulders, Gideon had decided that, despite Lain's generous offer, he would have to refuse. The man was apparently known in the region, and any chance they had of entering the city without commotion would be ruined by his company. When he broached the subject, however, Ivy thwacked him sharply on the head with her palm and explained to Lain that he had no idea how things worked around here. Gideon admitted it ruefully. Lain then offered to find Gideon a forestry costume if he felt too much out of place. Gideon voiced a liking for his own jeans. Ivy wanted to know if they were going to have a fashion show, out here in the middle of nowhere, for crying out loud. Lain, ignoring her outburst and pouring a dollop of colorless liquid from a canteen hitched to his belt into a cup he pulled from his quiver, asked to see the bat and was astonished when he couldn't lift it. Ivy recommended they all get some sleep. Tag pouted because he couldn't lead a nighttime raid against the hordes of Wamchu who were keeping him from his sister and the duck. Lain passed the cup around, and Gideon took a sip, waited for the burning, and realized it was only water. Ivy lay down and closed her eyes. Lain's men had created their own campfire and were now singing love songs around it. Tag joined them. Lain passed the cup again, and Gideon realized it wasn't water after all.

And it wasn't such a bad night.

The air was pleasantly cool, there were stars whose light was a gentle winking silver, and the songs that sifted toward him from the other fire were tinged with the right sort of melancholy that made women sigh and strong men remember their mothers.

With his hands pillowed under his head, he asked Vorden Lain about the duck.

"It's a duck," Vorden told him.

"So I gathered. But I'm told it's not really a duck—as ducks of my limited acquaintance go, that is."

"Well, that's true enough."

"So what is it?"

Vorden looked to Ivy and Tag. "But you don't mean to say they haven't told you yet?"

"No."

"Then it isn't my place to do it, then, is it."

He may have slept, or he may have merely gone catatonic for ten hours. Whatever the reason, he soon found himself unconscious on the grass, embroiled in a dream that featured no cartoons or trailers—simply a pair of slanted red eyes, mockery in their mien and evil in their cast.

When he awoke, sometime shortly after dawn, he was drenched in perspiration and his skin was taut and cold. Ivy was beside him, awake as well and holding his hand.

"You saw them," she said.

He couldn't speak; he could only nod and look westward toward the city still hidden by the morning mist.

"He knows," he said tightly. "He knows we're coming."

TWENTY-THREE

Incredible, Gideon thought, what one can find in one's pantry when one is hunting for one's sister's rotten preserves.

He was standing several yards off the road, at the crest of a low knoll lightly spiked with broad-spreading shade trees. Before him, the plain stretched level and unbroken to the horizon except for a number of farms, clutches of small buildings, and the city of Rayn, which, from here, seemed to be constructed entirely of a yellowish soft stone. It was by no means a metropolis, but certainly large enough for the purpose of drawing to it hundreds, perhaps even thousands, of merchants, traders, and buyers every day. From his angle, he could see a low wall surrounding it and the streets on the other side running in concentric circles; the buildings were flat-roofed, all of a color, and none more than a single story in height save for the three-story square structure in the center. Pennants, flags, banners, and wash were strung between houses and shops in rainbow contrast, smoke curled from a chimney or two, and faint music could be heard on the light breeze that pushed his hair back from his eyes.

"Quite a sight, don't you think?" Vorden said as he came up behind. "Stirring, actually, if you care for such things."

"And you don't?" Gideon asked without looking away.

"For me, my dear friend, the byways of the forest, the vines that swing, the branches that hold, the trails that one

177

must blaze before the sun settles in its nest. I do not hold
with such accumulation of bodies as you see there below.''

Gideon couldn't help a short laugh and slapped the
man's arm as they returned to the others, sitting under a
tree and watching the stream of people pass toward the
city.

Not an hour after they had started that morning they had
come to a crossroads, and their solitary journey was at an
end. Suddenly they were engulfed by caravans, pedestrians, men and women on, for want of a better word,
horseback, and long trains of carts and wagons drawn by
animals that Gideon called oxen only because he dared not
ask what their real names were. Chatter rose and fell, faces
were turned curiously toward them, and once in a while
a man would scowl at Lain's band of green-clad brigands as
if warning them off.

Gideon rode the lorra, a decision not his but Ivy's, who
declared that a creature like Red seen evidently on its own
would be fair prey for thieves and those who would want
to shear the animal of its luxurious coat. He didn't argue
and rather enjoyed being the object of curiosity that wasn't
backed for a change with a desire to slit his throat. He was
well aware that before the sun reached its peak he would
be facing a danger that increasingly made him wish he
could start looking for a handy Bridge; in the meantime,
he had no choice but to carry on, buoying himself with the
knowledge that whatever it was he was supposed to do
would soon be done. Rayn was ahead, and with it Glorian
and the white duck.

''. . . just whistle.''

''Huh?'' He looked down as Vorden pressed an alabaster penny whistle into his hand. ''What?''

''I said, I shall with great regret be leaving you now.
There below is no place for me, my oddly bedecked
friend. Boole and I will be off, green ghosts in the night,
and you shall never know our passing.''

''But the sun is out,'' Tag protested with a puzzled
frown.

Gideon ignored him. "Nice of you to come this far, anyway, but why did you bother?"

Vorden smiled broadly. "The lady, m'boy, the lady."

Ivy seemed to blush when the woodsman turned his gaze to her figure, but she scowled at the last and gave him her back. The band hummed five-part harmony to find their pitch, and with a final handshake all around they were off, tramping across the fields in search of a Snow White with a house built for twelve. Gideon watched them for a long while, listened to their songs, and when he turned around he saw half the travelers on the road watching and listening with him.

But as soon as they saw his face they were off again, the silence broken by the creak of wooden wheels, the snap of a whip, the cry of a woman pinched unawares.

A deep breath slowly released, and Gideon nodded toward the slope.

Almost an hour passed after they had reached level ground again, and he realized that Rayn was larger than he'd thought from his vantage point above, and farther away. The sights, however, kept him from being bored.

Aside from those walking and riding with him, there were increasing numbers of small wooden huts along the verge, neat and brightly painted and fronted by stalls and stands and tables filled with wares hawked by their makers. There was food, clothing, weapons, toys, utensils, figurines, jewelry, hats, boots, books, glassware, hardware, bats, candies, repairs-while-you-wait, palm reading, hair reading, artifacts . . .

"Hey!"

Gideon slapped Red to a snorting, annoyed stop, and Tag ran into the lorra's rump. Ivy, who had gone on ahead, turned at the shout and rushed back, her hand cupped around the hilt of her dagger as she scanned the crowds for signs of villains and mashers.

Gideon ignored her questions. He slid to the ground and headed back toward a small red shack, in front of which, on the ground, had been spread a brilliant white hide; and on the hide was displayed a collection of baseball bats whose price tags had been discreetly flipped facedown. The doorway was low, and he crouched in front of it, trying to peer into the darkness.

"What's the matter?" Ivy demanded. "We haven't got time for—oh, my goodness."

Tag stood with his back to the shack, glaring menace at those who might stop to watch, while Red sniffed around the bats, closed one eye, then strolled around the hut to graze for a while.

"Hello?" Gideon called through the doorway.

"Go away," a voice called back.

"I want to buy a bat."

"You can't afford it. Besides, you don't even know what a bat is."

"You didn't either, until I told you."

There was a startled pause, a rustling, and Gideon backed away as Whale popped outside. A moment was wasted in staring for identification before they grinned and shook hands, before Ivy sighed with relief and threw her arms around the former fat man, before Tag looked over his shoulder and gaped.

"Took your time," Whale said, gesturing that they should all sit on the ground. Then he rolled up the hides with the bats inside and tossed the bundle into the shack, scrubbed his mop of brown hair, and plucked at his wattles. "I was hoping you would find your way here much sooner. Time flies, Gideon, you know that, and we don't have that much time remaining before we must fly ourselves, in the manner of things."

"I fell in the ocean," he said.

"Oh my greens and stockings, how wet for you."

Gideon gave him a mock frown. "I suppose I should thank you, though, for getting me down at all."

Whale's long face swiveled questioningly to Ivy, who nodded sheepishly. "Ah, well, it was to be expected, don't you think? A man cannot truly hide his candle under the bushel if the basket is no longer empty, as the saying goes.''

Gideon, averting his eyes from a cloud of dust raised by a passing cart, waited for explanations, but Whale only brushed himself off and rocked on his buttocks, smiling at Ivy and Tag and every so often humming a tune that sounded remarkably like one of those Lain's men had sung.

"Whale,'' he said finally, "Tag thinks we ought to storm the city at nightfall.''

The thin man nodded thoughtfully. "They wouldn't be expecting it, I grant you that.''

Tag applauded; Gideon silenced him with a look.

"On the other hand, I doubt we will have to resort to such drastic measures. As you can see . . . ah, but you can't, sitting down here like that, can you?'' He laughed, and his cheeks flushed a faint pink. "I forget. You are a stranger. But you will see that one may just walk into Rayn as if one belonged there. As we all do, in one manner or another, so to speak. Getting in is the least of our little problems.''

"What's the biggest?''

"Finding that which we seek, I would say.''

Gideon mused, pondered, debated, speculated, concluded with an estimation of how long it would take him to climb back up Chey. All of it silently, and all of it in less time than it takes to spell it. "I don't suppose,'' he said after spitting out another round of dust, "there's something convenient like a palace or a governor's mansion or a tyrant's terrible tower in there. Like that building in the middle that I saw, the tallest one?''

"Could be.''

"Sure it is,'' Ivy said impatiently. "It's where Wamchu puts his ass when he's in town.''

Whale coughed with embarrassment at the language, but Gideon only nodded. "So then . . . what?''

"We overpower the guards,'' Tag said eagerly, "and—''

"Put a cork on it, huh?'' Gideon snapped.

"On the contrary, my dear Gideon," Whale chided gently. "The lad is merely exercising his military and intuitive potential. He sees the difficulties and seeks a solution. As do we all—oh my, yes, we do, make no mistake about it, and I suggest that we take a little time to understand more fully that which we are about before we move on."

So saying, he rose and went inside, stuck his head back out, and beckoned to them. Tag followed immediately. Ivy took the time to straighten her garments as best she could, spending, Gideon thought, an inordinate amount of time in sunlit profile. Then she looked toward Rayn.

"It isn't going to be as easy as Whale thinks," she said.

"I didn't think so."

"Clever," she said, and took his arm, leading him inside to a room too large for the walls he'd noted on the road. But he asked no questions. He only sat in a comfortable albeit sparse reed chair and waited as Whale bustled around a fireplace, stirring a huge cauldron and tasting the contents and smacking his lips. When he was satisfied, he disappeared into a back room, returned with a pile of dishes balanced on his arms, and, with what Gideon decided had to be a third and fourth hand, ladled out the soup.

"Eat," he commanded jovially. "You'll need your strength."

Tag, his expression telling them all he had expected something more than soup, barely ate at all before muttering something about Red and leaving. Gideon motioned Ivy back into her seat when she made to follow, finished his meal, and wasn't surprised when Whale, at Ivy's query, allowed as how the main ingredient was footh.

"You people do eat a lot of footh," Gideon remarked.

"A staple," Ivy told him. "They breed twelve times a year. If we didn't eat them, they'd kill us all."

"Lovely."

"Skinned, maybe."

He set the bowl aside and leaned back, his palms pressed lightly to his cheeks. "Whale, what are we going to do?"

He shouldn't have asked; he knew, somewhere deep in his heart and throughout the now frozen marrow of his brittle bones, that he simply should not have asked and should not even be listening as Whale explained that they must gain entry to the Wamchu Hold, face Lu himself, and attempt to discover through clever means or foul the whereabouts of the duck. When Gideon reminded him that, from all accounts, Wamchu was unsavory as well as unpleasant, Whale chuckled and assured him that all would be well once they were face to face with their adversary.

"You have a plan?"

"You," Whale said, "have the bat."

Gideon blinked. "So?"

"You will dispatch him."

"Lu?"

"You."

"No. I mean, Lu?"

"Of course."

"With the bat?"

"Naturally."

"I don't know."

"Third base," Ivy muttered.

Whale flicked his eyes toward her, retrieved them, and went on to say that their only problem would be the guards. Some of them were bribable, some were corruptible, and some were so loyal they would lay down their very lives for the highest bidder.

"We, however, being without sufficient funds, must resort to other things."

"Like the bat."

"Oh, no. That's for Lu."

"Then how about those little balls?"

"I never go to parties."

He pleaded with Ivy silently, and she reminded the armorer of the bombs he had had Gideon use against the Pholler. Whale closed his eyes to think before finally shaking his head. And again, until he rose, clasped his hands behind him, and strode into the back room.

"Another concoction?" Gideon asked softly.

"Sometimes," she said. "Other times he just falls asleep."

"Wonderful."

She gave him a rueful smile, then slipped off her chair and sat on the hearth. He followed a few minutes later, placing his hand beside hers, pretending to stretch a kink out of his fingers so that they brushed over hers. She sighed, apparently needing a lungful of air to clear her head of the unexpectedly heavy soup and the warm, comfortable glow from the dancing blue flames. He cleared his throat and raised his arms over his head, rolling his head about his neck, rolling his shoulders, arching his spine, lowering his arms again to sweep briefly over her shoulders. She took another deep breath and popped two of her buttons. He scrambled for them before they rolled into the embers. She scrambled after them, and they froze.

Their hands met.

Their gazes locked.

Their tongues flicked briefly over their respective lips.

"Gideon . . ." Her voice was hoarse.

"Ivy . . ." His voice was choked.

"My sleeve is on fire."

"Hey in there!" a voice shouted from the doorway as they leapt to their feet and proceeded to pound at her arm and the fire on her wrist.

Gideon whirled just as a scruffy little man with one eye patched darted in, stared, and finally blurted, "You the people with the kid and the big thing with all the hair?"

"The lorra?" Gideon asked.

"Yeah, that's the one."

"What about them?"

The one-eyed man pointed into the night. "They're gone."

"What?"

Ivy ripped off her blouse, dropped it on the floor, and began to stamp on it; the fire had moved to the bodice.

"I just saw them. The kid. The big thing."

"Where?"

"Out back there. The kid was on the lorra's back."

"So?"

Ivy cursed the blouse, the fire, and the fact that her bouncing braid was raising welts on her breasts.

"So these guys came up and took them."

Gideon took a single step across the room, grabbed the little man by his scruffy little jacket, and lifted him up to eye level. "What guys?" he snarled.

"Wamchu's guys. You know Wamchu?"

Gideon nodded.

"Bopped the big thing on the head, bopped the kid, and carried them off."

Gideon met the man's uneven gaze evenly, trying to ferret a trick, a conspiracy, a plan to separate them and thus render them helpless.

"When?"

"Half an hour ago?"

"And you just now came to tell us?"

"Hey," the man said, "it's dark out there, y'know? All these shacks look alike in the dark."

Gideon nodded, and as he turned to Ivy he threw the man out the door. "We're in trouble."

"No shit. I only have one blouse."

Whale came out of the back room, rubbing his eyes and yawning, saw Ivy partially undressed, saw Gideon wiping his hands on his jeans, and said nothing until Gideon passed on the message he'd just received.

"Oh dear," Whale said. "I suppose that means only one thing."

"No it doesn't," Gideon said glumly, "but I guess we don't have any choice."

"None at all, I'm afraid. We'll have to see Wamchu now. Tonight. Or we'll never see our friends again."

TWENTY-FOUR

"Bopped on the head," Gideon muttered as he strode down the road with Whale and Ivy following. "How the hell do you bop a giant goat on the head?"

There were no answers, either from his companions or from the few people they passed. The shacks were all dark, clouds had rolled in to bury the stars, and more than once he stumbled over a rut or into a hole; but Rayn itself was their beacon, aglow with hundreds of small lanterns hanging from lintels, from torches burning brightly atop intricately and hypnotically carved posts at each intersection they crossed. The glow cast shadows on the walls and the now cobbled road, which danced and writhed around them, blotted out the starless sky, and prevented them from seeing into the open windows and doorways of the buildings they hurried past.

But from the sounds they heard within, most of Rayn was having a fairly good time.

"I don't get it," Gideon said in amazement. "Why do they come here? Don't they realize what's going on? Don't they understand whose place this is?"

"Why, they most certainly do," Whale said, as if to think otherwise would be shocking and insulting to the parties concerned. "But you must remember two things. First, Wamchu has only recently decided to return and has therefore not quite put his full evil stamp on life as these dear folks know it. Second, the former mayor, if you will, is not capable of resisting him. And third—and I know what I said, so do not correct me—in spite of his odious and malicious presence, there are still businesses to be run, vices to be pursued, lives to be led, fortunes to be won and lost, tragedies to be enacted, birth, death, life, and things like that." He tugged lightly at his wattles. "It isn't a pleasant place these days, I'll grant you that, my heavens no, but it has its own certain charm if you're inclined to see beauty wherever you look."

Gideon looked up at him.

"Or not," the armorer retreated.

Despite Gideon's concern about a trap being laid for their pursuit of their friends, there had been no trouble getting through the city gates because there were none, merely a gap in a ten-foot wall guardless and unblocked. Once inside, Whale had suggested they take one of the back streets to avoid premature confrontation, but Gideon was too angry to listen to reason. He kept his hand near his enholstered weapon, and his fierce, uncompromising scowl readily cleared the way until, breathless but no less ill-tempered, he stopped at the Wamchu Hold.

Wonderful, he thought; now what do I do?

It was, as he had observed from the knoll that morning, a rugged three-story building, square and flat-roofed like all the others, but as far as he could tell completely without windows. The huge double doors at the top of the three steps were made of a deep red wood, and in the various panels were bas-relief carvings of all manner of exotic creatures in varying postures of menace and intimidation. In one at eye level a pacch was busily thumping a party of innocent travelers into the ground. Gideon examined it for a moment, then sniffed and took out his bat.

There were no guards.

There was no doorbell, doorknob, bellpull, knocker, or peephole.

A glance around at the broad-cobbled square that surrounded the building proved it inarguably deserted of pedestrians, merry-makers, drunkards, and thieves; the people of Rayn, apparently, avoided the Hold once the sun had gone down. He didn't blame them; this was no place to be at night without saying good-bye to your mother.

And there was silence almost total, as if a soundproof invisible wall had been suddenly erected between the Hold and the city. It was more than a little unnerving, and he smacked his lips loudly, clucked, stamped his foot, just to be sure he hadn't been magically rendered deaf.

Whale came up behind him then, examined the forbidding entrance with hands clasped behind his back, and muttered what was either a complaint about the weather or an incantation; either way, there were no results.

Ivy pushed them both aside and pulled out her dagger, attempting to slip it in between the doors in an effort to spring the bolt. Nothing happened except a bending of the blade, which she straightened with an evil look and a stomp of her boot.

Gideon brushed aside a suggestion that they walk around the rest of the Hold, that perhaps there was another way in. He stood sideways to the door, rested the bat on his shoulder, and waited for the pitch. Then he swung at the barrier and yelped at the stinging that was born in his hands and grew up to fire that coursed along his arm.

Ivy, on the other hand, cried out at the cracks that webbed across the panels, at the screech of tearing wood, and jumped back when the doors crumbled into fragments at their feet.

"There's that way, too," Whale said with a sigh, and stepped over the threshold into a large chamber from whose exposed beams two stories above hung hundreds of heraldic banners, from whose damp stone walls angled monstrous blazing torches, and on whose paving-stone mosaic floor were thousands of tiny rugs, each with a single red eye embroidered in its center.

There were no doors to either side, but directly ahead was a staircase that led to a short gallery.

There were no guards.

Gideon took a determined step toward the stairs, swinging the bat angrily, but Whale took his arm in a restraining grip.

"Now what?"

"There are no guards," the armorer said.

"I know."

"If you were the Wamchu, heaven forbid, would you let just anyone be able to walk across this magnificent hall and up those stairs and into your room without some sort of protection? My heavens, don't you see that there are probably any number of hidden traps around here, most of which, if I am any judge of hidden traps though without firsthand experience of them, are very likely on the fatal side?"

Ivy moved closer to Gideon and looked down. He looked down. Whale looked down. They were standing on an eye. There was a gap a single paving stone in width before the next tiny rug. When Gideon surveyed the floor more carefully, he realized that the carpets were arrayed in checkerboard pattern.

"One just doesn't rush into these things precipitously," Whale continued as one hand fumbled into his belt pouch and pulled out one of the tiny round bombs. "We shall have to discover in some clever way how to reach those stairs without coming to any harm, which will surely be the case if—if you'll pardon me for being so long-winded about it—we are not more cautious. Can you imagine the destructive power of one of those torches should it be loosed from its bracket? Or the speed at which a spear or arrow can reach when launched from a gap in those walls? Or the suffocating trauma of one of those banners if a single misstep should bring the lot down on our heads?"

"The door," Gideon said.

Ivy looked; it was still shattered across the threshold, and she could see straight up the street toward the gates. "What about it?"

"Could anybody else have gotten through that door but us if this Wamchu didn't want it?"

"Not unless it was opened," Whale conceded after a second's deliberation.

"Then what the hell are we worried about?"

"Dying," Ivy said.

"That's a good one," Whale agreed.

Gideon looked at them disgustedly, took a firmer grip on the bat, and took a step off his rug onto the bare floor. His legs tightened, his stomach lurched, his eyes watered only slightly, but nothing untoward happened. A second step, a third following a fraction more rapidly, and he was soon walking straight across the hall. At the staircase he looked over his shoulder and saw Ivy and Whale following, hesitantly, fearfully, but eventually reaching him and grabbing onto the newel posts.

Granting Gideon his moment with a nod, Whale scanned the gallery's length and frowned. He pointed, and Gideon looked up to see nothing but a blank wall. There were no doors, no tapestries behind which doors might be hidden, and there were no guards in front of what might have been doors that rotated on a hidden axis. Nor could he discern the presence of ropes for ladders, ladders folded into niches, or gaps through which an ant might crawl.

It didn't make sense, but neither did the feeling that he was being watched.

It occurred to him that the stairs themselves might be the traps, and with a deep breath for courage he took tight hold of the lefthand bannister and began to climb up, testing each riser with a kick, each flat with gentle pressure before moving on to the next. It was slow going, but he was no longer rushed. He didn't think that Wamchu would harm Red or Tag, that the taking of them—how the hell do you bop a giant goat over the head?—was merely to draw him and the others into the Hold before the night was done. It remained then to figure out just why this night was so important, why this all couldn't have waited until tomorrow.

Whatever the answer, he knew damned well he wasn't going to like it.

Just as he knew when he reached the gallery and waited for the others to join them that there was something odd about this whole thing. Nobody builds a front hall without any exits save for the way one gets in.

On the other hand, nobody has a place like this in his pantry, either, so why bother to look for reason when he had obviously fallen through the looking-glass?

He sighed loudly to signify his martyrdom for those who cared, then walked to the gallery's far end and began pressing against and tapping the wall, hoping that somewhere along the line he would uncover a clue to the next portion of the puzzle. Whale, seeing what he was doing, began at the opposite end. Ivy stood at the head of the stairs and glared down at the hall, dagger at the ready, every so often plucking distastefully at the baggy black shirt Whale had given her to replace her burnt blouse.

In the center the two men met, without success, and joined Ivy in her scowling.

"I don't get it," Gideon said. "There has to be a way."

"No, there doesn't," she answered tartly. "You just think there does because you're imposing your own cultural attitudes on a culture that has no connection with yours."

"No, I'm not."

"You are too."

"I am not. And there is so a connection."

"Name three."

He almost did, then shook his head angrily.

"Well, I think we ought to go back outside and do what Whale said in the first place."

Whale maintained a diplomatic silence, though his grin gave his deepest feelings away.

"All right, so I was wrong," Gideon admitted. "But you have to understand I'm new at this sort of stuff."

"This sort of stuff," Ivy said heatedly, "is going to save our world as we know it! If you don't want to help, just find yourself a damned Bridge and go back where you came from!"

"All right," he said. "Okay, don't get so huffy."

"I am not huffy," she said, and took a stamping step down.

Gideon moved to stop her, to apologize, and Whale hurried after them.

Not long after that, the steps gave way, dropping out from under them and plunging them into a darkness unrelieved by anything save their startled shouts and screams, suddenly developing a slanted floor that took their breath away on impact and sent them sliding and spinning downward in what Gideon perceived was a spiral chute of some sort, a tube made of highly polished and very slick wood that was, as he raced through total blackness, beginning to burn a hole in the seat of his jeans.

Christ, he thought, what a pain in the ass.

Below he could hear Ivy's high-pitched curses end abruptly, followed by a shout from Whale, and followed by himself when his soles struck a barrier, the barrier gave way, and he plummeted out of the chute onto a high pile of silk-covered multihued pillows.

He rolled down the uneven slope and landed on a floor littered with silk-covered, multihued pillows only marginally less thick than those he had landed upon, and came up against Ivy, who was sitting cross-legged and shaking her head.

"Are you all right?" he asked, taking her shoulders and looking deep into her eyes.

"Dizzy."

He was, too, and they held each other for a long time before the dizziness passed.

Then: "Where's Whale?"

Gideon looked around the room and saw no sign of their friend.

The room, however, soon distracted him.

It was a full twenty feet on a side, its walls of whatever composition hidden behind tapestries depicting beautiful garden scenes fraught and filled with unicorns, maidens, flowers, birds, kings and queens, and their richly attired retinues.

"Jesus," Gideon said with a slow shake of his head. "My god, I've never seen anything like it outside the third grade."

The tapestries were dreadful. There were gaps, mismatched colors, and disproportion; the sides were uneven even when they were bound, the fringes were ragged when there was any fringe at all, and even from where he was sitting he could tell that whoever had done them had used whatever threads had come along, thick and thin and without regard to origin of same.

He rose shakily and pulled Ivy to her feet. A check of the pillow tower behind them failed to locate Whale. A check of the ceiling hidden behind tapestries tacked to it failed to uncover anything but the chandelier that gave the room its soft golden glow.

"Electricity?" he said, his astonishment rendering his voice high.

"What?"

"You have electricity here?"

"You mean the stuff in the wires?"

He nodded, unable to speak.

"Sure. If you want to put up with it, all those holes in the walls, all those wires, all that little bitty crap running around in them and making you sterile."

Seven or eight immediate questions came to mind, but they were all shoved to the background when the tower of pillows began to crumble around them. Grabbing Ivy's hand, he backed away and watched, bat at the ready, as the landslide of silk and satin hissed and rustled and tumbled around their feet.

"Do something," Ivy whispered urgently.

"What? Have a pillow fight?"

They backed away again, wary and thin-lipped, until the tower was completely destroyed and there, in its midst, sat Whale.

Gideon's first reaction was to take a step toward him; his

second was to try to pry Ivy's fingers off his hand when they began to crush the bones; and his third was to look at her and then behind, where she was looking herself.

At a tapestry that had been drawn up into the wall, and at the doorway behind.

"Good evening," said Lu Wamchu. "Welcome to my house."

TWENTY-FIVE

The three walked in glum single file behind the imposing Wamchu, along a narrow, ill-lit corridor toward a bright, blinding white light.

Whale came first, nervously tugging at his hair and wattles, murmuring incomprehensibly to himself and holding tightly to the pouch into which he had replaced his tiny bombs. He stumbled several times along the way, perhaps as a result of his near suffocation in the mound of pillows, but refused any assistance from Ivy, who followed, fingering her dagger and braiding and rebraiding her hair to such distraction that Gideon, bringing up the rear, felt a great and uncharitable temptation to tear it out at the roots.

He also wondered why he didn't just grab one of the bombs and blow Wamchu up, or at least clobber the man with the bat and be done with it; and the answer, he knew, was painfully and ridiculously obvious—he had no idea what lay ahead or how to escape from the Hold. Nor did he know where Red and Tag were, and until that information was forthcoming, he was forced to play the tyrant's game.

He closed on Ivy after a few paces and put a comforting hand on her shoulder, raising himself slightly so that he could see the man at the lead.

Wamchu, his back rigid and head held high, was nearly seven feet tall, with a sickening abundance of hair almost as blond as Ivy's that fell in well-brushed ripples down his back. He had no mustache but sported a deep red beard neatly trimmed in a crescent moon beneath his chin. His taut skin was dark, much like a Navajo's, and his features the same except for the brilliant dark red, gold-flecked eyes that were somewhat Orientally slanted. A curious amalgam disconcerting at first sight and somewhat fearsome afterward, the intimidating effect heightened by the clothes that he wore—deep ebony silk of so many folds and ties and subtle tucks that it was impossible to tell whether he was wearing an elaborate shirt and trousers or a single flowing garment that hissed like enraged snakes as he walked, exposing with each stride night-green boots on whose toes had been tooled reflections of his eyes.

There was no question that his was the indistinct face Gideon had seen several times since his arrival, that his evil presence was the one felt when the sun went down and nightmares crawled out of his subconscious, that his was the upper hand until fortune returned from her inexplicable vacation.

Whale once or twice haltingly attempted to engage the man in conversation, but Wamchu merely flicked a disdainful hand over his shoulder and the armorer fell silent.

Ivy made once or twice to toss her honed dagger into the broad back, but Gideon hastily restrained her, whispering urgently that they dare not do a thing until the fate of the others had been discovered, not to mention learning the whereabouts of Glorian and her stupid duck.

Reluctantly she agreed and gripped his hand tightly until, at last, they passed from the winding corridor into the light.

It was a chamber twice as large in all dimensions as the pillow room, evidently carved out of solid rock some distance beneath the surface. A dazzling orange light was provided by torches throughout and a massive, twenty-tiered crystal-and-diamond chandelier that hung from a twisted black chain from the unseen vaulted ceiling. There were smooth-stone pews set up as though the place had once been a church that seated several hundred worshipers;

yet where the altar should have been was a raised dais upon which sat a throne of solid ivory, simple and unadorned and most impressive in its plainness. Behind it were draperies of the same execrable design as the pillow room tapestries.

The pews were empty.

Ranged along the bare walls were black-clad Moglar guards carrying weapons of several descriptions, all of which made Gideon grip his own bat more tightly.

Wamchu gestured that his so-called guests should take the front row, then climbed to his throne and, with a theatrical swirl of silk and satin that reflected none of the room's light, took his seat, crossed his legs, leaned forward, and smiled.

Whale looked away.

Ivy grew pale.

Gideon wondered if those teeth were really as sharp as they looked.

"You have come for your friends," Wamchu said, his baritone echoing solemnly throughout the massive chamber.

Gideon, seeing the others unresponsive and possibly paralyzed with fear, nodded.

"In good time," the giant said amiably. "In good time. But first I would like to know more about you." He leaned back and cupped his hands behind his head. "It is a tradition we in the Lower Ground have and would like to establish here in the Middle Ground. Don't be shy. Why don't you go first," and he pointed at Gideon.

It wasn't so much the man's arrogance, or his obvious power, or the cruel cast of his unusual face that made Gideon stick out his tongue in defiance; it was his uncanny occasional resemblance to the owner of the now disbanded football team, who had ruined his career, lost him his self-esteem and pride, and, as a consequence not to be ignored, cost him his house, his hometown, and the bottle of scotch in the sideboard.

Wamchu frowned with one eye.

Gideon turned sideways and glared.

"You have spunk," Wamchu said. "Lower Ground wisdom has it that spunk is stupid."

Gideon ignored him and peered around the room, seeing several exits flanked by the giant dwarves, seeing no others save for the one leading to the corridor they had just traveled.

"You ignore me at your peril," Wamchu said, his voice rising.

Gideon ignored him, standing now with hands on his hips and looking to see if there was some way he could loose the chandelier and cause havoc in the chamber, thus effecting their escape with a minimum of danger.

"I am not pleased," Wamchu bellowed. "Turn around! Look at me!"

Gideon did, and had no idea at all why he suddenly smiled, unless it was the fact that Wamchu truly had no idea who he was and therefore had no way of measuring how effective he would be as an opponent. The thought gave him a bit more confidence, and he touched the handle of his bat with one caressing finger.

"Where is Glorian?" he demanded in a soft voice.

Wamchu's mouth opened as if he were going to shout, then slowed into a thin pale line as his left hand thoughtfully stroked his cheek. "Glorian."

"Yes."

"I see."

"Do you?"

"Clearly."

Gideon nodded sagely as if he understood, then glanced at Whale in the forlorn hope that the armorer had somehow developed the power of telepathy in order to tell him what the hell he was talking about.

"I cannot help you there, my friend," Wamchu said smugly. "She is beyond your reach now."

Ivy leapt to her feet, and a half hundred Moglars growled a warning. "She better not be dead!"

"Not at all, not at all," the tyrant said with a wave of his hand. "I am not so crude as that. No, she is alive, though I cannot speak for the condition of her health." He laughed, low and slow. "My right hand, so to speak, Houte Illklor, has an affinity for women such as she."

"You wouldn't dare!" Ivy shouted.

"No, but Houte would."

"And the duck?" Gideon ventured calmly before Ivy did something stupid.

Wamchu slammed back in his seat. "What? How did you know about that?" he hissed.

"I have my ways," he answered enigmatically.

Wamchu gathered some folds about him huffily and narrowed his eyes, gnawed pensively on his lower lip, and recrossed his legs. "Interesting."

"I wouldn't know; I haven't met it."

"No. I mean, it is interesting that you should ask me now about the duck." A cruel smile parted his lips. "And, I'm afraid, a little too late. You see, my mysterious friend, events have already been set in motion. The Blood—"

"You wouldn't!" Whale interrupted fearfully. "That's rather drastic, don't you think, Lu? Certainly as a teaser it's most effective and you've done it well, without bloodshed, I might add." He grinned then. "My heavens, I think I've made another joke." He looked at Ivy, who smiled wanly. "I must remember that one, I really must."

"It is too late, as I've said," Wamchu snarled. "The Blood is already beginning to turn. With time, it will rise, and then the Ceremony will begin and all . . ."

He laughed again, maniacally, the room reverberating with his madness while the guards chuckled and the drapes rippled and the very pews seemed to rock on their foundations.

"What the hell is the Blood?" Gideon asked in frustration.

"Hush!" Whale admonished.

Wamchu sobered and eyed him as a snake would a bird with a very large beak and nasty little claws. "The Blood, my inexplicable friend, is, as you well know, the third river of the Middle Ground. Called thus—the Blood, that is, not the Middle Ground—because of its color when certain portents come to pass. It will soon fill to overflowing, spreading its diseased and vile contagion into the Tearlach Sea, which will then become a cauldron of flooding that shall destroy all it touches! It is inevitable! It has begun!''

Gideon did his best to understand, but it did not make sense to destroy a land one was attempting to conquer. Unless, he thought suddenly, by destroying the Middle Ground Wamchu thus had a golden opportunity to then move his operations successfully to the land above Chey.

His eyes widened.

Wamchu chuckled.

His eyes became slits at the diabolical implications.

Wamchu nodded.

"That's crazy," he said.

"You have your methods, I have mine," Wamchu said primly.

"You won't win, you know," Whale said quietly. "This man is a hero. You anger him at your own risk."

Wamchu leaned forward. "Whale, you will not stop me."

"It's been done."

"I didn't have the Blood or the duck before."

"And I didn't have Gideon Sunday."

Wamchu frowned. "Sunday? What kind of name is that?"

"Pious," Ivy grumbled, anxious to stop the talking and get on with the adventure.

Wamchu rose, and Gideon stepped back as the tyrant pointed an unwavering finger at him.

"I asked you once and I ask you again for the last time—where do you come from, my unrevealed friend? I know you were with Glorian. I saw you on the Ekkler Meadow. But where did she find you, eh? Where did she find you?"

For some reason, Gideon understood that his origin was vital to the madman's plans. And that same instinct told him that Wamchu wasn't going to like the answer a bit.

For the second time, then, he smiled. "I," he said softly, "have come across a Bridge."

Wamchu gasped in horror, dropped to his seat, and gripped the armrests so tightly the ivory began to crack. "What? A Bridge? That is impossible!" His face shaded slightly darker. "I control all Bridges, all Tunnels, all roads to every place in this land! What you say is a lie!"

Gideon shrugged.

Wamchu bared his teeth. "Just tell me who you are, where you came from, how that little bitch in the white dress came upon you and brought you here."

"A Bridge," Gideon said, beginning to think that perhaps he ought to change his tactics to something a bit closer to cooperation and submission.

But Wamchu gave him no time. He clapped his hands once, and from behind the draperies suddenly appeared three of the most striking women Gideon had ever seen. His immediate attraction, however, was rather dampened when Whale muttered, "Oh dear," and Ivy said, "Oh shit."

No introductions or fanfares were needed—these were the infamous wives of Lu Wamchu, and despite their snugly clinging black silk dresses with just a hint of flare at the bare ankles and a daring slit at each hip to expose a wink and a nod of soft pliable flesh, they were quite clearly as dangerous as the man himself.

"Chou-Li," Wamchu said to the tallest, "tell me if this man is telling the truth."

Chou-Li, her straight black hair parted in the center and framing an alabaster face of most exquisite Chinese beauty, stared at Gideon with deep blue eyes, and he felt a chill around his heart, a fence of ice rise around his lungs. It was impossible to breathe. His vision blurred. He tried to step away, but the pew behind pushed into his legs, and he had to force himself to remain upright, to keep from falling abjectly to his knees.

"He is," she said, her voice high and sweet and laced with deadly sugar.

Wamchu waved her away angrily, refusing to believe her. "Thong," he ordered.

Thong was of middle height and an exact twin of Chou-Li, her hands kept coyly folded at her waist, the glint and glitter of a dozen rings of a dozen different stones and settings causing Gideon's eyes to water, his bones to turn to rubber, his tongue to swell and blacken in his mouth. He could not swallow. He could not hear. He tried to step away but could only stumble at the force that emanated from those blue-ice eyes.

"He is," she said, her voice high and sweet and laced with deadly sugar.

"I swear," Wamchu said with a dismissing wave, "you women are helpless. I don't know why I didn't leave you home." He took a deep breath and turned to the remaining woman with a silent command.

She was short, lithe, busty, well-hipped, well-ankled, with wiry brown hair, a pug nose, freckles, soft chin, outstanding ears, and an emerald-frame monocle in her right eye.

So, Gideon thought as his vision cleared and his lungs returned to normal and his bones permitted him to stand upright again, this is Agnes.

TWENTY-SIX

I am not fool enough to think I am not in serious trouble here, Gideon thought as Agnes Wamchu stepped around the throne and bowed slightly to her husband. Wamchu bowed back, albeit a little tentatively, and gestured her to get on with it.

"Lu, I beg you not to do this," Whale implored. "This most assuredly goes beyond the bounds of decent behavior, don't you think?"

Wamchu silenced him with a glower.

Ivy, her lips taut and her eyes narrowed, turned her dagger over and over again in her hand, clearly wanting to bury its blade in the tyrant's chest and just as clearly unsure whether she ought to take the chance. If she missed, the consequences didn't bear thinking about, but she did all the same and changed her mind reluctantly.

Agnes put her hands on her hips and stared dispassionately down at Gideon.

He braced himself for another onslaught of psychic torture, which, he had barely time to realize, had not injured him physically at all, though several parts of his body weren't entirely positive they were still functioning, much less present to be accounted for.

"You have one more chance to answer me correctly," Wamchu said pleasantly.

"I've already told you the truth," Gideon repeated sternly.

"It's not my fault you don't believe me or your precious little wives."

"Agnes," Wamchu said, "fry the little prick."

She took off the monocle.

Wamchu hissed and averted his face.

Whale shouted, "No!"

Ivy began to cry.

Gideon lunged to one side, throwing himself to the floor and, at the same time, snatching Whale's purse from his belt. A penetrating heat began to form in the middle of his spine as he fumbled for the ball-bombs; an acid flame began to trace through his veins, swelling his shins and forearms; a vision of doom and destruction filled his brain as he suddenly rolled over and lobbed one of the spheres at the throne.

He missed.

Wamchu cried out a warning.

The explosion was muffled and partially absorbed by the drapes into which the missile had been thrown, but it was enough to break the woman's spell. Gideon leapt to his feet, weapon in hand, and whirled about to meet the challenge of the Wamchu.

And he gasped.

As smoke and dust showered over the dais, he could see that the throne, slightly askew but still intact, was empty. Wamchu and his wives were gone.

The Moglar, however, after initially deciding to panic at the explosive violence, changed their minds and charged down the aisles, screaming their war cries, grunting, brandishing their weapons, and barely managing not to trip over themselves in skidding halt when Gideon whirled again and faced them, the bat describing a smooth circle over his head.

He grinned.

Ivy whipped out her dagger.

Whale whipped out another bomb.

Together, shoulder to shoulder, they advanced down the center aisle toward the Moglar guard. Bluffing, Gideon knew now, was out of the question. This was not merely traipsing through forests, dropping into oceans, or riding on Red's back like some sort of idiot conqueror; this was the real thing, and if those guards didn't move soon, he was going to find out just how well he knew himself.

They didn't.

He did.

The first one broke ranks and ran screaming toward Ivy, a particularly fierce-looking triple-bladed battle axe spinning deftly in his hands; Ivy slit his throat. The second through eighth ones broke cleverly into the spaces between the pews on the left, intent on a flanking maneuver that would soon have the trio surrounded; Whale tossed them a bomb. The ninth through fifteenth charged in a body, and Gideon shoved his friends to either side, took a swing that took off a head and part of a shoulder, then jumped out of the aisle and began hopping from pew to pew toward the back, the bat whirring through the smoke and dust, his legs braced for each blow, his eyes racing to either side in order to keep track of the others.

Screams of carnage and defeat filled the chamber.

The aisles turned red and green.

The torches danced crazily, and shadows darting across the walls made them all slightly dizzy.

Several of the implacable guards ran for the exits in order to alert the rest of the battalion in case Wamchu had other things on his mind.

Several more decided to avoid the fool with the alien weapon and concentrate on the old man.

Whale tossed another bomb for good measure.

Ivy found a Moglar's weak spot and kicked him there, sending him writhing to the floor.

Gideon bounded from the top of the last pew and put his back to the first exit he reached, waiting until Whale had joined him, then calling to Ivy, who speared one last guard before racing through the doorway.

"Where are we going?" she called over her shoulder.

"Follow me!" Gideon called back as Whale ran agilely

around him when a second contingent of giant dwarves burst after them from the throne room.

They ran toward a wooden door, opened it, slammed it shut behind them, and ran again, angling left, always left, through dank and choking air, over bones scattered on the floor, around rusted iron cages in which skeletons reposed with jaws slack and eye sockets empty, through clouds of tiny insects that parted like the Red Sea when Ivy swatted at them with her fists, through a series of unlocked doors, until, at last, they found themselves at a dead end.

"Damn," Ivy said. "A dead end."

The room was small, its wall bare and made of wood. No light save from the corridor penetrated it, and despite a frantic pressing and shoving and kicking and yelling, no doors appeared or traps in the floor.

"Now what?" Whale asked, leaning against the door, trying to catch his breath.

"We go back," Gideon said, "and try another one."

"You're not serious!" Ivy said.

"What else can we— Wait! Listen!"

They listened.

And they heard, muffled behind one of the walls, the faint but unmistakable sound of Red's bleating.

"Red!" Gideon shouted. "Red!"

The bleating returned to a purring.

"Stand back," Gideon warned the others, picked up his bat, and leveled the wall.

"You're getting pretty good at this," Ivy said cheerfully as they rushed through the hole.

He managed a smile as portions of the ceiling began to crumble behind them, not sure he wanted to "get good" at this at all. So far, all it had gotten him was several severe headaches, a few new dyings, and an intense yearning for the humiliations and boredom of the unemployment line back home.

As it was, however, he stumbled into what was obviously a makeshift jail cell, in the far corner of which cowered Tag. When the lad saw the trio burst through, he gaped, grinned, and unabashedly threw his arms around Ivy, who hugged him back, kissed his skull several times, then backed away when Gideon put his bat against the lefthand wall.

Another cell, and Red was cramped inside, his eyes black and his head shaking with helplessness against the confines of the shackles that held his four legs and neck to a dripping stone wall. When he saw Gideon he purred so loudly the others had to hold their ears until the shackles were dispensed with. Then Gideon wrapped his arms around the animal's neck and did his best not to weep.

"A man and his lorra," Ivy said. "A hell of a sight."

"How," Whale asked Tag, "did this happen?"

"I don't know," the boy said as he attempted to yank open the thick doors of both cells. "One minute the lorra and I were in the field watching the city, and the next I was in here."

"You felt no blow?"

"I felt awfully tired, I think."

"Ah-hah!"

"Chou-Li," Gideon guessed as he extricated himself from Red's fur.

"No, I think it was Thong," Whale said.

"What about Agnes?" Ivy suggested.

"Never," said Whale vehemently. "She seldom deals in measures less than full—as Gideon here, in his own private way, which cannot readily be shared by anyone, will attest to."

"It doesn't matter," Gideon said, lifting the bat again. "We have to get out before that whole damned army comes down here. I don't suppose," he said to Tag, "you heard anything about Glorian or the duck."

"Nothing," Tag said glumly. "I wasn't even tortured, so I couldn't tell them anything. I just woke up in this dumb cell and they didn't even ask me what my name was."

"Did you see Wamchu?"

Tag shook his head.

"Any of the wives?"

Tag shook his head again.

Gideon knew then what he'd known before, and had tried not to think about because it made him feel wanted as he'd never been wanted before—the only reason the lorra and the boy had been taken was to bring him here, to the Wamchu. Yet the tyrant had been curiously lax in preventing an escape, almost as if he'd wanted it. But for what purpose? Gideon sure as hell didn't know where the duck was, and if Wamchu didn't know, then there was someone else playing this game. Someone neither of them knew about. Someone Wamchu thought Gideon was working for. Someone involved in a devilishly complicated plot of intrigue and counterintrigue; someone who knew of stakes far greater than Gideon could possibly imagine; someone who was determined to see both adversaries dead, or at least put permanently out of commission for the duration of whatever crisis he was preparing for this world.

It was dizzying.

Or, he thought suddenly, Wamchu had just been incredibly and stupidly careless.

It happens.

"Now what?" Ivy asked reasonably.

He didn't answer. He had no answer. He had only the remains of a wooden door to step over, into a dimly lit corridor filled with dust, cobwebs, torches sputtering on the dank walls, Moglars at the far end, and spiders and rats scurrying for cover as he and Red led the way in the opposite direction.

It was difficult to run because of the moss and the trickles of slippery water on the uneven floor; the best they could do was move in a rapid trot while the Moglar shouted death threats and destruction behind them, eerie sounds rebounding off the stone and filling their minds with images of mutilation and cannibalism, premature burials and unannounced death.

Red, stockpiled with energy from his unnatural confinement, edged past Gideon and took the first door they came to with a slam of his thick skull and spiraled horns; it shattered at the second blow, and they found themselves heading upward, the corridor widening and the light brightening, the spiders and rats and cobwebs gone. The Moglar cries faded behind them. Ahead they could hear faint music, atonal and punctuated with the sharp rap of a gong. Ivy stumbled and Gideon took her arm. Tag puffed and Whale pushed him gently ahead. Something dark and nasty flew at their heads from a crack in the ceiling, but they ignored it as a danger they could live with, as opposed to what the danger behind them could do.

The corridor twisted to the right, back to the left, up a steep slope, then around to the right again. Red was beginning to growl with impatience, and Gideon could do nothing about it. He wasn't conversant with underground tunnels and had no idea if there was a trick one had to use to keep one's direction, or if one simply ran on, and on, hoping to come to the end before one dropped from exhaustion.

And just before he dropped from exhaustion he saw a doorway. A large doorway. At least twelve feet high and guarded by two of the ugliest dogs he had ever seen—they were large and white, and their black teeth were covered with dripping saliva as they snarled at the enemy heading in their direction; they had no tails, and their claws gouged into the stone flooring as they prepared themselves for the charge.

Red shrieked.

The dogs shrieked.

Red lowered his head, and the dogs vanished down a side corridor, yelping, whimpering, snapping at one another in canine recrimination for desertion of their post.

Gideon stroked Red's neck thankfully and took hold of the large iron loop affixed to the righthand door. He pulled, and the door opened so easily he nearly lost his balance, the sight beyond so startling he almost pinched himself to be sure he wasn't dreaming.

TWENTY-SEVEN

The bare-floored chamber they found themselves in was as tall as the building itself, as wide, and took up fully half the total living space that protruded aboveground. Other than that, it was completely, totally, absolutely, and inarguably empty of furniture, decoration, and creatures even marginally living. At the back was a normal door, closed and perhaps locked; at the wall through which they had just passed there was a second pair of banded double doors; near the vaulted ceiling there were several round windows through which sunlight shafted and laid a faint gold hue over the room.

There was no sound but their own labored breathing.

Slowly, then, not daring to speak lest some device disclose their whereabouts, testing the parquet floor every step of the way to be sure they would not fall into yet another trap, they made the slow journey to the rear entrance. They next arrayed themselves in a defensive semi-circle around Gideon, who took hold of the latch and, with breath held and eyes partially closed, lifted and pulled.

The door was unlocked. And once opened, it revealed the city of Rayn before them, no guards in sight, the cobblestone square as devoid of life as if it were midnight.

Though Gideon was unaccustomed to such circumstances, he had the definite feeling this was entirely too easy. It was not unlike dropping back to pass, seeing his offensive line stoutly preventing the defensive from touching him, seeing his receivers in balletlike precision breaking into the open for a clear touchdown—all he had to do was choose the man to reap the glory and lob the ball to him. Too easy. Much too easy. Somewhere in that crowd of grunting, swearing men there was someone destined to take off his head.

"You're thinking the same thing I am," Whale said quietly as he examined the empty streets.

"It can't be anything but a trap."

"Then let's go," Tag declared. "You go out and spring the trap, and we'll save you, destroy the guards, and go get Glorian before it's too late."

"Assuming," Whale said before Gideon could use the bat, "we do all that, where do you propose we go?"

"I told you—to get Glorian."

"Where?"

Tag opened his mouth to answer, shut it again, and looked helplessly around him. Complications such as that had a tendency to dampen his enthusiasm, but not, happily, for long. "We'll ask Wamchu."

"He already knows," Ivy said, leaning against the wall as she dusted her blade against her side.

"No, he doesn't," Gideon said.

"Sure he does. The only reason he brought us all here was to see if we knew. And we didn't. So now he can let us go and get on with it because he knows we'll never find her in time to stop the Blood. He doesn't care. He has all the cards, and he's dealing from the bottom of the deck. He's your typical multibreed, polygamous sonofabitch, and the worst part about it is, he's right." She gave Gideon a curious look, then, one he could have sworn held a fleeting bit of affection before it was stifled. "I think we should go back and gather an army, that's what I think."

"And leave Glorian?" he said, astounded.

"Sure, why not? She can take care of herself."

"That's . . . that's crazy!"

"Suit yourself," she said, pouting. "You just like her because she's skinny."

He looked to Tag, to Red, then back to Ivy in utter disbelief. Was it possible she had somehow overcome her revulsion of him and had fallen for him? Was it possible she was jealous of Glorian and didn't want her saved after all, no matter the consequences as long as she achieved her primary goal, which was to ensnare him in an emotional tangle so devious he would never be able to escape? Could it be that she had noticed something in him that no other woman had, and that certain something had addled her reason to such an extent that she was willing to desert the band because of a few slippery hormones?

"Ivy—"

"But it makes sense, right?" she said. "If we stay here, all we'll be doing is running around falling into traps. Up home, we'll be able to set up a deliberate and effective defense."

On the other hand, he thought, maybe she just wants to retreat to more defensible ground.

Shit.

"No," Whale said softly, a curious expression on his face. "No, Ivy, you're wrong. Returning to the Upper Ground is not the answer, and a moment's thought will prove it to you."

She thought a moment.

Whale continued, "We do, in fact, know where Glorian is. And Wamchu knows that I know, and he knows that I know how to get there. He also knows that I know that I don't know whether or not I have the courage to go." He sighed heavily and shook his head. "This is all my fault, you know."

"How can that be?" Gideon asked.

"Well, if I had conquered the world when I had the chance, none of this would have happened."

Gideon stared at the wattled, lean man and decided he didn't want to know what Whale knew about world conquering and population subjugation, nor did he want to know what Whale knew about Glorian. That clearly portended another round of fighting, several instances of unpleasant danger, and not a little discomfort in the process. Despite his apparent prowess with the bat now back in its holster, he was more convinced than ever that he was not cut out for this sort of thing. There was no longer any difficulty in believing it—his bruises, cuts, and scratches were proof enough of the reality of his situation, all things considered—but there was also a lessening sense of obligation to the woman who had wanted him to find her duck. She had failed to inform him of the forces that would be arrayed against him, had failed to explain the complexities of the mission, and had failed to provide sufficient motivation for his continuing.

I think, he thought, I want to go home.

Whale put a hand to his arm, and he smiled wanly and allowed himself to be drawn apart from the others. Struck as he was by the change in the man's demeanor, nevertheless he was rather unsettled when he saw the gloom in Whale's watery eyes and the nervous tic that pulled at his right ear.

"We are in trouble," Whale told him confidentially.

"It's a way of life, I'm beginning to think."

Whale frowned, then brightened suddenly. "Ah! A bit of humor in dire tragedy, yes? Oh, Gideon, my friend, you don't know how much I appreciate the gesture. It tasks one, you realize, to have such responsibility as you do, and to still have a way with words, a kind of . . . well, I'm sure you understand what I'm driving at. Especially now that we're on our way to something more dreadful than this place."

"Then you do know where Glorian is."

"Didn't I say that already?"

"You did, but I was hoping you were speaking metaphorically."

Whale's smile faded only a shade. "Refreshing. You are most refreshing, Gideon Sunday. But yes, I am speaking from certain knowledge, not fanciful."

Gideon nodded fatalistically and listened as the armorer explained that there could only be one place Glorian and the duck could be that would build such confidence in Wamchu that he did not kill them outright. The mention of Houte Illklor had given that much information away—it was the villain's vile summer place, long fallen into disrepair when he was, many years ago, exiled after an abortive attempt to drain the Tearlach Sea and turn Chey into a desert testing ground for his wives. Since there was, as far as Whale knew, no other place as large or inhospitable for Wamchu's activities, it must be there that he had sequestered the means for his new thrust for conquest. It was there that he intended to hold the Ceremony.

"And what is this Ceremony you keep talking about?"

Whale swallowed hard and gnawed at his lower lip. "It has to do with . . . the duck."

"I gathered that."

"The down, you see. It's the down Wamchu needs."

"Down from a duck?"

"Is that a joke?"

"Whale, please, not now."

Whale nodded, doubly miserable now. "When the Blood reaches the tops of its banks," he explained in a hushed voice, "the down from a very special fowl, scattered over the river's surface, will bring it all the way up. All the way, Gideon; once started, it cannot be stopped."

"And if the down isn't used?"

"The Blood will recede and not rise again for a hundred years."

Gideon nodded, shook his head, nodded again. "A special duck, you say."

"Exactly."

"The one Glorian has."

"Precisely."

"And what's the name of this place where we can find it?"

"Umbrel, a miserable hovel and one I wouldn't wish on my worst enemy," Whale told him.

"Umbrella? What kind of a place is that?"

Whale seemed puzzled. "But I never heard of it."

"You just told me the name."

"But I said, 'Umbrel, a miserable place and I wouldn't wish it on my worst enemy.' That's what I said."

"And I said, 'Umbrella?' "

"I still never heard of it. A certain similarity, perhaps, but not where we're going at all. Heavens, no. Your place is bound to be nicer than mine."

Gideon put a hand on the man's shoulder and looked deep into his eyes for signs of senility and deafness, then ran the double conversation back through twice, with varying punctuation and inflection, until, at last, he allowed himself a smile for his own inability to grasp the local nuance and provide the proper comma. "Ah," he said.

"You've heard of it?"

"No. Do I want to?"

Whale shook his head, then glanced fearfully around the room. "I fear for our lives, Gideon. I truly do. If we do not succeed, then this entire world as we know it and as you are learning to know it will vanish."

"I see."

"The rise of the Blood will, directly and in after-effect, destroy everything I and our friends hold dear."

"All right."

"And once that is gone, we will be left at the mercy of Wamchu and his wives."

Well, Gideon thought, so much for going home.

"Are you two finished with your secrets?" Ivy asked after a nervous glance outside.

Whale nodded. Gideon nodded. Red stopped trying to nibble on the walls. Tag squared his shoulders and took a step over the threshold, leapt back, and fell pale-faced against the wall.

"Too late," he gasped. "They're waiting for us out there."

"It could be worse," Gideon said, hefting the bat once again.

It was. The second door opened, and the Moglar poured out.

"You know what it's like being caught on the wrong end of a blitz?" Gideon said to Whale as they raced through the door.

"No. I've never been to London."

He's on your side, Gideon reminded himself, and hurriedly scanned the options as they raced across the square surrounding the Hold. There were only a handful of guards waiting for them here, while ten times that amount were filling the vaulted room with feral cries of discovery and triumph. It seemed best to avoid them all and run around the corner, duck up a deserted street, and head as fast as they could for the walls.

Which they did, using their superior strides to keep them well ahead of the giant dwarves and their brandished weapons to prevent the occasional pedestrian from attempting to think of stopping them for questioning.

And for the most part it worked.

They successfully made it to the city walls with only one minor incident involving an old woman and her aged wolfhound, broke through the gateless gaps, at which there were no more than five guards, who scattered when Red unleashed his clawed hooves and deftly trimmed one of their beards, and headed rapidly southward across broad, rolling farmland toward a forest that broke the plane of the horizon. As they ran—and Gideon rode on Red, who wouldn't let anyone else on his back—the armorer pantingly explained that Umbrel was at the far edge of Chey, just before the descent into Choy, in a land protected from invasion by any number of incredible beasts and subhumans in the sole employ of the Wamchu. It would be their task to break through that defense, get into Umbrel, search for Glorian and the duck, and bring them both out alive. Only this, with a little more thrown in in order to stop the Blood's rise, would save the world as they knew it.

Gideon suggested they not go quite so fast. To preserve

their strength, he added quickly when they all turned to look at him scornfully.

Tag, over the course of the next hour, suggested and developed suicidally effective plans for a frontal assault, one the enemy surely would not be expecting. Such a battle would undoubtedly produce casualties, but the survivors would then be able to assault Umbrel. The remaining survivors would then be able to make their way to his sister and the fowl, and the survivors of that would be able to complete the mission in time and halt the Blood's devastation. When Gideon asked how many that would leave at the end, Tag admitted they could use a few more people, though he refused to estimate the numbers; Gideon thought the kid couldn't count that high.

Ivy and Whale were silent, the former in the lead and watching the trees for signs of treachery as they grew nearer, the latter running almost backward to keep his eye on Rayn and the certainty that Wamchu would surely not permit them to reach the dubious safety of the woodland without at least one final attempt to stop them. Wamchu was not, despite his recent ignominious failure, an entirely stupid man; once he understood that the hero from across the Bridge was indeed going to Umbrel, he would move heaven and earth to prevent it.

Whale was right.

They had just reached the trees when the earthquake struck.

TWENTY-EIGHT

It was no ordinary earthquake.

There was no abrupt silence, nor did the birds suddenly take flight from their forest roosts and wing to safety in the skies; no canines or their relatives barked preternatural warnings, nor was there a growing cold feeling that stability had hopelessly lost its definition; the ground itself neither rippled nor heaved, and there was a conspicuous absence of locomotive grumblings beneath the surface; the leaves did not tremble, the boles did not sway, and the grass was perfectly still in the afternoon sun.

But as Gideon and his friends plunged into the woodland twilight, Whale threw up his hands and yelled for them all to drop to the ground and cover their heads. He would have suggested a few urgent prayers as well, but there was no time. As Gideon did as he was ordered, he glanced over his shoulder and saw a massive bolt of pulsing white light streak toward them from Rayn. He had no time to yell his terror and only barely heard Whale shouting Thong Wamchu's name before the lightning-not-lightning slammed into the earth.

There was a silence that took on tangible weight.

A tiny cloud of dust wafted on the breeze from the spot where the bolt disappeared beneath the grass.

Somewhere, behind one of the distant farm buildings, a dog began to bark hysterically.

The birds took flight and winged with eerie quiet into

the sky, the only sound the frantic beating of their wings.

Then the ground began to writhe in a series of rhythmic undulations that seemed to turn the very earth to a horrid green liquid. Leaves snapped and trembled; boles swayed and snapped like the crack of a palm slapped against another. There was a sensation of intense dry cold, and stability as it relates to the crust of earth lost all definition when the grass began to part and the surface broke open.

Ivy flung herself at Gideon, landing at his side and hugging the breath from his lungs. Red's eyes darkened, and his great head swung back and forth in his limited caprine attempts to understand why his long silky fur was standing on end. Whale covered his head with a moan. Tag began to whimper.

And still the ground split, into zigzagging chasms arrowing their way through knolls, rises, humps, and burrows, dropping entire trees into their black mouths, spouting clouds of smokelike dust into the air, filling the land about with the deafening roar of a locomotive bent on slamming itself into the side of a granite mountain, the thunderous rush of water newly released from a dam, the voice of the gods pounding their fists on celestial tables.

The ground humped, and Gideon was thrown into the air, landed four feet from Ivy, who gaped in dismay at her empty arms.

The ground rolled, and Tag was slapped against a tree, crying out once before he dropped unconscious.

The ground twisted in anguish, and Red raced into the open, not about to be thumped by a falling trunk, adroitly spanning the cracks and canyons, stubbornly digging in his hooves to prevent being toppled.

There had been only seven or eight moments of more exquisite terror since he had arrived, and Gideon thought of them all with something akin to nostalgia as he watched in victimlike fascination a gap in the ground making its way toward him. He was caught in a thorned bush, and try as he might to thrash his way free, he only managed to entangle himself further. A call for help was useless, he knew; the others were too busy attempting to save their own lives.

The gap widened.

An uncovered grey boulder toppled slowly into it.

A branch fell from the tree nearest him and smashed part of the bush.

The gap tore at the ground and advanced more rapidly.

Another branch landed close to his legs and pinned one ankle beneath it with a thicket of smaller limbs and twigs.

He caught a glimpse of Red hopscotching across the field.

He saw Ivy crawling toward him, her face lined with scratches, her hair disheveled and clotted with beads of black earth.

The gap was less than a man's length away, and the ground heaved again, wrenching the bush from its roots and tossing both it and Gideon into the air. He flailed, reached to grasp the air and land on the gap's lip, felt himself slipping, and did not look down into the bottomless dark.

A hand closed on his wrist; it was Ivy, and she was weeping as she tried to pull him free. The toes of his boots kicked into the instant cliffside, slipping, then giving him tenuous purchase when he threw up his free hand and grabbed her arm. Together, then, they pulled and climbed, exhorted and cursed, until, at last, he rolled free onto his back and stared into her eyes.

The ground fell still.

The birds wheeled in a great flock, calling for a weather report so they could return to what was left of their homes.

The dog shut up.

Red rolled on the grass to flatten out his hair.

"Thanks," Gideon said, aware that his voice sounded anything but manly.

Ivy said nothing. She only pushed at her hair, nodded once, and sat cross-legged beside him.

"The others?"

She shrugged; she was getting a little fed up having to keep saving the damned hero.

Then Tag came into his line of sight, smiling bravely as he pulled a quivering Whale behind him. It didn't take long, however, for the smiles and expressions of gratitude to fade, replaced with the grim knowledge that proximity was not healthy when it came to Wamchu's wives. Nor were they surprised when a monstrous dark bird rose from the center of the city and coasted on the currents over the field. Its single cry of anger was all they needed to know to understand that Thong had seen her failure.

"We'd best go," Whale said without enthusiasm or spirit.

"So it is written," Gideon muttered, and accepted Tag's hand to pull him to his feet.

The way was less difficult once they'd left the area of the earthquake's devastation, but it was not easy. Red took the lead, using his claws and horns to tear them a trail when the paths they found vanished. Whale and Tag came next, keeping their eyes on the foliage for instances of ambush, while Gideon and Ivy brought up the rear, checking behind, to either side, and watching as the light shaded to dusk. They stopped to rest frequently, but only for a few minutes at a time; they ate what they could find, none of them daring to try the red berries Gideon and the lorra popped into their mouths; and they each brought out one of the floating blue globes to keep the shadows at bay when they reached a clearing surrounded by the dark green trees.

There was little talk. Whale had assured them that it wouldn't be long before they'd pass beyond the range of Thong's particular powers, yet even once that had been reached, none could quite keep from an occasional glance over a shoulder, a pause to listen for footsteps or something streaking at them from Rayn. When Tag asked if the wives just couldn't follow them on foot, Whale told him no. Wamchu seldom let them out of his sight while he was away from the Lower Ground; the man would obviously be confident that he could entrap them, or annihilate them, once they'd reached Umbrel.

A good thing to know, Gideon decided as he chopped at a low-hanging branch with his arm. It would, he thought, give him time to prepare his will and settle his mind to the fact that he wasn't ever going to leave this mad place.

They forded a stream.

They climbed a low hill on their bellies and waited nearly an hour before moving on.

They slept in a series of depressions—footprints, Whale explained, from some of the creatures living in the deepest part of the woods, near their destination. Gideon wanted to know if they were carnivores; he was told that meat was only supplementary to their diet.

During the second day they began to hear rumblings in the distance, as if something, or a number of somethings, was preparing to explode. Whale led them far to the east before returning to their initial direction. Gideon didn't ask why; he didn't want to know.

The second night was spent in the trees.

Midway through the third day, Gideon spat out some berry seeds and wondered aloud at Ivy's ability to hunt the dreaded poisonous footh with only her knife. She explained that she had good aim and knew when to duck. He told her not to use that word and ate another berry.

Toward the end of the fourth day, he decided Whale was lost, then stopped when they broke into a glen and he saw the other side.

Behind him, though not precisely pastoral, the trees were tall and lush and the air redolent with the scent of unseen blossoms and flowing sap; ahead, the trees were dark, nearly black, and they were stunted, twisted, a march of vegetation perpetually blasted by unholy lightning. There were no shrubs, no grass covered the ashen earth, and he knew he wasn't imagining it when he saw shadows moving contrary to the wind.

Whale suggested they stop and wait until they had a full day ahead before pressing on. Tag scowled his impatience, but a one-eyed glare from Ivy had him on the ground, stabbing his dagger repeatedly into the earth. Red grazed, though he never turned his back on the land they faced.

It was long after dark, then, and Gideon was sitting against a bole, his knees drawn up and his hands tucked under his arms. It wasn't cold, or even chilly, but he couldn't help thinking that winter had somehow overtaken them when he wasn't looking.

"Thinking about her, right?" Ivy asked, plopping down beside him and offering a footh steak.

He took it, blew on it, and began to nibble. "About who?"

"Glorian."

He shook his head.

"I would, if I were you. She's very pretty. She's a pain in the neck half the time, but I suppose she can get away with it because she's so pretty."

He looked without turning his head. If she was fishing, she was using a harpoon.

"I mean, this"—she swept a hand toward the glen's other side—"is silly. We can't go in there. We'll get killed."

"I wouldn't know."

"Oh yes you would, if you'd been in there before."

"Have you?"

"No. I've just heard stories, that's all."

"Want to tell me about them?"

She told him with a look he was out of his mind.

He watched Red nestle down on his other side and stretched out a hand to bury it in the lorra's hair. "Can I ask you about the duck?" he said then. "I don't want to offend you, mind, but I think it's about time someone let me know, don't you?"

Ivy lay on her stomach, her head by his crossed boots. "I already did."

"Right. It's a duck. A white duck. Nothing more, nothing less."

"See?"

"Ivy, it isn't enough."

She refused to answer for several minutes, but he had a rein on his impatience and he merely stared at the back of her head until, at last, she sighed and rolled over, her fingers drifting to the buttons of her blouse.

"And no," he said, "it wouldn't be better if you took off your clothes."

She sat up, indignant. "I wasn't going to suggest it!"

"You did once."

"You had your chance."

He pointed at her chest. "It looked to me like you were giving me another. If I was wrong, I'm sorry."

"Well, you weren't," she said. "But it's too late now."

"For god's sake, too late for what?"

"To hear about the duck!"

"You mean I can't hear about the duck unless you're naked?"

"Naked!" Her voice broke. "Naked?"

"It's what happens when you take off your clothes."

"Who said anything about taking off your clothes?"

"You did."

"I did not."

"The hell you didn't."

She raised a fist and he leaned away, causing Red to grumble in his sleep.

"I was going to take off my clothes, not yours," she said in a dangerously low voice.

"That's what I said."

"No you didn't. You said you were going to take off your clothes."

His voice lowered now. "Ivy . . ."

"And it's too late. Besides, who'd want to see you naked?" And she flopped down again, cradled her head on her arms, and closed her eyes decisively.

What do you mean, who'd want to see me naked? he thought as he thumped against Red's side and fluffed the hair into a pillow; lots of women want to see me naked. Jesus.

He tried to curl himself into a ball, stretched out, curled again, rolled over onto his right side, his left side, pushed at Red to move over, draped himself over the lorra's back, neck, and finally haunches.

Jesus.

Red lifted his head slowly, reached out a front claw, and shoved Gideon away.

"Well, damn," he grumbled, and stretched out on the ground, not realizing he was next to Ivy until she shifted to her side, propped her head up on a palm, and grinned at him.

"Men are all alike," she said.

"I am not."

"Sooner or later they come crawling."

"Ivy, I am here because Red wants at least one hour's sleep tonight."

"Sure, I understand." She unfastened the blouse's first button.

"Besides," he said, lowering his voice to a whisper, "there's the boy to consider."

"The boy," she said, undoing the second button, "is less a boy than you think, and knows his place when the adults get down to business."

"And Whale?"

"He ain't stupid." The third button popped open.

"Ivy, listen, you are undeniably an attractive woman, and it is certain that some of us may not survive this madness, and we may even be dead by morning for all I know, and life is too short to waste haggling with convention when that convention demands a certain amount of propriety even in the most desperate of situations, but I really don't think this is either the time or the place to demonstrate our mutual if somewhat jaded attraction for each other."

She stared at him.

He stared at the tantalizing expanse of her chest barely

visible, but visible enough, in the blue glow hovering slightly behind them, marveling at the faint wink of gold he saw snuggled against her skin.

"On the other hand, this may be the only opportunity we have to—"

"Are you married?" she asked suddenly.

"What? No."

"Do you have a lady friend?"

"No."

"I didn't think so," she said sourly, rebuttoned her blouse, and went back to sleep.

I've missed something here, he thought glumly.

But as he pulled out the alabaster penny whistle he found in his pocket and played it tunelessly to himself, he didn't miss the singing that suddenly erupted behind him.

TWENTY-NINE

Gideon was instantly on his feet, bat in hand and eyes scanning the surrounding trees through the glow of the bluelight he had neglected to extinguish. Ivy was slower to her weapon, Tag couldn't find his knife, and Red only swung his great head around, growled in a lorralike fashion, and fell back asleep.

"Who?" Ivy whispered huskily, wiping the sleep from her eyes with the back of a hand.

"I don't know. First time I ever heard of a raiding party accompanied by an overture."

"My goodness, for heaven's sake," Whale said as he came up beside them. "Put those nasty things down. Don't you recognize the intricate five-part harmonies? The tune? The fat man in front?"

Gideon stared into the forest and finally, slowly, and very cautiously, relaxed.

"Oh great," Ivy said in disgust.

It was Vorden Lain and his band of twelve, boisterously entering the glen with much laughter, more singing, and a goodly quantity of edibles, which they immediately set to roasting over an open fire. Though it was late, and though Gideon knew he should sleep in preparation for the morrow, he couldn't help but grin at the smell of nonberry food. Even Red stirred himself with a rippling shake and wandered over, sniffing each offering until he found something he liked.

And once they were seated around the fire, the forest a black screen around them, Gideon asked what fortuitous stroke of fortune had brought him here.

"You whistled," Vorden said in surprise. "It was you, was it not?"

"Well . . . I suppose," he answered, looking down at the whistle in his hand, then back up to the woodsman.

"Then here we are!" Lain said expansively. "Ready and willing to remain at your side, my dear fellow, until such time as we have roundly defeated the Wamchus. Not a pleasant task, I grant you, but one does have one's duty, doesn't one."

Croker Boole, who was busily pouring rations of the woodsman's potent water, inquired innocently where they were heading.

"Umbrel," Whale said before emptying his cup in a single swallow.

"On the other hand," Vorden said, "there is rather a lot of forest to be guarded hereabouts. And we being only a baker's dozen, it doesn't pay to stretch one's forces too thin, does it." Before anyone could answer, however, he clapped his hands once and swept off his emerald tricorn. "But let no man say that Vorden Lain is a coward, nor his men. If Umbrel is the goal, then Umbrel it shall be."

Whale expressed his gratitude with a broad smile and a broader belch. "Every man will be needed, Vorden, believe me. I'm pleased you've consented to go with us."

"He has, I haven't," Croker Boole said from the shadows beyond the fire. "No offense, but there's nothing that will make me go in there, day or night." The other lads murmured their assenting rebellion. "I'm really sorry, Vorden, but that's the way it is."

Lain's meaty hand closed briefly on the gold hilt of his foil, then dropped away slowly. "Have I ever asked you to do something you didn't want?"

"No," the younger man said.

"And I shall not ask you now. Eat, drink, and in the

morning, if you still feel the same, you and the others are free to go.''

"Do I get the sword?"

"Over my dead body."

"Just asking," Croker said with a smile.

"A good man," Vorden said in an aside to Gideon. "He has the makings of a fine leader someday. I suspect he'll have his own band before long."

"Do you—" Gideon cut himself off and looked up at the dark sky, puzzled because he thought he had heard a loud buzzing up there.

"It's not your imagination, my friend," Lain said, gesturing to his men to arm themselves.

Gideon stood while Whale and the others moved closer to the fire. None seemed to know what the sound was, but they all knew it meant them no good at all.

And they were right.

A sudden bellow from Red, and the air was instantly filled with large flying things, which reflected the firelight on their glasslike bodies, which filled Gideon's ears with an horrendous chainsaw whine, which ducked and darted around his blows while they snapped with astonishingly large teeth at everything that moved that wasn't them.

Lain laughed and sliced several in half, one of the pieces landing on Gideon's arm and, to his amazement, melting almost immediately. Ice! he thought then; these things are made of ice!

It was a keen observation his sister would have been proud of, and then she would have asked, *So what? You gonna use them as ice cubes?*

One of Lain's men screamed as an icewasp took a chunk of his shoulder, another groaned when his wrist was gouged; Whale danced about trying to make use of his bombs, and Ivy slashed at the air with her dagger, swearing so hotly none of the creatures even tried to chomp her face.

Gideon arched his back when something landed on his spine and drew blood, smiled quickly when Lain thrust home. The icewasp cloud thickened, Red bellowed in pain, and suddenly Gideon realized how stupid he had been. He tossed the bat aside, to Ivy's alarm, and yanked a flaming brand from the fire. The icewasps buzzed in panic as he swung the flames at them, their attack swiftly becoming a rout when the woodsmen saw the tactic, approved, and even improvised by setting afire a few of the local bushes. In five minutes it was over, five minutes Gideon thought had lasted at least five years.

He looked to Whale, who was shaken and pale. "Thong?"

"Chou-Li," the former fat man said. "A cold bitch if I ever knew one. One last chance to stop us, I would assume, before we reach our destination."

Croker Boole said nothing, but any chance there was of his changing his mind was lost now, and Gideon knew it. Just as he knew that the wings he heard overhead were one of Chou-Li's manifestations, checking on her success. A prolonged angry screech told him she knew she had failed.

"Well," Lain said heartily. "What a night, what a night!"

But as he and Gideon sat together while wounds were bound and comforts were given, the fire snapped sparks at the night sky and a keening wind passed harmlessly overhead, and a shade of melancholy slipped over the man's face.

"Are you all right?" Gideon asked.

"Just thinking of my son," the woodsman answered.

"I didn't know you had one."

"Sometimes, when I have a bit of trouble with Croker, I remember him." He poked at the fire with a stick. "Bela is a good boy, really, but somewhere along the line I failed him in his teachings. He left me some while back to make his way in the world, and I haven't seen him since."

"Do you know where he is?"

Vorden nodded sadly.

"Do I have to guess?"

"Can't you imagine?"

Gideon followed his gaze eastward, into the ashen forest. "Oh damn." He touched the man's leg then. "This wasn't just a fluke, then, was it."

Vorden shook his head.

"If you hadn't found us, would you have gone on?"

The woodsman gave him a smile, brief and wise, and Gideon grinned back before taking a sip of the man's unbelievable brew and lying down to stare at the dark. The position of loyalties was odd in this odd place, and he wondered as he drifted off to sleep, with Lain's men humming in the background, what his own companions would do when this was over. If it was over. If they survived whatever waited for them tomorrow. If they ever had a peaceful moment again when they weren't pursuing or being pursued.

He thought then of home. Of the house. The living room with the overaged television set, the bottles of liquor in the cabinet, the kitchen, where dishes were done when needed, not when used, the bedroom and its shadows past midnight, the newspapers and their sports sections, the telephone that seemed to ring only when a stranger tried to sell him a subscription to a magazine he didn't read or never heard of.

He thought of the world carrying on without him.

He thought of his sister.

"Shit," he said, and rolled onto his side.

By noon the following day, his thoughts were much less charitable.

The border between Chey and Choy was more dismal than he had imagined. Despite the sun above, the grey-ashen trees and the powdery ashen ground were no lighter, no more appetizing than they had been the night before. It was a dead land through which wound webs and tentacles of mist that distorted perspective and buried shallow depressions into which he stumbled with monotonous frequency. There were leaves on the contorted black-boled trees, but of the same color and texture that reminded him of peeling dead skin, and he had no desire to see the life-forms he heard prowling up there—harsh, guttural birdcries, low mutterings to which Red replied with growls of his own, and a constant scraping as though a band of creatures were following them only a few paces behind.

The air smelled faintly of sulphur.

And though protests were made, Tag was placed on Red's back. Gideon knew the lad was afraid, and that fear had produced a bravado destined to bring down the worst of the land on their heads. By having him ride the lorra, Gideon hoped he would at least tone his challenges down.

Vorden Lain stopped singing.

Whale and Ivy each held one of the tiny bombs, the supply of which had been reduced to less than a dozen after the escape from the throne room in Rayn.

Gideon held his bat and drew some comfort from its warmth, its heft, and the fact that when he accidentally bumped it against a bole, the tree shattered into glasslike shards that turned to dust the moment they reached the ground.

And just past midafternoon he realized with a start he had been listening for some time to a continuous hoarse rumbling behind them. He stopped, looked back, and nudged Vorden urgently with an elbow.

"Ah," the woodsman said, "you've noticed."

"What is it?"

"Very likely a zed; perhaps a pair of them."

Gideon peered into the mist, which, over the past mile or so, had been rising steadily to waist height and growing thicker. "I don't see anything."

"They're short."

Ahead of them, Whale and Ivy had slowed to flank Red, who was tossing his head from side to side and grunting. Tag, with one hand buried in the lorra's hair, was trying desperately not to look around. When Whale glanced back and caught Gideon's questioning look, he shrugged and displayed one of the bombs.

"What is this zed likely to do?" he asked when Lain

unsheathed his foil and whipped the air with it to limber up his arm.

"Attack."

"I gathered that. Could you be more specific?"

"From all that I have heard," the woodsman said, "it will first go for the most helpless of the group. Rather powerful, so I'm told. Hideous, most hideous. Its very look is rumored to turn a man to stone. Not, you understand, dear fellow, that I am opposed to ornamental statuary in my honor, but I much prefer choosing my own time and place, if you catch my meaning."

"Then we have to avoid looking at its eyes?"

"Rather difficult to do, as I gather it."

"Why?"

Vorden opened his mouth to explain and gave a warning shout instead, leaping backward toward Red, who had wheeled about with lowered head and a coarse grumbling in his throat. Ivy and Whale were at the ready, Tag had slipped to the ground and was beginning his war dance, and Gideon could only swing his bat to his shoulder before the mist began to roil and crest as something charged toward him just below its surface.

"Go for the eyes!" Vorden shouted as Gideon backed toward him.

"How? I can't see them!"

Another ripple in the mist as a second zed began its charge.

"No," Whale said, "you must take it in the throat!"

Ivy put her hands on her hips. "The snout," she said in disgust. "You have to do the snout first. Then the throat. Then the eyes. God, you don't know anything, do you?"

"M'lady," Vorden said in gentle contradiction, "with all due respect to your fair sex and wondrous beauty, it is the eyes to blind, then the throat to stifle, then the snout to kill. So it has been for generations, don't you see."

Gideon swung at the first shape, black and slender as it propelled itself through the mist. He struck something hard and heard a faint squeal of pain.

"The throat first," Whale said, edging his way forward. "If you take the throat first, it can't use its teeth. Then you blind it, then snout it. Goodness, it can't be more obvious than that."

"The snout," Ivy declared in a fierce whisper, "kills the lungs, you idiots. Then you strangle it. Then you blind it. The eyes, if you knew anything at all about zeds, are actually its heart. If you do the eyes first, it dies!"

"Well, isn't that the point?" Whale asked.

Gideon leapt to one side and swatted the second creature over what he thought was its head. It reeled and fell back, squeals of agony rising to a pitch that began to hurt his ears. The first one returned from his left, and he was nearly knocked off his feet when it collided with his legs. He swung wildly and groaned when his jeans were ripped and something stabbed into his calf.

"The point, my aged friend," said Vorden, "is not in the killing but in the process of the killing. One simply does not dispatch an enemy without first giving the enemy a sporting chance."

"Hey!" Gideon called as he brought the bat down on the skull of the second zed and saw its dim shape crumble to the ground.

"Sporting chance?" Ivy yelped. "With a zed? Are you crazy?"

Vorden bowed. "I grant you a certain element of danger—"

"Danger isn't the word for it," Whale grumbled. "You have to understand the anatomy of a zed before you can attempt to destroy it before it destroys you."

"Can't we just chop it up?" Tag asked as he whirled about to find the danger.

"The lad is hasty," Lain said.

"The lad wants to stay alive," Whale said primly.

"Jesus!" Gideon yelled when the remaining zed came at him from behind, butting him behind the knees and bringing him down. He flailed into the mist and brought his weapon around one-handed, catching the zed on the side of its skull. There was a sickening soft noise as the head imploded, and the animal dropped instantly on its back. And not wishing to examine the creature more closely, he staggered to his feet and limped toward the others, feeling a rush of blood spill warmly from his wound.

"You can't stay alive unless you do the snout first," Ivy declared vehemently. Then she uttered a short scream when she saw Gideon lurching toward them. Immediately, they surrounded him, realized he was injured, and put him gently on the ground. Whale, however, understood in an eyeblink that the maneuver wouldn't do since he was now rendered effectively invisible. Again hands took his arms, and this time they placed him on Red's back while Whale reached into his pouch for medicinal contrivances. Ivy hovered worriedly. Vorden hovered around Ivy. Tag wanted to know if he had hit the snout, the eyes, or the throat first.

"How the hell should I know?" he said, wincing when Whale poured a vial of stinging cool liquid over the slash. "I just bashed their heads in."

"Very dangerous," Vorden said, looking over Ivy's shoulder.

"Are you all right?" Ivy asked, holding his hand tightly enough to collapse two veins and a few dozen capillaries.

"I don't know," he answered honestly. The liquid and subsequent balm Whale used to staunch the bleeding did little for the firepain that filled his leg to the knee. But it wasn't the pain that bothered him so much as the fact that this time, with the zeds, he knew that he could have died.

THIRTY

"You're limping," Ivy said the following morning.

Gideon allowed as how that was probably true, since Whale's ministrations were not entirely effective. The bleeding had stopped, and the flesh had closed miraculously over the wound, but there was an ache deep within the muscle that made him long for the whirlpool baths in the locker room, the deep heat of a hot tub in his own house; as it was, he knew that many more attacks like the one last night, and he was going to be more than a little useless to the group.

Though the sun was up, the heavy mist still lay over the ground, and he could barely see Whale and Vorden forging the way ahead. The two men were talking quietly, Lain every so often looking up to the sky.

"I don't like this place," Ivy said, rubbing one arm briskly.

He agreed, but it wasn't because they were nearing their destination. Even in daylight, the closer they came to Umbrel, the more dismal the forest became. The grey became more lifeless, the black less reflective, the trees themselves larger and more hovering. And it affected them all to such a degree that he hadn't heard a single laugh since they'd broken camp and said their good-byes to Croker and the others. It was as if every mote of humor had been drained out of him, and not even Red's occasional affectionate butting could bring him a smile.

236

"You don't like us either, do you?" she asked quietly, looking up at him sideways.

"Don't be silly."

"I'm not. You think we're crazy and selfish. Or worse."

He brushed a hand down his rumpled shirt and sighed. "Well, I have to admit, I'm not exactly inclined to give you all medals for your forthrightness."

"Is it Whale?"

"Part of it. What I mean is, if he's a magician, why doesn't he just magic Wamchu out of the way so we can all go home?"

They were ten paces farther on before she answered, nodding toward the thin man whenever she mentioned his name, telling Gideon that a long time ago, before she was even born, Wamchu and Whale had some sort of confrontation in the Lower Ground. Whale was victorious, but he had somehow failed to recover completely—either mentally or with his spells. No one knew the true story; they only said that things weren't the same.

And why, he asked, was Glorian so important? As far as he could tell, she certainly wasn't royalty or anything similar.

"She comes from Whale," she said, lowering her voice still further. "You're not to know that."

"His . . . Jesus, his daughter?"

"Of course not," she said. "If she was, then Tag would be his son."

"Oh."

"Granddaughter."

"Oh . . . brother." He batted a hand idly at the mist, half listening for anything that sounded like the approach of a zed, half wondering what other marvelous revelations were in store for him now. "And the duck?"

She said that Glorian had found it some while ago, and it wasn't long after she'd taken it into her home that Wamchu first began making trouble.

"Where did it come from?"

"Only Glorian knows."

"And why does Wamchu want it?"

"Only Glorian knows."

"What about Whale?"

"If the Wamchu wants it, Whale knows it can't be good. It's all to do with the Blood."

He wondered why none of this had been told to him earlier, decided to forgo more questions when the mist thinned, the trees grew more closely together, and they found themselves on the bank of a wide, rushing river.

It was red.

And it was obviously much higher in its bed than usual.

"The Blood," he said, pushing between Whale and Vorden to look down at the water.

Whale nodded.

Gideon hunkered down and reached out toward it, pulled back his hand quickly, and wiped it dryly on one knee. He could not see to the bottom, nor did he want to. Despite the fact it was clearly water, its color in the deepest regions was too dark, too red, too much like its name. And though he could detect no unpleasant scent or see anything vaguely or otherwise threatening beneath the surface, there was an electric tingling at his fingertips that told him more forcibly than anything Ivy or Whale had said that the Blood River beyond its banks would be deeply and evilly dangerous.

Hell, he thought then, it's just nerves.

Until he realized with a silent gasp that the river made no noise.

There were traces of whitewater, there were boulders poking through in the shallows, but the Blood had no voice. It flowed like smoke without the crackle of fire.

He stood quickly and shuddered, looked around, and saw Red picking his way along the bank, the others falling into a line behind him. Looking, he imagined, for a way across, and trusting to the lorra's instincts to get them there safely.

Curiouser, he thought, and curiouser. What are they

going to do when they get the duck, throw it in the river and turn it to wine? That made as much sense as sprinkling down on it as Whale had told him.

Twenty minutes later they discovered the crossing.

A darkstone natural bridge stretched between the banks, the river itself slipping under it in a shallow waterfall and emerging back in its bed some fifty yards farther on. There was no mist from the fall. There was no sound. Nor was there consultation—the five and the lorra rushed across without a word, looking neither left nor right behind them. And once in the forest again, they virtually ran for the next half mile to put the sight and image of the Blood River behind them.

The ground mist was gone.

The land began to rise.

Gideon thought of home again and wondered just how desperate one had to be before a Bridge opened. He supposed there must be some sort of link between whatever worked the Bridges and the emotional state of the seeker, or perhaps with the seeker's mind. If you think hard enough about it . . . And he stared at a spot just off to his left, willing the glow to appear, and with it the way home and out of this mess.

"You see it too?" Whale whispered.

Gideon blinked. "See what?" He looked around then and saw the others bunching up as they walked, all of them including Red keeping a wary eye on something moving parallel to them back in the trees. He squinted through the odd shadows, not realizing he was still walking until he collided with Red's rump. The lorra eyed him with a grunt, and he patted the animal's flank absently.

"What is it?" he said, whispering as Whale had.

The armorer shrugged, looked back to Vorden, who was keeping close to Ivy. Tag was ahead, dagger at the ready, slicing the air and muttering to himself.

What it was, he soon discovered, was fast, whatever it was.

One moment it was alongside them, the next it was blocking the path at the top of a rise. The trees on either side darkened in its presence, and Tag scuttled backward, suggesting they surround it and cut off its legs.

"Which ones?" Gideon asked.

If it was a spider, it was abnormally large, abnormally round, abnormally covered with shifting, hissing fur; if it was a centipede, it was abnormally tall, abnormally multilegged, abnormally possessed of two sets of dripping mandibles that would have done credit to the Spanish Inquisition; and if it was insectoid at all, it seemed to have forgotten that most of its kind did not have a larynx.

It roared.

Its spherical head lifted above the trees and bellowed at the sky, trembling the branches, scattering the clouds, causing whirlwinds of dust to lift from the ground into instant choking fog.

And when it rose on several of its hind legs, Gideon caught a glimpse of blacklight flaring off claws thin enough to be razors.

"Nothing to be afraid of," Whale assured him, plucking one of the bombs from his pouch.

"What the hell is it?"

Red lowered his head and pawed at the ground, adding to the dustclouds that hovered around them.

"If memory serves, an ant."

Gideon snatched the bomb from the old man's hand and stepped to Red's side. "You've got to be kidding!"

"At a time like this?"

Gideon lobbed the ball without aiming to the top of the hill and turned away as it exploded. Vorden, who hadn't been warned, threw himself to the ground and rediscovered the foxhole; Ivy, however, only brushed off the twigs that showered around her and snatched at Tag, who had decided he wanted to join Croker's band instead.

When the dust cleared, the creature was gone.

"It's gone," Gideon said with a grin.

"Right," Ivy said, whirling around when the ant appeared behind them.

Tag ducked as a leg awkwardly tried to decapitate him, cutting wildly with his dagger and shouting his surprise when the leg came off neatly and thudded to the ground. The creature roared again, but this time at the loss of a second leg to Ivy's swift weapon. Vorden, who had seen the ant's vulnerability, took foil to hand and proceeded to slice away, ducking nimbly away from the claws as he reached Ivy's side and laughed. She glared at him and took another leg. Tag jabbed at the thing's exposed stomach, then raced around to its back to bedevil it there.

"What the hell kind of thing is that?" Gideon said.

"Stupid," Whale told him after Red lowered his horns and charged.

"You think we ought to help?"

Whale pointed at his chest. "Too old. I could be killed."

Gideon felt as if he should be doing something, but the ant was the one in trouble, not his friends. They were standing knee deep in furry limbs, still fighting, and the longer they attacked, the slower the ant moved.

"Why doesn't it disappear, the way it did before?"

Whale shrugged. "I told you it was stupid."

But not so stupid that it didn't, finally, whip one remaining claw around and slash it across Tag's chest. The lad screamed and fell back into a bush, and Ivy cried out, leaving Vorden to drag the boy off to one side. Immediately, Gideon put bat in hand and ran forward, just as the gallant woodsman saw his shoulder opened to the bone.

Stupid? Gideon thought, cocking the bat and letting fly against the ant's abdomen; stupid enough to have a few dozen pairs of false legs, that's how stupid it was.

The ant staggered under the blow, and a fair portion of its chest cavity caved in.

Gideon struck again at its supporting legs, and it began to topple, slowly enough for him to back out of the way, not slow enough to allow Vorden to crawl out of its path. It landed directly atop him.

And broke in half.

Gideon wiped a hand over his eyes, not only to clear them of a sudden rush of perspiration, but also to watch as both halves of the ant seemed to crumple to dust, leaving behind a creature no taller than his shin. It darted into the trees before he could smash it, its bellow no less loud but rather ludicrous now.

Whale, pouch in hand, ran to Tag while Gideon brushed off the remains of the ant's camouflage from Vorden and did his best to bind the wound, wincing at the blood and at the man's pale face.

"Hurt bad?"

Vorden managed a brave smile. "Like hell, what do you think?"

"Whale'll be here in a minute."

The ground darkened with blood, and Vorden's eyelids began to flutter. Gideon demanded help at the top of his voice, yet had to be shoved aside when the armorer arrived with his balms and medications. He had to watch despite the queasiness in his stomach. He had to know that the woodsman would be all right, and he had to know that even in this place it was possible for someone to die. It had nearly happened to him, but he'd never given much thought to it happening to any of his friends.

An hour passed.

Ivy sat on the ground with Tag's head in her lap, wiping his face and scolding him lightly for being so clumsy.

Whale had done what he could with Vorden, assured Gideon the man would be well enough to travel the next day, all things considered and if they weren't killed first, and then walked to the top of the hill. Slowly. Agedly. Scratching his head and talking angrily to himself. Gideon followed a few minutes later.

"I'm sorry I yelled at you," he said, putting a hand on the other's shoulder.

Whale lifted a hand and let it drop to his side. "I wish I knew how to make jokes."

"I don't know if it would help, now."

"I suppose you're right. It certainly won't help them,"
and he pointed behind Gideon, who turned and got his first
look at Umbrel.

THIRTY-
ONE

"If Glorian is down there," said Gideon, "she's crazy."

Umbrel squatted beneath the grey sky in a deep valley whose slopes were barren, whose fields were dust, and whose bleak, colorless features were relieved only by the garish east-west flow of the Blood, in such a contrast that the whole looked to him like some festering wound.

And a second look showed him it wasn't a city at all, but a single sprawling building broken by open corridors very much like streets that connected each of what he supposed were rooms in such a haphazard fashion that maps were surely needed to find one place or another. It was virtually formless. Its components were low and square and made entirely of stone, and the hallways meandered, some stopping at a blank wall, others winding mazelike until they were lost among the others. And unlike Rayn, there were no colors visible, no pennants or flags or hints of flowers. It was a dark unshaded grey, relentless in its sameness from the tiles in the halls to the low wall that did its best to surround the unguided sprawl. A single narrow road broke out of the forest below and to their left, entered the palace through open gates that even from this distance appeared more rusted than solid, and somehow made its way to the back, where it straightened again and stretched to the farthest slope. Monsters hunkered there with folded black wings, no two hideous faces alike, claws dug into the stone, flat black eyes watching the treeless plains around them.

"Damnedest place I ever saw," he said with a shake of his head. "It's hard to believe someone could actually live there."

"I wouldn't really call it living."

Gideon nodded and thought with a wry smile what a challenge something like Umbrel would have been for his sister. Monica Freeman the actress had always been a frustrated decorator, interior or otherwise, and though she had never touched his own home, she had done wonders with many others. So much so that she made it a policy never to return to the scene of her triumphs lest she find that the Philistines had invaded during the night.

Slowly, then, they walked back to the others. Tag was sitting up against a tree, wincing at the pull of his healing injury and trying to keep Ivy from fussing. Vorden, on the other hand, was already on his feet, complaining about the rip in his immaculate green jerkin; his arm was in a makeshift sling, his face was still pale, but he didn't seem as near to death as he had been an hour before. And one by one they made their way to the hilltop, when they saw the look on Gideon's face, returned, and sat glumly around a pitfire Whale had somehow managed to coax into life beneath the spreading branches of what could only be a willow that substituted sobbing for weeping.

A slight wind rattled the branches, and the ground dust stirred without rising.

An ant roared a mating call in the distance.

"I honest to god don't see how we can do it," Gideon said at last, resting his head wearily against Red's side and stroking the lorra's foreleg absently. "I really don't. This isn't Rayn by a long shot. There are bound to be a zillion guards like those . . . those things down there. And they definitely don't look as stupid as a Moglar."

"I agree," Ivy said with a brisk nod. "And if you want my advice, we'll start back for home. If we hurry, we'll be there in time for the party."

"What party?"

"The annual Handicraft and Nuptial Fair," she said eagerly. "An event no one misses, that's for sure."

"Except the bachelors," Whale told her with a grin.

She scowled. "I still think it's a good idea. We were stupid to come this far, if you ask me."

"And what about Glorian?" Gideon said quietly.

"Why do you always have to bring her up?" she demanded, slapping an angry hand on her thigh. "Hasn't she caused enough trouble already?"

"I sort of thought she was the point of all this," he said without looking at Whale.

"The point is," Ivy said, "that we not get killed, that's what the point is. We can't do her or us any good at all if we're not around to take care of things. God!"

Tag wrinkled his nose at her and swiftly, if painfully, drew a diagram in the dust with the point of his dagger. "That's silly and you know it. What we should do is put a man here, here, here, here, here, and here. At a signal— maybe Gideon can do it—we climb over the walls, rush to where Glorian is, kill those garks—"

"Garks?" Gideon said.

"Sure. The guards on the wall are called garks. Haven't you heard of them?"

"Not until now."

"They're easy," he said confidently. "You can take them without any trouble at all."

"They have wings, Tag."

"So you duck. No problem. Then I'll get Glorian, Gideon'll take the duck, and Whale can blow the place to smithereens. We can't take any prisoners, but that doesn't matter. They wouldn't want to come, anyway. Then Ivy will—"

"Not," she said. "Ivy will stay here and watch you all get slaughtered."

"Jeez," the lad pouted. "You never want to do anything."

"What about it?" Gideon asked Vorden. "What do you think?"

The woodsman shrugged his good shoulder. "I would like to see my son again, it's true and I shall not deny it, but I had hoped it would be in a place rather more hospitable than this. Something of the old gloom about it, wouldn't you say?"

Whale, when he was asked, offered no opinion save to say that he was in an awkward position, chasing after the man who had, after all, taught him everything he knew.

Hell of a teacher, Gideon thought sourly, and suggested they have another look at the place to seek out its weak points, find its Achilles' heel, hunt for the underbelly as a place to strike. Tag was all for it, though he reminded them that all the best generals didn't waste time worrying about their men; they just went ahead and did it and wrote their memoirs later.

Vorden, claiming weariness from the effects of the battle with the camouflaged ant, remained behind and, when Gideon knelt by the fire to drop more twigs into the pit, asked him what he thought.

"You really want to know?"

"It's the polite thing to do."

He grinned. "Well, to be honest, what I really want is to go home, fix my pantry wall, have a good stiff drink, and then go get a job as a sportscaster on some lousy little station that never heard of me or football. That shouldn't be too hard to find. They do it for baseball players all the time."

Vorden frowned his puzzlement. "What's baseball?"

"A game."

"Have you played it?"

"When I was a kid. Never professionally."

"And what was your profession?"

"Football."

"What's football?"

"Exactly," he said, and sat back with Red to listen to the others on their return begin their arguments again. By the time the sun had set, Whale was proposing an under-cover assault while Ivy was demanding first crack at pluck-ing the duck and Tag was using as many trees as he could reach to demonstrate the best way to demoralize a gark. Several times the boy and Ivy nearly came to blows, and Gideon sighed as he scratched the lorra between its ears.

"Y'know," he said, "I am not optimistic."

Red, who had eaten the last of the berries, belched.

On the other hand, he thought glumly, I don't know if I could just up and leave if a Bridge came along. Not now, anyway. After all, someone had to teach Tag a little restraint without diminishing his enthusiasm, and Whale, for all his flakiness, wasn't quite as dim as he made out to be, and Ivy . . . He sighed again and watched as she stalked back and forth along the path, gesticulating, debat-ing, once taking her braid and slamming Tag across the head. He was more than a little flattered that her jealousy— and he wasn't stupid enough to think that it wasn't— tended to save more than her own skin. But suppose there was no conflict, no danger, no threat to life and limb and the avid pursuit of healthy breathing? Would she care then? And did he care enough to find out if she really cared?

Jesus, he thought, these quest things are a bitch.

Finally, as the last of the medicines were applied to Lain and the boy in order to hasten their healing, Whale pre-vailed, though not without a certain amount of dissatis-faction.

"A slave?" Ivy said, choking as a result of trying to keep her voice down. "The hell I will."

"But my dear, it won't look right otherwise, don't you see? What good is a reputable slavemaster if he doesn't have at least one delectable female to offer to the bidders?"

"Over my dead body," she declared, and demanded with a look that Gideon defend her.

He, however, wasn't so sure about his own role. It reminded him too much of his quarterback days, when every season he was aware that his contract—and his body along with it—was up for grabs for anyone who needed someone to hold the end of the bench down. It was, to be sure, demeaning, ego-damaging, morale-squelching, and at the same time a part of the game. It never occurred to him until now that "slave" was also a good word for what he was. Paid well, but ultimately a trading-block slab of living meat that was—

He stopped before he slit his own throat.

"Well, I think it's a capital idea," Vorden said with a snap of his fingers. "I'm not so sure I'll be much good at the groveling and fawning parts, but I think I can give it a good try if that's what we need."

"No," Ivy said. "No. And no. And in case you weren't listening, no."

"You're just mad because you're not down there instead of Glorian," Tag said.

"What?"

"Sure. If you were down there and Glorian was up here, then Gideon would be after you, not her."

Gideon checked on the condition of his leg.

"Tag," she said, leaning toward him with her fingers clenched, "if Glorian was up here and I was down there, there would be no need for you or anyone else to go down there because you'd have what you wanted up here."

"Say, Tag," Gideon said.

"You keep out of this," Ivy told him.

"Well, you are," Tag insisted.

"I most certainly am not."

"Are too."

"Am not!"

"Jesus!" Gideon exploded. "What's the big goddamned deal, huh? For god's sake, it's only until we get inside. It isn't like it's going to be forever."

Ivy folded her arms across her chest. "Then why can't I be the slavemaster?"

"Because I am," Whale said simply. "It was my idea, and I'm too old to be a slave. You, Gideon, the others, are young and healthy enough to make it work. My goodness."

"It's demeaning," she said, though less firmly.

"It's only for a while, child."

"It's sexist."

Gideon blinked.

"It's my wish," the armorer said gently.

Ivy took a deep breath, held it, released it, and reluctantly nodded as she rose and walked up the path toward the hilltop. Gideon followed after a few moments and took her arm. She did not protest. And in the pallid moonlight they looked down on the darkened city.

"Why are you so nervous?" he asked.

"I'm not," she said, her lie too evident to be comfortable.

He let it pass; to go further would be to invite confidences he did not think he was ready to accept or willing to share.

"And what about that 'sexist' remark?"

"What about it?"

"I don't know. It just seems to me that this doesn't seem the right place for it. I don't mean the situation," he said to her puzzled look. "I mean, this world of yours. That's a my-world kind of word. Where did you hear it?"

"Around," she said with a shrug.

"Around where?"

"Around Glorian, if you must know," she answered testily. "She was always talking about the rights I'm supposed to have, and how men are always taking them away from me."

"Do they?"

"How should I know? I didn't know what the hell she was talking about."

They stayed for a few minutes more. Then Ivy suddenly leaned over and kissed his cheek, snarled at him to be sure he didn't take it the wrong way, and hurried back to the fire.

Gideon watched Umbrel.

And for the first time in days he saw the red eyes watching him.

THIRTY-TWO

Shortly after what passed for dawn in this seldom traveled part of the Middle Ground, Whale asked for permission to ride Red, which was given with a doubtful nod of the lorra's head. Makeshift chains had been improvised from vines Vorden had discovered under a suspiciously dead tree, and once all had been tenuously linked to a central strand Whale held in his left hand, they were off.

Halfway down the slope, Tag asked a question: "What about the wives?"

They stopped as one, quickly considered as many answers and implications as they could, and immediately returned to camp. Once there, the armorer attempted to convince them that despite all the powers exhibited in Rayn against their persons, prescience wasn't one of them. They were almost perfectly safe as long as they weren't in eyeshot of the three women. When Gideon reminded him sourly that Thong and Chou-Li seemed to have damn good eyes, he was told that the women, diabolically and perhaps even preternaturally clever as they were, could not see through walls. The light-bolt was meant to cause an earthquake. It did. They could have been anywhere in the vicinity and still have been affected.

"And the ice critters?"

Whale shrugged; he could not, after all, be expected to know everything.

Ivy shyly allowed as how she had been working for

several years on a double-sided needlepoint tapestry for the Handicraft and Nuptial Fair, and this year was to have been its debut. When she was asked what the point was, she told them it was at the end of her dagger, and if they didn't get moving in one direction or another, she would prove it.

Halfway down the slope, Tag asked a question: "How do we know which of those rooms to look in?"

They stopped as one, considered Umbrel laid out before them, and returned to camp, where a hasty map was drawn in the dust and suggestions were made as to which sectors should be their starting and ending points. No one paid attention to Ivy, whose comments were somewhat bloody in the extreme.

Finally, when it appeared as if they were stumped and would have to fly it blind, Whale admitted to having been at Umbrel once before, many years ago, and admitted further that he had a vague idea just where they might begin looking, assuming they managed to get that far. When Gideon asked him to clarify the term "vague," Whale made a vague gesture somewhere between *I think it's over there* and *close your eyes and pick a number*.

"Sounds chancy," Lain said.

"Do we have a choice?" Gideon told him.

"Do you want an answer?" Ivy said.

Halfway down the slope Tag snapped his fingers and started to ask a question, but Red, who was rather tired of all the climbing back and forth and getting hungry enough to eat a dissident, growled to shut him up.

The road, when they reached it, was deserted and, from the layer of omnipresent grey dust, had not been traveled for many days. Nevertheless, they managed a good impression of reluctant slaves as they approached the rusted, half-hinged gates and had no quarrels at all when Whale told them he would do all the talking.

The nearest garks, and there were too many of them for Gideon's peace of mind, swung their heads around slowly. One had a parrot's beak stocked with a dozen more fangs

than were necessary, another flicked a serpent's tongue at
them, and a third rose from its squatting position to stretch
its wings and show them a muscled chest and corded
thighs no barbarian should be without. All of them appeared to walk on hind legs, with a pair of forelegs as long
as a man's arm ending in three clawed digits. When the
standing gark's wings flapped lazily in the tepid air, they
sounded like attic doors closing raspingly on a heroine
who should have known better.

Gideon, hands tied ahead of him, kept an eye on the
guards as they neared the gates. Beyond, he could see the
central hallway and the rooms off it, and he wondered how
in hell Whale was going to get them to Glorian, not to
mention back out again. He also wondered how they were
going to get through the gate without tripping an alarm.
And wondered thirdly, when they were through the gate
and nothing happened, why the garks had only stared at
them and had not even mounted a token challenge. He
was, however, in no position to ask questions. Whale was
busily urging the lorra to a faster gait, and they were
genuinely stumbling now as they found themselves trotting
between roomwalls, peering fearfully into open doors that
revealed nothing but darkness. They could hear no sound
save their own passage, and once the hall began the twisting he had seen from above, he had no idea where in the
open palace he was.

Suddenly, Red stopped.

Gideon managed to halt before he collided with Vorden
but too quickly to prevent Ivy from charging into his back.
There were grumbles, a few curses, and a poke in the
middle of his back before he was able to walk to the
lorra's side and look at what lay ahead.

Nothing.

They were at a dead end.

Whale shrugged, turned them around, and they tried
another direction.

And found another dead end.

"There's a trick to it," Whale muttered as they wandered helplessly along.

"Should've used the doorbell," Gideon said.

"Oh, he knows we're here," Whale said brightly. "The garks told him as soon as we were spotted."

"He? Who he? Wamchu?"

"Oh, I doubt that. Wamchu has other things to do aside from the Ceremony. No, Houte Illklor—his majordomo, as it were. I suspect Wamchu will only show up if there's trouble."

"But there will be."

"Then I guess we'll see him later."

Later, as far as Gideon could tell, would be in about four years at the rate they were going. And just as he was ready to suggest a halt for a little rest, Whale grinned and pointed to a doorway whose lintel was topped with a row of tiny skulls.

"Footh," he said triumphantly. "Well, friends, I guess it's time to go in."

Since Red insisted on following them, the room was rather crowded by the time they were all inside. None of them noticed it, however, because they were busily gawking at the ceiling, which was covered with hundreds of tiny electric light bulbs merrily glowing a delicate shade of red. They had been activated when the first one crossed the threshold, and so fascinated were they that it wasn't until Tag exclaimed aloud that they noticed the door in the far wall. A large door surrounded by gold-leaf design and topped by a semicircle around whose perimeter ran a series of quaint Art Deco numerals.

Gideon ignored Whale's hissed warning that they might be under surveillance and approached the door cautiously. A poke, a rap of his knuckles, and a look to one side, and he wondered what had happened to his resolution not to be surprised by anything else in this place.

"It's an elevator," he announced.

"Of course it is," Whale said, dropping his end of the

vine and joining him. "You see, you push this button here and you wait a few moments, and pretty soon, if all goes well and of course I can't guarantee that, a little room shows up on the other side of this door. Then you get in—"

"I know how an elevator works," Gideon snapped. "But what the hell is it doing here?"

"To get down," he was told.

Gideon took gentle hold of the man's scrawny shoulders and smiled. "Correct me if I'm wrong, but what you're saying is that Umbrel is not what we have seen on the surface, but is rather something which lies even now below our feet."

Whale nodded.

"And we have to use this elevator to get down there."

Whale nodded again.

"And when the door opens once we're down there, there's a good chance there'll be some sort of reception committee waiting. A small army would be a good guess."

He stopped Whale from nodding a third time by walking back to the corridor and looking up at the sky. There was no help. It was bright and grey and perfectly miserable; divine intervention even of the symbolic sort was not forthcoming. Then he heard a shout and raced back into the room, pushed Tag and Vorden aside, and edged around Red to look at Ivy and Whale.

Who were looking at the open elevator door, and the wide stone stairs revealed behind.

"I don't know," Whale said when Gideon mouthed the question, and none of the others were willing to speculate. All they knew was, the elevator was gone, the stairs were broad and low, and they seemed to stretch farther down below the surface than any of them were willing to travel at the moment. On the walls were lights in the shape of flickering torches, exposing close-set stone streaked with discolorations that ran haphazardly toward the floor. There were no spiderwebs, no scurrying rats, no unspeakable creatures hovering in the shadows above their heads.

Only the stairs, and a distinctly damp feeling of unshakable dread.

On the other hand, Gideon decided, we're almost done with this thing one way or another. And once done, I can go home.

The thought cheered him so much that he began to whistle silently to himself as he stepped onto the top stair and looked behind him—Ivy was nervous, Tag was thumbing his nose like a punch-drunk boxer, Whale was fumbling in his pouch, and Red's eyes were slowly turning black; Vorden Lain was at the back, somewhat morose at his upcoming reunion. And they were all of them silent, watching him so intently that he began to wonder what part of him was showing that shouldn't have been, or if he had something small and ugly crawling through his hair. He smiled at them, cocked his head, and took the first step.

They followed, the distance between them determined by courage, seniority, and the length of the vine still tied to their waists. Thirty-nine steps and several tight turns later, the stairwell straightened and he could see the bottom landing. There was no door, only an arched entryway that led, as far as he could tell, into a corridor apparently rather wide.

Ivy came up beside him, and together they took the rest of the steps with exaggerated care, each pressed tightly against a wall, weapons out and ready to use in case they were surprised by anyone except Glorian. At the bottom they halted, exchanged glances neither could read, and poked their heads cautiously into the hallway.

It was, in fact, nearly twenty feet wide and extended in both directions for several dozen yards before veering out of sight. There were no doors that he could see readily, no light except for the occasional false torch, and no sound at all to indicate anyone was nearby.

The entire underground city could easily have been judged deserted were it not for a faint throbbing he could feel through his boots. Machinery or people, he could not tell. But it meant life in some form, if they only knew where and how to find it.

He gestured for the others to join them quickly, then used a series of referee hand signals to suggest they begin their search to the right.

Ivy signaled that they might do better heading to the left.

Gideon shook his head. He had a feeling, no more than that, which told him that going in her direction would mean disaster for the entire expedition.

Ivy disagreed silently.

Tag tried to intervene with a series of complicated hand waggles that directed them all to charging in both directions at once in order to take the enemy by surprise, but Vorden, whose eyes were glazing, grabbed the boy's arms and pinned them behind his back. Whale, meanwhile, was flipping a coin and whispering a compass spell whose words he almost remembered, and by the time Gideon stopped counting, he was up to twenty-six out of fifty.

Right, he commanded at last, fed up with the discussion that was starting to hurt his wrist.

Left, Ivy countermanded, one hand on her hip.

He sneered at her and stepped into the hall.

She followed and grabbed his shoulder.

He grabbed her wrist to pry the hand away.

She pinned his left hand in a sinister fashion and tried to drag him toward her.

He resisted.

Whale dropped his coin.

Red, with a disgusted shake of his head, bulled through them all and started down the hall to the right, his nostrils flaring at the clear scent of food, the vine dragging behind him and, eventually, dragging the others as well.

And around the first bend they came to the first room.

And in the first room Vorden Lain found his son.

THIRTY-THREE

"This is really very embarrassing," said Bela Lain as the others crowded into the room behind Gideon. "You weren't supposed to be here for ages."

Gideon ignored him for the moment when he suddenly realized where he was. "This is a kitchen!" he said. "It's a goddamned kitchen."

Red already knew that, and he was busily sniffing around the various tall cabinets, low cupboards, the two dozen large tables scattered about the even larger room, the storage bins that completely lined one wall, and the ovens that completely lined another. The air was heavy with the scent of cooking, aging, curing, and waiting meals. From the ceiling a full twelve feet above them dangled hundreds of utensils, pots, pans, skillets, jugs, and two slaves.

The kitchen was, unquestionably, as spacious as any baronial hall.

Bela, who had managed to put a table between himself and the intruders, fussed with a green-hide apron, then snatched off his cocked chef's hat and slammed it down. "Very embarrassing!"

"Embarrassing?" Vorden said in a cracked voice. "Embarrassing, you say?"

When he approached the table it was clear that despite their sartorial and philosophical differences, they were father and son, from the extension of their waists to the cut of their features. It was also clear that Vorden was mightily disappointed.

"Now, Father—"

"Don't you 'Father' me, you hash-slinging traitor! Going out to see the world, you said. Going to find my fortune, you said." He sagged a little, his palms pressed to the tabletop. "All those letters you wrote. All those letters. Moving up in the world, Father, you said. The Organization has a real place for me, you said." He gestured to the room. "This is a place? You're a lousy cook?"

"Well . . . not exactly lousy."

Vorden swung around to Gideon. "A son's gratitude, eh? Big man in the Organization, and he's a *cook*!"

Gideon made no attempt to understand the paternal attitude but understood perfectly that a place this size was not the basic kitchen nook of a summer home. It fed hundreds daily from the look of it, and they had evidently been lucky enough to stumble in between shifts. The more he scanned the room, however, the more he realized that Bela Lain was not preparing just any simple sit-down for a few lucky thousand; he was setting up for the Ceremony. From the looks of it, there wasn't much time left.

And when Red started for the far side and began dragging them with him, Tag quickly set about sawing them free of the vines while Vorden raged on the inequities of fatherhood, parenthood, and the obligations a son has about telling the truth to his only living relative.

"A cook?"

Bela drew himself up and put on his hat. "A chef, Father. Please don't call me a cook. And this," he said huffily, "is my establishment."

"Gideon," Whale said.

Ivy had been checking the two pair of doors at the room's back, flinging each one open and stabbing forward blindly in hopes that someone foolish was hiding there. By the last one she was wearying, but she had found nothing save another corridor, this one twice as wide as the first.

"Gidoen," she called.

Tag was rummaging around the tables, sampling bits of bread, meats, fruits, cookies, salads, and things to which he could put no name but looked and tasted fine after his mouth had had little but dust over the past few days. Then he stopped, looked away, looked back, and swallowed, hard.

"Gideon," he called.

Vorden vaulted nimbly onto the table, strode down to Bela, and belted him across the head with his tricorn. "And take off that stupid hat when you're talking to me! I am still your father, and I demand a little respect!"

Gideon stood beside Whale, who was thoughtfully examining a large map tacked to the wall. It was of Umbrel and appeared to show that the city was five levels deep, with uncountable rooms on each level and a number of ways to achieve descent and ascent. They had apparently stumbled in through the back door. Whale pointed to what seemed to be the middle level, where the rooms were considerably smaller than any others he could locate—and there was, apparently, only one way in and out.

"The dungeons, I think."

"Glorian," Gideon said.

"Unless she's being kept in Lu's private quarters, I can't think of anyplace else she might be."

"She'd have to stay there until the Ceremony."

Whale nodded.

"Your mother would die!" Vorden yelled, belting his son again.

"I didn't even know her!"

"You never stayed around long enough for me to introduce you!"

Gideon stood beside Ivy and peered into the corridor. It was more like a boulevard, and along each high and wide wall were doors to shops whose signs and banners hung over their entrances. A fair number of people were evident, carrying baskets, goods, weapons, and in one case each other from what was obviously a bar. There were also creatures that looked like one-eyed horses pulling a curious variety of carriages and carts. There was also a definite air of festivity about the place—the colors were not exactly bright, but they were colorful, and the citizens bustled gaily about as though working against a tight schedule.

"It's a city!" he exclaimed quietly. "What about those other doors?"

"Dining rooms. The kid's running a restaurant, not a private kitchen. This stupid Ceremony is probably the best thing that ever happened to him."

Gideon took a deep breath and shook his head, then told her what Whale had discovered.

Ivy looked pained, but she touched his arm gently. "We haven't much time, you know. The Blood was already near the top of its banks. And those people out there aren't exactly getting ready for somebody's birthday."

Bela picked up a meat cleaver.

Vorden whipped out his foil.

Gideon stood beside Tag and looked down at the elaborately decorated platter the lad had uncovered, one all too clearly meant to be a showcase presentation. On it was a delicate arrangement of greens, fruits, and nuts. In the center it was blank, but there was a handwritten note to mark what it was to be used for.

"I don't think Glorian will like this," Tag said glumly.

"I doubt she even knows."

"But who would want to eat a duck?"

"Where I come from, lots of folks."

"What do you do with the feathers?"

Grabbing Vorden by the belt, he dragged the woodsman off the table to Ivy's door. Whale and Red followed, each munching in his own way on apples the size of softballs. "Bela will take us down," he said with a glare to Lain.

"Down?" Bela said loudly. "I haven't got time to breathe! Do you realize what it takes to feed those animals out there? Do you realize the reservations I have? My god, even Illklor is coming to dinner." He repositioned his cap and plunged his hands into a large bowl of flour. "I'm sorry. I haven't time for this silliness."

"Bela!" Vorden snapped.

"Sorry, Father."

Vorden shook Gideon's hand from his arm and stalked across the kitchen to his son, who took up an instant defensive posture with a double handful of overcooked scones. Vorden said something to him none of the others could hear. Bela blanched. Vorden snarled. Bela looked helplessly around his domain and sighed.

Gideon checked the outside again. "There doesn't seem to be any alarm raised, so I doubt we're in immediate danger. I don't know who the garks told, but it seems that's the least of our worries, for the moment."

"What do we do when we get Glorian and the duck?" Tag asked nervously.

"I don't know. We'll cross that bridge when we come to it."

"You're going home?" Ivy said in shocked amazement.

"Who said anything about going home?"

"You're staying?" she said delightedly.

Whale suggested further discussion of their plans, but Gideon was too apprehensive. He gestured Vorden and Bela over, the latter still protesting how absolutely furious Illklor would be if his ceremonial repast wasn't ready on time, not to mention the absolute temper Houte Illklor would be in when he discovered that his master chef had decided to go for a walk in the middle of the busiest day of the century; when he was once again apprised of his options in return for leading the group to the dungeons, he decided that Houte was putting on a little weight anyway and didn't know a pacch pie from a footh-patty, and what was an hour or so when he had finally been reunited with his long-lost father?

Whale then gathered them about and muttered a few words over their heads—a spell, he explained, to render them invisible for the trek across the boulevard to the next way down.

Gideon held out his hands, his arms, checked his legs and still saw them. But trust had to begin somewhere, and he was in no position to argue. With a nod, then, and a tight smile, he led them into Umbrel.

"Hey!" a pasty-faced man grumbled when he collided with Gideon. "Watch where you're going, huh?"

A pair of miniature dwarves danced mockingly around Red until a well-placed hoof sent one of them tumbling into a cart.

Two men standing outside a bar whistled at Ivy, one of them making a gesture so obscene that Gideon was too angrily embarrassed to do anything about it. Ivy wasn't. The man doubled up.

"Invisible, huh?" Gideon muttered as they shouldered their way toward a black-rimmed arch beyond the next intersection.

"It's been a long time," Whale apologized.

Gideon didn't doubt it. Nor did he doubt any longer Ivy's story that something dreadful had happened to the armorer as a result of his conflict with the Wamchu. He could only hope that the man's obvious nervousness wasn't going to hinder his ability to help once the going got rough.

Which it did when they reached the arch and saw the variety of elevators they had to choose from. There were extraordinarily long lines, many of them with animals as noisy as the people they mingled with, and when one of the doors hissed open they were able to see the stairs on the other side leading in both directions. The only one that had no line at all was at the back, and its door was red, and flanking the red door were two sullen garks.

"Three guesses," Gideon said sourly. He turned to Whale, who was smiling inanely in a vain attempt to seem like just one of the crowd. "How do you fight them?"

"Not terribly simple, I'm afraid," came the whispered answer. "You have to neutralize the wings, the claws, the beaks, the hind legs, and the eyes."

"One at a time, or all together?"

Whale started to answer, then checked himself with a

laugh. "I see. A joke to dissipate the stress, yes? My goodness, you heroes are clever, aren't you?"

With a growl not unlike Red's, he led them along the far wall, edging behind the elevator lines until they had reached the corner. The garks seemed to pay them no heed, but there was no question that however they communicated with the master of this place, it wouldn't be long before they added slavemaster and goods together and came up with Gideon.

Time, he thought then; there's no time anymore.

"All right, let's go."

Before the others could stop him, he strolled boldly across the mosaic floor, reached around one of the guardian garks, and pressed the summons button. The guard made no move to stop him. The doors opened. He stiffened his spine and took a step forward. The gark on his left whistled low and harshly, a sound soon strangled into silence when Red came up on its blind side and pressed it firmly between his bulk and the wall. The second gark turned slowly, its wings beginning to spread, the rusty sound sending the rest of the hall into abrupt, shocked, and fearful silence. Gideon wasted no time. He dashed into the stairwell, the others behind him, and could only listen as Red lured the second one in after him, then butted it until the doors closed and sliced the thing in half.

There was no opposition on the next landing.

Nor on the third level.

But the doors wouldn't open until Red used his ramhorns to splinter them. A race, then, down a dingy corridor barely wide enough for two of them abreast. The air was stale, the footing treacherous, and at the first turning they stopped and listened.

To wails of agony, screams of pain, cruel laughter that signaled a torturer's heaven.

Bela asked if he could just draw them a map.

Vorden slapped his shoulder and ordered him to lead them on and make no mistakes, or his mother would have no children.

Gideon's throat dried and filled with sand; swallowing helped not at all, and he was sure his hand was palsied when he waved them on, noting how the floor dipped downward, minute after minute, as the screams grew louder, then faded, then grew again as they made their way past iron-banded doors behind which they heard grunts and groans and beggings for mercy. He looked in none; he did his best to ignore the vile odors that crept like invisible fog from the tiny barred openings and the cracks in the walls; he brushed aside a silent suggestion from Ivy that they begin testing each cell to see which held their goal. He knew none of them did. For someone as important as Glorian and her possession, nothing but the best would do, and though he granted the Wamchu a great deal of bastardy and nastiness, there was also a sense of style about him.

No. No ordinary cell would do for the means to conquer the world.

He was right.

Almost an hour later, most of it spent hidden in niches and shadows from patrolling Moglars with garks on leashes, they came to a door made of gleaming brass. It faced the corridor like a dull embossed sun, and it was flanked by two of the same ugly dogs he had seen in Rayn.

Bela nodded at the entrance. "She's in there, the little bitch. Do you know she thinks she knows how to make a desh mousse? She couldn't boil water in a volcano. Why, only last week—"

Vorden silenced him with a snarl.

Bela looked hurt and crushed his chef's cap in his hands.

"I don't like it," Gideon said.

"It is awfully tacky, isn't it," Bela said.

"I mean the lack of guards. It doesn't make sense."

"He is a confident man," Whale said. "I truly don't think he expected us to get this far."

Red edged his way to the front, and the dogs yelped, whined, and took off.

"It's a trap," Ivy said when Gideon reached for the polished latch.

"Of course it is," he told her. "But do we have a choice?"

"Why the hell," she said, "do you keep asking stupid questions?"

THIRTY-FOUR

If this is a cell, Gideon thought as the doors closed silently behind them, I'm going to rob a bank.

The room, and it was massive, was an entrapped rainbow of elegant silks billowing from the ceiling, polished satins billowing from the walls, fringed and intricately designed Oriental carpets strewn thickly across the floor, and deft combinations of Edwardian and Victorian furniture, solid and dark and carved with grape leaves, cherubs, and mythical creatures; the scent of freshly picked roses filled their nostrils, exotic perfumes smoked from gold censers hanging from silver chains, platters of fruits added the touch of an orchard, and the music of dexterous harpists was soft and inviting and psychologically relaxing.

On the lefthand side was a tall archway hung with glittering pearls on strands of silver; on the right a dais upon which stood a four-poster, its closed draperies a deep wine velvet.

Red sat on his haunches and scratched behind one ear.

Gideon and the others rushed across to the bed, flung aside the coverings, and stared.

It was Glorian, in her long white dress, her dark hair disheveled on the five brocade pillows set beneath her head. Her hands were folded modestly across her stomach, and on her feet were silken emerald slippers whose toes curled up and back toward her shins.

"It's her!" Tag exclaimed in delight.

"Wonderful," said Ivy, plucking at the velveteen coverlet with a moue of disgust.

Glorian's eyelids fluttered.

Gideon held his breath.

Her eyelids opened, and she gasped.

"Good god," she sputtered, "is it you?"

"No, it's the tooth fairy," Ivy snarled. "C'mon, Glorian, move yourself, huh?"

She sat up by degrees, dazed by the sight of her friends crowded around the bed. "Oh my heavens, it really is you. It really, really is." She clasped her hands to a grateful bosom and smiled beatifically.

"Glorian, please, we're running out of time," Gideon told her urgently. "Hurry and get up. We have to get out of here before the guards find out."

Glorian nodded vigorously, leapt from the bed, and embraced Whale, weeping; then she thrust herself away and embraced Tag, weeping; then she thrust herself away and shook Ivy's hand; then she stood in front of Gideon and said, "I knew you were a hero." And she punched him in the stomach.

He stumbled back, blinking, then slammed Ivy back with one arm to prevent her from tearing out the other woman's throat. "What the hell?"

"Do you know what time it is?" Glorian demanded. "Do you have any idea how long I've been in this miserable, rotten place waiting for you to rescue me? Some hero. My god, have you any idea of the danger?"

He gulped for air and nodded.

"Well, thank heavens for that."

"Gideon!" Ivy called from the beaded curtain. "Here it is!"

With a ragged smile, he left Glorian to explain to the others what had happened since she'd been taken from the Kori forest, and ran through the curtain. And stopped.

"Fascinating, isn't it," Ivy said.

"I almost didn't believe it," he admitted.

The adjoining room was bare save for a huge silver-and-gold table in its center, gently bathed by well-aimed streams of golden light originating somewhere in the high reaches of the ceiling. On the table was a round golden cage nearly eight feet high and eight feet in diameter, its bars spiraled, its top a filigree representation of all things bright and beautiful, however abstract they may be; and in the cage was one of the largest ducks he had ever seen.

A white duck.

It was real.

With a look to Ivy, he approached the cage cautiously, staring, peering, finally reaching out to tap a finger on one of the delicate bars. The bird, which had been sleeping with one wing wrapped around its head, stirred. He tapped again. It shook itself and rose onto its great webbed feet, waddled about to shake the stiffness off, then leaned its long slender neck toward Gideon's face.

"Hey, fella," Gideon said with a grin. "Don't panic now. We're gonna take you out of here."

"For god's sake, let's go!" Glorian said anxiously from the archway.

But the others, having come so far and through so much, pushed her aside and came in to examine what they had been after all this time. The duck, sensing that it was the center of attention, preened a little and did its best to look marginally aloof.

"This is it, huh?" Tag said, shrugging his disappointment at not finding something a little more majestic.

"Gideon," Whale said in a breathless voice, "we don't have much time."

"Right," Ivy said. "Let's beat it with the bird before we get killed."

Gideon walked slowly around the table, examining the cage until he found a large door. A tentative tug; it seemed locked. The duck, meanwhile, followed him closely, every so often turning its head to stare at his face. Gideon smiled. The duck closed one eye.

"Bela," he said without taking his gaze off the bird, "how can we get out of here in a hurry?"

There was no answer.

"Damnit, Bela—" He looked over his shoulder and saw Vorden shrugging toward the door—his son was gone, slipped out while the others were greeting Glorian.

The duck quacked.

Gideon looked back.

The duck pressed its face as close to the bars as it could.

Crazy, Gideon thought; but damnit, I *know* this thing.

The duck reared back, opened its bill, closed it.

Gideon wiped a hard hand over his face. This whole thing was getting to him, no question about it. He knew a lot of people, to be sure, but a duck wasn't one of them. Yet there was something odd about this bird, some . . .

And the duck said, "Giddy, for god's sake, is that you?"

Almost a full minute passed in silence.

Gideon gripped the edge of the table with both hands, stared at the bird staring back at him, and closed his eyes tightly. Opened them and glared at the ceiling for several seconds before releasing a harsh breath.

"Hello?" the duck said.

He rose slowly to his full height. Another look at the duck, and he stepped around the table as if afraid that if he moved too fast, he would keel over.

The duck waddled hurriedly after him. "Giddy? Giddy, don't just stand there, say something!"

He swallowed hard and turned to face the others. When they saw the rage in his face, they fell back a step; when they saw him take his bat by the middle in his left hand and raise it almost over his head, they took another step back; when his right hand formed a fist nearly as large as the weapon he held, Tag tried a smile.

"It is not funny," he said, his voice so deep it began to reverberate in the room and set the silks to swinging gently. His eyes were narrowed, and Ivy could have sworn she saw the hint of a tear welling in one. "If this is your idea of a joke . . ."

"Not mine," Whale said quickly.

"Gideon, for crying out loud," Glorian said impatiently. "We haven't the time . . ." The scolding trailed off when his face darkened and a muscle began to tic at the side of his neck.

"Gideon Sunday, for Christ's sake!" said the duck.

Gideon whirled and stared. "It can't be."

"Who said so?"

"But you're dead!"

"I might as well be. Of all the colors, this thing had to be white. Damn, you know how I hate to wear white."

"Who's dead?" Ivy asked.

Gideon dropped to his knees beside the table. "My sister," he whispered, and reached a finger between the bars to stroke the duck's feathers. "She died . . . a long time ago."

"But what does that . . ." Ivy turned to Glorian, who lifted an eyebrow in a *beats me* gesture.

"It isn't funny," Gideon said. "It isn't funny at all."

"Gideon," the duck said, "it's me."

He looked at the feathers, at the feet, at the bill, at the eyes, at the lines, at the tail.

"You're a duck."

"Tell me something I don't already know."

"No," he said, frowning. "You tell me." He leaned forward and whispered something in what he hoped was the general area of the bird's ear. The duck closed one eye, lifted its gaze to the ceiling, and snapped its bill once.

"Three hundred and seventy-two yards, against the Rams. No touchdowns, and you still ought to be ashamed of yourself. Sacked five times. Third rib from the bottom."

"My god, it's Tuesday," he said, staggering to his feet and back until Ivy caught him.

"Look," Glorian said, "I am not sure what the day of the week has to do with anything, but we aren't going to see the rest of today if we don't get the hell out of here now."

"It's not a day of the week," Gideon said weakly.

"Today? It most certainly is."

"It's my sister."

They broke into unison protest, broke off instantly, and stared at the duck.

"Tuesday?" Ivy said in a small voice.

"Tuesday," the duck confirmed. "My mother had a thing about an actress of the time."

Gideon began to grin.

"Tuesday?" Ivy said in a small voice, almost laughing.

"You want to make something of it," the duck said, "just come a little closer."

"I'll be damned," Gideon said.

"She . . . she told me her name was Monica Freeman," Glorian protested in a struggle for belief, and more than a little peeved that she'd been lied to by a duck.

"That was her stage name. Her real name is Tuesday."

The brass door suddenly rang with harsh pounding.

Glorian looked wildly about her and shook her head violently when Whale asked if there was any other way out of this cell. Ivy immediately grabbed Vorden's arm and dragged him to the other room, Tag running puzzledly behind—their weapons were drawn and at the ready when the door began to split apart.

"Tuesday?" Gideon said, shaking his head to clear it of the fog that had enveloped his thinking. "I don't get it. I accept it, but I'll be damned if I get it. What about the car? The accident?"

"It happened," the duck said with a nervous eye toward the tumult in the next room. "But when I hit the bottom of the river, everything went white. I thought I was dead. Then I opened my eyes and saw that woman over there standing over me."

"A Bridge," he said, the answer clear at last.

"Smashed it to hell, I think," Tuesday said.

"Wamchu," Glorian explained.

And could explain no further. Suddenly, the doors shattered and the cell was filled with screaming Moglars, squawking garks, and two snarling ugly dogs that hung back by the threshold to cover the rear.

THIRTY-
FIVE

Gideon grabbed one of the bars and tried to run with the cage, but his arm was nearly yanked from its socket when the cage wouldn't move. He looked down while the duck quacked its panic and saw that the bottom had been securely fastened to the table. Quickly, he raced around to the door, pulled on it, pulled harder, and snapped its flimsy lock. He fumbled it open and reached in. The duck cowered for the moment, cocked a head to listen to the battle raging in the front room, and flung itself into his keeping.

With his sister tucked under his left arm and his bat firm in his right hand, he swung around the table . . . and stopped.

There was silence in the front.

There were people and things facing him.

He lifted the bat for them to see.

The Moglars and garks surged slightly forward.

Through the slow-dancing pearls he could see Tag and Ivy held in the grip of four guards, Whale on the floor shaking his head from a stunning blow, and Vorden sneering at a gark that was eyeing his thighs hungrily. Red was by the door, eyes black but pinned by ropes about his neck and legs, and a Moglar standing by his muzzle with a four-bladed knife tickling his throat.

I could, Gideon thought, wade in. After all, I do have the bat, and I could probably lay waste to a dozen or so of the Moglars and smash the wings and beaks of a few garks, free Ivy and Tag so they could help me fight my way to the door, where we could get Red and Whale, use Vorden for a diversion in the hall, and then retrace our steps back to the kitchen, where Bela will tell us another way to get out of here if he knows what's healthy for him.

A gark sneezed, the points of its parrot-beak snapping together and causing sparks to flare into the air.

A rough count, before the rescue of his friends, put the odds at something like thirty-nine to one, not counting the garks.

He looked at the duck.

"Don't look at me," she said. "I'm just a duck."

Reluctantly, he lowered the bat and began to walk. The Moglars, grunting their approval of his good sense, made way for him. Ivy and Tag fell in behind, rubbing various parts of their somewhat bruised bodies; Whale, back on his feet, sighed and allowed Vorden to hold his arm to keep him upright; and Red, snorting and not purring, gave his captors a look that told them he'd be good, but he'd be damned if he was going to be treated like a dog. Glorian followed behind, demanding that somebody *do something* before they were all killed.

Ivy suggested something Gideon didn't catch, but whatever it was, it shut Glorian up.

The doors opened.

Gideon revised the odds to seventy-three to one and followed the vanguard, which, he assumed, was going to take him to some miserable and dingy cell where he would spend the rest of his life developing the perfect offense for a team he would never play for again.

On the way—and it seemed to him that they were, oddly, heading back up—Tuesday explained how she had come to be in her predicament. That she tried to whisper wasn't bad; that she kept her bill close to his ear and several times nearly nibbled it from his skull made him flinch.

She had been drinking, she said, the night of the accident. Her agent had tried to arrange for a part in an historical epic in Spain, but the deal fell through when it was learned she had principles about appearing in nude scenes with Hannibal's elephants. Distraught, furious, self-rightcous, and filled with self-pity, she went for a drive. As she approached the bridge she saw a curious glow over the water and thought she was about to be kidnapped by Martians, experimented on, and returned to her home a gibbering idiot. She lost control. The car smashed through the wooden railing. She screamed. The car landed in the water, and she landed on a hillside in the middle of nowhere she recognized.

Naturally, she thought she was dead.

Naturally, when she saw a herd of giant goats in the distance, she knew she was dead and in a peculiar sort of purgatory where she was doomed to be a goatmaid for all eternity.

Then she saw a woman coming toward her from the east and a tall, red-bearded, blond-haired, Oriental-looking gentleman coming toward her from the west. She struggled to her feet. She considered her options and took a step toward the man. The man smiled at her, raised a hand, and the next thing she knew she was a duck.

Then the man tripped, fell, rolled down the hill, and the woman—who was none other than Glorian herself—snatched her up and ran with her to a small village, where it was explained to her that the man's name was Wamchu, world domination was his game, and he needed an otherworldly duck's down to bring something called the Blood River over its banks.

Quite naturally, she didn't believe a word of it until someone stepped on her foot and she realized she wasn't dead, and she wasn't still drunk, and she wasn't ever going to see her home again because she had somehow become an object of supremely flattering veneration. Without, she added smugly, ever once taking her clothes off.

Then, she recalled with a shudder, nightmarish creatures rose out of the ground and attacked the village. In the middle of the fighting, a monstrous bird swooped down out of the air, plucked her from her perch in the backyard, and carried her off here, where she languished for god knows how long until Glorian was brought in to keep her happy, to feed her, and generally keep her from molting out of despair until she was needed for whatever ceremonies were to be performed in, she was sure, a revolting manner upon her duckhood.

"Funny, isn't it," she said as the small army and its prisoners reached what Gideon surmised was the uppermost level and marched toward a pair of golden doors guarded by a quartet of really ugly dogs, "how you can be just driving along, drunk as a lord and minding your own business, and zap, out of the blue, you're a duck."

"Yeah," he said. "Funny."

"It makes you wonder, doesn't it."

"About what?"

"About the meaning of it all. Of life. Of fate. Of chance. Of coincidence."

The ugly dogs saw the army, checked among themselves, and took off.

"What it means is," Gideon said, "life is a bitch."

"Well, I know that, but it makes you wonder, doesn't it."

The doors opened.

The army marched in.

They were placed in an antechamber whose walls were covered with tapestries depicting the same woodland landscape at different times of the year. There were three padded benches, not large enough for all of them, so Gideon sat on the floor against the back wall, Tuesday on his left, Red curled as best he could on his right. As he watched, Glorian huddled with Whale, no doubt planning a strategy for escape, while the others sat opposite them and scowled at the walls, the ceiling, the floor, and him.

He did not feel the slightest bit apologetic. After all, it wasn't his idea to attach an alternate world to his pantry, drag him through, and try to turn him into something he wasn't. If anyone should feel bad, it was Glorian. It was her world. Her impending disaster. Her duck.

Well, not exactly her duck in the sense that it belonged to her feather and foot, having been raised from an egg and living on an ornamental pond on the back forty. The duck, if he were going to be honest, was his sister. That, he supposed, gave him some sort of obligation, though for the moment he couldn't think of what it might be other than getting her returned to her rightful state.

Glorian rose, stretched, and walked to the door, tried the latch futilely, and sighed. Whale stretched out and fell asleep. Vorden whispered something in Ivy's ear, and Tag punched his shoulder.

Gideon looked up when Glorian approached, stood there for a moment, then sat cross-legged in front of him. She was still lovely, despite the now soiled white gown and the tangles in her dark hair, and he remembered the hour in his living room, after he had driven off the black beast. It was, he thought, about the only peace he'd had since he'd started this thing.

"I'm sorry," she said at last, her violet eyes downcast. "I shouldn't have hit you."

Tuesday ruffled her feathers, but he put a restraining hand on her back until she calmed, snorted as only a duck can, and tucked her head under her wing to grab a few moments' sleep.

"You're all right?" he said quietly.

She nodded. "It was Wamchu, or rather, one of Wamchu's creatures that took me off that night. I didn't wake up for days, and then I was . . . here. Down here in the bordello." Her smile was quick and strained. "I thought I was going to die."

"You didn't. You won't."

"Are you so sure about that?"

"No," he said honestly. "But then, what is there about this whole thing I can be sure of? Nothing. So while I'm sure I'm in a hell of a mess, I'm not sure yet I can't get out of it.''

Red purred in his sleep.

She touched his knee with a hand.

Ivy growled.

''Gideon, I think we've had it. There's no way out of here that I know of. There are too many guards, too many weapons, too many places to get lost in, too many ways Wamchu can get us.''

''Is he here?''

''Good grief, no. I suppose he's still back at Rayn.''

He shifted uneasily. ''I don't understand. Why doesn't he just come here, take care of us, and do the Ceremony and be done with it?''

''Because he's stupid.''

''I know that. But this just doesn't make sense.''

She smoothed a hand over her chest, toyed with the gold girdle that bunched her gown at the waist. ''I heard things over the past couple of days. Something about his wives.''

''Wonderful people.''

''He's annoyed with them.''

''Furious would be more like it.'' At her look he smiled. ''They told him I was from across a Bridge, and he refused to believe it. I guess he finally did. One of them tried to do us in with an earthquake. Another one sent some weird insects after us. That didn't work either.''

''Oh.'' She nodded. ''Now I begin to see.'' She nodded again. ''I knew there was something odd when he didn't show up right away. It isn't like him to leave things to the last minute.''

''Things like what?''

She shrugged. ''Things. Killing us, destroying the world.''

''Oh.''

She inched closer, knees touching now, and he could see the conflict in her eyes between enjoying some discomfort on the enemy's part and knowing that it would all end the same, anyway.

''You going to tell me?''

She laughed lightly, softly. "He and his wives don't really get along, you see. Whenever he tries to come up to the Middle Ground, they always want to go with him. He usually doesn't let them. I guess they won this time, but when they failed him, he wanted them to go back. They didn't want to. It's really lousy down there in the Lower Ground, you know. You think this place is bad? You should see what passes for flowers down there. You'd want to step on them, but you wouldn't want to lose a foot doing it, if you know what I mean."

"The wives," he said.

"Oh, right." She shifted again, her hand idly tracing over his thigh. "Well, I guess he had to persuade them to leave Rayn for home. They don't persuade easily. He reminded them of their failures. They reminded him who was boss. As I get it, he probably has a black eye."

"I see."

"But he'll still get here in time for the Ceremony."

"I see."

She gripped his hands then, tightly. "Gideon, what are you going to do?"

"What?"

"What's the plan?"

"Me?"

"We must get out of here, you know that. We have to take the duck and get out of here."

"The duck has a name," the duck said, opening one dark eye.

"How?" he said.

"How?" Glorian echoed. "What do you mean, how?"

"How," he said. "As in, by what means? Isn't that what you and Whale were talking about?"

"For heaven's sake, no. He had the hiccoughs. I was trying to help him. Danger always does that to him when he doesn't eat properly."

He leaned back against the wall, folded his arms over his chest, looked at the duck, looked at the lorra, looked at Ivy, who was unraveling one of the tapestries, and sighed.

"You're the hero," she reminded him.

"Yeah. Right."

"Maybe you can talk Houte into letting me go. Then I can round up an army, come back, and storm the place. You can hold out in here until we break through and rescue you. Then you can take care of the Blood before it's too late."

"You know something?" he said. "I've just found out why Tag is the way he is."

She frowned, not sure if he was complimenting her or not, and decided he wasn't. Before she could slug him, however, there was a muffled commotion at the door.

"And who is Houte, by the way? Houte Illklor?"

"You know him?" she asked.

"Only by reputation."

The door opened at the sound of a gong.

"Then get up, hero. He's here, and we're about to die."

THIRTY-SIX

Houte Illklor, First Lieutenant to the Wamchu and Guardian of Umbrel, stood on the threshold. He was dressed in a dizzying yet effective array of colorful hides, furs, and silks, which served to add a great deal of bulk to an already bulky man. His face, however, was unpleasantly cadaverous, and the long stringy hair that dangled from the sides of his concave skull added to the impression that someone had just disturbed him in his coffin.

"Which one of you is the hero?" he demanded in an ordinary but commanding voice.

Gideon stood up. Tuesday ducked behind him.

Illklor, casting a disdainful glance at the others, who were pressed fearfully against the walls, strode confidently into the room, a group of garks and Moglars remaining outside amid a screen of scowling and wing stretching. Behind him, the man was dragging the bat, and before he reached Gideon his face was flushed with the effort.

"What is this weapon?" Illklor said.

"A bat."

Illklor dropped it and shook his head. "Things certainly have changed since I left the surface." Another shake of his head. "A pitiful group you have assembled here, hero. Did you really believe you would be able to defy the might of Lu Wamchu and get away with it? Did you really believe you could stop the Blood from its destiny? Did you really think, deep down in that hero's heart of yours, that you could stem the tide of fate with a petrified bat?"

The man put his hands on his hips and laughed, looked over his shoulder to encourage the Moglars and garks to laugh as well. And when the display of arrogance was done, he sniffed, took a foothcloth from his sleeve and blew his nose, replaced it with a flourish, and kicked the bat. Grimaced when the bat didn't move. Winced when a message reached the proper lobe. And shook his head again.

"I understand," he said, "that you come from across a Bridge."

Gideon nodded.

"Amazing," he said. "I've always wanted to use one myself, but I just don't have the time. It isn't easy running a summer palace. Lord, you wouldn't believe the details I don't dare leave to others."

"Try me," Gideon said, hoping that by stalling for time he could think of something to do.

"No. But if I change my mind and don't have you killed, you must come to dinner sometime and tell me all about it."

"Like hell."

"Oh, that wasn't nice at all. But then"—he gave them a long sigh and sorrowful look—"Wamchu told me you had spunk."

"He didn't like it."

"As well he shouldn't. It bespeaks a certain lack of critical thinking, which otherwise might bring one safely out of a situation like this—which, I should add in case you've started to think of something, isn't going to help you one bit."

Shit, Gideon thought, and stopped.

Illklor looked to Glorian and smiled nastily. "None of this would have happened if you had married me, you know."

"What?" Gideon said.

"But of course, naturally, and didn't you know?"

"Marry you?"

"I've asked several times."

"And every time," Glorian said, "I told you what you could do with the proposal, the marriage bed, the vows, the honeymoon, and that funny little bulby thing you keep in a suitcase under your chair."

"That funny little bulby thing would have made you very happy, my dear," Illklor said.

"You mean, all this is because she wouldn't marry you?" Gideon said.

"Don't be stupid," Illklor told him. "What does raising the Blood from its banks have to do with my marrying Glorian?"

"I don't know. That's what I asked you."

"Why don't we just kill him?" Tag said suddenly. "Gideon can use the bat, I can use my bare hands, and Glorian can use her fists. We could kill him, rush the guards, get out, go to Rayn before Wamchu leaves, and kill him, too. Then we could—"

"Tag, shut up," Gideon ordered.

"Don't talk to my brother that way," Glorian said. "There's something in what he says."

"The something is suicide," Gideon told her.

"Way to go," Ivy said approvingly. "I told you she was—"

"You mind your own business," Glorian snapped. "When I want your opinion, I'll rattle your cage."

"Ladies, please," Vorden said, palms raised in a gesture of peace.

Illklor pulled on a string of hair impatiently, whirled around and shouted, "You will be quiet!" They were. "You will accept your miserable fates like the other peasants do. You will stop this—" He cut himself off, tilted his head slightly, and walked to Ivy.

She had winked at him.

He smiled.

She toyed with the top button of her blouse.

"Ivy," said Tag, aghast. "What are you doing?"

Vorden drew himself up. "She is hysterical, sir," he said to Illklor. "I must ask that you refrain from taking undue advantage of her weakened condition."

Ivy winked again.

Illklor rolled his shoulders, adjusted his hides, furs, and silks, and took a step closer.

Ivy saw what she thought was her reflection in his hair and had second thoughts; she rebuttoned the button.

"Giddy," Tuesday hissed, "do something!"

Illklor batted Tag aside and reached for Ivy's arm. She slapped the hand away; he laughed and grabbed it, pulling her away from the wall. She slapped his cheek; he slapped hers. She slapped again; so did he.

"Hey," Gideon said, squirming at the heat taking fire in his chest.

"Shut up," Glorian whispered. "She's distracting him so we can get away."

Gideon pointed at the doorway. When she counted the waiting guards, she adjusted her roped girdle and decided that Ivy would do anything for a laugh.

Illklor grabbed her by the throat; Ivy's face went red.

"Wish I could blush like that," Glorian muttered.

"Hey!" Gideon said while the guards at the door began their own peculiar brand of giggling.

With a groan, Tag struggled up from the floor and was kicked back down. Whale and Vorden immediately reached for their weapons, remembered they didn't have any, and rushed Illklor from either side. With his free hand, the Umbrel guardian batted them aside as well.

"Well, shit," said Tuesday, stretched her wings, and flew right at the man's head.

Illklor snatched her out of the air by the neck, laughed, and shook her until feathers began to fly.

Gideon picked up the bat.

The guards began to murmur.

Vorden pushed himself to his feet and reached out to stop him from doing anything foolish.

Gideon looked down at him, and the woodsman backed away.

Ivy gurgled a protest; Tuesday tried to beat the man to death with her wings.

Glorian said something rapidly, but Gideon couldn't hear it. There was a rush in his ears, stormy surf trapped in a shell, and he felt no compunctions at all about bringing the bat across the man's back. He yelled and dropped Ivy and Tuesday, and turned just in time to receive a forward thrust just below his sternum. There was no air left for another yell, so he simply gargled a bit and pointed to the guards.

Gideon brought him to his knees with a light tap to his skull, to his face with a not-so-light tap on the back of his thick neck.

Red growled then and lumbered to his feet.

Glorian ran to the limp, gasping duck and gathered it up in her arms while Tag, glowering at Illklor's unconscious body, put his arms around Ivy and held her close.

Gideon saw none of it.

He advanced on the door, hesitated only a few seconds, then began flailing at the first face he saw, and the second when the first disintegrated, and the third when the second split into two others. He only had time for a glance to his left, where Vorden was doing his best to nail garks into the floor with one of the benches, before he strode boldly, and somewhat precipitously, into the hallway, the bat little more than a green, hissing blur. He barely felt the blows he received in turn—the pricks on his legs from garks' needled beaks, the stings on his back from Moglar's swords and stickers, the bruises raised on his arms when pikes and planks were thrown to stop him, at the headache he was getting because he couldn't move fast enough, couldn't swing hard enough to vent the rage that drove him forward.

Alarms were raised.

Screams filled the hall.

Vorden forsook the bench for a sword snatched from a fallen Moglar; Tag grabbed up a sword with a ball of spikes on the end; Whale found a crescent dagger; Ivy found a two-headed pike hinged in the middle; Red used his hooves, his horns, and his teeth.

Illklor, his eyes slightly crossed, staggered to his feet, to the doorway, and shouted instructions to his guards.

Ivy kicked him between the legs and blew him a kiss when he screeched and fell backward. Then she slammed the door and locked it, and headed for the fight. Returned, unlocked the door, and waited with a disgusted look for Glorian and the duck to hurry out. Then she kicked Illklor again and relocked the door, fought her way through a mass of indecisive garks and decidedly unhappy giant dwarves until she was at Gideon's side. She said nothing because the dark look on his face told her he wouldn't be listening.

Whale and the others saw it, too, and could only do their best to make sure he hacked the fastest way toward the exit.

Within minutes they were in the center square, citizens scattering at the carnage, a few leaning out of windows and calling bets to four men on a scaffolding hastily scribbling in steno notebooks while a fifth stood behind them chalking the odds on a blackboard.

Within minutes more, they were at the door to Bela's kitchens and once inside slammed it shut and piled tables against it. Then Vorden turned to his son, pointed a finger, and said, "Not a word, boy. Not a single word or you're dessert."

Bela nodded unhappily.

Ivy dropped her pike and grabbed a pot of water from a stove, clambered onto a table, and dumped its contents on Gideon's head.

Gideon, who was busily battling a butcher's block to the death, stiffened, blinked, and slowly holstered the bat. Ivy jumped down to his side and put an arm around his waist, bracing him while he regained his breath, his composure, and a better clarity of vision. When it was done, he could hear the shrill alarms still sounding throughout Umbrel, the footsteps outside, the pounding and scratching on the door.

"We have to leave."

"Where to?" Ivy said.

"When we get there we'll know. But we can't stay here."

"Good idea," Bela seconded.

Vorden grumbled at him.

"Well, it is," his son said defiantly. "What are you going to do when they break in, sauté them to death? This kitchen is not big enough for all of us."

Gideon stopped Vorden's murderous advance with a word, then took the duck from Glorian and stroked its neck. With a quacklike purring, it nuzzled its head against his side, then suggested that the sooner they leave Umbrel, the sooner pursuit would stop. While Houte Illklor was one of Wamchu's minions, he was also aware that he couldn't be expected to hold off an army for two days, until Wamchu arrived. Therefore, it made sense, and a perverted kind of logic, that once into the ashen woods, Houte would send word to Rayn that the duck had flown the coop, the prisoners were on the loose, and what with the Ceremony to prepare for and all, what was a lieutenant to do?

Ivy mentioned rather sarcastically that once the duck was gone, there would be no Ceremony, Wamchu would hold Illklor responsible, and it would be worth considerably more than the man's life to see to it that the duck was returned.

"The duck has a name," the duck said grimly.

"You're all missing the point," Glorian said.

Ivy examined her hinged pike closely.

"I forgot something, you see."

"Forgot what?" Whale asked fearfully.

"The army."

"How can I forget it, I can hear it right outside the door."

"Not that army, the one in Rayn."

Gideon slowly turned his head.

"The one," Glorian said in a small voice, "Wamchu is going to send against the Upper Ground when the Ceremony begins."

He saw it then—why Wamchu wasn't here, why Houte had so many guards for a lousy summer palace, why his sister had been here instead of in Rayn. There were still a few unanswered questions—such as what the hell was he doing here in the first place—but they would have to wait.

Meanwhile, Ivy said to Glorian, "Nice of you to tell us now."

"I forgot."

"You forgot?"

"Well, there was a bit of excitement, you know. I can't be expected to remember everything."

"But who started all this in—"

Gideon, beginning to feel the effects of the weapons, teeth, fists, feet, nails, hands, and hips used against him, shut them up with a mirthless smile and sent them to the exit. When they were gone in a flurry that belied their casual arguing, he turned to Bela.

"Are you going to be all right?"

The young man guessed he would be, as long as no one connected him with any of the raiders.

Gideon considered the problem and solved it to his own satisfaction by putting his sister down, walking over to the chef, shaking his hand, and giving him two black eyes and a slightly cracked jaw. If that doesn't convince them, he thought, let him stew in his own juices.

Then he rushed to the elevator stairwell just as the kitchen door burst in and the room flooded with troops.

THIRTY-SEVEN

It was relatively easy to escape the surface city, considering the leaderless forces ranging below them. Red skewered five garks, Ivy decapitated one, and the rest scattered for reasons best known to them and their instinct to survive in a hostile environment. The worst part was pushing through the crowds of decidedly unsavory people who were beginning to arrive for the end of the world. Long caravans, large groups, the occasional carriage of trollops and gamblers all conspired in some way to prevent them from taking full flight. But when they reached the side of the road, they were able to race over the grey, dusty plain to the nearest slope. Climbing was not difficult once they got the hang of slipping back two paces for every four forged ahead, yet they were thoroughly exhausted by the time they reached the safety of the dismal forest atop the hill and had reached the campsite they had used before their foray into the heart of the enemy.

They dropped to the ground, gasping, thirsty, suddenly aware of all the injuries they had taken during battle. Whale did his best to spell the wounds away, and though his efforts were weak and somewhat confused, the results were sufficient to ease much of the pain and staunch the worst of the bleeding.

An hour later they moved on, goaded by the knowledge that though the duck was with them, they had not yet completed their onerous task.

By nightfall, however, there was no sense in taking another step. Their legs were stiff, their lungs burning, their heads aching from the unwholesome atmosphere of the woodland that pressed ominously close about them. Agreeing that carrying on would do them more harm than good, they stopped to build a fire and collapsed into puddles less animated than the branches above, dancing in a wind tainted with the stench of nightmares.

Finally, when the horrid roars of prowling ants prevented their sleep, they huddled around the fire and watched the sparks reach for stars that never shone in this part of the world.

Gideon kept an arm around Tuesday, every so often scratching her neck and stroking her back to remind himself that she was indeed real—or as real as anything could be in a world where his best friend was a red-haired giant goat.

"I'm glad you came," she said at last, her words slightly clipped because of her bill's action. "I was getting tired of all that luxury."

An eyebrow lifted. "Luxury?"

"Hey, don't knock it. I was treated like a queen, you know."

"They were going to pluck you, then serve you for dinner."

A wing shifted in a shrug. "You want perfection, go to heaven."

"I'll settle for my living room, thank you very much."

"And I," said a shamelessly eavesdropping Ivy, "will settle for knowing what we're going to do next."

"That's easy," said Glorian. "We go home."

Ivy, in spite of herself, nodded agreement.

"Why?" Tag asked in disappointment.

"Because Gideon has done what we've asked him to. He found the duck, he found me, and now I can proceed with stopping Wamchu on the Upper Ground."

"You?" Ivy leaned away from her. "I think you're right that Gideon has done more than his share, give or take, and we can't in good conscience ask him to do more. But where do you get off saying *you'll* proceed?''

"Well I am who I am, after all."

Ivy mouthed a word that brought a blush to Glorian's cheek and a cough to Whale's throat. "Ladies," he admonished gently. "As much as I know you hold your country's best interests at heart, I should like to know how you propose to stop Wamchu from taking over."

"Well, that's easy," Ivy said quickly. "We station men at the edge of Chey and push them off the ladders when they climb up."

"Lots of ladders," Whale suggested.

"Nonsense," Glorian said sweetly. "We raise the armies, fortify the villages, boobytrap the Scarred Mountains, and beat them to a pulp in a war of attrition."

"Waste of manpower," Ivy said.

"I think that's all wrong," Tag interrupted, and looked startled when everyone turned to listen. "I mean, don't you think we ought to go right now to Rayn? We can lay down a siege or something. Or we can attack it the way we did Umbrel, knock it all to the ground, hang Wamchu in the square, and torture the guards until we find out the secret way down to Choy. Then we go get the wives and hang them." He smiled. "That's a lot easier than going back up home, and a lot more fun. I mean, have you counted the ladders we have to climb? I did on the way down. It's a lot, I can tell you. We'll be so tired when we get there, we won't be able to kill a single one of them."

Ivy waved the suggestion away with a limp hand and turned to Vorden. "You do a lot of fighting and stealing, right? What do you think?"

"I think," Vorden said sadly, face cupped in his palms, "I am a miserable excuse of a man who has just lost the only son he's ever had. And to think . . ." A hand shifted to his brow. "A cook. The man's a cook."

Gideon tried twice to break in and was twice shouted down with the reminder that they were only trying to spare him further danger, heartache, and injury, and if he didn't appreciate what they were doing for him, he could take his silly little bat and go home.

Even Whale, though he felt obligated to come to his defense, did so in such a halfhearted manner that Gideon could only push himself back into the shadows, where he tried, for one more time than he could count, to understand these people. He realized he was, essentially, an alien and could therefore not be expected to fully grasp their mental, cultural, and psychological aspects; nor could he be expected to be understood himself because of his unique, to them, character and background. But surely there had to be some common ground, some midpoint of compromise, some logical median along which they might travel as one instead of as a mob.

Tuesday waddled back after several minutes and sat down in front of him. "Would you mind telling me how you got into this in the first place?"

He told her, as simply and quickly as he could. When he was finished, he discovered an ache in a curious space between his lungs.

"Well, I personally think," she said judiciously, "we ought to go home. God knows I could get a Bridge fast enough, if all it takes is desire and need. You really don't owe them, you know, big brother; not when you get right down to it. They dragged you into this—for which, I must say, I am very grateful—and like they say, you've done your bit."

"I suppose."

"I should also like to add that I am not pleased with the reference to my preserves. They were much sought after in my time, in case you've forgotten."

"Yeah, I know. Aunt Beth used them on flypaper."

"That," Tuesday said with a toss of her head, "is a damned lie, Gideon Sunday."

"And Uncle Howard waxed his cello with them."

"God, you *are* cruel." She spread her wings and covered her eyes, sobbing a bit before peering through the feathers to see him grinning. "You're a creep, too. And if

my misery, which you see displayed before you, its bill
toward your hand, isn't enough to move you to tears, I
might also add that I'd kill for a good steak about now.
And the only way I'm going to get it is by going home.''

"Right.''

"Home, Gideon. Remember that?''

She left him with that thought and returned to the campfire to mediate the growing acrimony between Ivy and
Glorian, Tag and Ivy, Whale and Glorian, and to tell
Vorden some jokes that did not brighten his dismal mood
in the least.

The fire burned down.

Whale announced that clearer heads in the morning
would better solve the dilemma, whereupon he curled up
next to the embers and fell asleep, snoring. After much
positioning, the others did the same, and Gideon was left
to stare at the dying sparks.

An hour passed, and Glorian crawled over to him and
put her arms around his neck. "I need your help,'' she
whispered silkily into his ear. "They won't listen to reason.''

"What can I say that you haven't mentioned already?''
he said, tensing against the attempts of her tongue to wash
his lobe.

"You could tell them you're the hero and you think I'm
right.''

"What if I don't?'' he said, tensing against the attempts
of her left hand to memorize his chest.

"I could break your jaw,'' she said with a laugh. "But I
won't, because you will.''

He said nothing and let out a muffled groan when she
finally crawled back to her place. He wasn't sure, but he
thought he heard Red sniggering behind him.

He dozed and was awakened sometime later by a hand
that insinuated itself into his shirt and began scratching his
stomach lightly.

"Ivy,'' he whispered harshly, "cut it out.''

"But I only wanted you to wake up so I could tell you what to do tomorrow."

"I'm awake."

Her fingers stopped; her thumb moved on. "Then you'll help me?"

"Do what?"

"Do what? Where have you been, Gideon? Get the others back home where they belong, of course. We can't begin to do anything down here and you know it."

"It does seem more practical," he said, wondering just how long that damned thumb was.

"Then we can dump Glorian and I can show you my scars."

His eyes closed.

"I can also show you how to summon a Bridge."

"That's a lie," he said.

"Sure it is. But desperate times demand desperate measures, don't you think?"

Gideon wriggled as politely as he could out of her grasp and reach, and promised he would sleep seriously and without delay on it and talk to her in the morning. She did not like not having an answer and told him so in a husky whisper, but when her hand closed sensuously over Red's hoof instead of his knee, she grumbled something about sacrifices and tribulations and crawled back to her place.

Gideon mopped his face with a sleeve.

An hour later Tuesday flapped over and snapped at his nose until he woke up. When he reached for his bat, she hissed at him and nipped the back of his hand. He groaned. She cackled.

"Just remember, brother," she said, a too familiar voice, though somewhat hoarse, floating out of the dark, "I want a goddamned steak."

When she left, Gideon lay back, closed his eyes, opened them again, and said, "Damn."

*   *   *

After ten minutes of trying, he managed to coax a feeble bluelight from his bat and sat morosely in front of Red's head. The lorra's eyes were barely open, and what they saw they didn't like.

"Listen, old pal," he said, keeping his voice low so as not to be overheard, "this is dumb. The way things are now, they can't take on Wamchu alone, and they can't take him on back up there, and they can't go down to Choy and take on the three weird wives, either. They're dreaming, Red, and they don't even know it."

The lorra grunted.

He rubbed the back of his neck, but, knowing there was nothing else he could do: "I think, if it's all right with you, that I'd better do something now, or we aren't going to be alive long enough to enjoy whatever it is we're going to live long enough to enjoy if we live long enough, if you catch my drift."

The lorra grunted.

Gideon stroked the animal's muzzle and the flat, silken hair between its eyes. "So what I'm going to do is, I'm going to head out for Rayn now. They'll never catch me in time, I don't think, and when I get there I'll . . . do something."

Red lifted his great head and stared down.

"No," Gideon said. "You can't go. They need you here."

Red grunted.

"You've convinced me, you can go. But I really would be grateful if you'd let me ride, okay? And it might be better if we went as fast as you can go. If, that is, you don't mind."

Red shook himself to his feet and nodded.

"You're a hell of a pal," Gideon said as he swung onto the animal's back.

And you, he said to himself, are a goddamned idiot.

THIRTY-
EIGHT

It didn't take long for Gideon to change his mind, but by
that time Red had gotten into the spirit of the thing and
wasn't about to stop for anyone.

They had eased out of camp without waking anyone,
Gideon not getting aboard the lorra until he was positive
they were out of earshot. Once on the animal's back, he
took a good grip of the hair on its neck and asked for
speed.

That's when he changed his mind.

Red, with a snort, a growl, and a flamboyant toss of his
horns, leapt forward and didn't seem to come down for at
least twenty yards. And when he did, he was running, the
long legs sweeping them through the night not quite as
silently as the wind. There were grunts when they collided
with trees, a groan now and then when a branch gouged a
side, but none of it deterred the lorra from making as much
haste as his great strength could manage.

Gideon finally had to lie cheek down on the animal's
back and close his eyes, praying that Red knew the way
back, while he attempted to figure a way to turn him
around. This was ridiculous. This was suicidal. This was
less an end run than a power play straight up the middle,
where, the odds dictated gleefully, he would sooner or
later be pulverized.

And to make matters worse, he was unable to decipher
his own reasoning. If the group of seven (eight, if he

counted the duck) would be incapable of taking on such a powerful tyrant, why should a group of one (two, if he counted the goat) do any better? Logic would assume just the opposite, in fact.

Red veered sharply around an unseen obstacle. Gideon held on more tightly and held his breath as well.

Maybe, he thought, I'm just punishing myself for my perceived but not necessarily accurate succession of failures; maybe I think I must prove myself to those who have depended upon me and my talents for so long, through so many perils; maybe I'm showing off for Ivy.

He sat up suddenly.

Now why, he said to himself, did I say Ivy and not Glorian?

A branch missed taking off his head by mere inches.

He lay down again and sneezed when some of the lorra's soft hair tickled his nose.

In point of fact, both women were attractive in their own idiosyncratic ways, and the notion that he might be playing the foolish prancing male for either of them was remarkably disturbing, under the circumstances. Could it be that his ego was such that he would threaten the safety and existence of an entire world just to display his better qualities to a couple of women, one of whom had a boxing fixation and the other so clearly disdainful of him that she pretended moments of affection simply in order to humiliate him later?

Red raced on, muscles stretched and corded, neck and head bobbing, missing all threats to balance now as his vision adjusted to the dark around him.

They reached the perilous mist-land of the zeds, and Gideon was positive a few were trampled in their zeal to attack the intruders.

By dawn they were within sight of the Blood River, and Red unerringly swung right to the stone bridge that led across the silent water.

There was only the sound of his hooves, nothing more.

Through a blur of time later they were into greenery

again, and Red slowed to take a few swipes at the leaves hanging in front of him, nourishing himself before he regained speed.

Gideon didn't realize where he was, in fact, until the first pure lance of sunlight warmed the back of his neck. He blinked, was shocked to realize that he had actually fallen asleep, and, when he cautiously lifted his head, was further shocked to realize that they were not far from the plain outside Rayn. In fact, at the rate they were going, he thought they would be there shortly after sunrise the following day.

"My god, Red!" he said in naked admiration.

What had taken almost six days to traverse on foot, the lorra would manage to cover in less than three.

With that thought in mind, he asked Red to stop, please, so that he might attend to several base and necessary functions, not the least of which was getting himself something to eat. The lorra stopped. Gideon picked himself up off the ground and suggested strongly that stopping meant stopping, not stopping. Red didn't understand. Gideon brushed himself off and was soon seated at the roots of a berry bush, gorging himself and not caring, while he considered a plan of action.

He also hoped the others wouldn't be too angry with him. Most likely they were rushing after him now, cursing the loss of Red, extinguishing a few zeds, and generally thinking of ways to pay him back for his thoughtlessness.

He belched.

He fell asleep.

He awoke when Red cuddled next to him in the moonlight, and he listened to the nightbirds stirring in the foliage, to the night creatures rustling in the brush, to the sound of his own heart.

Jaw tight, then, he waited for the homesickness to come.

When it didn't, he fell asleep again, frowning.

They emerged from the woods just before noon.

The sun was high, the sky a deep blue unsullied by clouds.

And the moment their shadows fell upon the grass, the birds ceased their singing, the breeze retreated, and in a distant farmyard a dog began a mournful howling.

Gideon reviewed the several dozen reasons why he should turn back and wait for his friends, and he discarded them all. He didn't care if this was showing off, he didn't care if this was only pride, and he didn't care if this was extremely stupid. All previous attempts at forcing logic and reason into this world had failed, and there was no reason to think it would work now.

What counted, when all else was considered and found wanting, was how he felt.

And he felt this had to be done, and it had to be done alone.

A squeeze of his legs, and Red began walking across the field.

The dog still howled.

The sun climbed and grew warm.

The walls and rooftops of Rayn broke the horizon.

Red's hooves clumped loudly on the hardened soil, his occasional snort and growl gunshot sharp.

And halfway to the city, atop a low rise, Gideon whispered the lorra to a halt and took out his bat.

There, on the flatland ahead, stood Lu Wamchu.

He was alone, though Gideon could see much activity along the walls—hundreds of concerned citizens anxious to learn the outcome of this final confrontation.

Red backed away nervously.

Gideon slid off his back and took a deep breath.

He hoped luck was with him, that Glorian was right when she said that the three wives had been returned to Choy. If not, he was going to die. Out here. No less alone than he had been back home.

Wamchu raised a hand in greeting, his flaxen hair catching the sun brightly, his black silks absorbing the light, his red beard flaring as if it were afire, his slanted eyes narrowed in satisfied anticipation.

"Please stay, Red," Gideon said when the lorra moved to stand beside him. Red seemed perplexed, and his eyes darkened briefly. He purred, and Gideon patted his neck, stroked his nose, pulled playfully at an ear. "Just stay, Red. Just stay."

He started down the slope slowly, the bat loose in his right hand. His boots were as loud as hooves, the crinkle of his jeans the husk of a wind that remained hidden in the forest. He did not think. He did not plan. He neither slowed down nor sped up when Wamchu advanced at the same steady pace.

They were fifty yards apart when Wamchu stopped and put his hands on his hips.

"You have arrived," he said, his voice as clear as if they were standing nose to nose. "You know I am annoyed."

"I know the Blood will not rise," Gideon told him.

"I have other ways, my friend; don't doubt it for a minute."

"I don't. That's why I'm here."

Wamchu laughed, thunder that rolled across the grass beneath the clear blue sky.

Then his hands disappeared into the folds at his chest, reappeared with the glint of hard silver surrounding them. Gideon stared, and almost stared too long when the arms drew back and snapped forward. He leapt to one side just in time and gaped at the four knives that embedded themselves hilt deep into the ground where he had stood.

Wamchu laughed.

The thunder rolled.

He pulled two sabers from the folds at his hips and sent them lightning swift, sun-blindingly off their razored blades. Gideon leapt to his left, and they sank into the ground and vanished.

Wamchu laughed.

He gave Gideon a mocking bow of appreciation, turned his back, and looked for a full minute at Rayn, at the crowds on and in front of the walls. He waved to them.

They waved back. He turned around swiftly and sent a dozen spiked spheres humming through the air. Gideon threw himself forward, flat on the grass, as the missiles landed in a perfect ovoid pattern, which would, had he moved to either side, caught him perfectly, and lethally.

Thunder rolled.

Wamchu laughed.

Gideon raised his head and saw a rock, pulled it from the ground, and stood. Hefted it. Noted the imperfections of its surface, its weight, how it fit into his hand. He dropped the bat and put the rock in his right hand. He drew back his arm, and he threw it as hard as he could.

Wamchu blinked, his jaw dropped, and he turned slowly as the missile sailed over his head to smash into the wall. There was a mild explosion of stone dust and a slow spectator.

"Just a warning," Gideon said while he swore at himself. "Don't toy with me, Wamchu. You won't get away."

Wamchu nodded once and began to advance.

Gideon picked up the bat and matched him, step for step.

At forty yards they stopped again.

"I don't suppose," Wamchu said, "you would be at all interested in a negotiation?"

"You mean a deal?"

"No. I cheat. I mean a negotiation. I'll spare your life if you'll go back where you came from."

It was temptingly immoral. "And what about my friends?"

"If they survive the journey back, they will not survive the journey home." He spread his hands. "I am not a complete idiot, you know. I do have my standards."

"Such as?"

Wamchu reached into his belt and in a motion too fast to follow sent several short but deadly silver spears toward Gideon's heart. Gideon sidestepped with an angry hiss, reached for another rock, and sent it straight at Wamchu's head, which turned in admiration as the missile screamed into the city wall and created a gate for the lower and shorter forms of life. Then he snapped back with a brace of iron platters studded with spikes, which sizzled past Gideon, one slicing a lock of hair from above his left ear. Gideon touched his scalp gingerly, then scrambled for another stone, threw it, and followed it with another before the Wamchu could watch the first take out a cart and horse on its way to market. The second fell short of the city, and the citizens cheered.

"Enough," Wamchu said venomously. "My neck is getting sore."

Gideon felt the sweat creeping down his cheeks, his forehead, the length of his spine. He held the bat more tightly now and watched in dismay as Wamchu pulled from yet another fold a four-edged broadsword, which, amazingly, he held in one hand and whipped around in tight circles so rapidly a wind began to rise and his figure became a wavering blur.

He stepped forward, and Gideon did as well, turning his head slightly from the high-pitched whine the spinning sword emitted, trying to keep his eyes from watering, telling himself the man was not lifting off the ground.

Wamchu laughed.

Thunder rolled.

Red bellowed at the cloudless sky and reared to kick at the air.

Gideon felt a rush of heat as the spinning sword began to glow, yet he brought the bat to his shoulder and continued to move.

Wamchu seemed puzzled when his opponent refused to back away, then glared, hissed, and finally lunged.

Gideon swung Whale's bat.

The weapons collided with the sound of ripping sheet metal, the flash of an explosion that threw both men to the ground. The sword flared into slivers that showered on the grass, the bat burst into splinters that burned to cinders in the air.

"Sonofabitch," Gideon said, shaking his head and hands, wiggling his arms to banish the electric tingling.

Wamchu only stared, then scrambled to his feet and began sprinting for the city. Gideon watched dumbly for a moment, then took off in pursuit, keeping his eye on the man's arms in case they had something else up their sleeves. And it took only fifteen yards before he launched himself into the air and wrapped his hands around the man's legs. He then rolled aside and jumped onto his back as soon as they were grounded again. An arm slipped around his throat and drew his head back. Wamchu's eyes widened, his tongue protruded between his lips, and his face went as pale as the moon above Choy.

"Mercy," Wamchu gasped.

Gideon drew back his lips, but not in a smile.

"Mercy!" Wamchu begged.

Gideon pulled back a bit more.

"Please!" Wamchu pleaded.

Gideon tossed a mental coin.

Two out of three, he asked himself, and shook his head angrily. Weapons were one thing; hand-to-hand murder something else. He would regret it in the morning, but it was still afternoon.

Quickly, he released his hold and grabbed a handful of the man's luxurious hair, dragged him to his feet, and pinned his left arm behind his back. Then he walked Wamchu to the city, to the citizenry's jeers and sneers, into the Hold through the back door, where the Moglar were packing.

"You have a way to get back," Gideon said harshly. "Show it to me."

Wamchu did not resist. He guided them through a door into a hallway, into a large chamber whose floor was centered by a large grating. Gideon threw the man down, lifted the grating, and saw a cart and bald lorra waiting underneath. The driver, a scrawny man in a frock coat and top hat, looked up and said, "There's room for one more."

Gideon turned, grabbed Wamchu's ankles, and tossed him bodily down.

And the last thing he saw was Wamchu rubbing his neck thoughtfully, his arm painfully, his hair soothingly, his stomach needlessly.

"You haven't seen the last of me!" was the voice he heard as the cart pulled away. "I'll get you for this, Sunday! I won't rest until you're dead! I swear it! I swear—"

Then the driver said, "Duck!" Wamchu cursed, and Gideon heard the sound of a skull striking a stone beam.

THIRTY-
NINE

The Moglar paid no attention to him when he returned to the back hall. They only hurried their packing, bid each other good-bye, and rushed out to catch the last coach to the forest.

Incredible, he thought; and, *what the hell?* when he saw Red coming down the street toward him, Ivy and the others trailing behind. A flurry of greetings, hugs, kisses, and laughter forestalled his attempts to discover how they had managed to get here so fast. And when he did, he turned on Whale.

"I thought you weren't spelling properly anymore."

Whale smiled sheepishly, his neck beginning to turn red. "Off and on, my friend, off and on."

Then Gideon explained with as much modesty as he could muster how he'd managed to send Lu Wamchu back where he belonged. They were pleased, and they were solemn when he told them of the warning. It was done, but not over, and for the rest of the day they wandered about the city, curiously unhappy until, that night at their camp in the field outside Rayn's walls, the realization of their predicament finally struck home.

Gideon was out beyond the campfire, watching the lights of the city glow, listening to the celebrations, and smiling to himself. A footstep behind him made him turn. It was Glorian.

"I'm leaving tomorrow," she said softly, slipped her

hands around his waist, nestling her head beneath his chin. "You'll come with me, I hope."

"To be honest, I don't know."

"It'll be wonderful, I promise you. I'm going to start up Kori again, bigger and better than ever, and this time they'll listen to me when I tell them what needs to be done." She giggled and pressed closer. "It's going to be a grand place, the best in all the Upper Ground." A tilt of her head, an examining eye, and she kissed him soundly, hard, making sure he was tactilely aware of what waited beneath the gown that wasn't quite silk. "You could be my lieutenant."

"Maybe," he said.

"Men," she said, pulling away. "Give 'em an inch, for god's sake, they want the whole goddamned kingdom."

He looked up at the stars; they were still unfamiliar.

A footstep behind him; it was Whale.

"Well?" the former fat man said.

"I don't know."

"Home is never easy," the armorer said.

"You know?" he said, surprised and pleased.

Whale nodded toward Rayn. "They want me to stick around. I think they think I would make a decent mayor."

"You would, you know, as long as you didn't try to make it rain."

Whale frowned, then laughed. "My heavens, Gideon, you've made another joke. If only I could do the same, I'd die happy and sane."

"No one dies happy, Whale," he said. "They just die."

"That's not a joke," Whale said, patted his shoulder, and walked off.

Gideon watched the moon; it was full and had no face.

A footstep behind him; he sighed and wondered if someone was handing out numbers.

"I need your help," Ivy said, holding his hand but not squeezing.

He waited, watching her and the play of golden hair unbraided on her shoulders.

"You remember Shelt and the others?"

He did; he said so.

"I want to beat the shit out of them for what they did to us, me and Tag and Whale. I want them to remember Kori." Her hands were fists, her eyes dark and squinting. "They don't deserve getting away with it, you know. I don't want them to sleep at night for fear of retribution."

"Pretty harsh," he said. "I would think they'd be very happy indeed when they find out what you've done."

Her head pressed against his arm. "I didn't do it, you know. You did."

"Whatever I could, but too many people got hurt."

A moment passed. "So what are you going to do, hero?"

"I don't know yet. It's hard."

"Do me a favor, then?"

He nodded.

"Talk to Tag in the morning? He wants to follow Wamchu and bring his head back for his wall."

"I'll talk."

"You'd better, or I'll cut off your arms." Then she kissed him lightly on the cheek, hugged him, and walked off.

"Lord," he said as he sank to the ground. "Give me strength."

He slept with his arms folded over his knees, his cheek in the cradle of one elbow. It was a fitful sleep with too many dreams and too many nightmares, and when he opened his eyes again light was filling the eastern sky.

Then Tuesday waddled up to him, nudged his arm around her neck, and sighed. "This is a weird place, Giddy. I think I want to go home."

"So do I, sis."

They were silent for several minutes, watching Red graze and looking longingly at the distant clouds that marked the climb back to his home pasture.

"On the other hand," he said miserably, "what is there to go back to?"

"The house, decent food, decent clothes, and old movies on TV," she answered without hesitation.

"For me, maybe," he said, "but what about you?"

"Whale can fix me up."

"He's already tried three times, as I understand it."

"He's a dear, sweet old man who has . . . well, who has—"

"A problem."

She agreed.

"So do we, sis, so do we."

But no matter how often they added the pros and the cons, the pluses and the minuses, they were unable to decide what to do next. Tuesday suggested it was only because they were used to excitement, and the humdrum was somehow no longer appealing.

"It is safe, though," he reminded her.

"Sure. So was sitting on the bench all those years." And she yawned.

At midday they wandered back to the camp, surprised when they saw that the others had already been to Rayn for supplies and fresh clothes, were packed and were only waiting to bid them farewell.

Glorian kissed him, her cheeks damp with tears. "You saved us, you know. We don't owe you a thing."

Whale shook his hand and walked off to Rayn, his shadows somehow larger than the former fat man who cast it.

Ivy just stared at him, searching his eyes and sighing. Then she kissed him and hugged him and punched him gently on the arm.

Red wandered up, Tag nervously on his back.

"You watch the ladies," Gideon said sternly to them both.

"Don't worry," Tag assured him. "I have a great way to slice a desh, and pacchs don't scare me a bit." He reached down for Gideon's hand, then looked quickly back toward his sister.

Red's eyes were dark.

"You don't want to stay, not really," Gideon said, wrapping his arms around the lorra's neck and burying his face in the soft hair. "You miss home. I know it."

Red purred and bobbed his head.

"Besides, I'll be around. And if I . . . if I go, I won't do it without coming up to see you."

Red purred and butted him gently, then swung free of his grip and started toward the road. Glorian walked beside him, her hand on Tag's leg. Ivy trailed, hesitated, turned suddenly, and ran back.

"The Bridge," she said.

He waited.

"You won't get it if you don't need it."

"Ivy—"

"Shut up," she said, and ran back to the others.

He watched until the sun began to burn his eyes. Then he returned to the dead campfire and sat beside his sister. "Did you hear her?" he asked.

"Sure I did," the duck said.

"So are we in need?"

"Well, I certainly am," Tuesday said, flapping her wings to remind him of her condition. Then she stared at him and smiled as only a duck and sister could. "But you're not, are you? You don't need home at all, anymore."

"That's a little harsh, sis."

"What harsh? Like the lady said, look around you. Do you see a Bridge waiting to whisk you home?"

He did; there wasn't.

"You don't need it, Giddy," she said. "Something's changed, and you don't."

"I'm beginning to believe that," he admitted.

"Well, if that's the case, you'll have to promise me something."

"What's that?"

"That you'll find some way to turn me back. I had flat feet before, but this is ridiculous."

Gideon laughed and hugged her.

She was always right before, and she was definitely right now. If he were home, what would he be doing besides the crossword puzzles, listening for the telephone that probably wouldn't ring, and nursing his bottle of scotch? At least here he could feel as if he were doing more than taking up space and marking time; at least here he could make some difference, not only to others, but, more important, to himself.

A little pompous, don't you think? he thought with a wry smile.

A little, he said silently; but what the hell, right?

"A deal," he said at last.

"Great," she said. "God, it's hell when I have to wait for you to make up your mind to do what I knew you were going to do all along. And while you're at it, you might as well figure out how the hell I'm going to get a man looking like this. Do you have any idea, Gideon Sunday, what having feathers can do to a passionate woman's love life?"

He didn't, but he nodded anyway, not caring because now it was just like home.

No, he thought then. Not *like* home. *Is* home.

And he spent the rest of the day grinning, and most of the night dreaming about Ivy and her buttons.

THE BEST IN FANTASY

ANDRÉ NORTON

Buy them at your local bookstore or use this handy coupon:
Clip and mail this page with your order

TOR BOOKS—Reader Service Dept.
49 W. 24 Street, 9th Floor, New York, NY 10010

Please send me the book(s) I have checked above. I am enclosing
$_____ (please add $1.00 to cover postage and handling).
Send check or money order only—no cash or C.O.D.'s.

Mr./Mrs./Miss _____

Address _____

City _____ State/Zip _____

Please allow six weeks for delivery. Prices subject to change without notice.

CONAN

☐ 54238-X   CONAN THE DESTROYER $2.95
  54239-8   Canada $3.50

☐ 54228-2   CONAN THE DEFENDER $2.95
  54229-0   Canada $3.50

☐ 54225-8   CONAN THE INVINCIBLE $2.95
  54226-6   Canada $3.50

☐ 54236-3   CONAN THE MAGNIFICENT $2.95
  54237-1   Canada $3.50

☐ 54231-2   CONAN THE UNCONQUERED $2.95
  54232-0   Canada $3.50

☐ 54246-0   CONAN THE VICTORIOUS $2.95
  54247-9   Canada $3.50

☐ 54248-7   CONAN THE FEARLESS (trade) $6.95
  54249-5   Canada $7.95

☐ 54242-8   CONAN THE TRIUMPHANT $2.95
  54243-6   Canada $3.50

☐ 54244-4   CONAN THE VALOROUS (trade) $6.95
  54245-2   Canada $7.95

Buy them at your local bookstore or use this handy coupon.
Clip and mail this page with your order

TOR BOOKS—Reader Service Dept.
49 W. 24 Street, 9th Floor, New York, NY 10010

Please send me the book(s) I have checked above. I am enclosing
$_____ (please add $1.00 to cover postage and handling).
Send check or money order only—no cash or C.O.D.'s.

Mr./Mrs./Miss _____
Address _____
City _____ State/Zip _____
Please allow six weeks for delivery. Prices subject to change without
notice.

PIERS ANTHONY

☐	53114-0	ANTHONOLOGY		$3.50
	53115-9		Canada	$3.95
☐	53112-4	HASAN		$2.95
	53113-2		Canada	$3.50
☐	53108-6	PRETENDER (with Francis Hall)		$3.50
	53109-4		Canada	$3.95
☐	53116-7	PROSTHO PLUS		$2.95
	53117-5		Canada	$3.75
☐	53110-8	RACE AGAINST TIME		$2.95
	53111-6		Canada	$3.50
☐	53118-3	THE RING (with Robert E. Margroff)		$2.95
	53119-1		Canada	$3.75
☐	93724-5	SHADE OF THE TREE (Hardcover)		$15.95
☐	53120-5	STEPPE		$3.50
	53121-3		Canada	$4.50

Buy them at your local bookstore or use this handy coupon:
Clip and mail this page with your order

TOR BOOKS—Reader Service Dept.
49 West 24 Street, 9th Floor, New York, N.Y. 10010

Please send me the book(s) I have checked above. I am enclosing
$_____ (please add $1.00 to cover postage and handling).
Send check or money order only—no cash or C.O.D.'s.

Mr./Mrs./Miss _____
Address _____
City _____ State/Zip _____
Please allow six weeks for delivery. Prices subject to change without
notice.